W9-BNP-589

DATE DUE

SEP 0 6

Pinky & Stinky

by
JAMES KOCHALKA

IOWA CITY
DISCARDED
from Iowa City Public Library
JUL 2006
PUBLIC LIBRARY

TOP SHELF PRODUCTIONS
MARIETTA, GA

PINKY & STINKY
COPYRIGHT © 2002 BY JAMES KOCHALKA

PUBLISHED BY

TOP SHELF PRODUCTIONS
P.O. BOX 1282
MARIETTA, GA
30061-1282

www.topshelfcomix.com

TOP SHELF PRODUCTIONS AND THE TOP SHELF LOGO
ARE TM AND © 2002 TOP SHELF PRODUCTIONS, INC.

EDITED BY CHRIS STAROS
PRODUCTION DESIGN BY BRETT WARNOCK
AND JAMES KOCHALKA

THE STORIES, CHARACTERS AND INCIDENTS FEATURED IN THIS
BOOK ARE ENTIRELY FICTIONAL. NO PART OF THIS BOOK
MAY BE REPRODUCED WITHOUT PERMISSION, EXCEPT FOR
SMALL EXCERPTS FOR PURPOSES OF REVIEW.

KOCHALKA, JAMES
PINKY & STINKY / JAMES KOCHALKA
ISBN: 1-891830-29-5
GRAPHIC NOVELS, CARTOONS,
YOUNG ADULTS

FIRST PRINTING, PRINTED IN CANADA

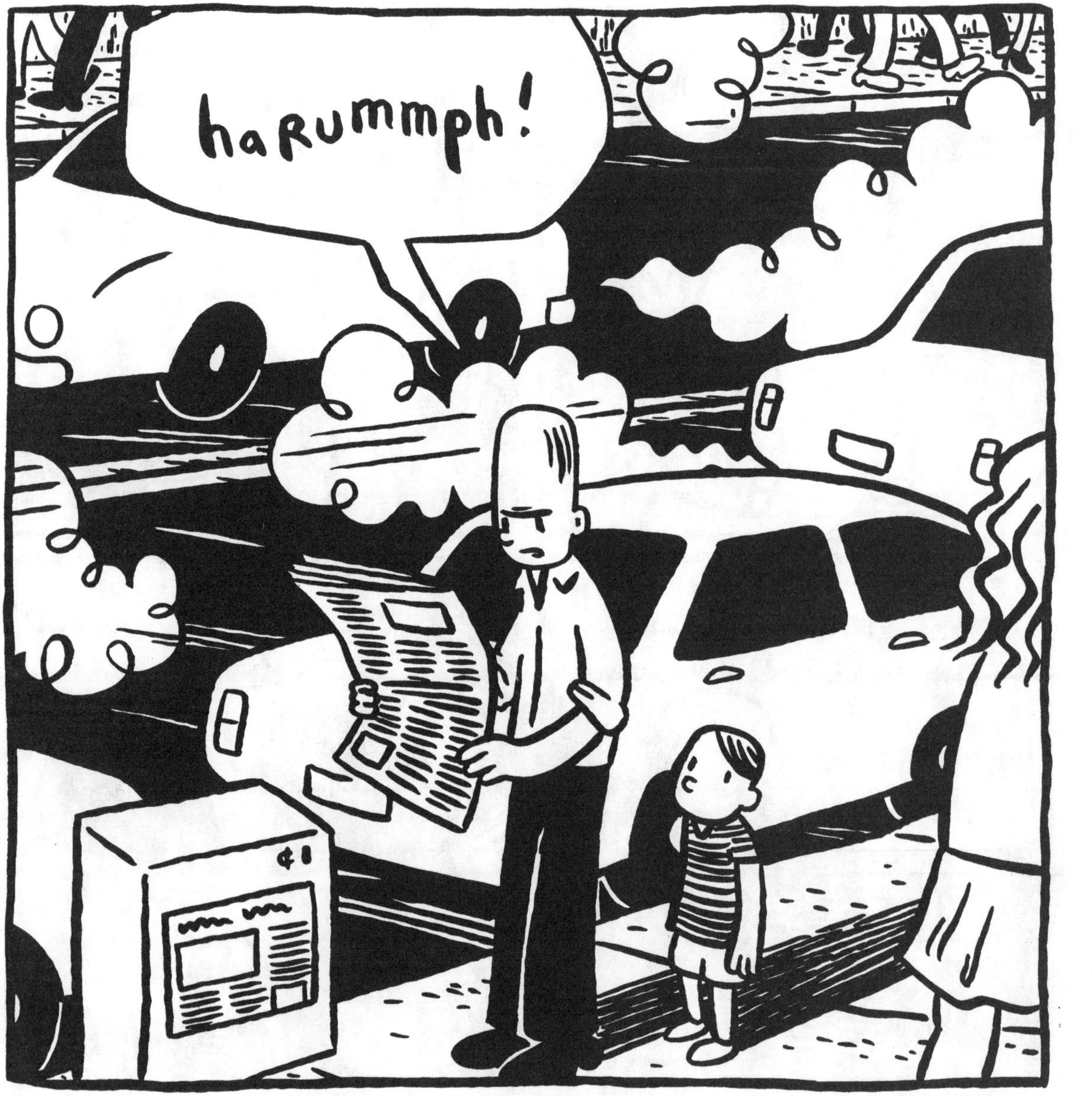
haRummph!

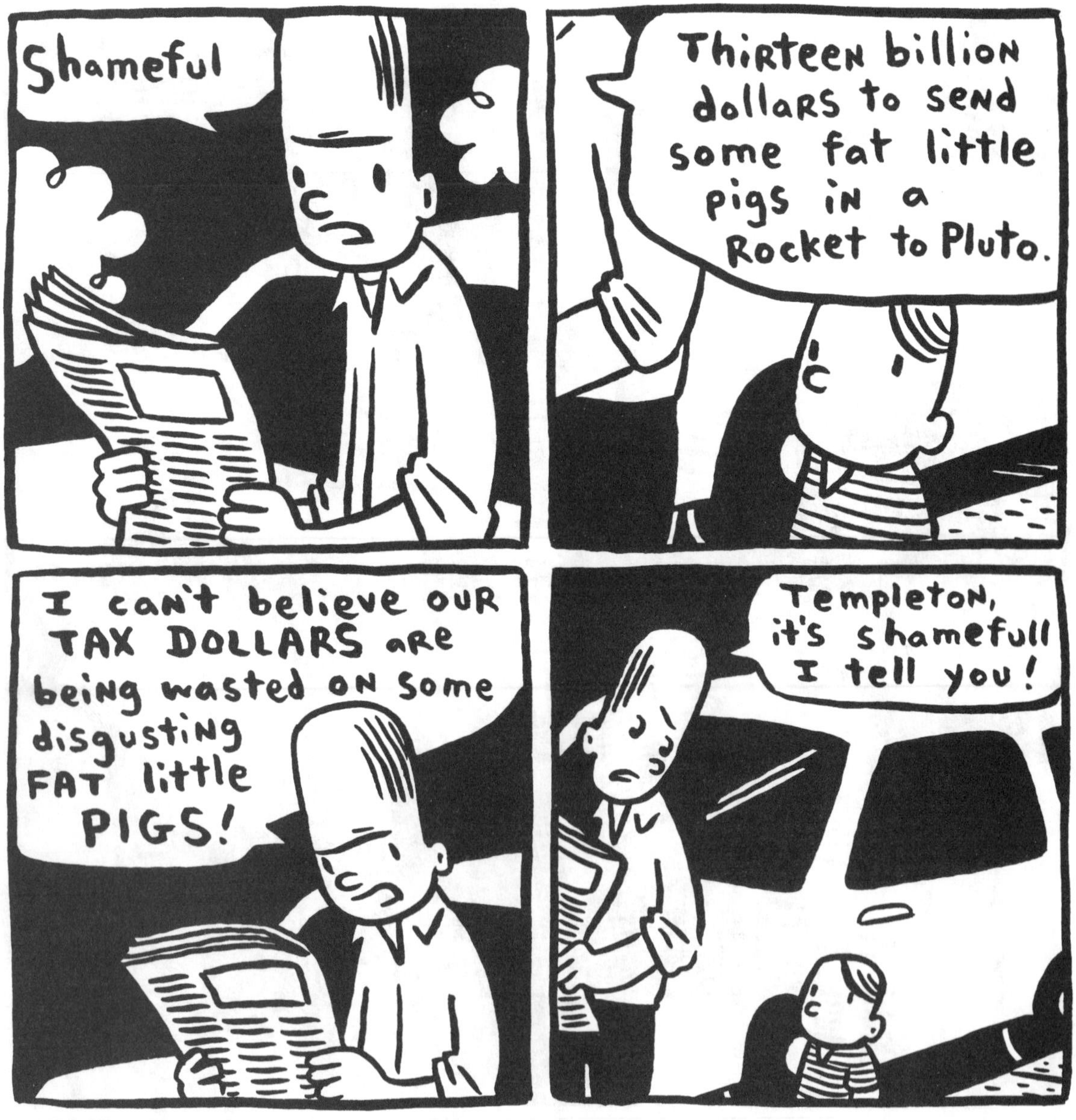
Shameful
Thirteen billion dollars to send some fat little pigs in a Rocket to Pluto.
I can't believe our TAX DOLLARS are being wasted on some disgusting FAT little PIGS!
Templeton, it's shamefull I tell you!

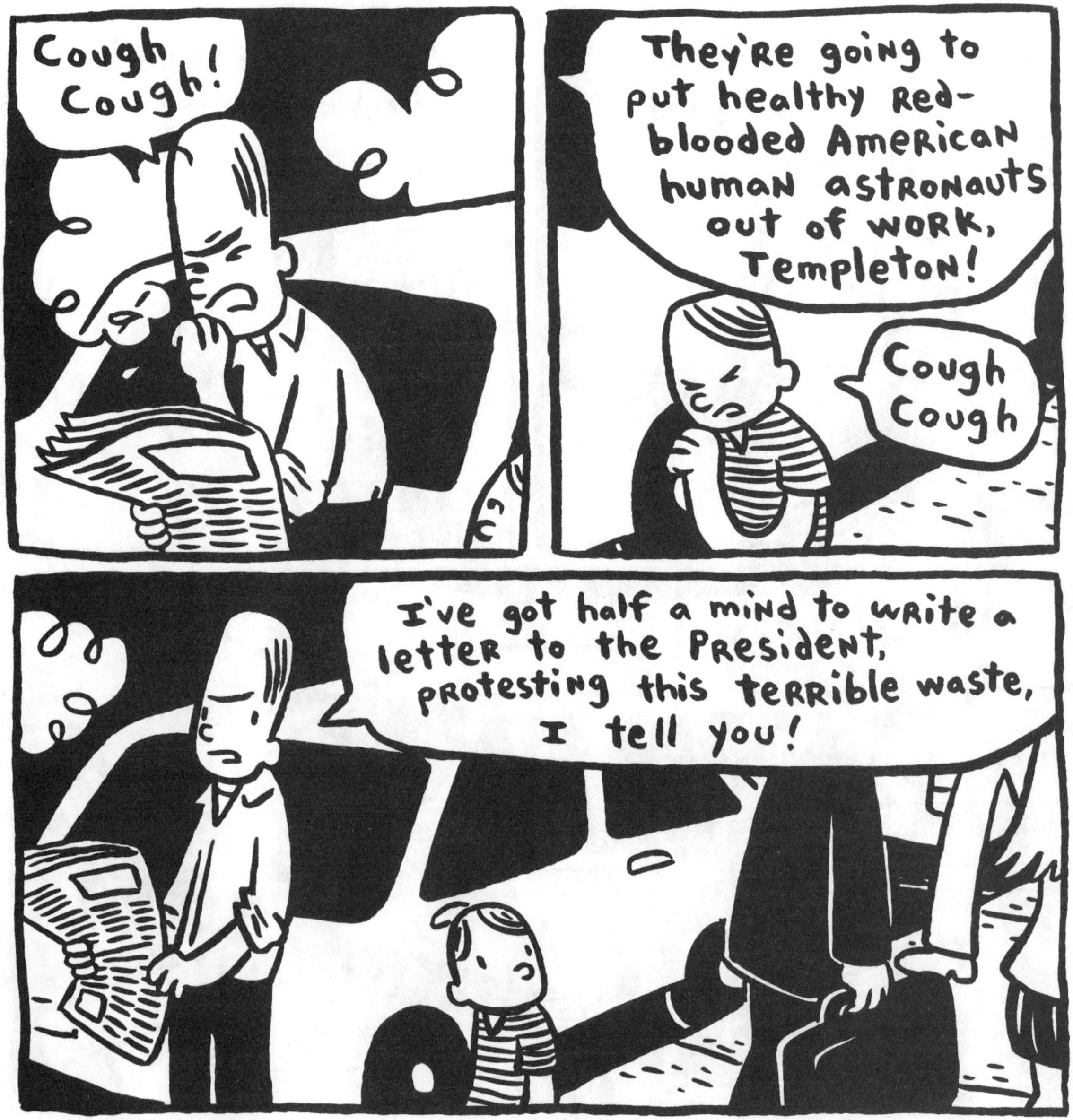

Cough Cough!
They're going to put healthy red-blooded American human astronauts out of work, Templeton!
Cough Cough
I've got half a mind to write a letter to the President, protesting this terrible waste, I tell you!

Are the pigs up there right now, Uncle?
Yes, their rocket launched today. It's shameful, I say!
honk
honk
hon
hrumph.

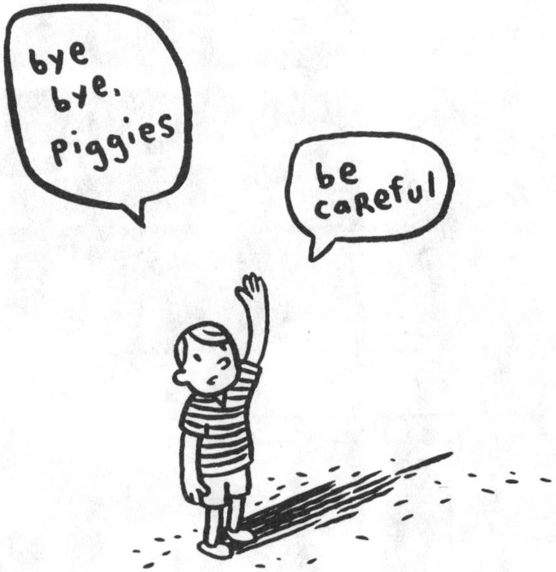
bye bye, piggies
be careful

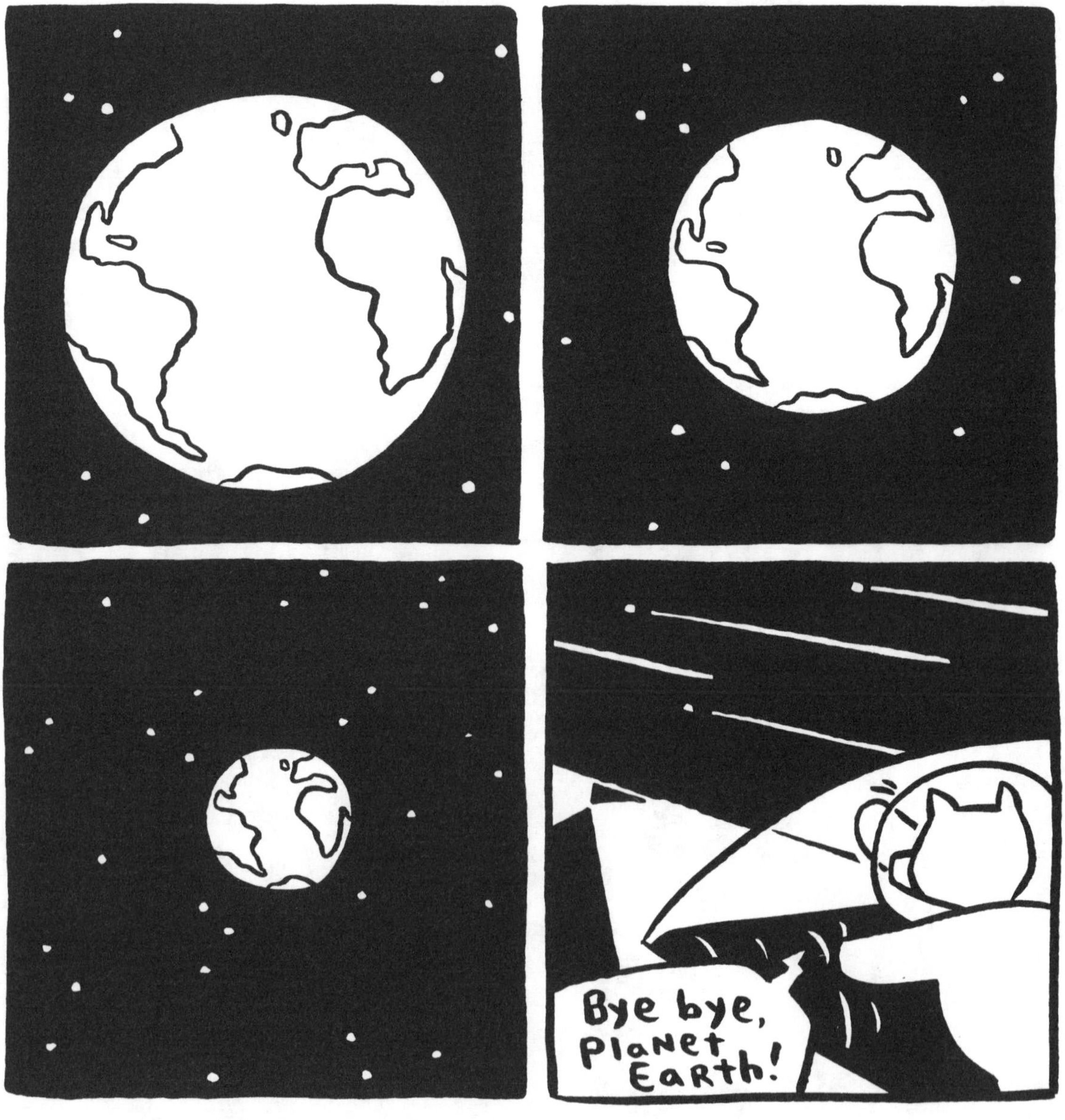
Bye bye, planet Earth!

Stinky! Sit down!
Help me steer
Sorry Pinky
Hmph

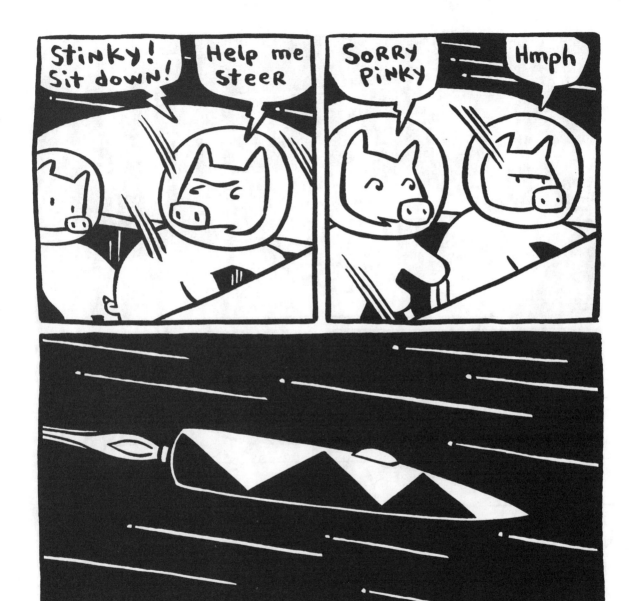

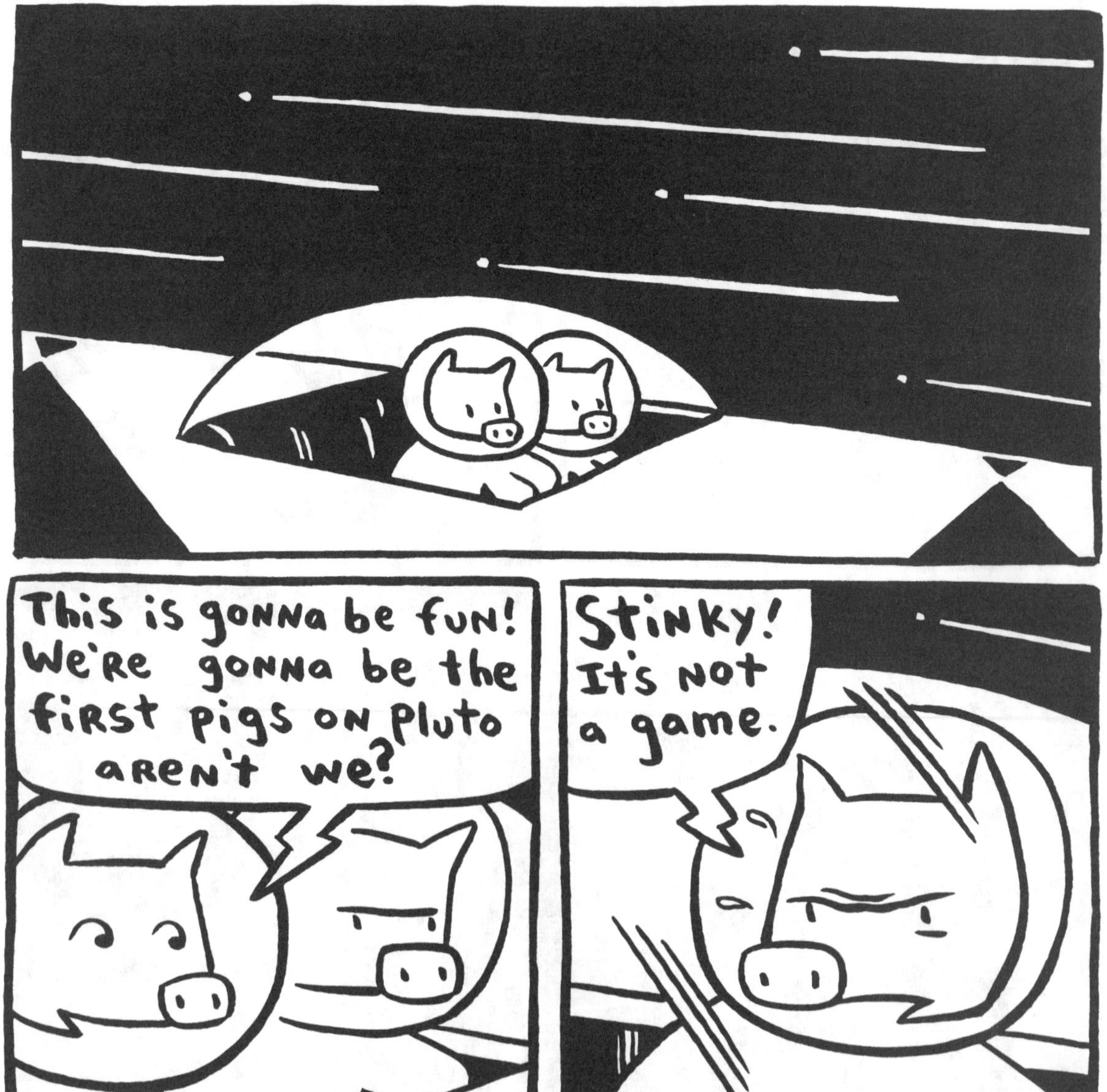
This is gonna be fun! We're gonna be the first pigs on Pluto aren't we?
Stinky! It's not a game.

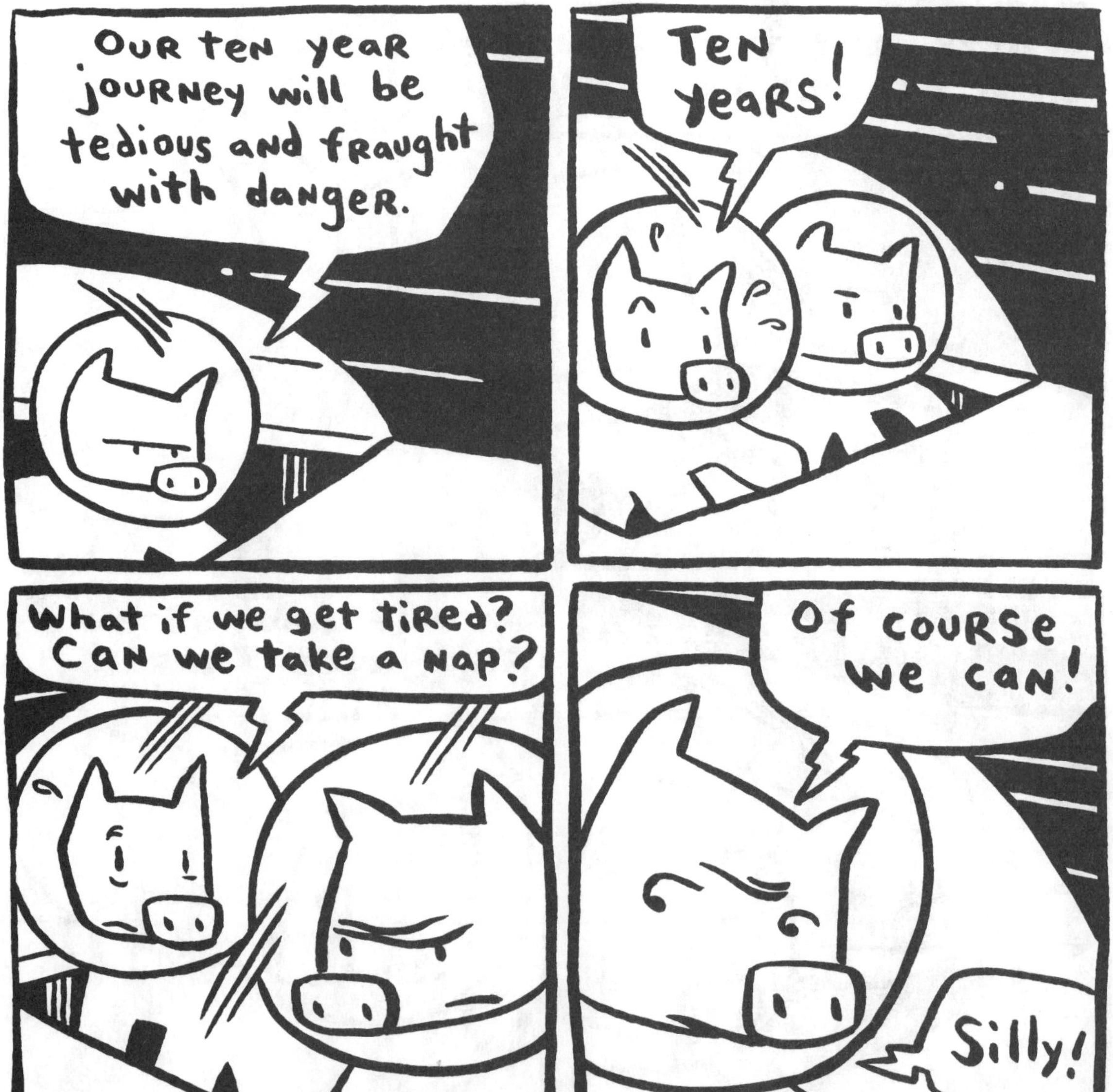
Our ten year journey will be tedious and fraught with danger.
Ten years!
What if we get tired? Can we take a nap?
Of course we can!
Silly!

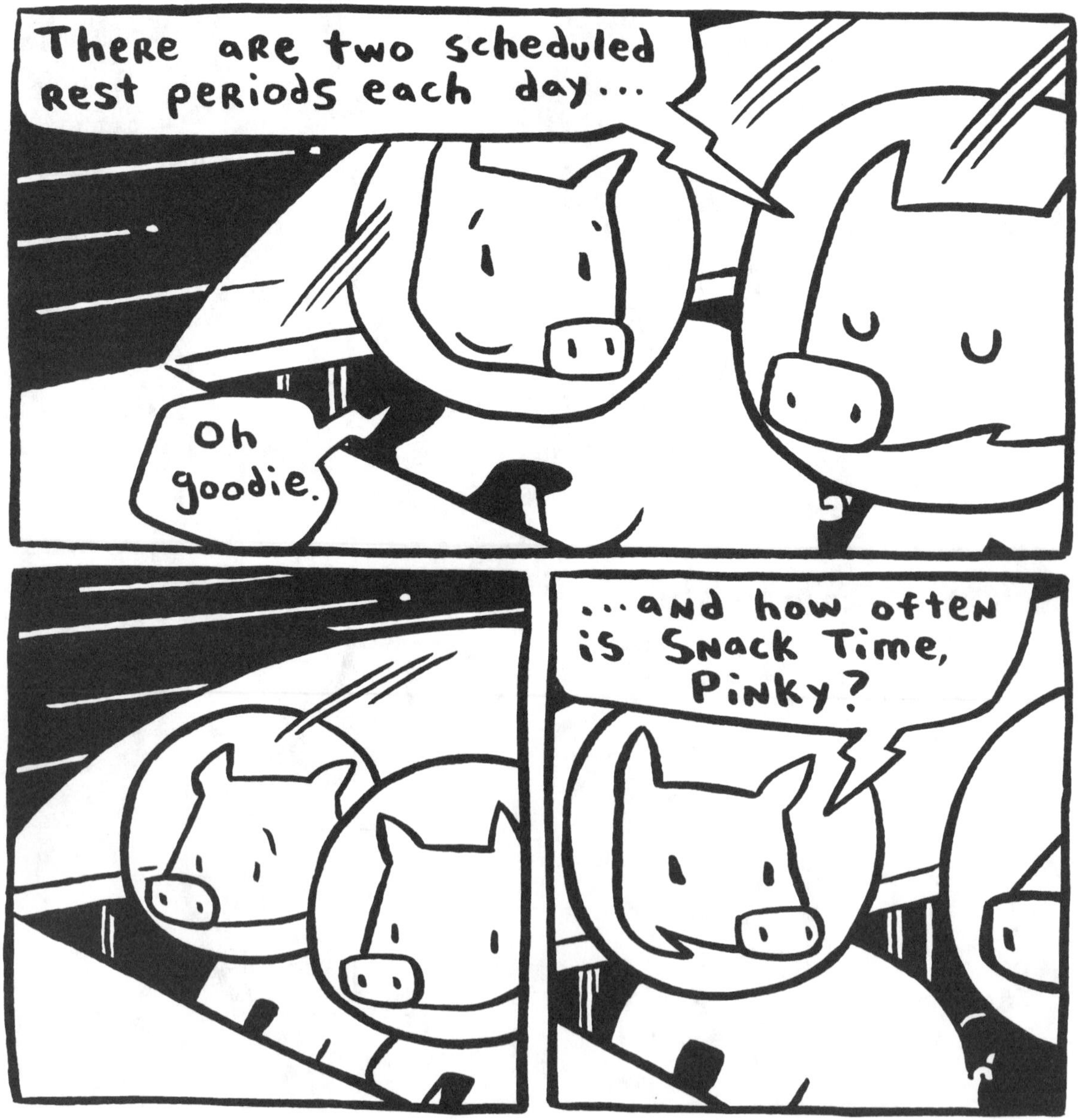
There are two scheduled rest periods each day...
Oh goodie.
...and how often is Snack Time, Pinky?

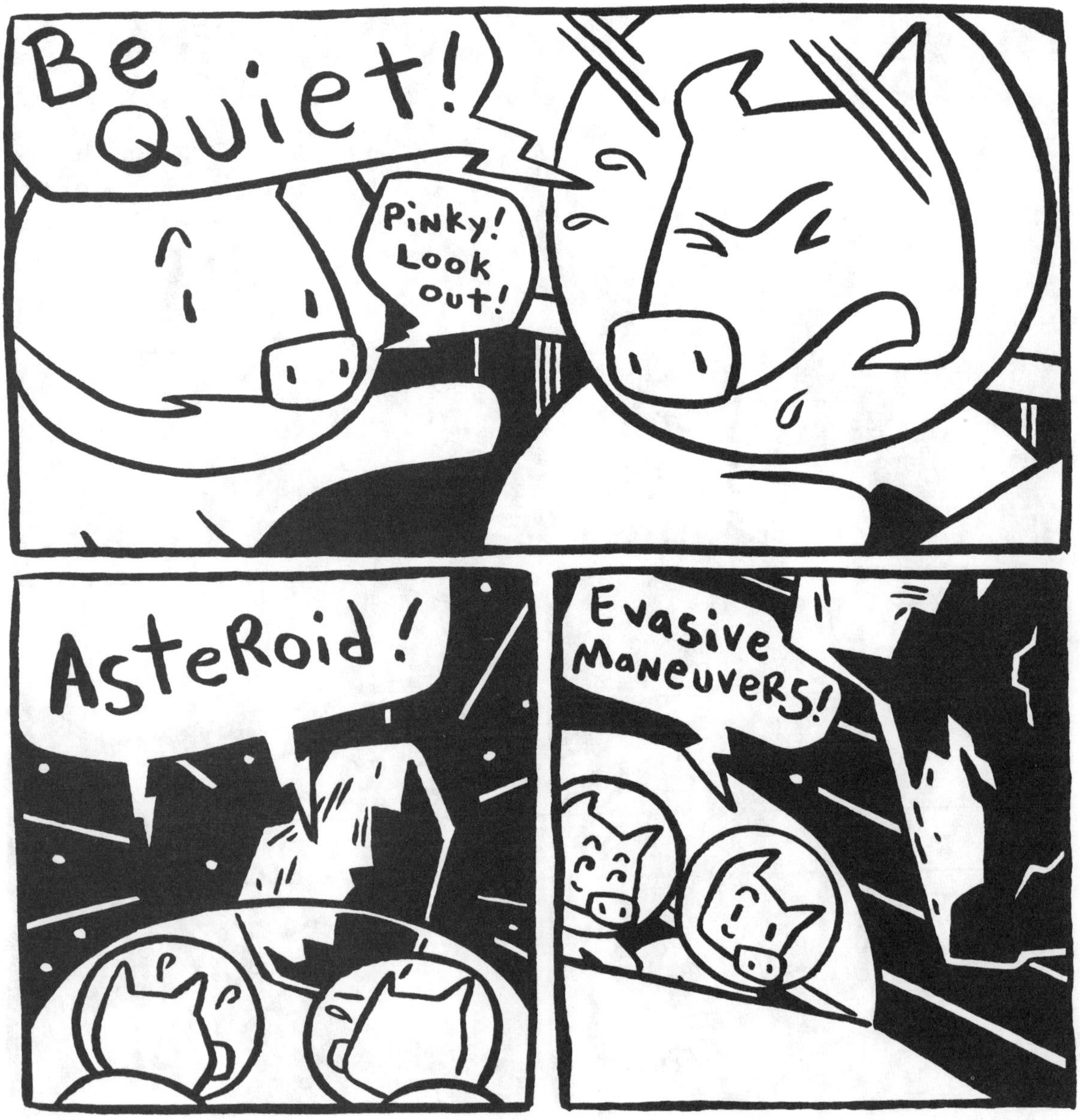
Be Quiet!
Pinky! Look out!
AsteRoid!
Evasive Maneuvers!

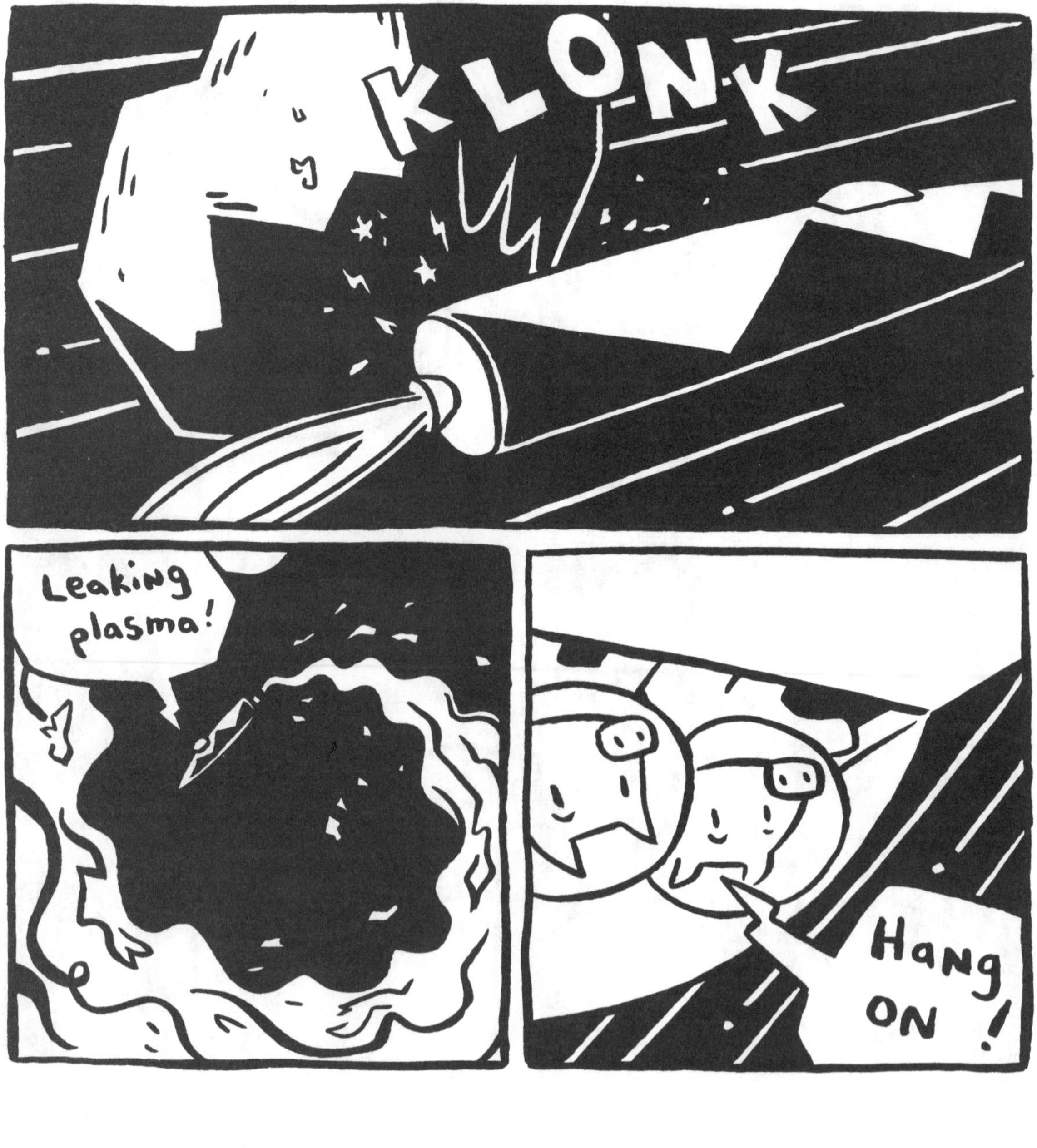
KLONK
Leaking plasma!
Hang ON!

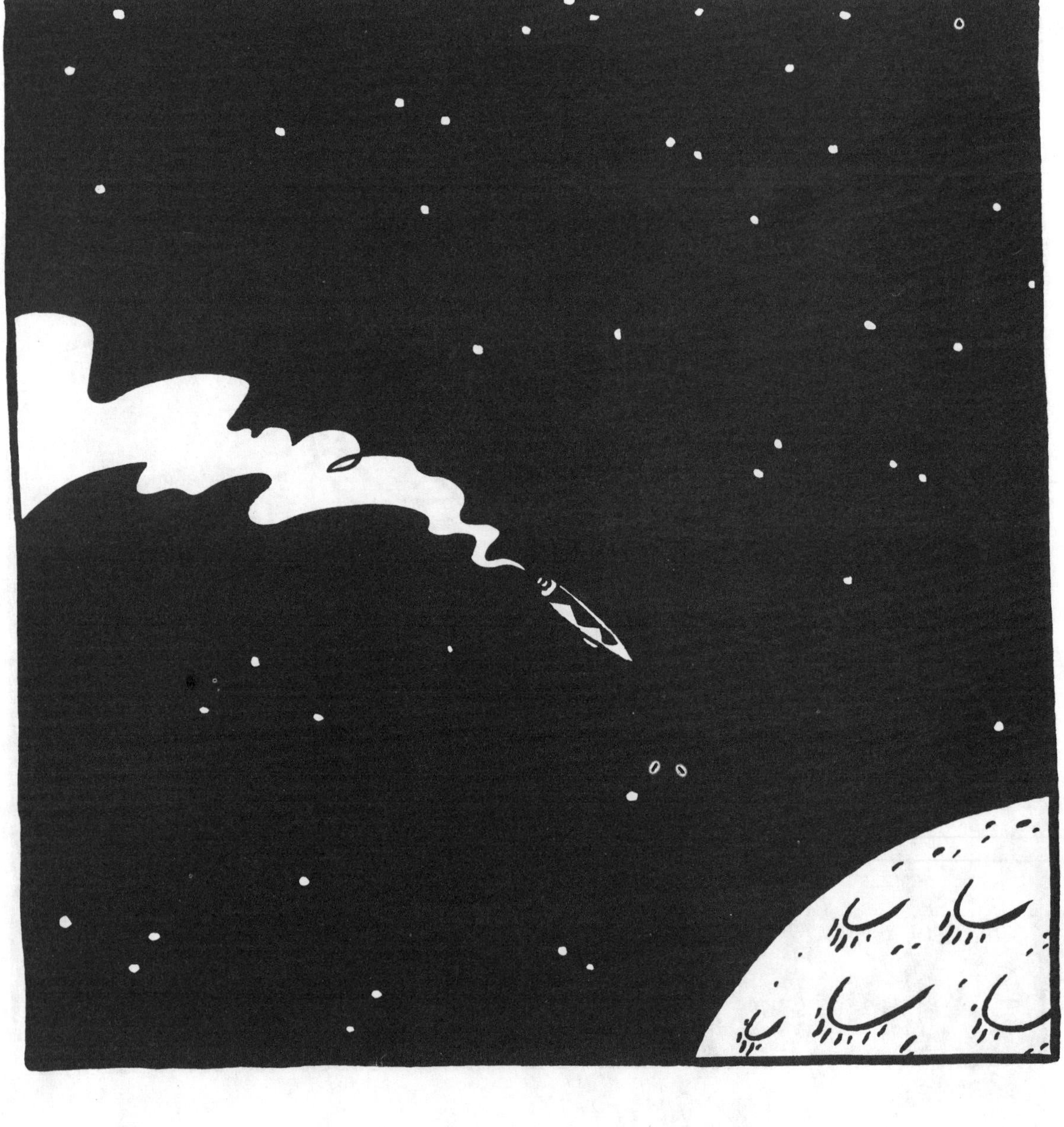

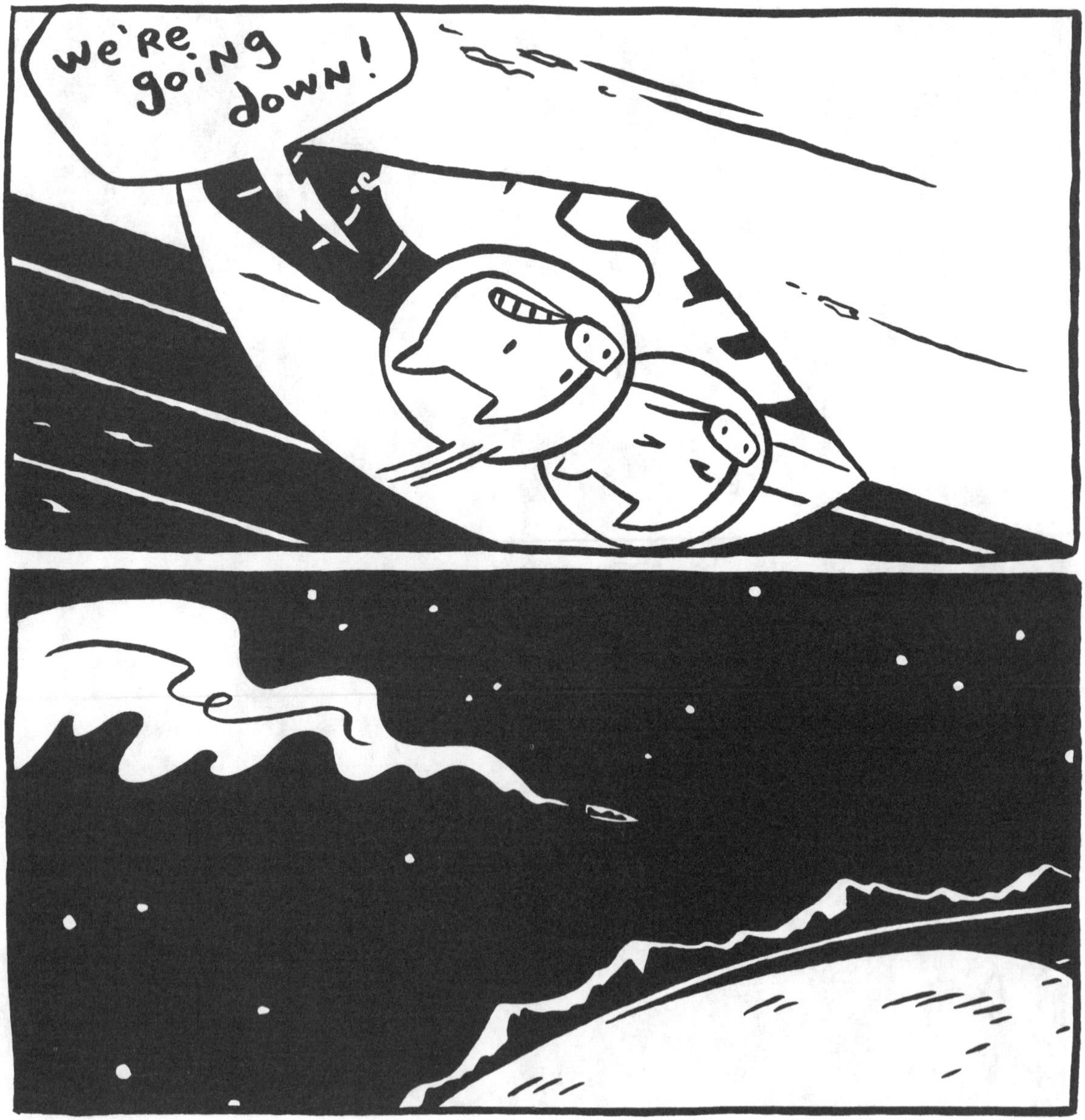
we're going down!

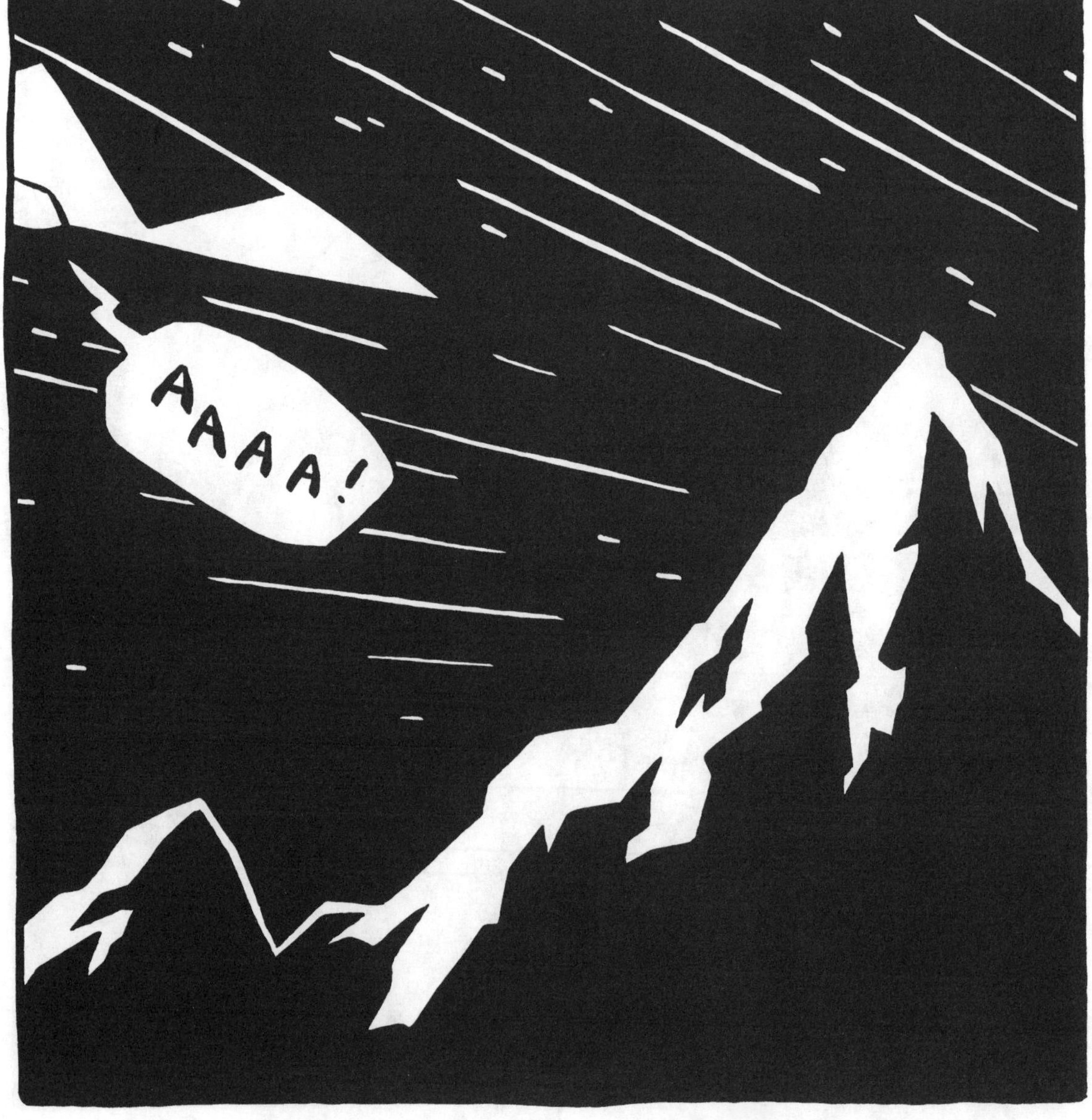
AAAA!

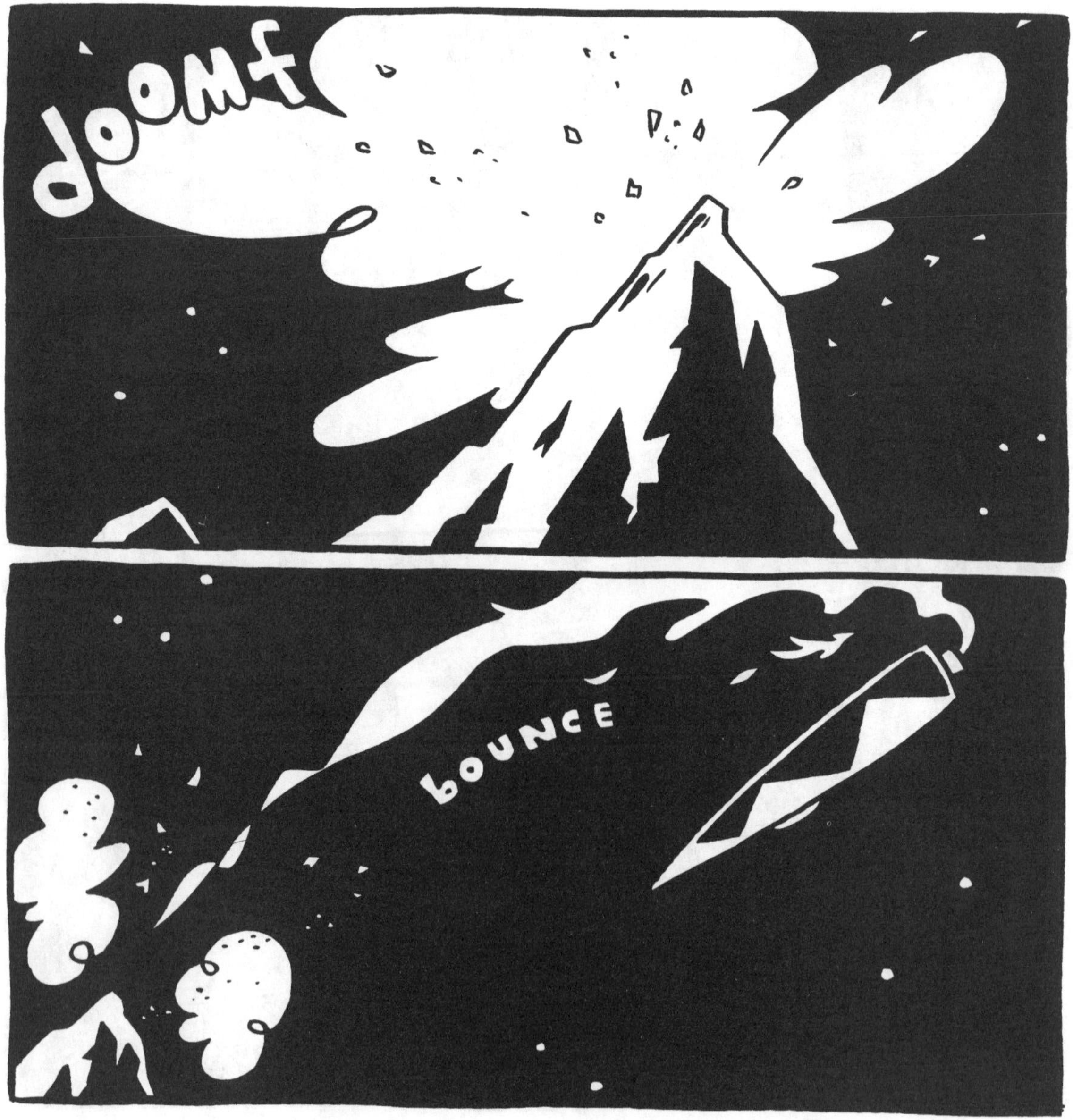
doomf
BOUNCE

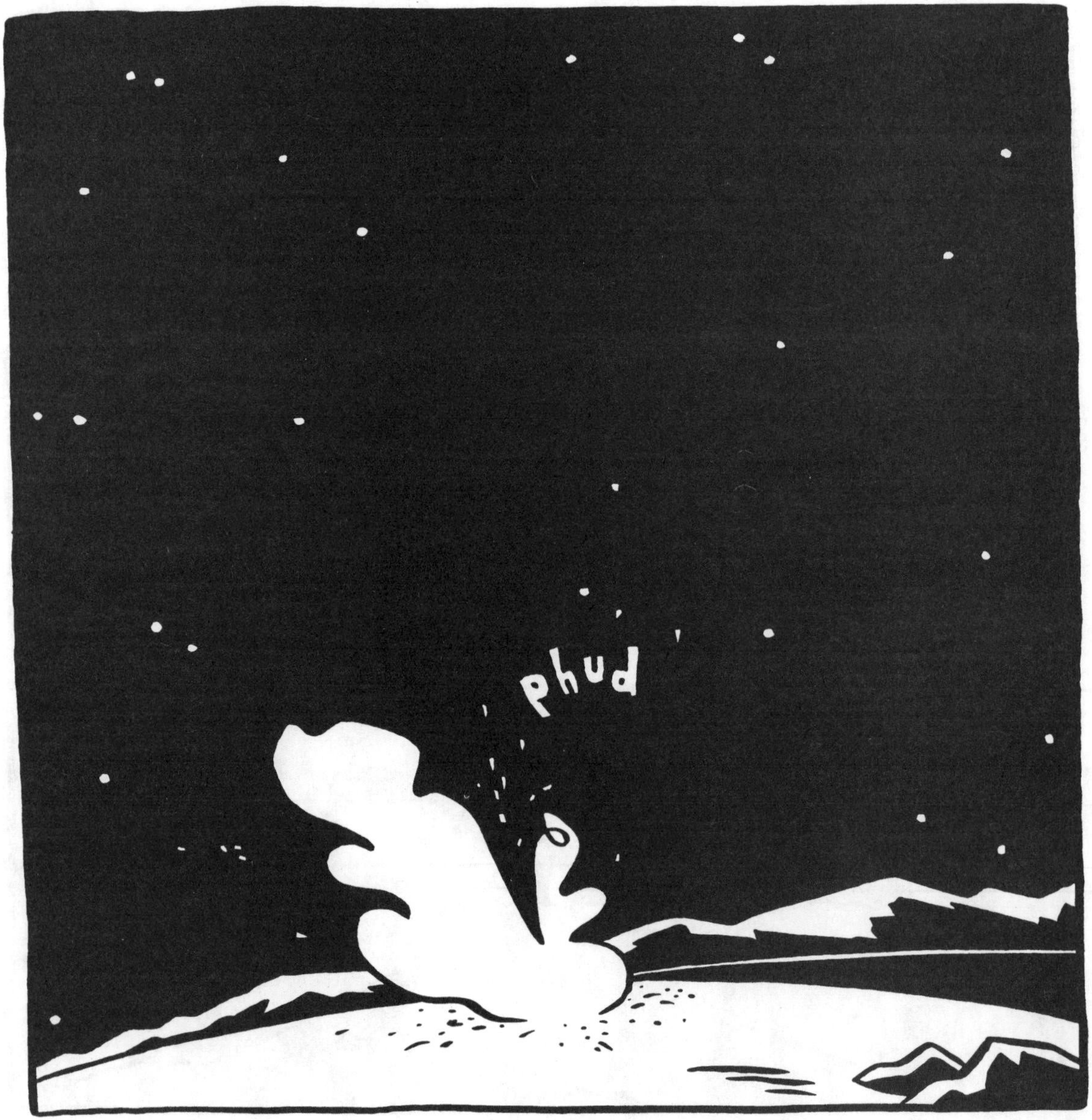
phud

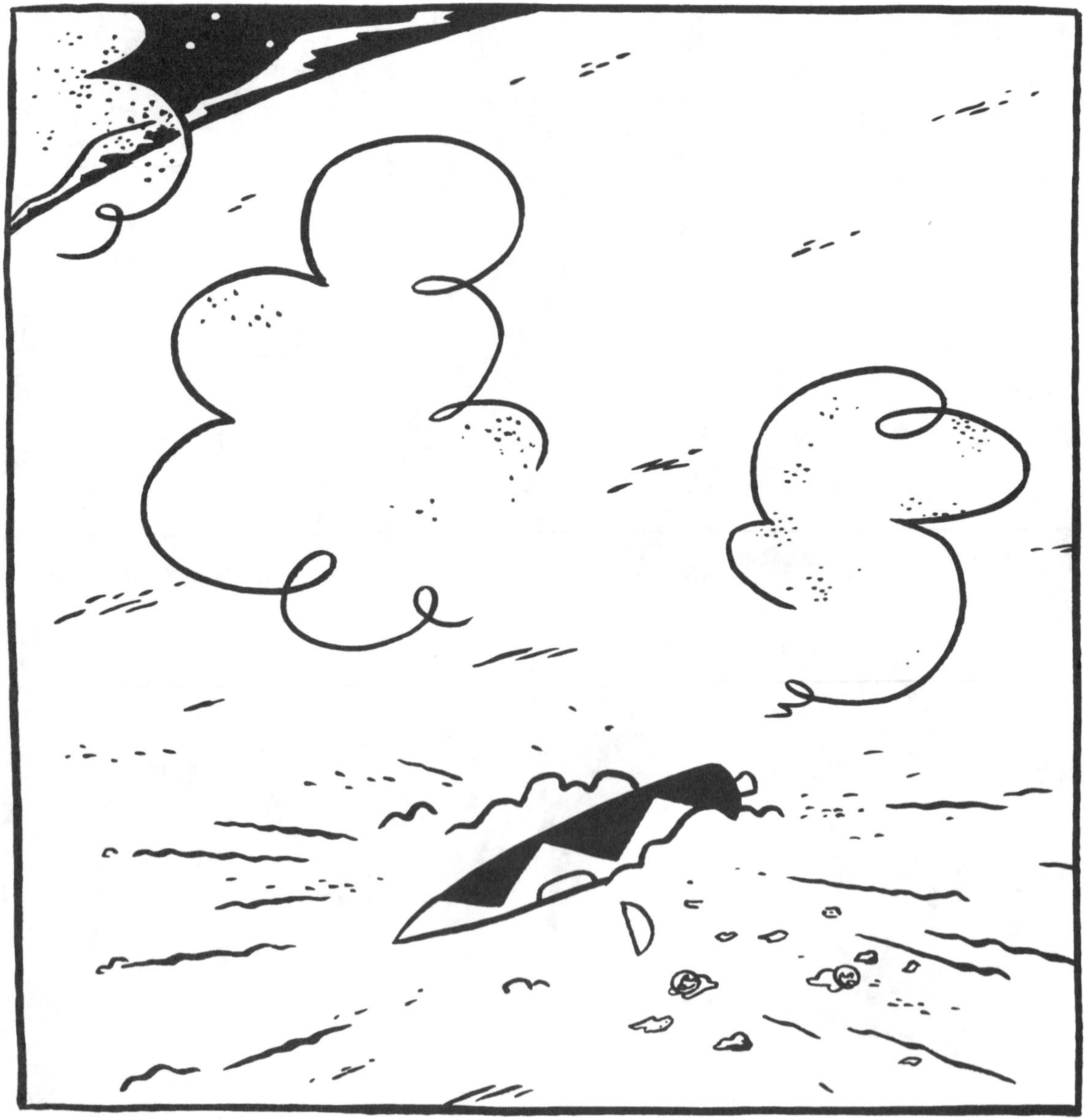

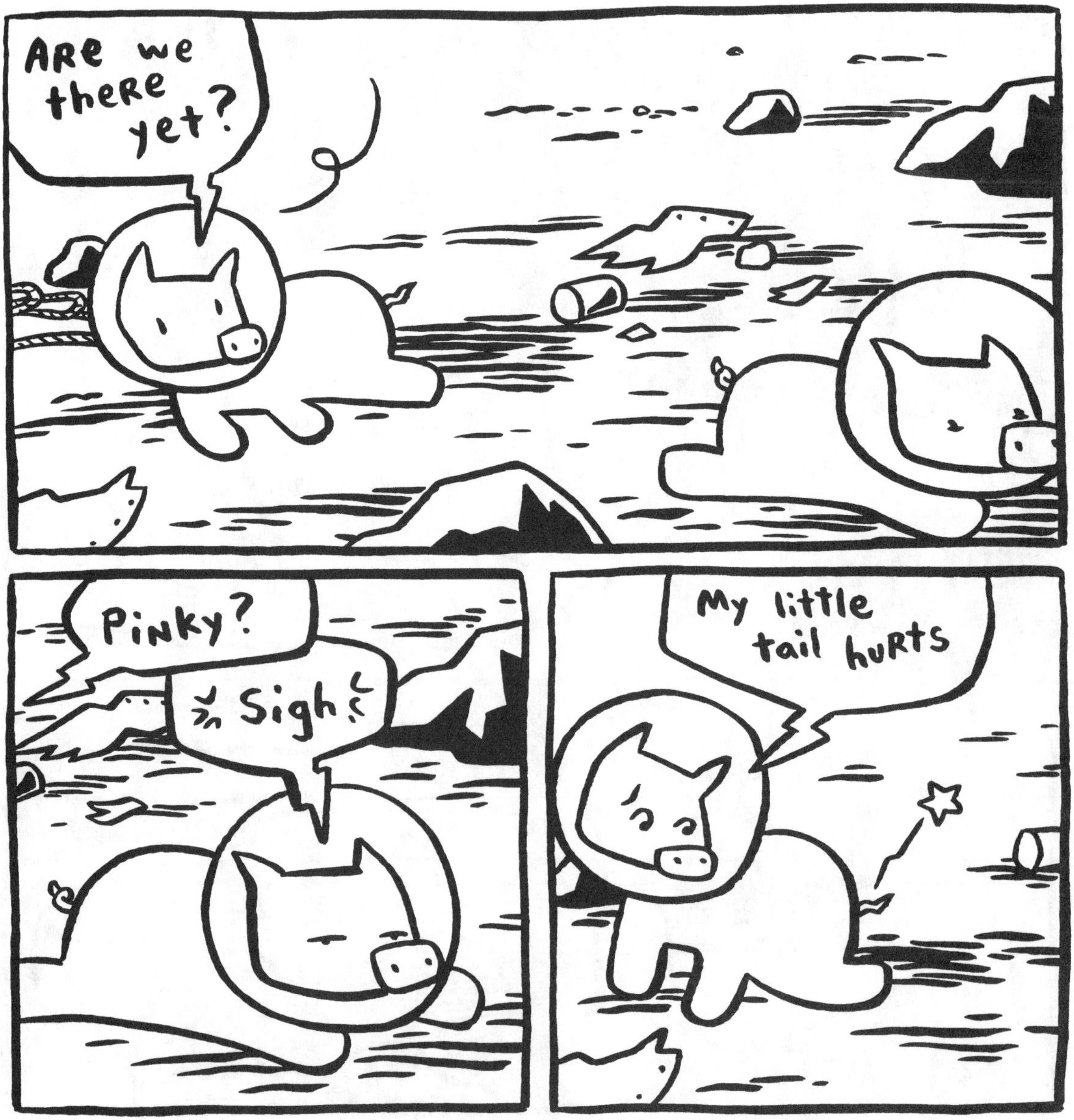
Are we there yet?
Pinky?
Sigh
My little tail hurts

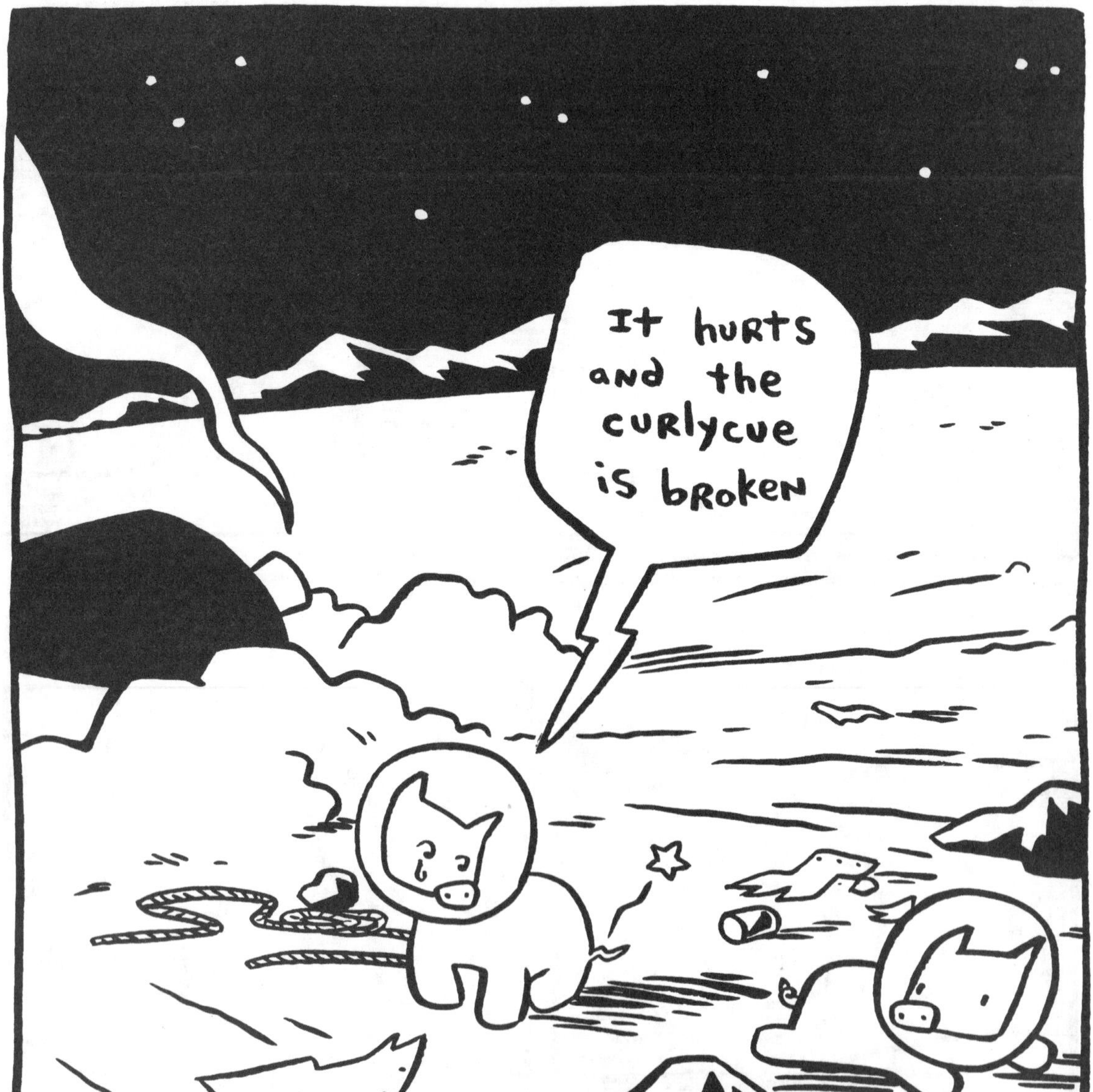
It hurts and the curlycue is broken

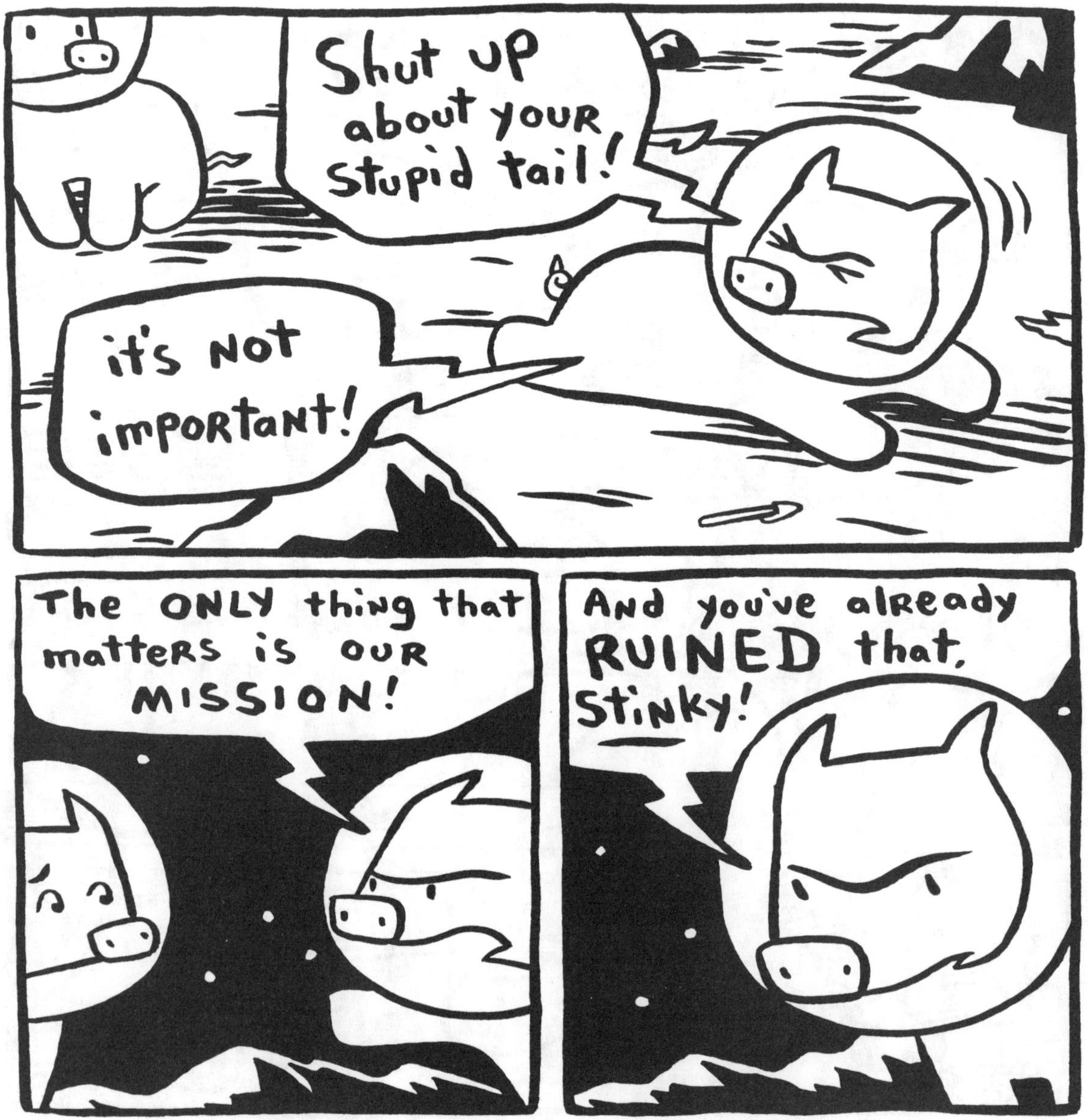

Shut up about your stupid tail!
it's not important!
The ONLY thing that matters is our MISSION!
And you've already RUINED that, Stinky!

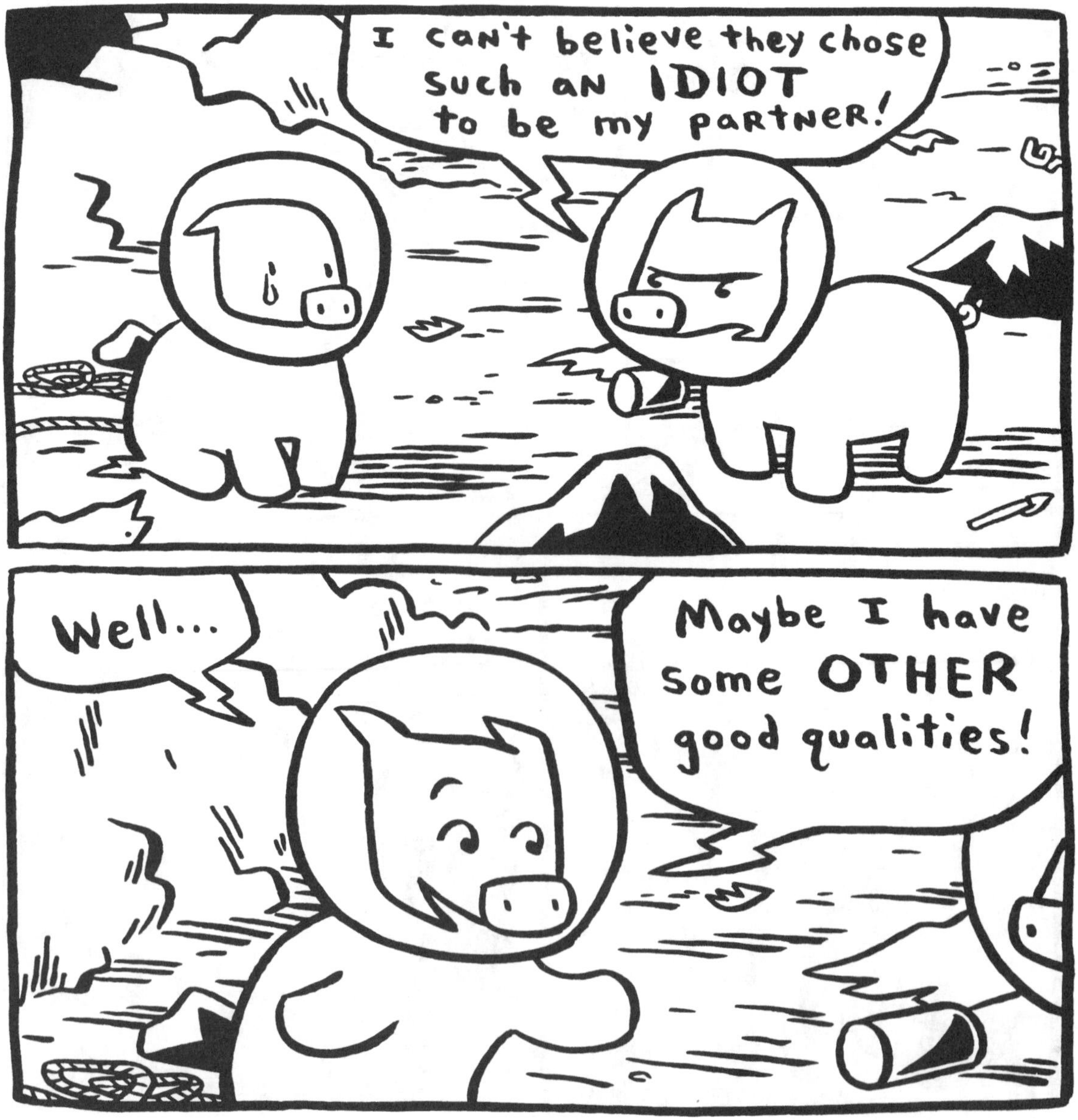
I can't believe they chose such an IDIOT to be my partner!
Well...
Maybe I have some OTHER good qualities!

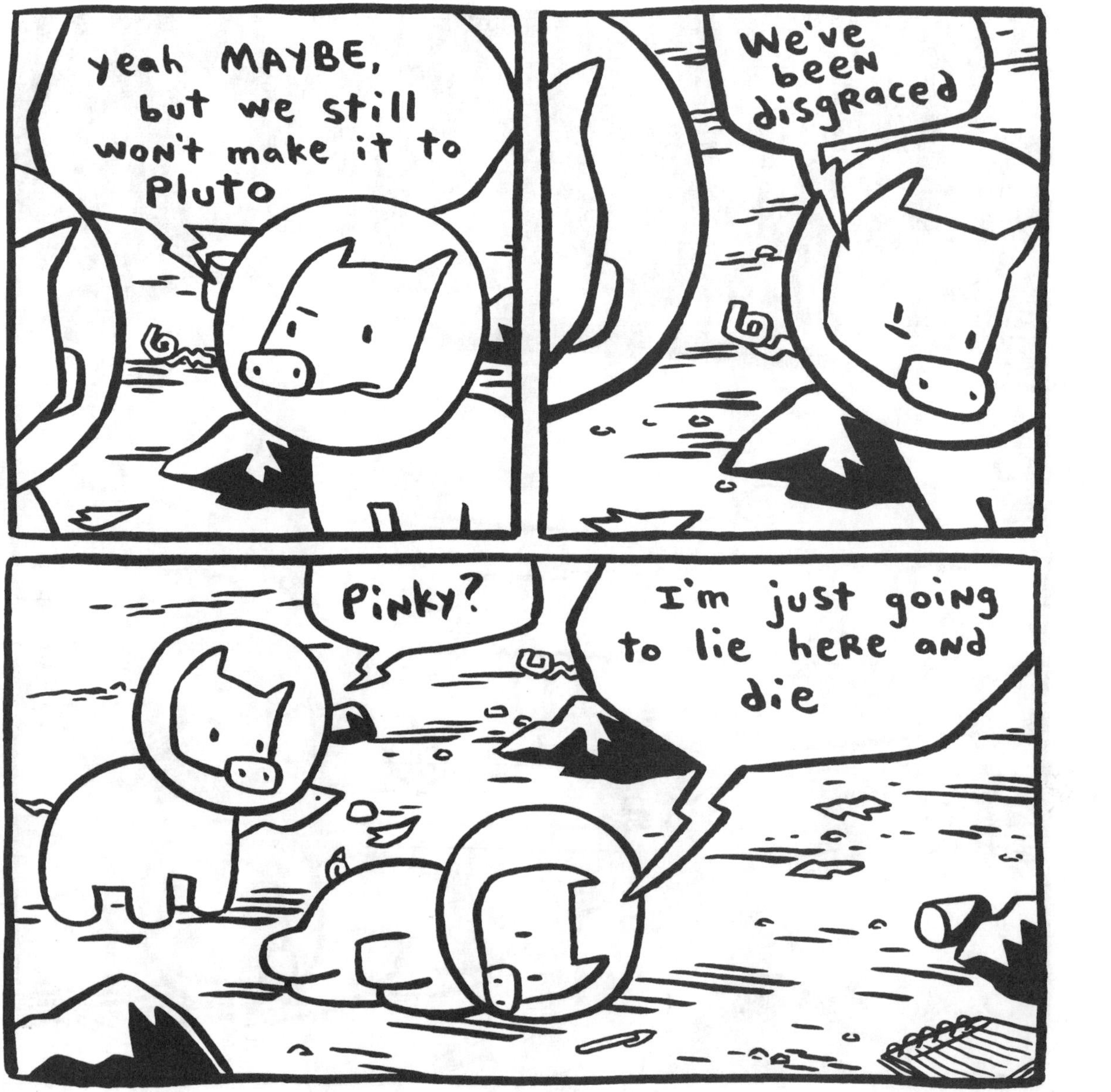
yeah MAYBE, but we still won't make it to Pluto
We've been disgraced
Pinky?
I'm just going to lie here and die

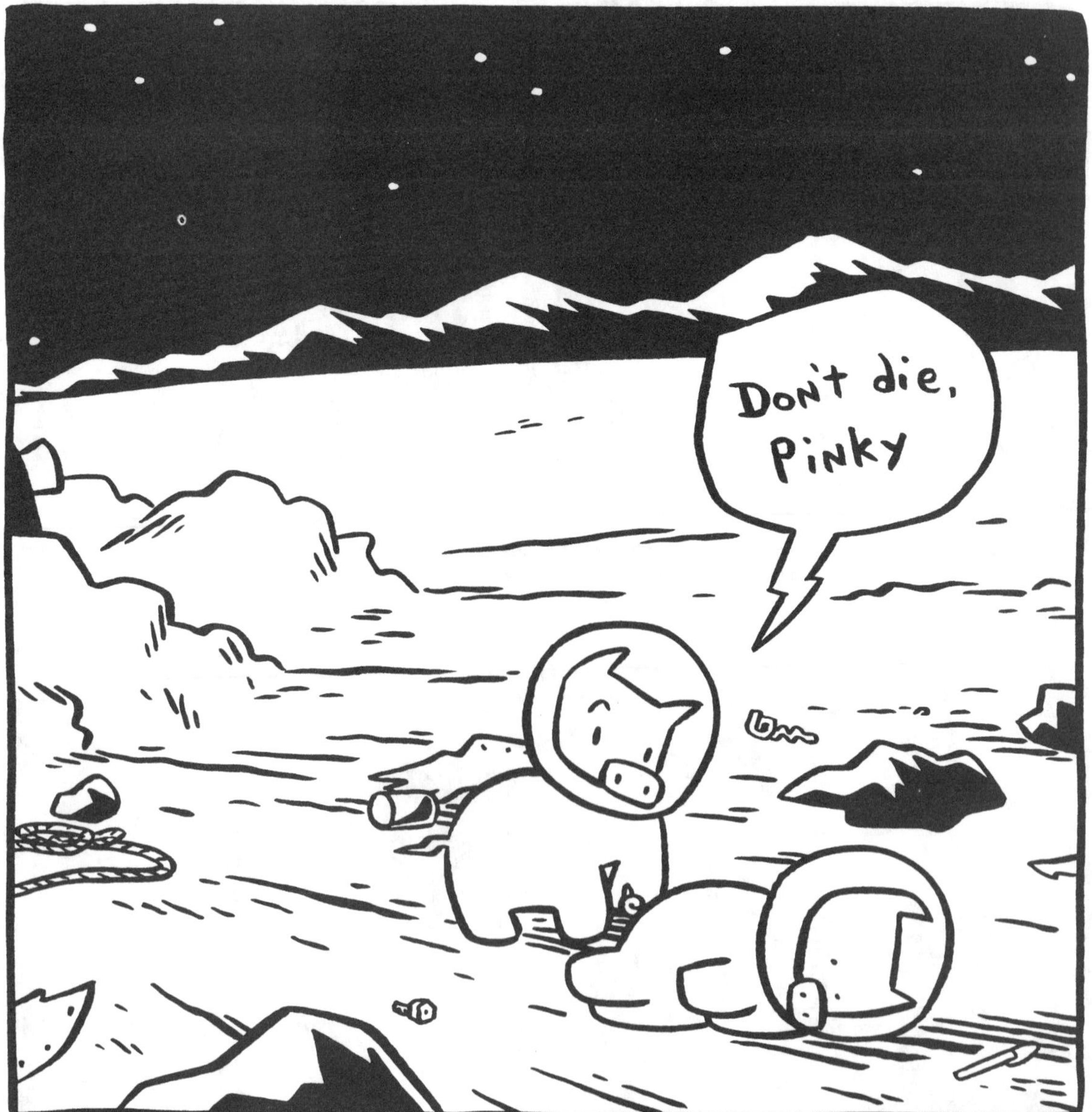
Don't die, Pinky

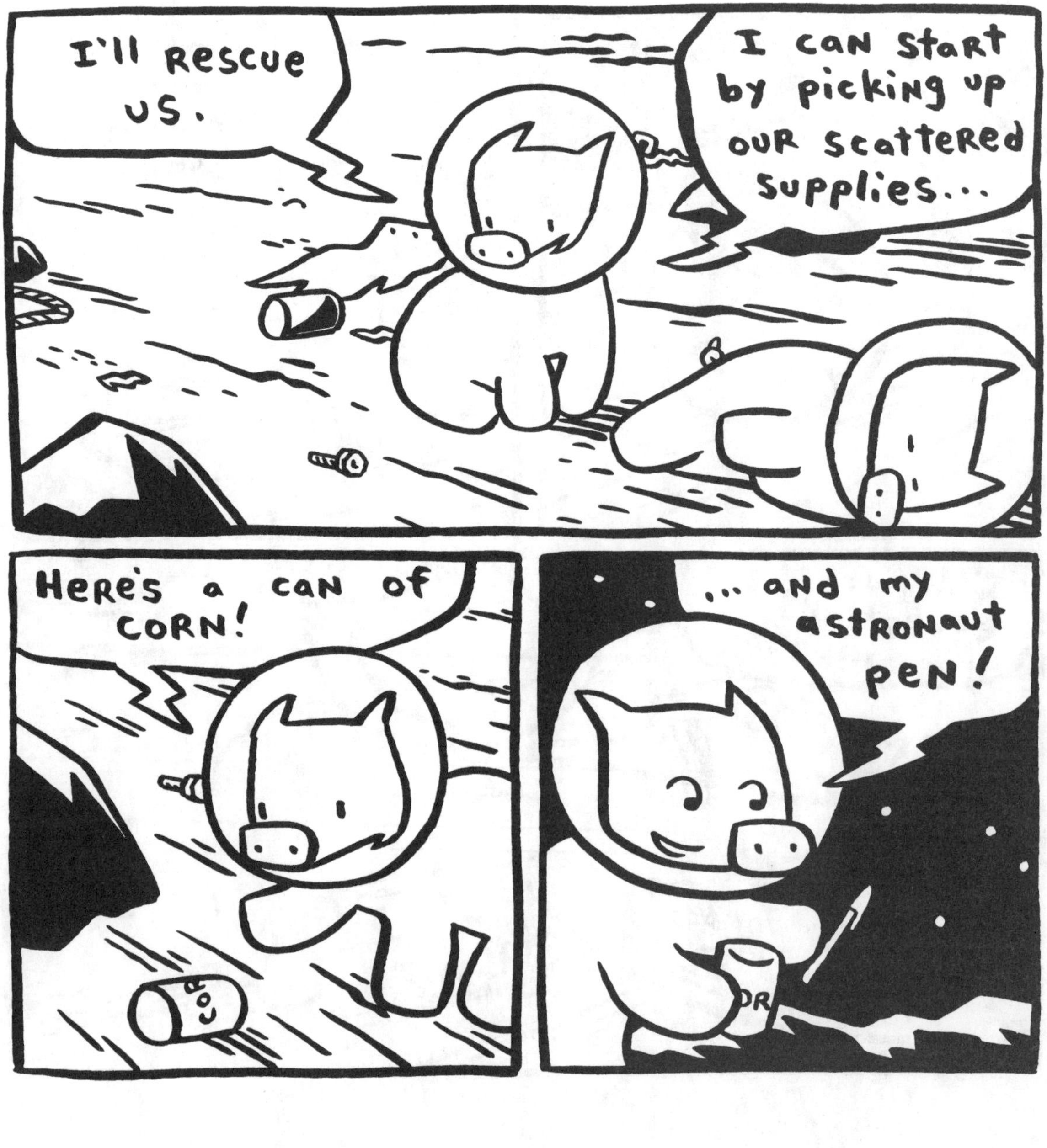
I'll rescue us.
I can start by picking up our scattered supplies...
Here's a can of CORN!
COR
... and my astronaut pen!
OR

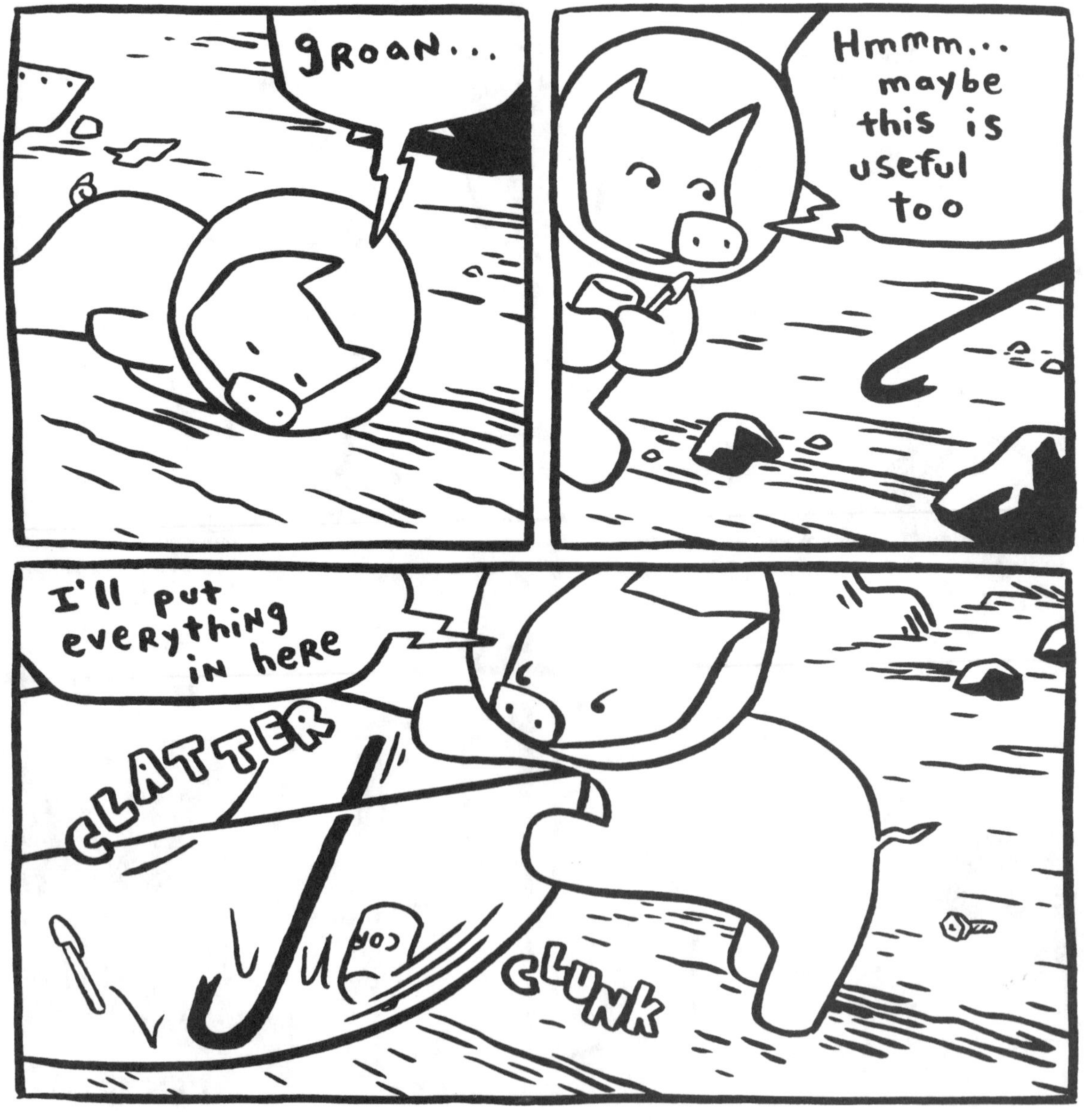
groan...
Hmmm... maybe this is useful too
I'll put everything in here
CLATTER
CLUNK

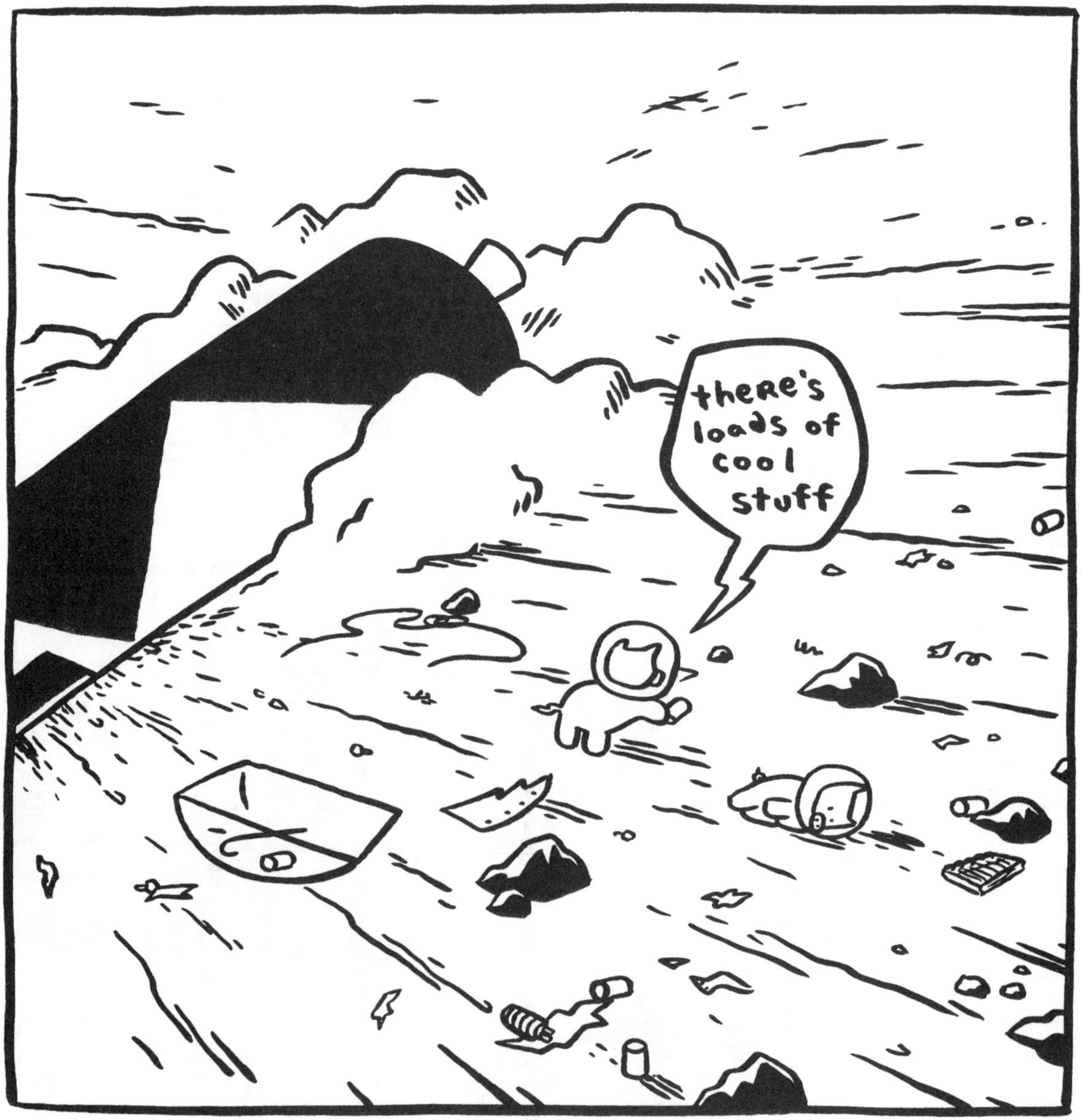
there's loads of cool stuff

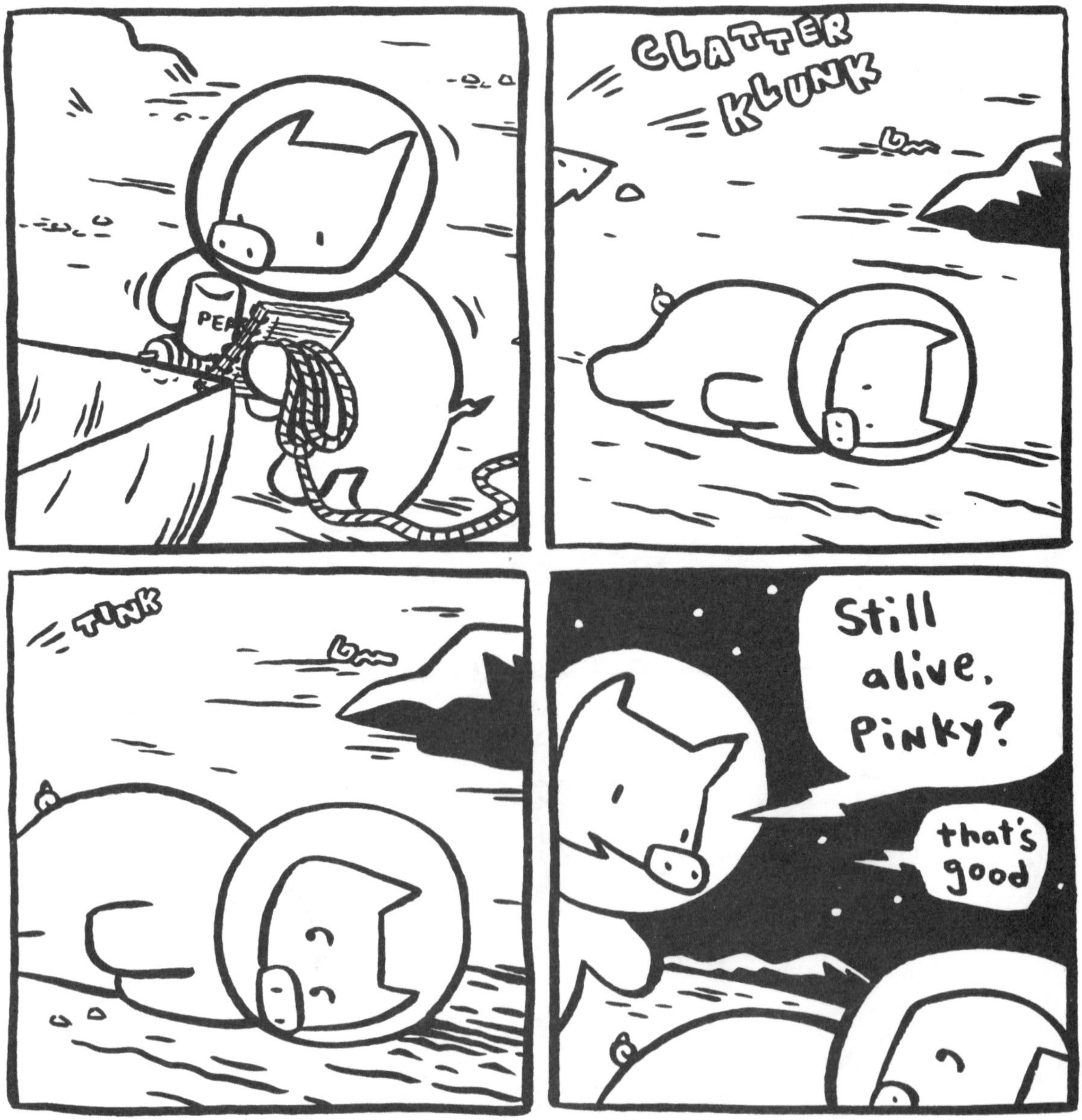
CLATTER
KLUNK
TINK
Still alive, Pinky?
that's good

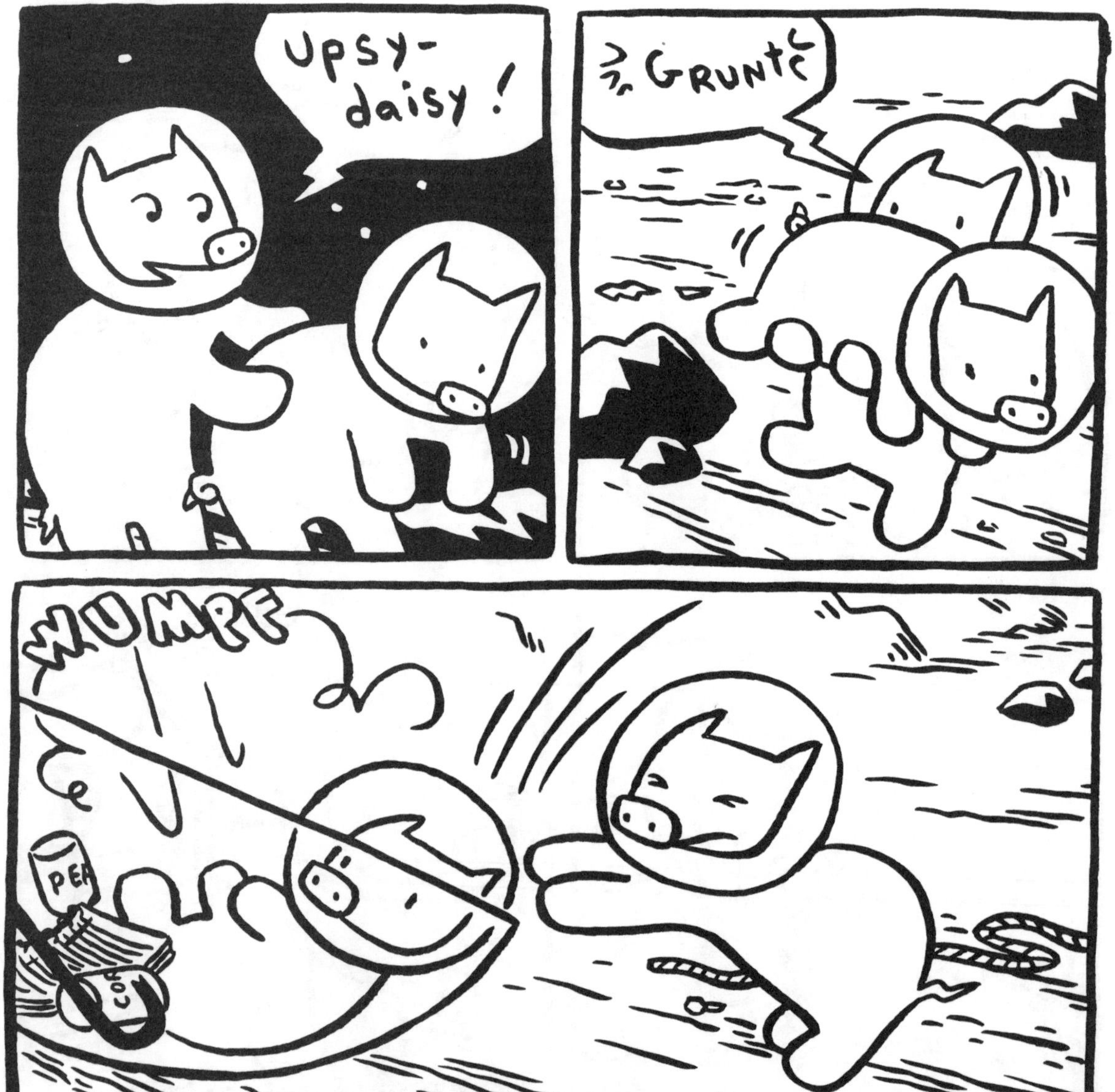

Upsy-daisy!
GRUNT
WUMPF
PEA

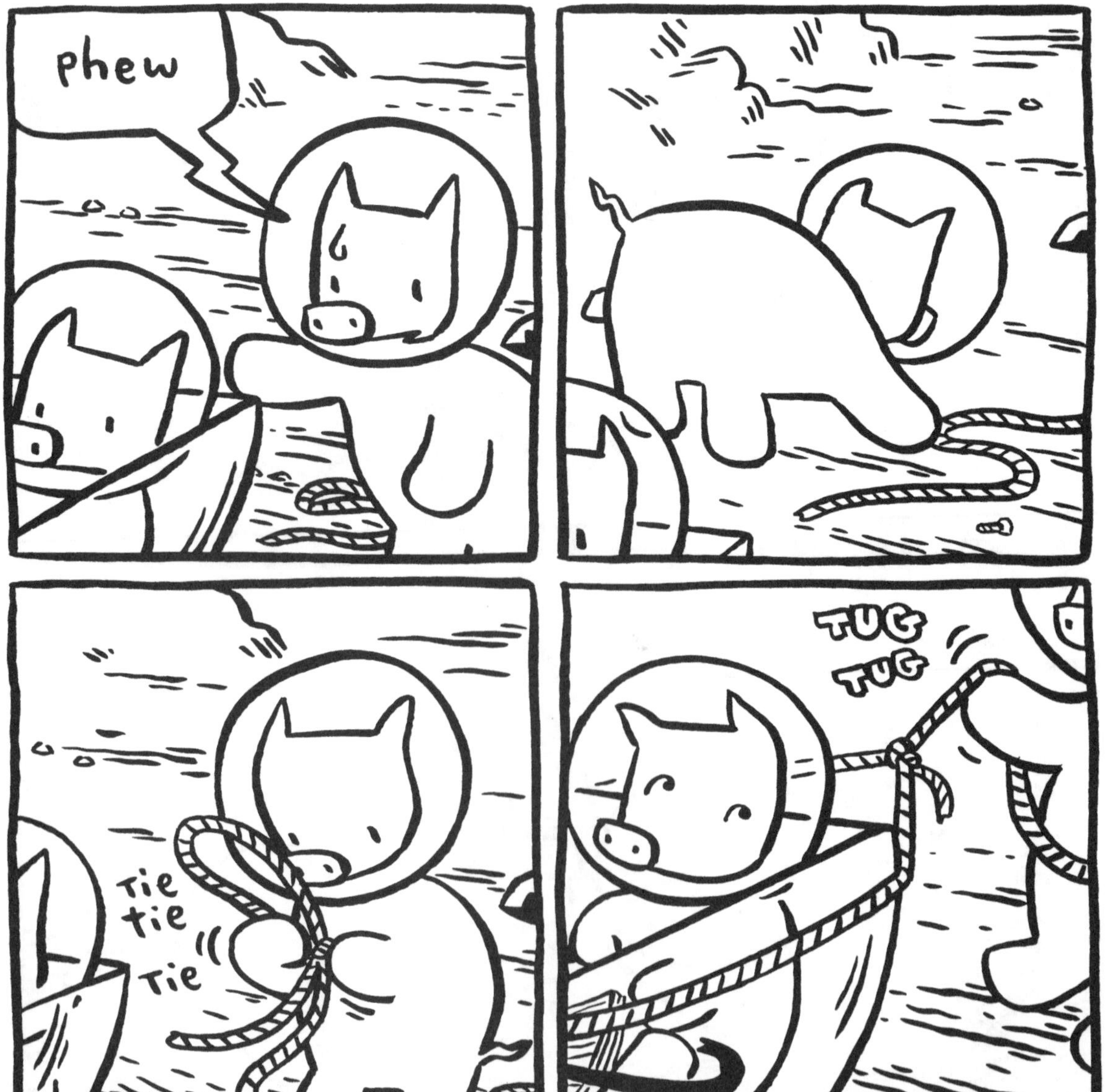
phew
tie
tie
tie
TUG
TUG

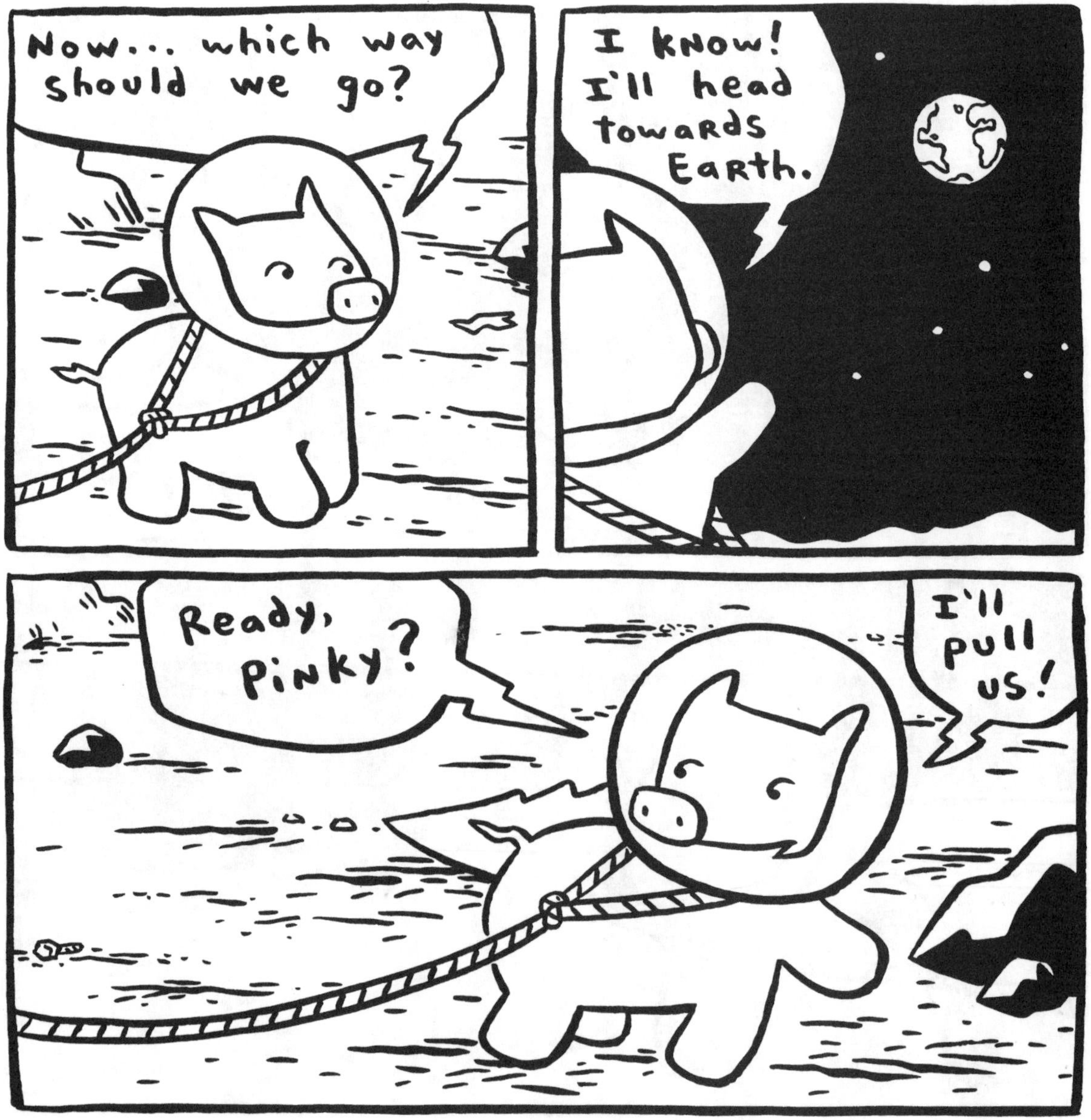
Now... which way should we go?
I know! I'll head towards Earth.
Ready, Pinky?
I'll pull us!

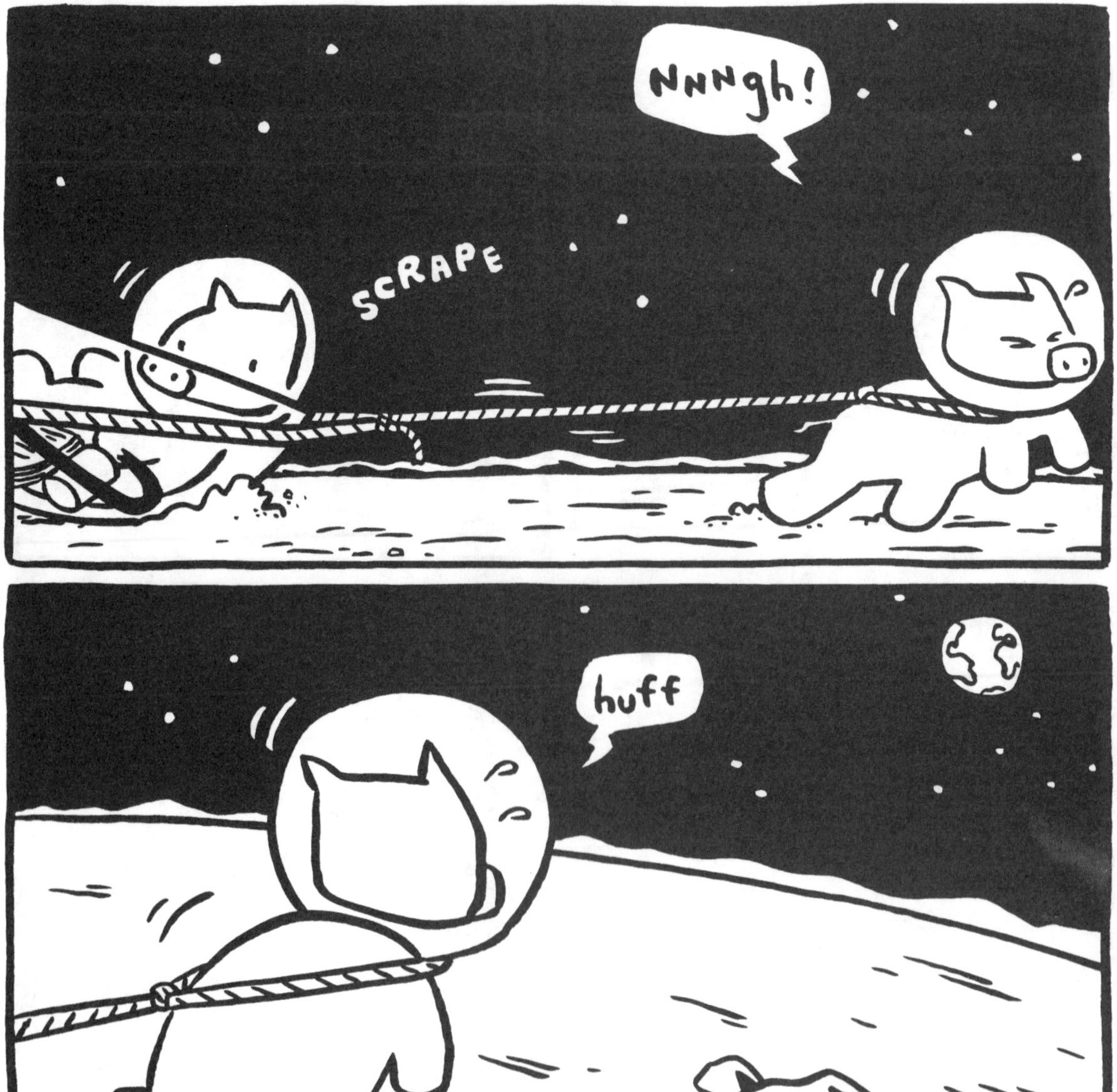
NNNgh!
SCRAPE
huff

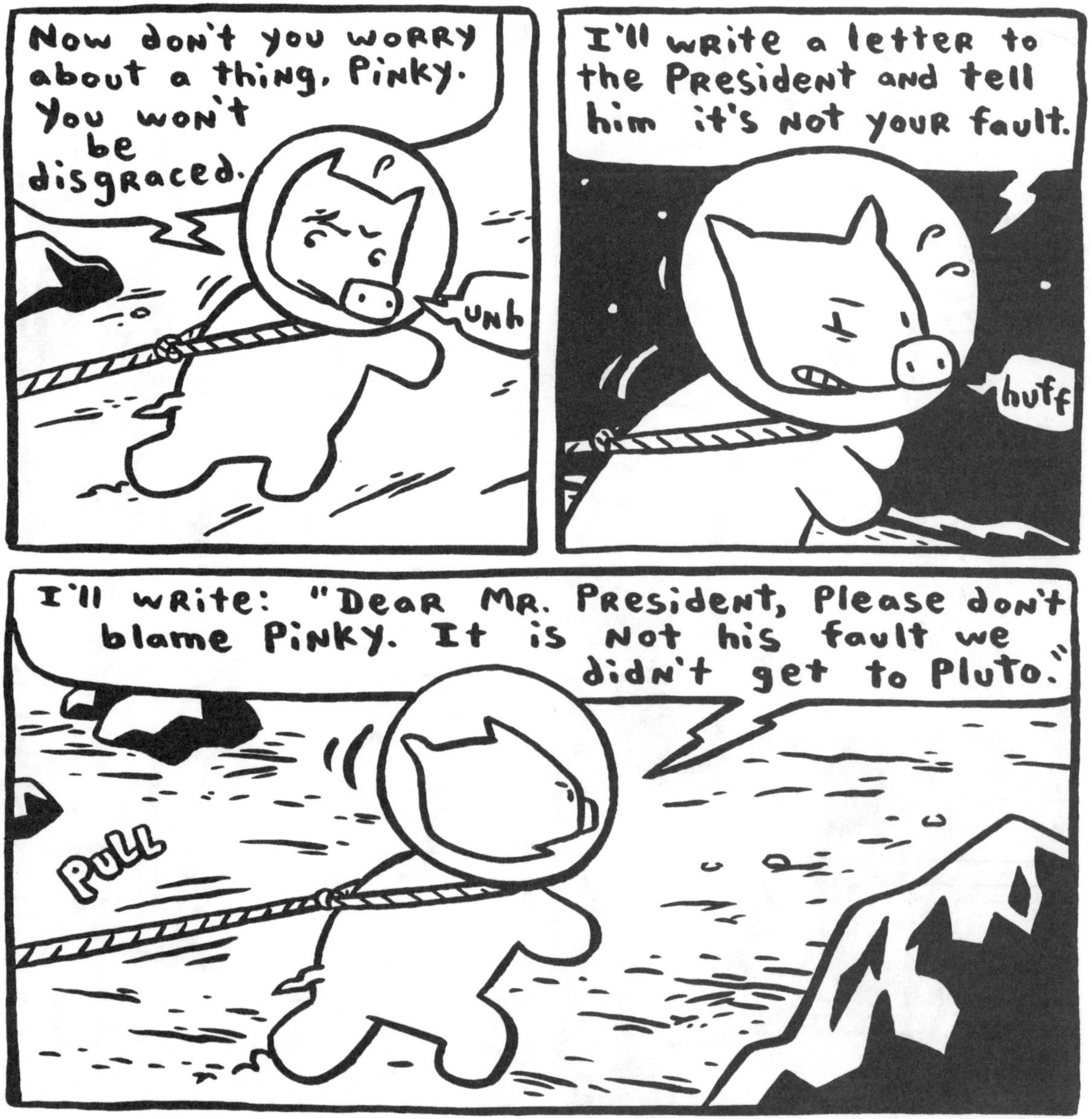

Now don't you worry about a thing, Pinky. You won't be disgraced.
UNH
I'll write a letter to the President and tell him it's not your fault.
huff
I'll write: "Dear Mr. President, Please don't blame Pinky. It is not his fault we didn't get to Pluto."
PULL

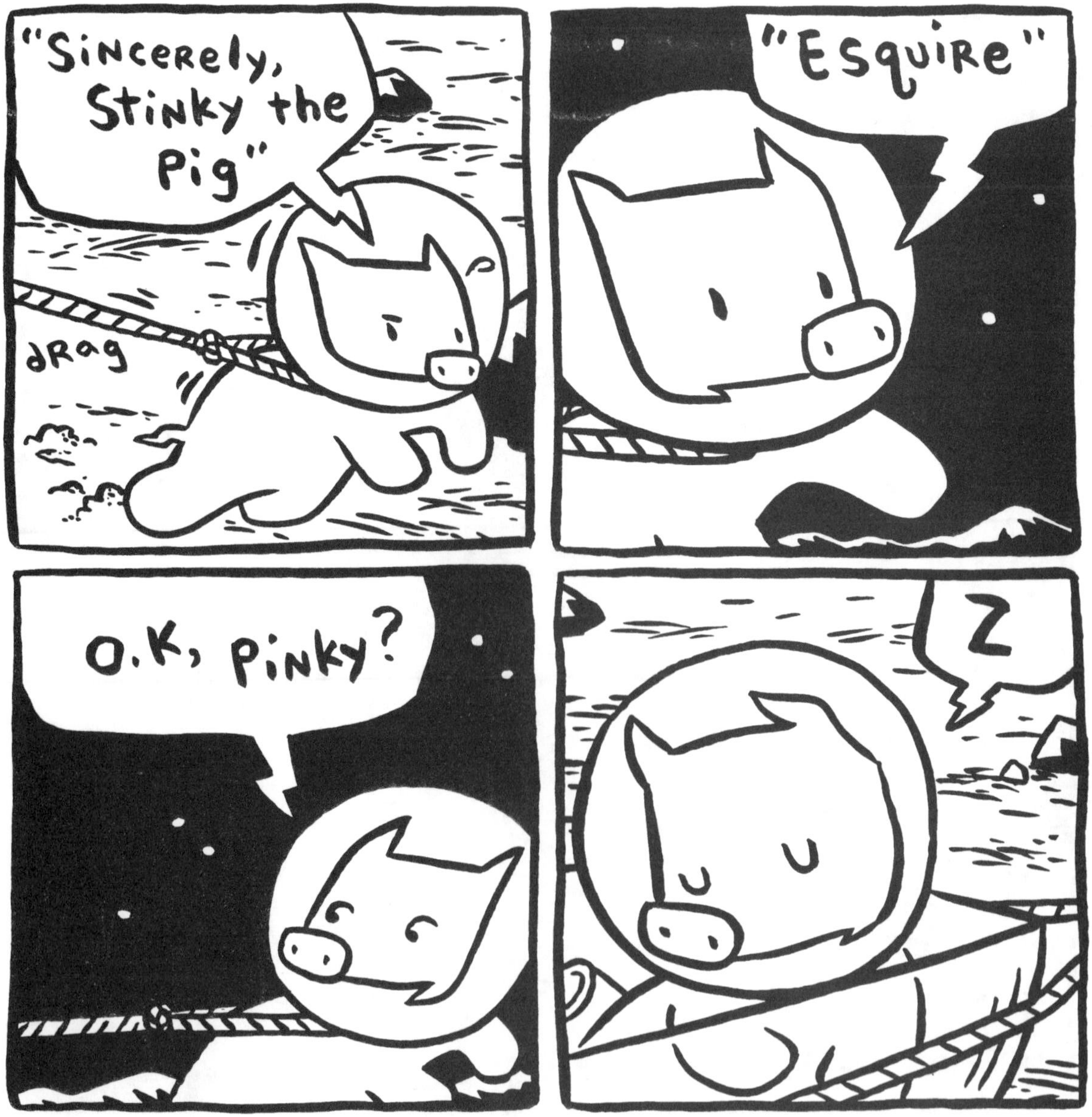
"Sincerely, Stinky the Pig"
dRag
"Esquire"
O.K, pinky?
Z

Oh, you're sleeping
That's good. Maybe you'll be less depressed when you wake up.
GRUNT
Pull
ZZZ
SCRAPE

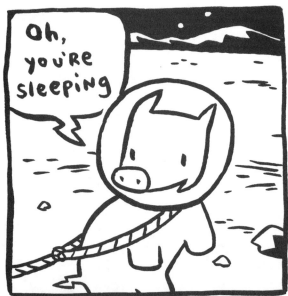

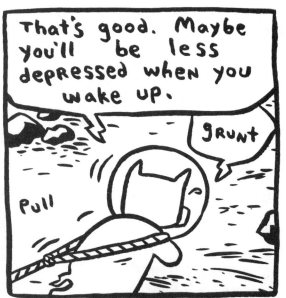

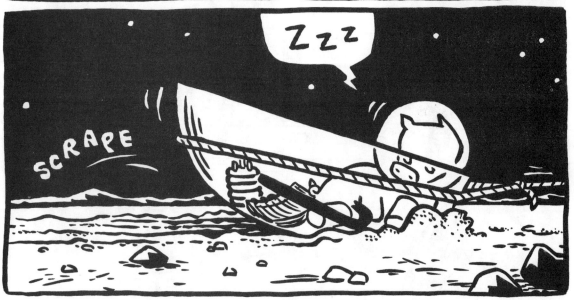

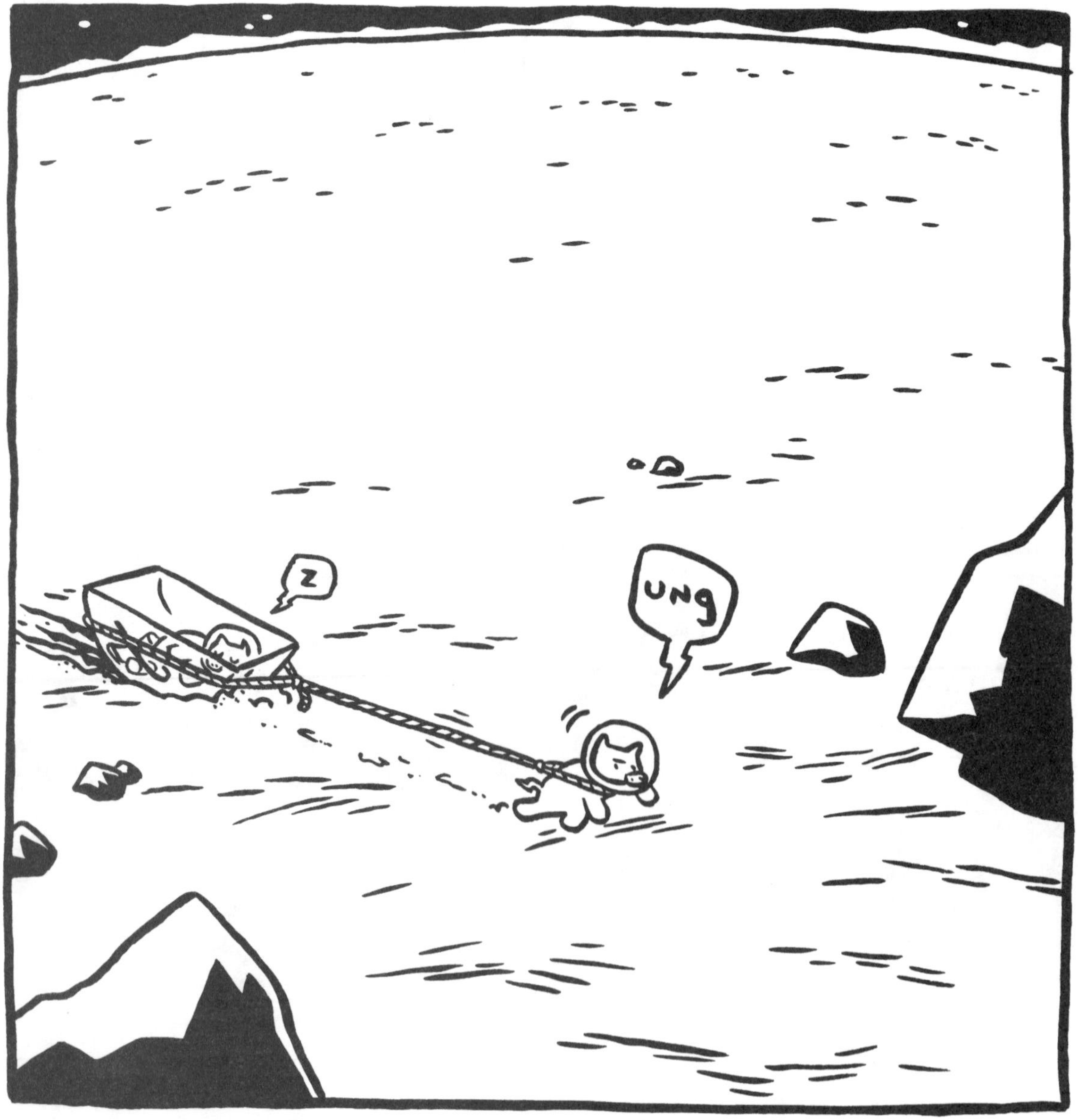
Z
UNG

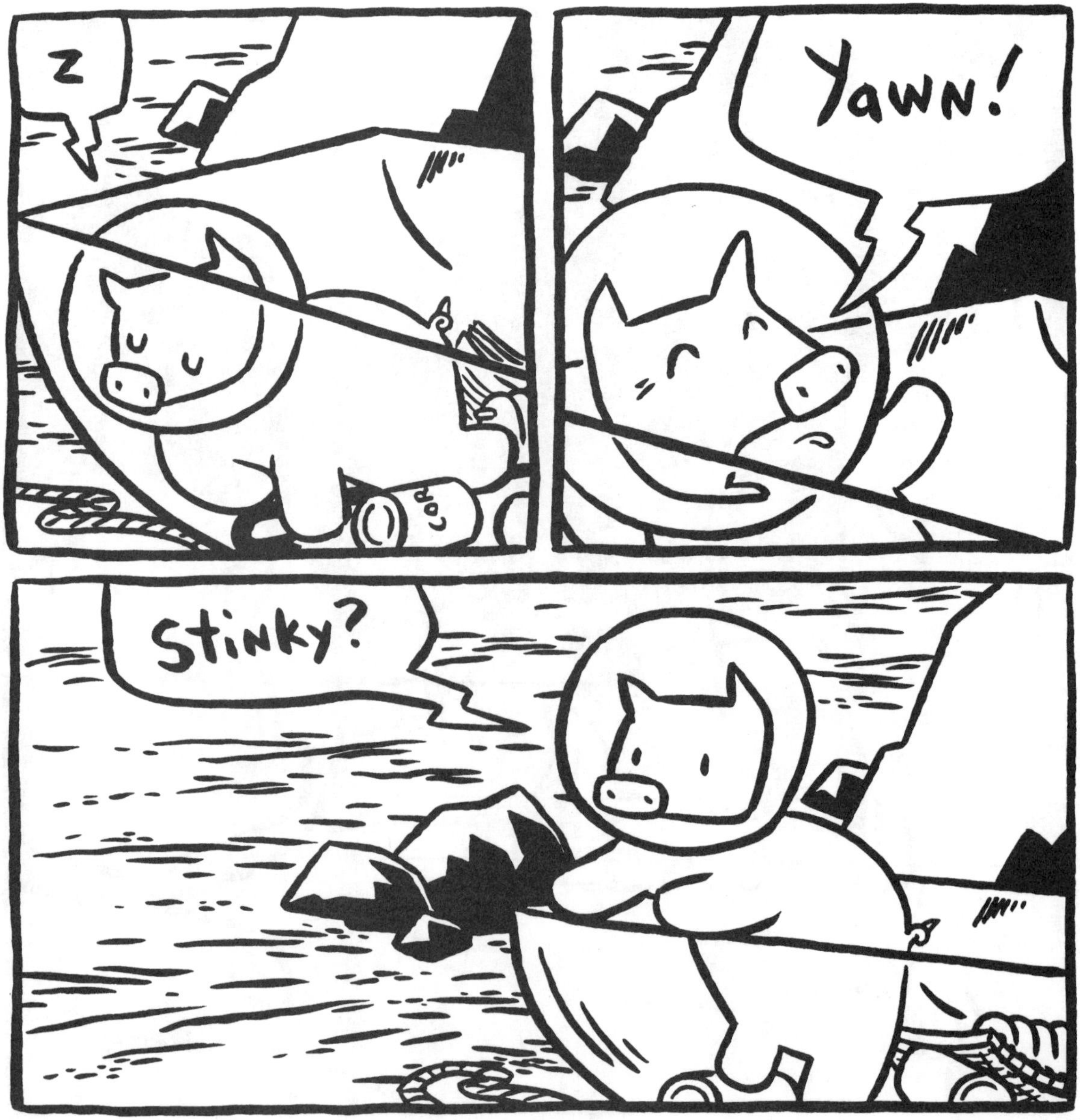
z
Yawn!
Stinky?

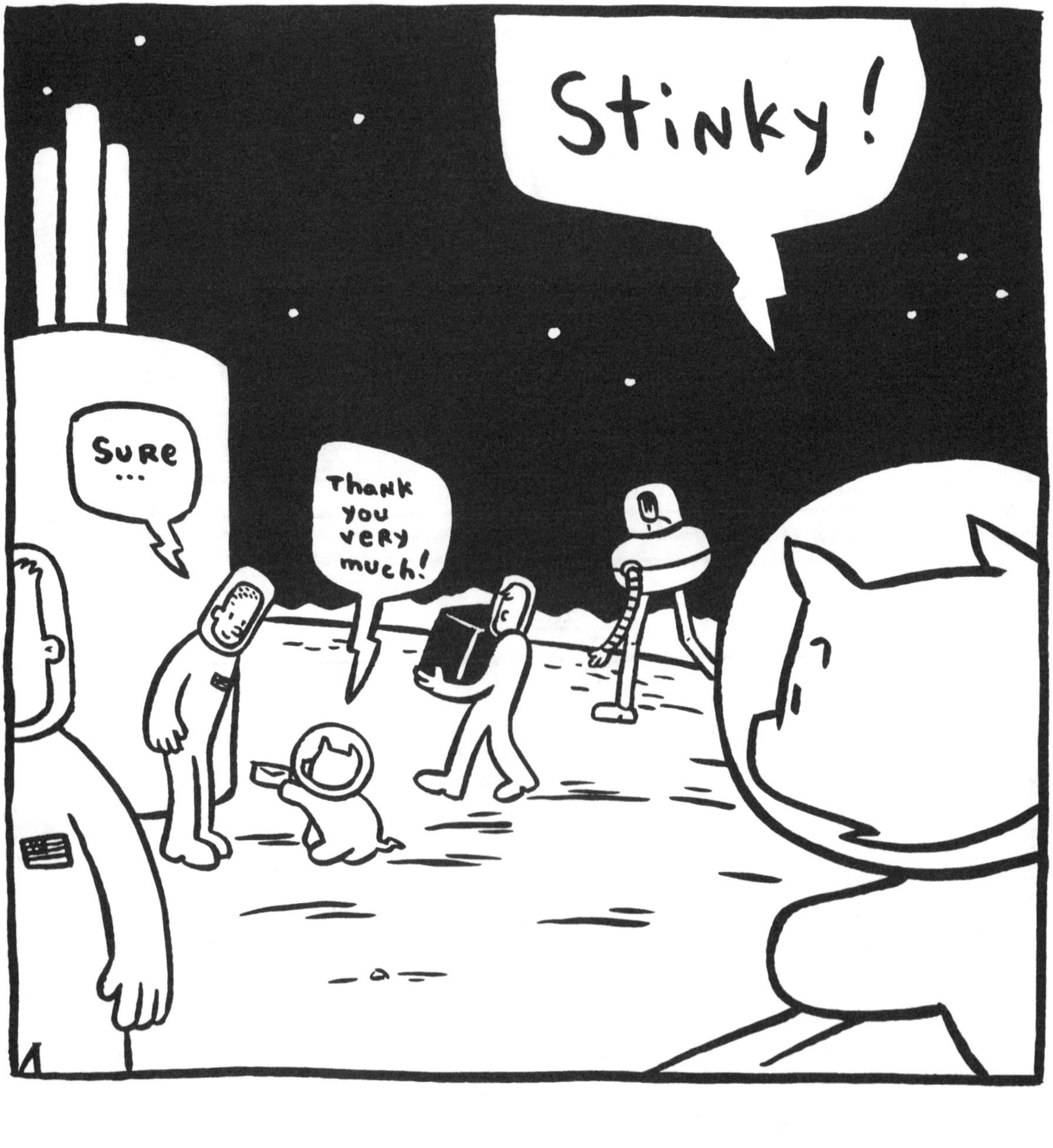
Sure ...
Thank you very much!
Stinky!

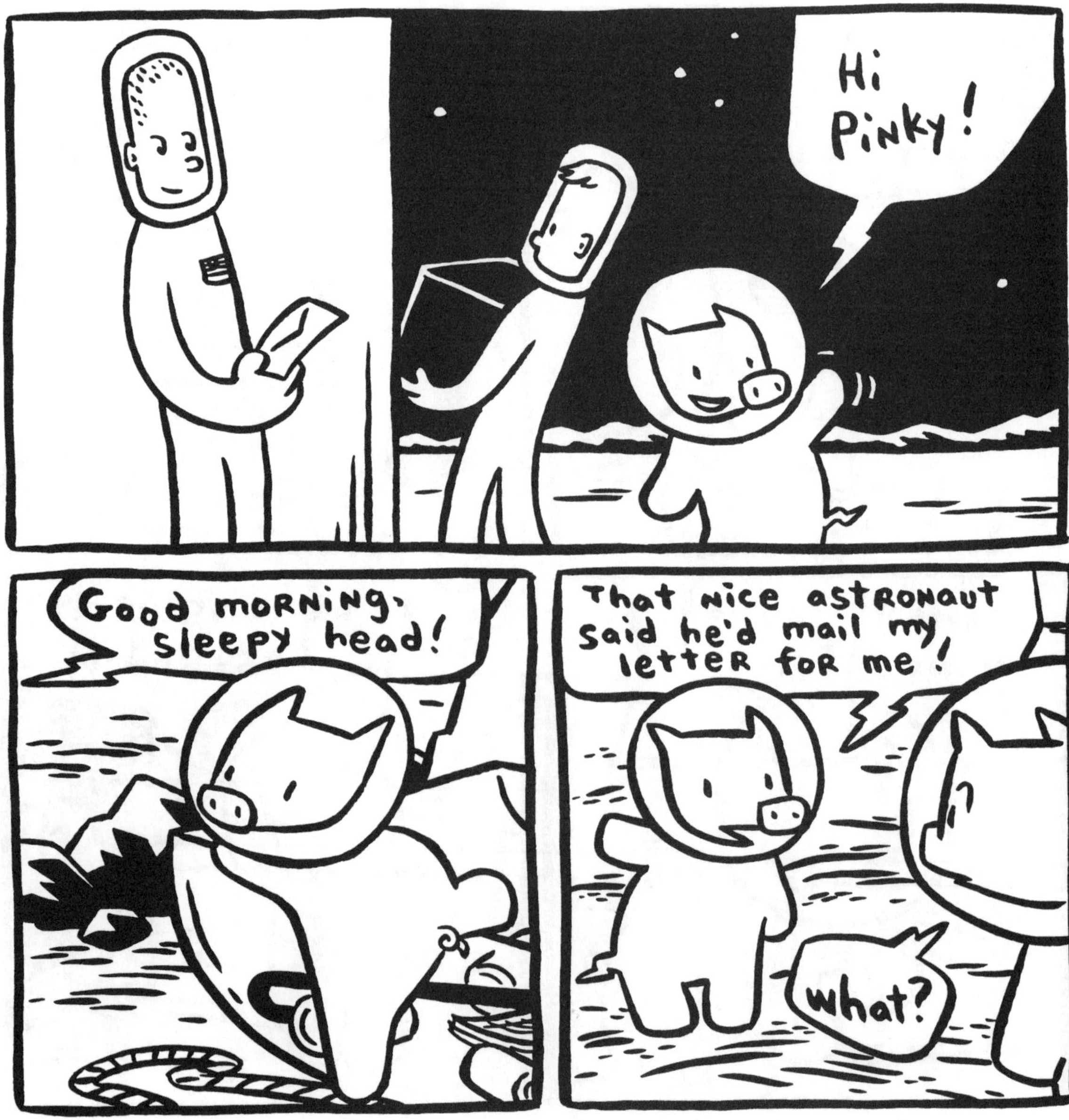
Hi Pinky!
Good morning, sleepy head!
That nice astronaut said he'd mail my letter for me!
what?

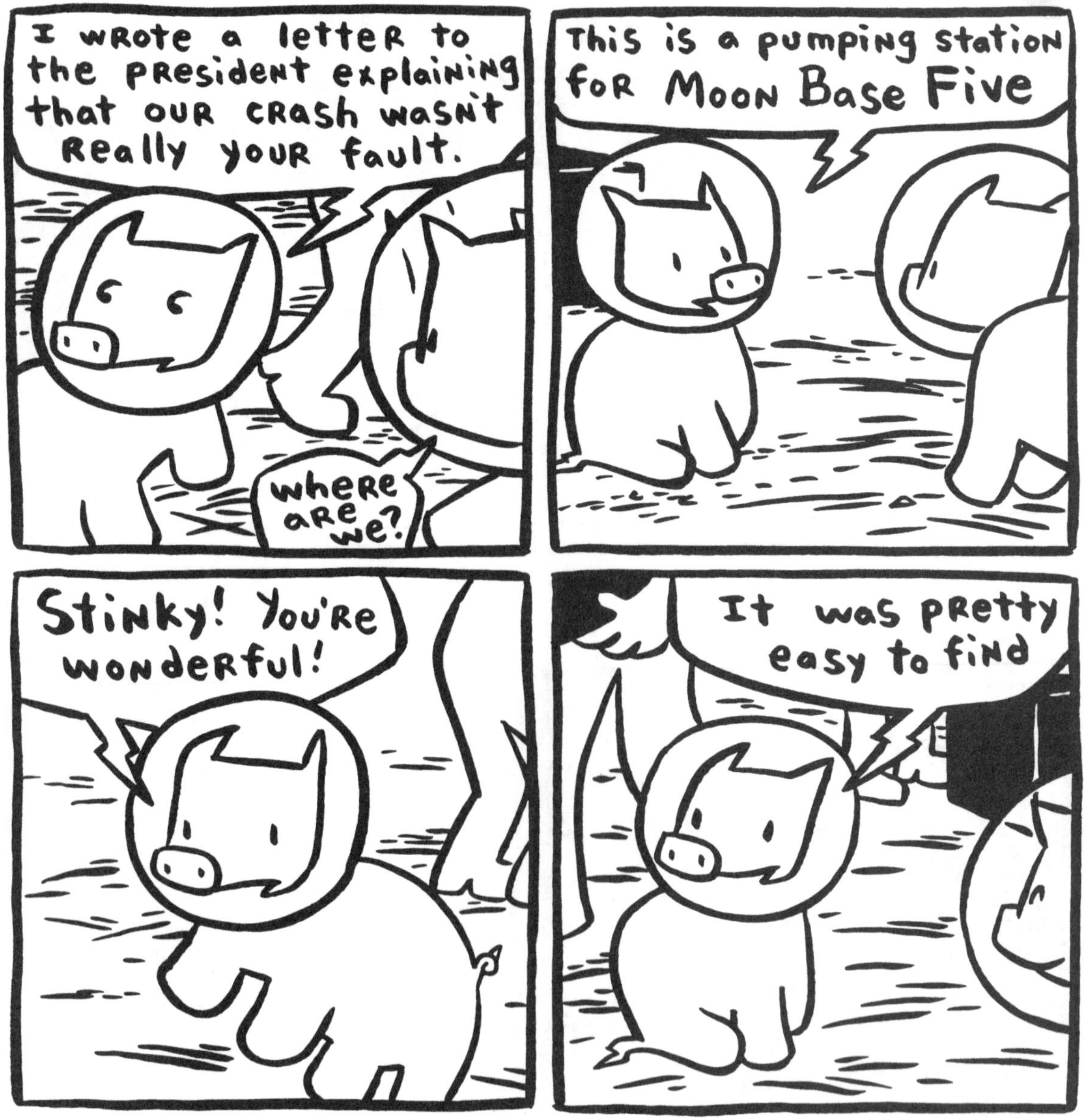
I wrote a letter to the president explaining that our crash wasn't really your fault.
where are we?
This is a pumping station for Moon Base Five
Stinky! You're wonderful!
It was pretty easy to find

All right piggies,
Move along.
We MEN have work to do here and we don't need little piglets scurrying about!
Getting in our way
We're not scurrying!

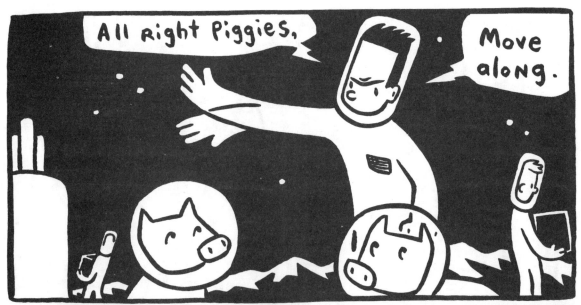

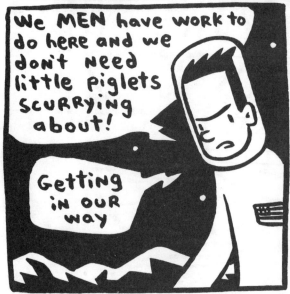

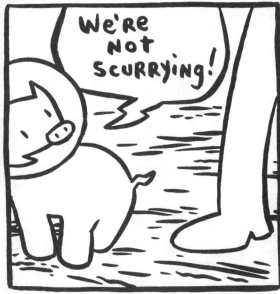

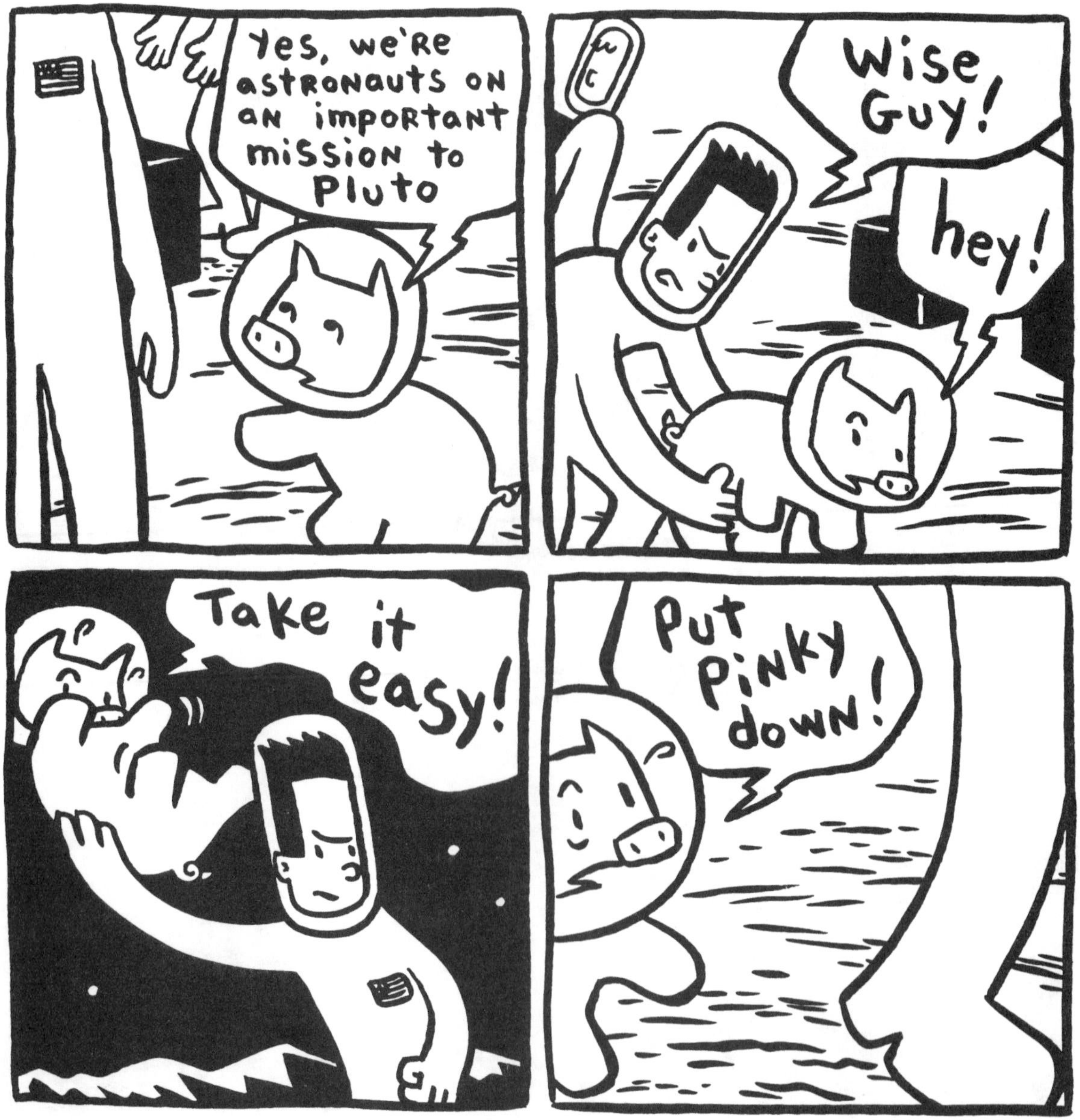
Yes, we're astronauts on an important mission to Pluto
Wise Guy!
hey!
Take it easy!
Put Pinky down!

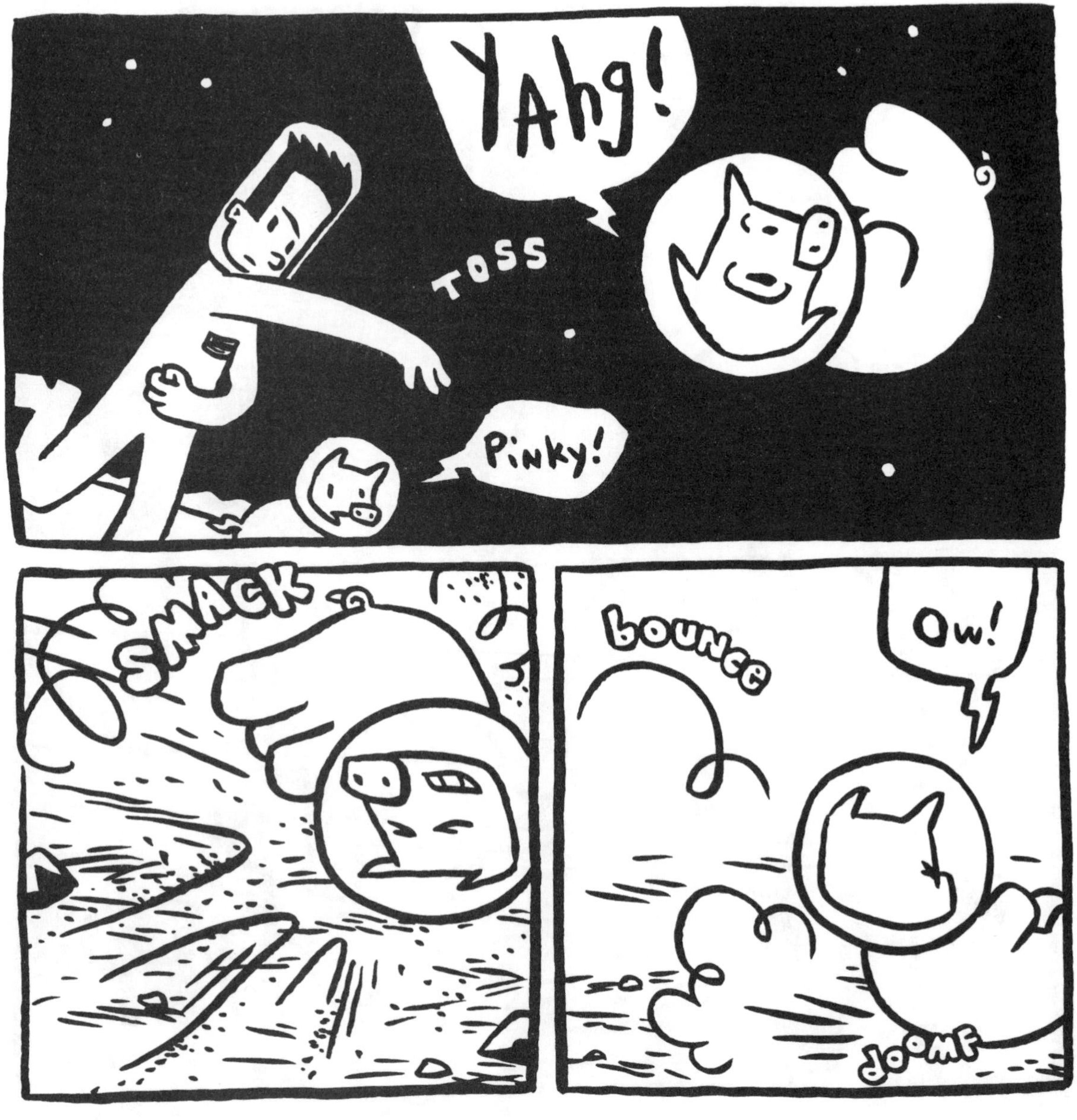
Yahg!
TOSS
Pinky!
SMACK
bounce
Ow!
dOOMF

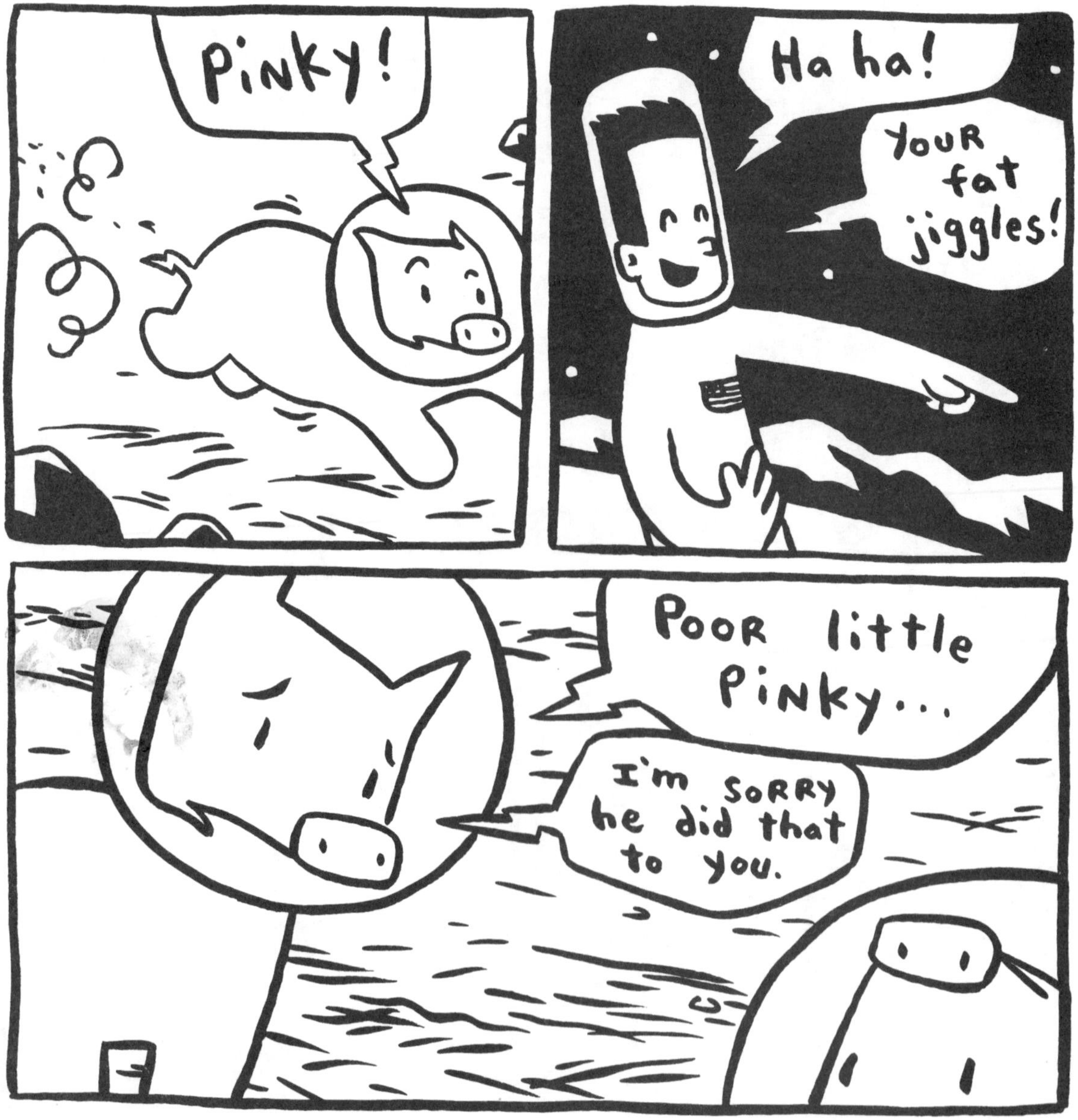
Pinky!
Ha ha!
Your fat jiggles!
Poor little Pinky...
I'm sorry he did that to you.

Are you going to get all depressed again now?
No... it just hurts a little.
That astronaut wasn't as nice as the other one.

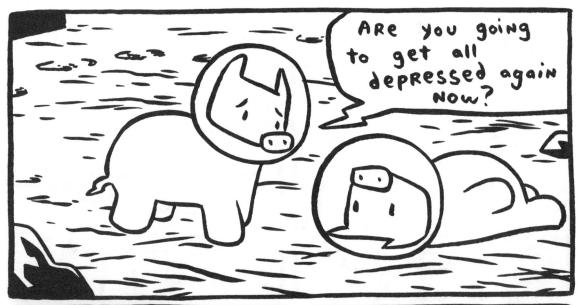

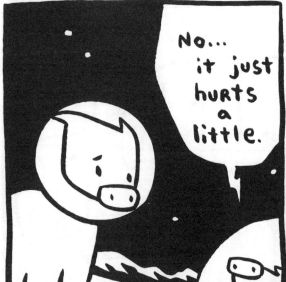

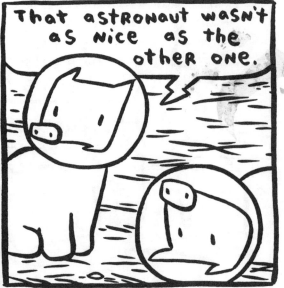

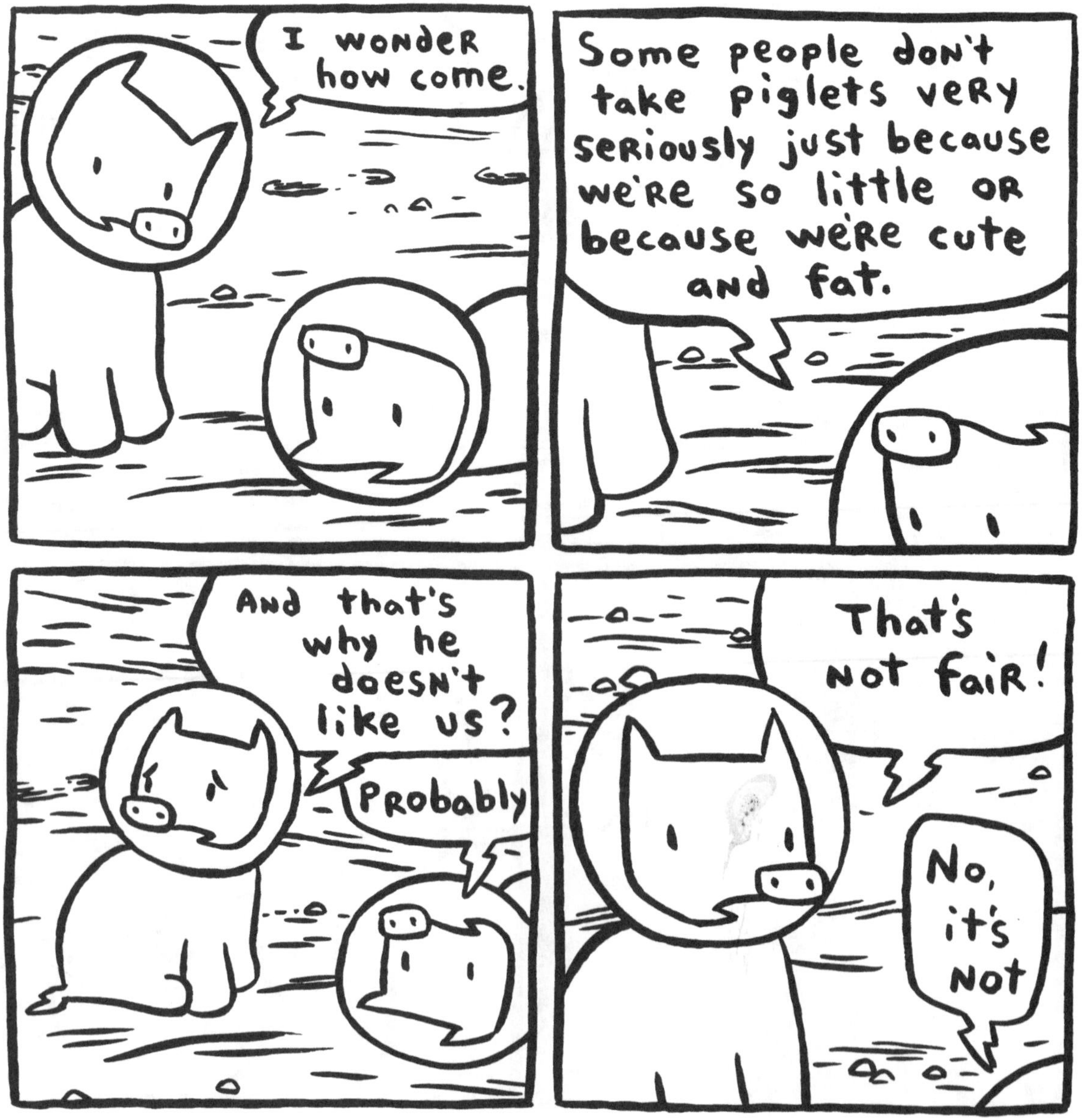

I wonder how come.
Some people don't take piglets very seriously just because we're so little or because we're cute and fat.
And that's why he doesn't like us?
Probably
That's not fair!
No, it's not

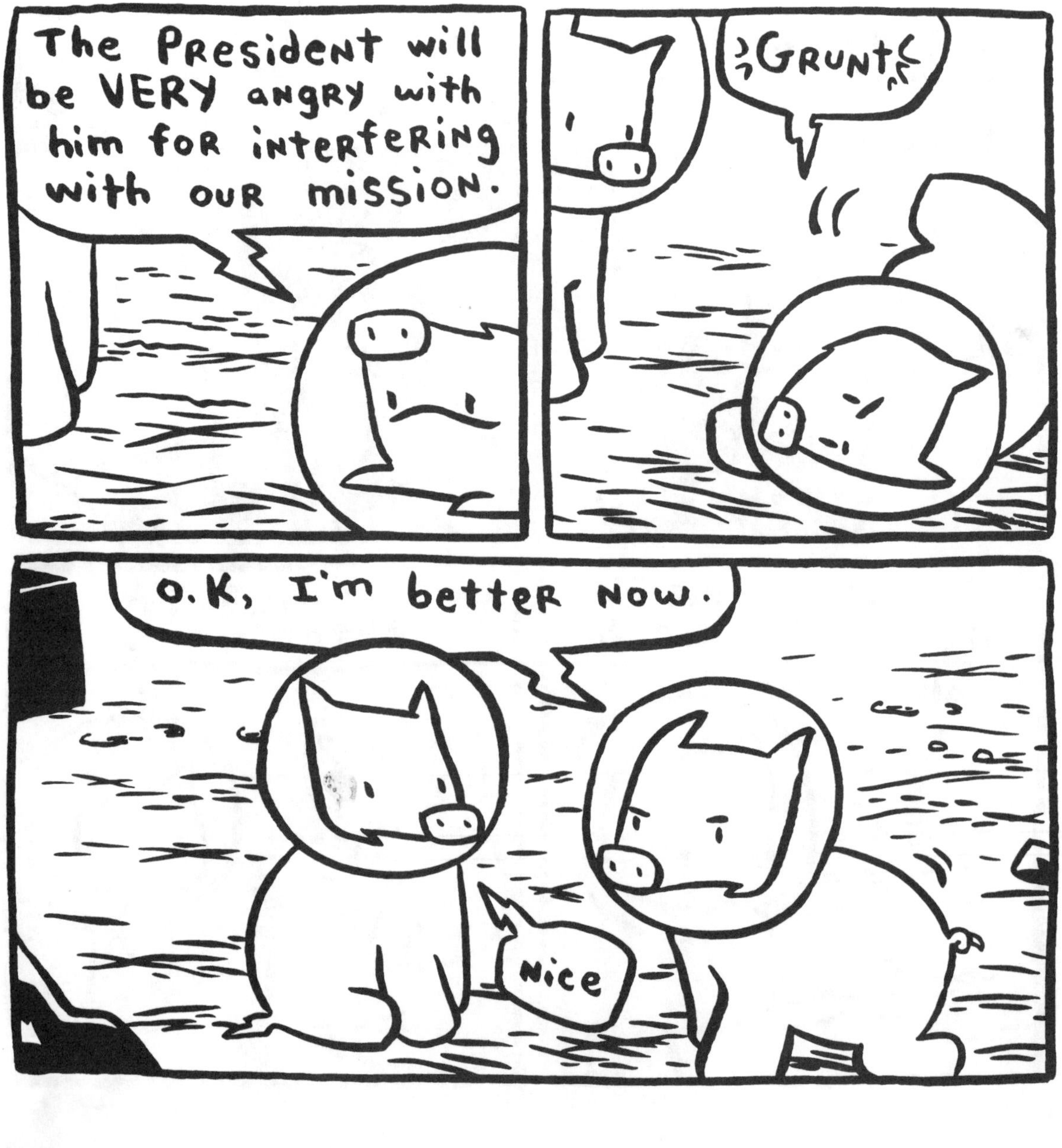
The President will be VERY angry with him for interfering with our mission.
GRUNT
O.K, I'm better now.
Nice

We'll follow the pipeline to Moon Base Five where the President will probably have a new Spaceship waiting for us.

...but, Moon Base Five might be too far to walk...

How will we get there?

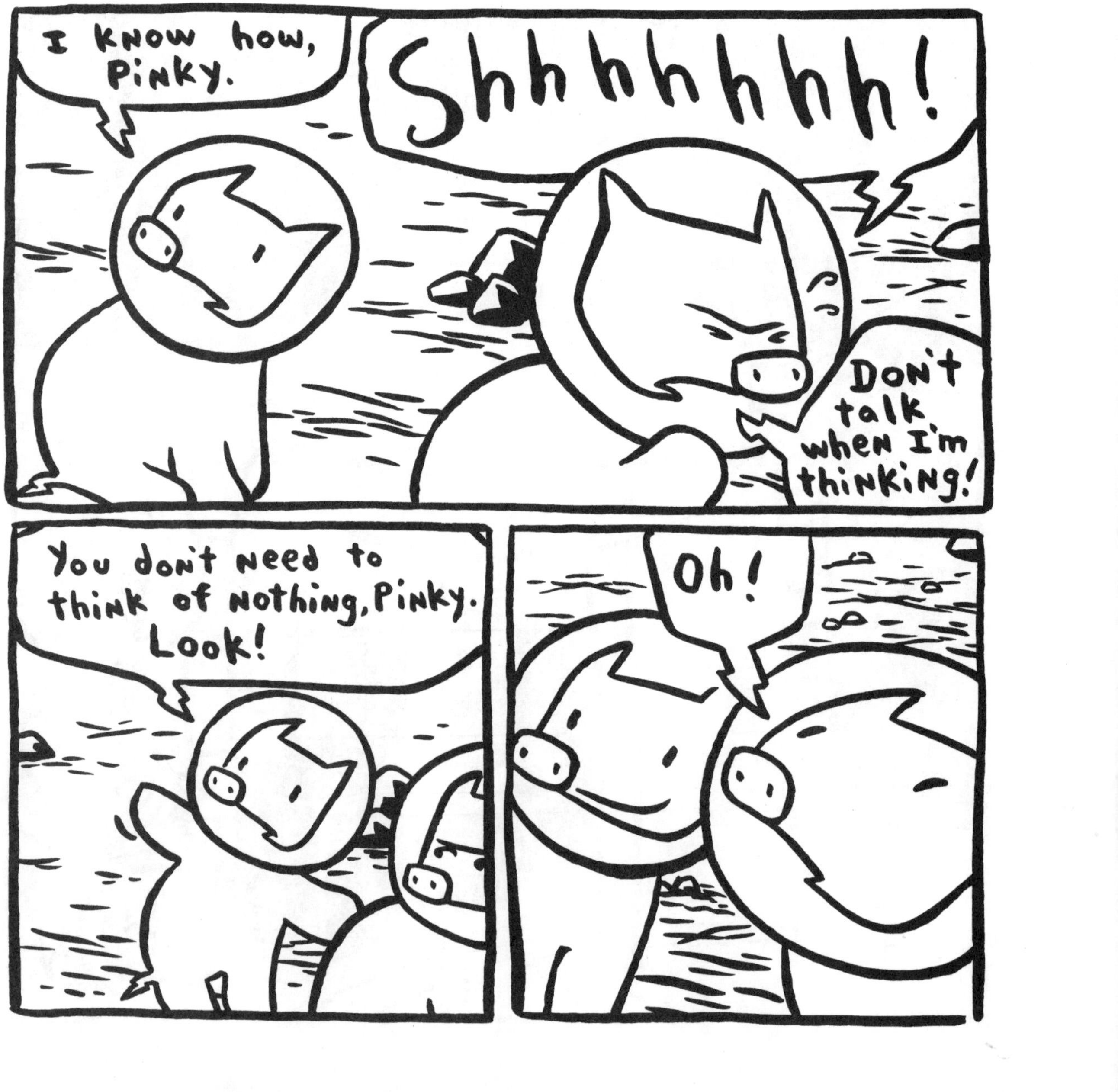
I know how, Pinky.
Shhhhhhhh!
Don't talk when I'm thinking!
You don't need to think of nothing, Pinky. Look!
Oh!

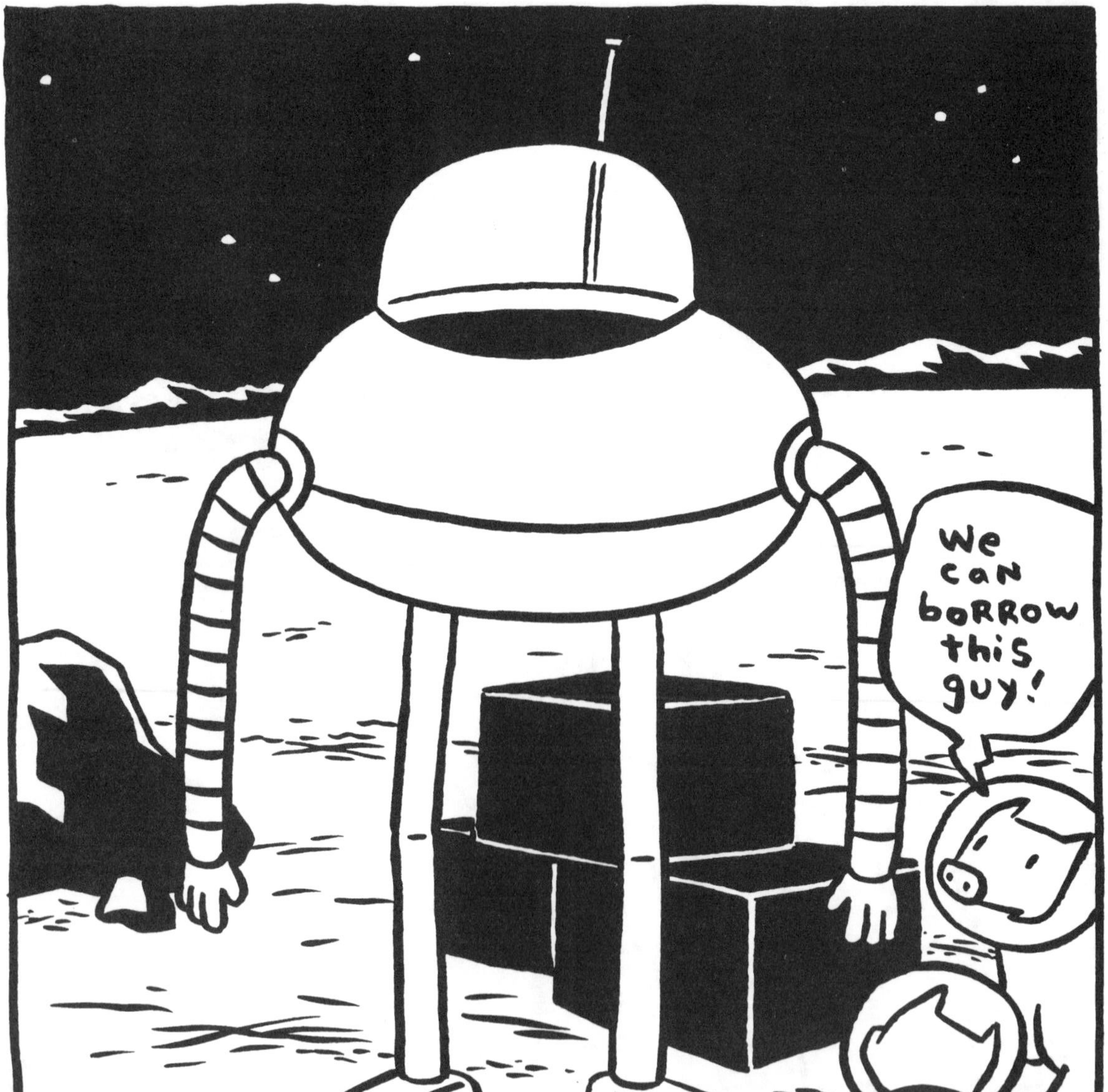
we can borrow this guy!

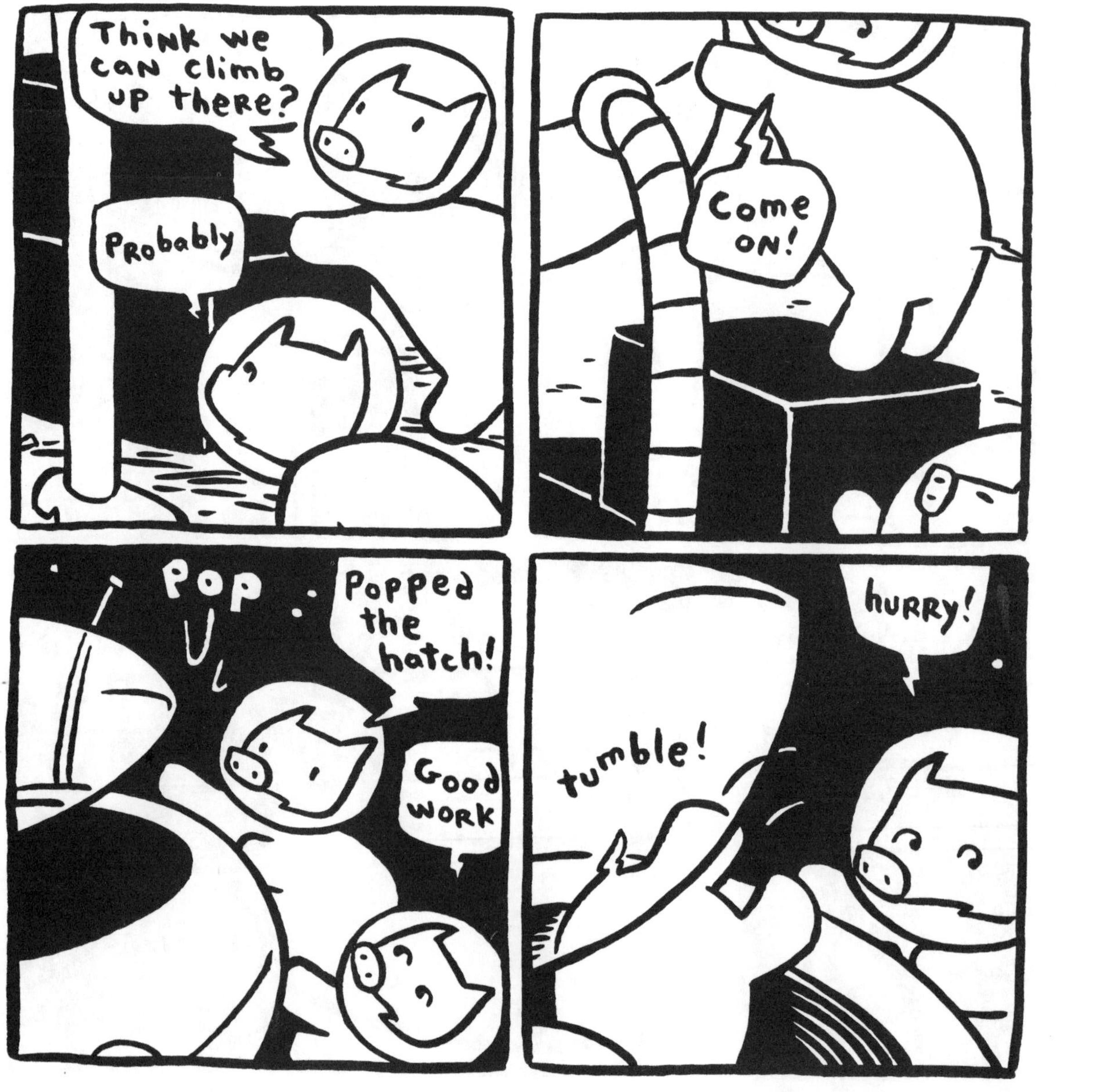

Think we can climb up there?
Probably
Come ON!
Pop
Popped the hatch!
Good work
hurry!
tumble!

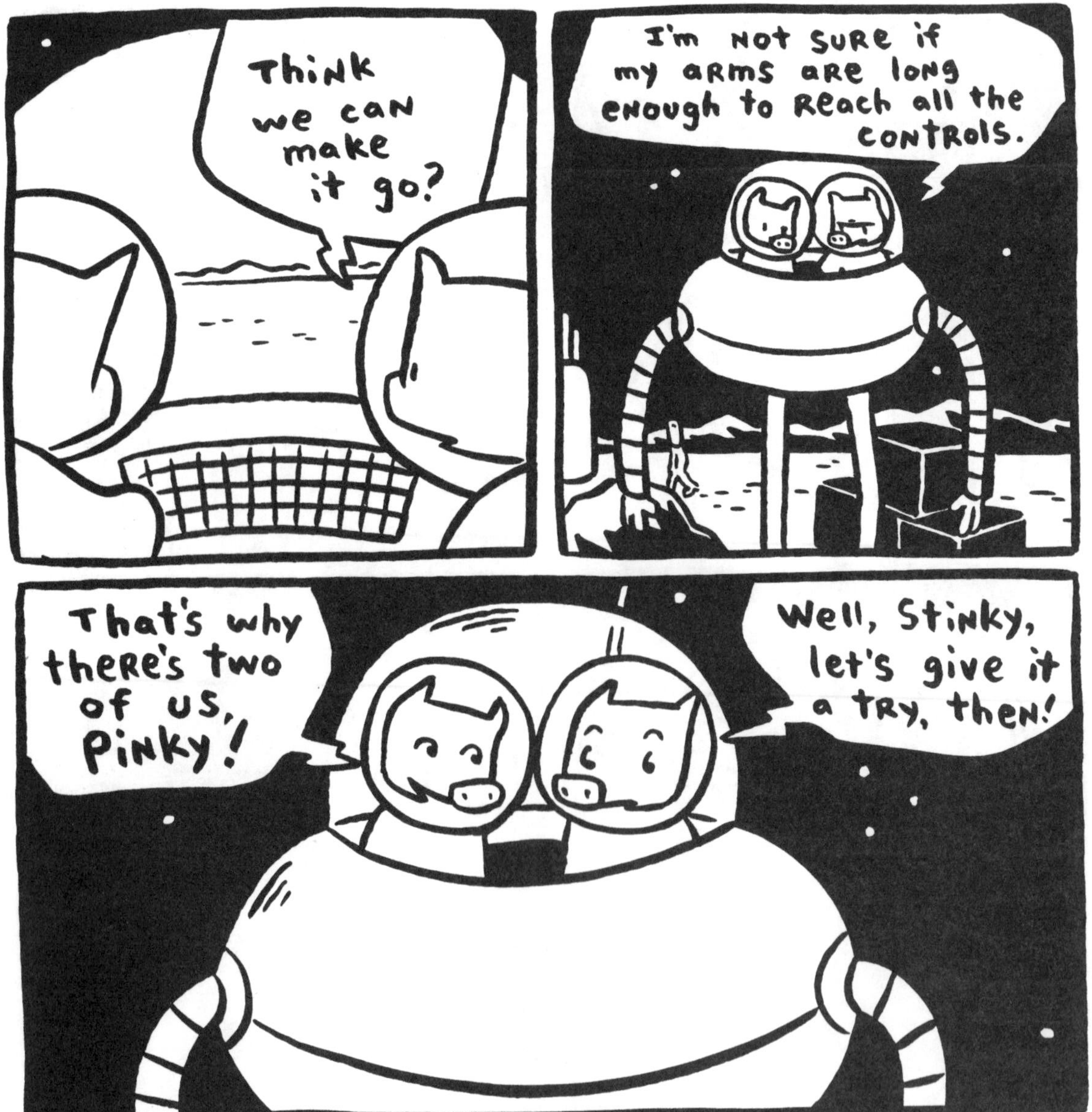
Think we can make it go?
I'm not sure if my arms are long enough to reach all the controls.
That's why there's two of us, Pinky!
Well, Stinky, let's give it a try, then!

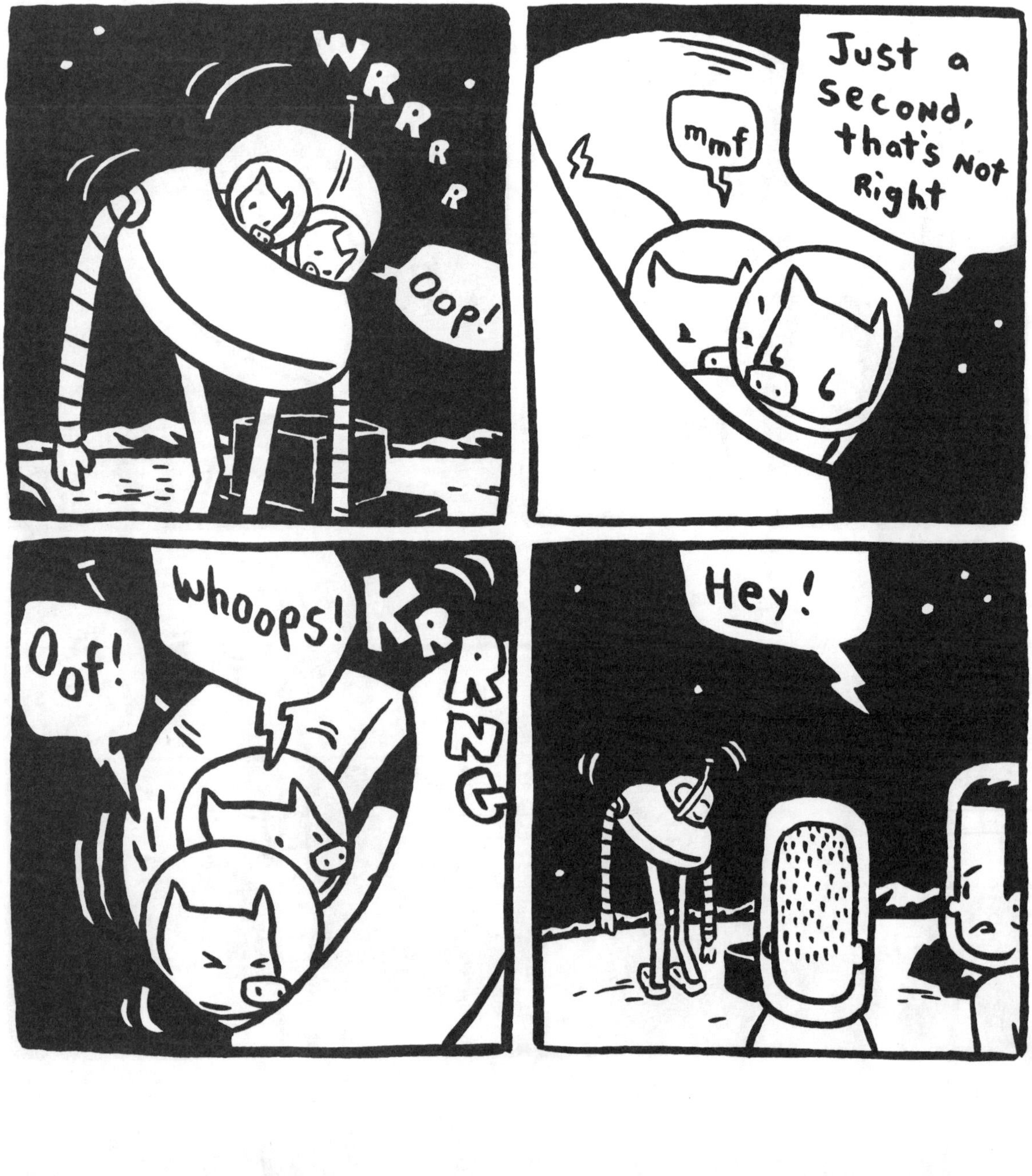
WRRRRR
Oop!
mmf
Just a second, that's not right
Oof!
whoops!
KRRRNG
Hey!

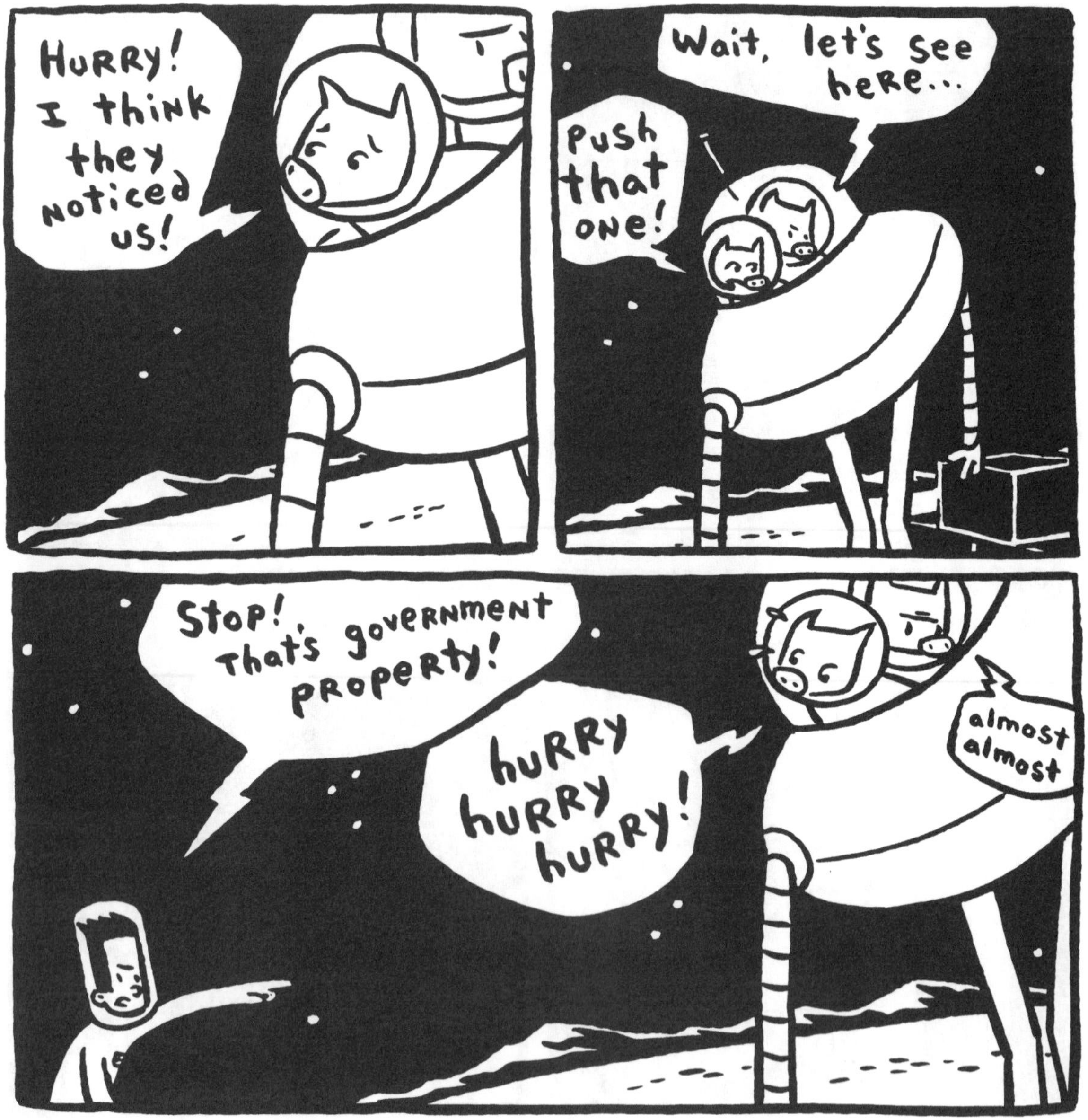
HURRY! I think they noticed us!
Wait, let's see here...
Push that one!
Stop! That's government property!
hurry hurry hurry!
almost almost

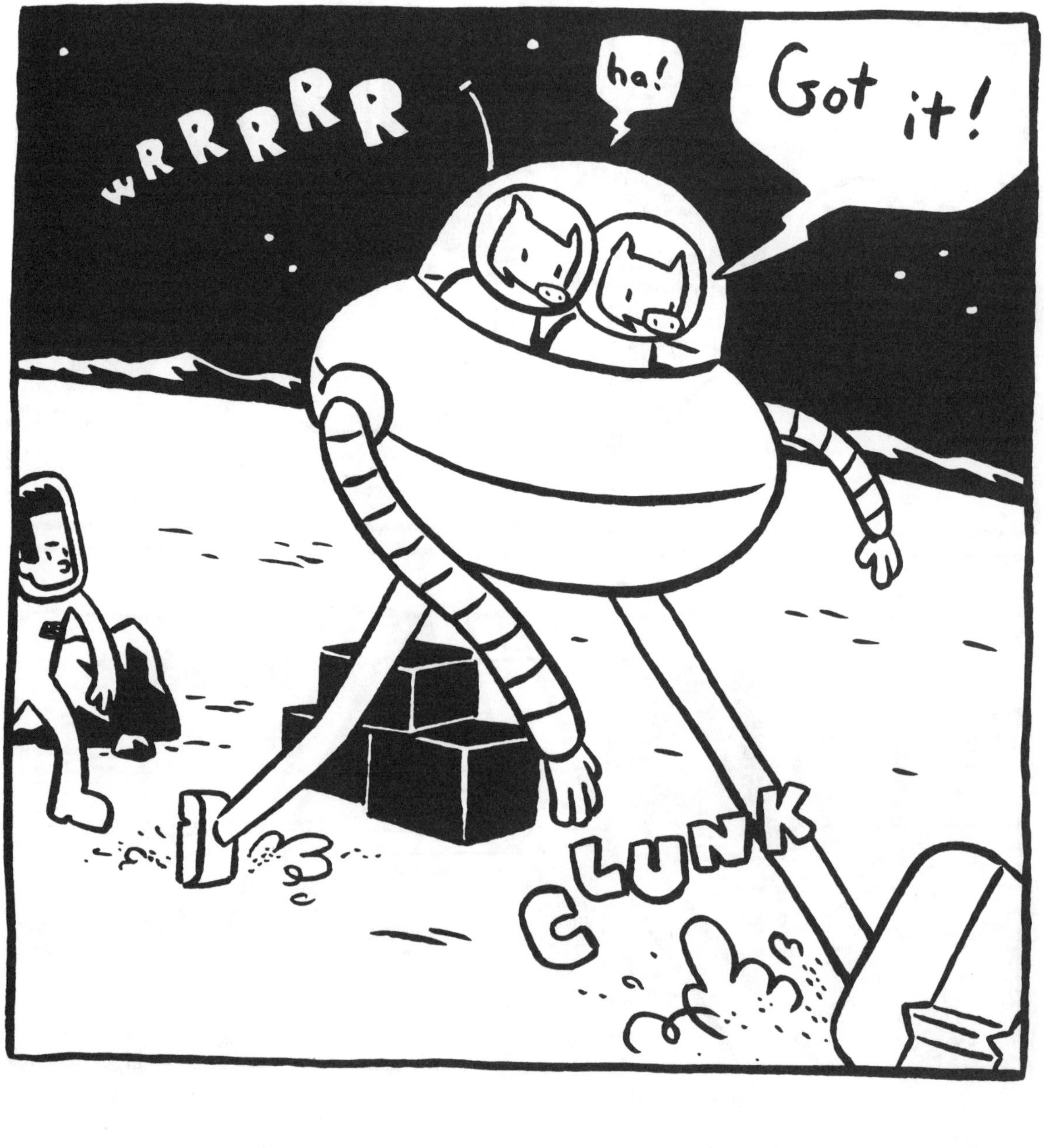
wRRRRRR
ha!
Got it!
CLUNK

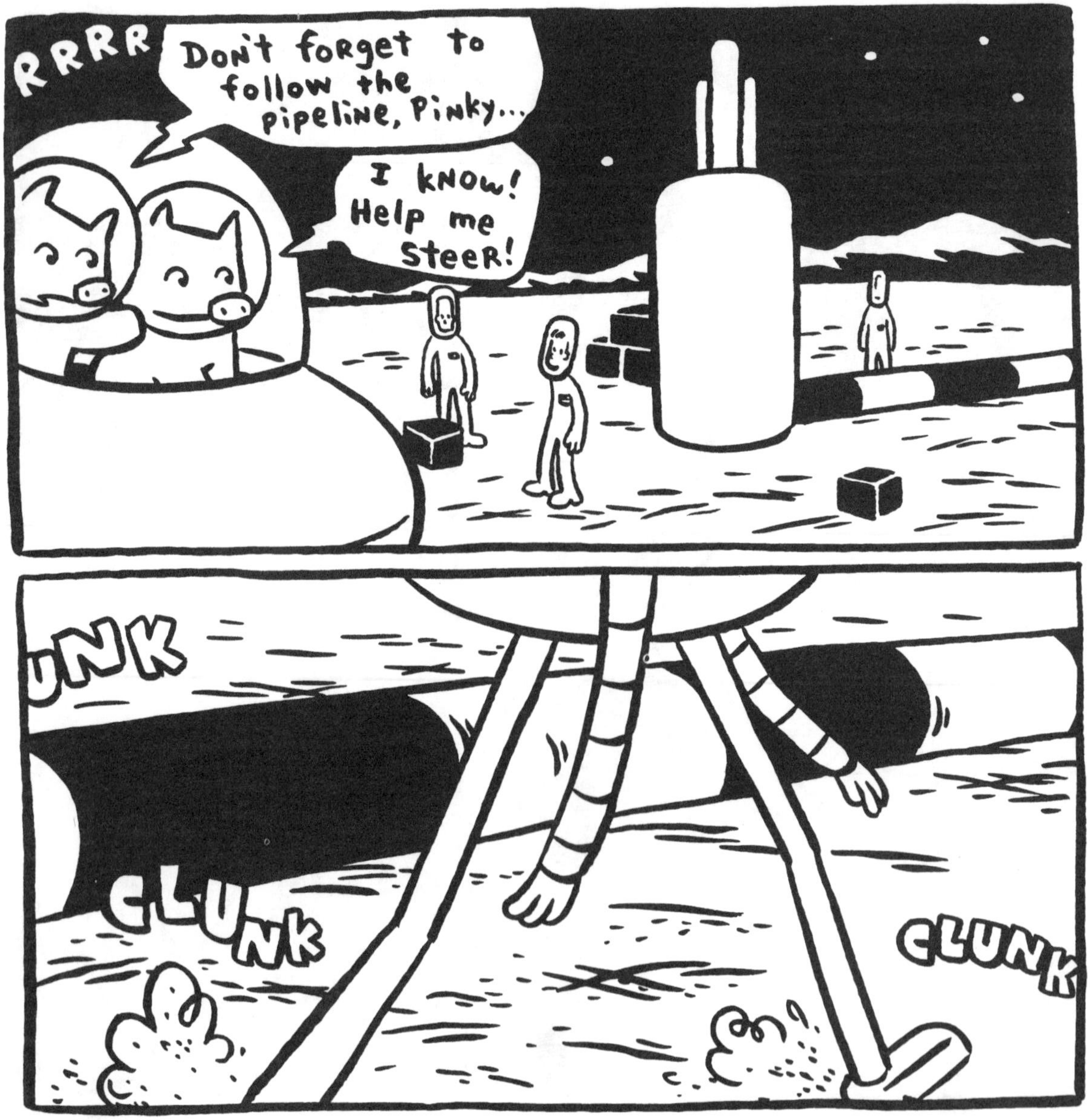
RRRR
Don't forget to follow the pipeline, Pinky...
I know! Help me steer!
UNK
CLUNK
CLUNK

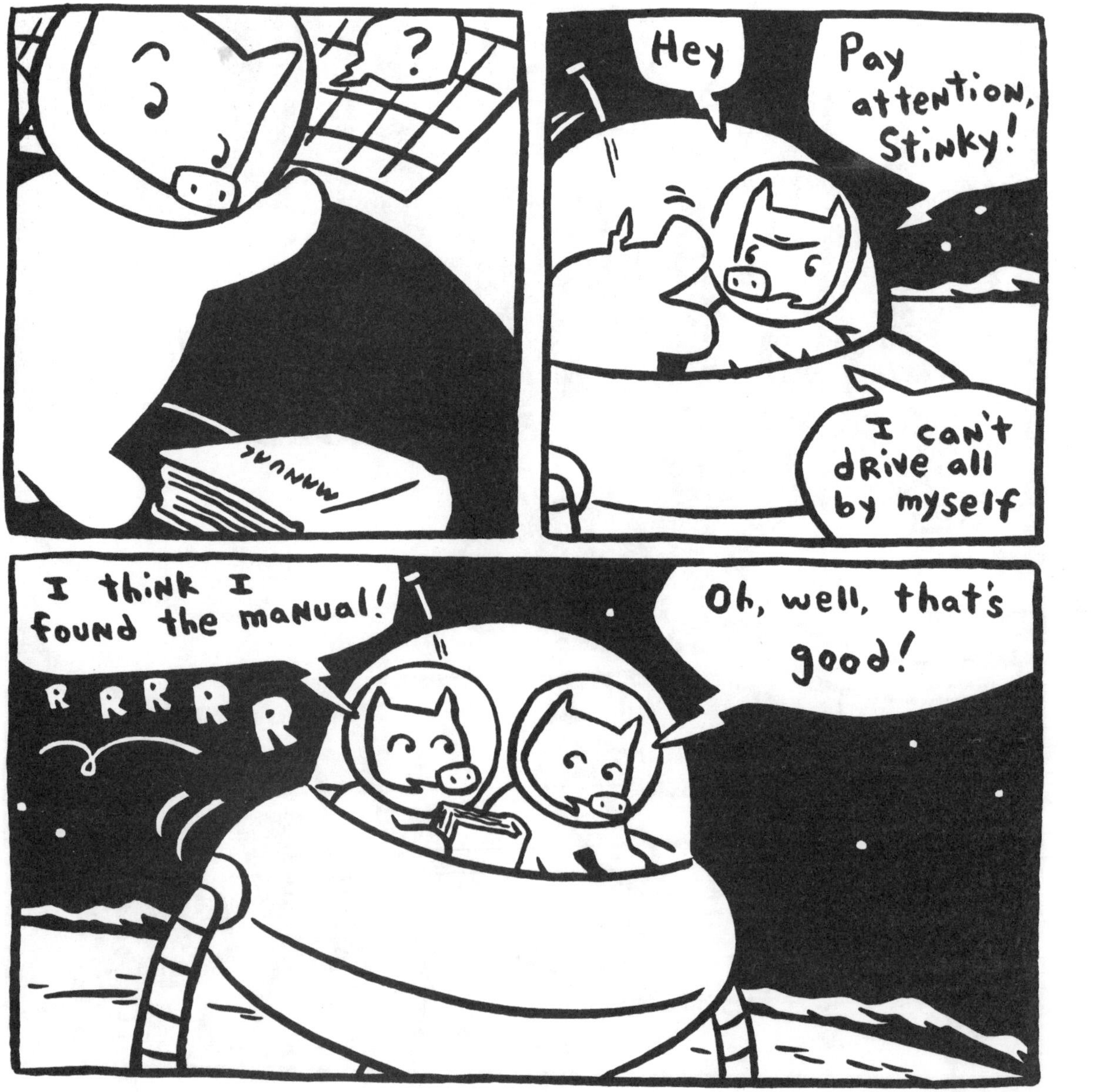
?
MANUAL
Hey
Pay attention, Stinky!
I can't drive all by myself
I think I found the manual!
Oh, well, that's good!
R R R R R

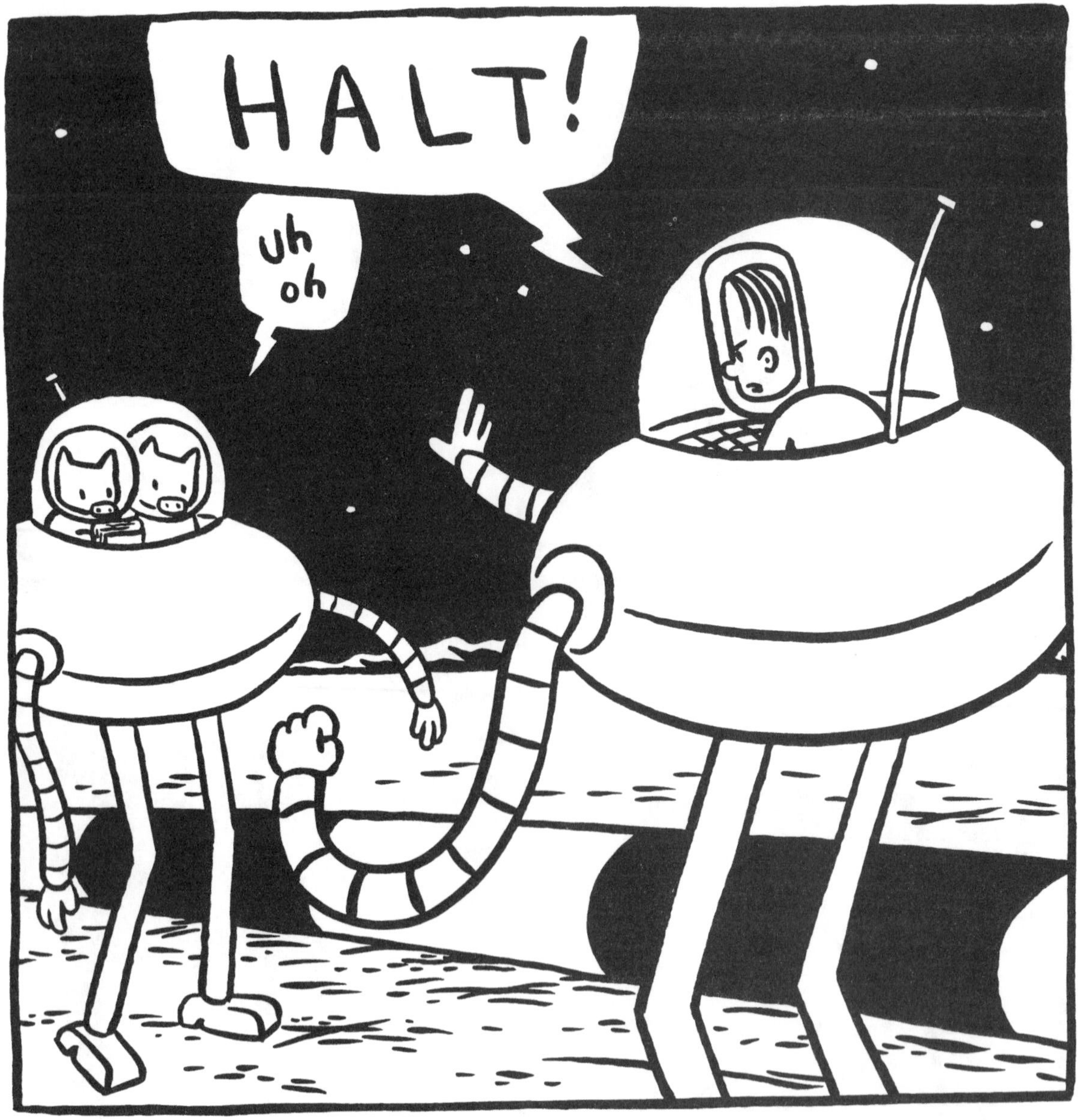
HALT!
uh oh

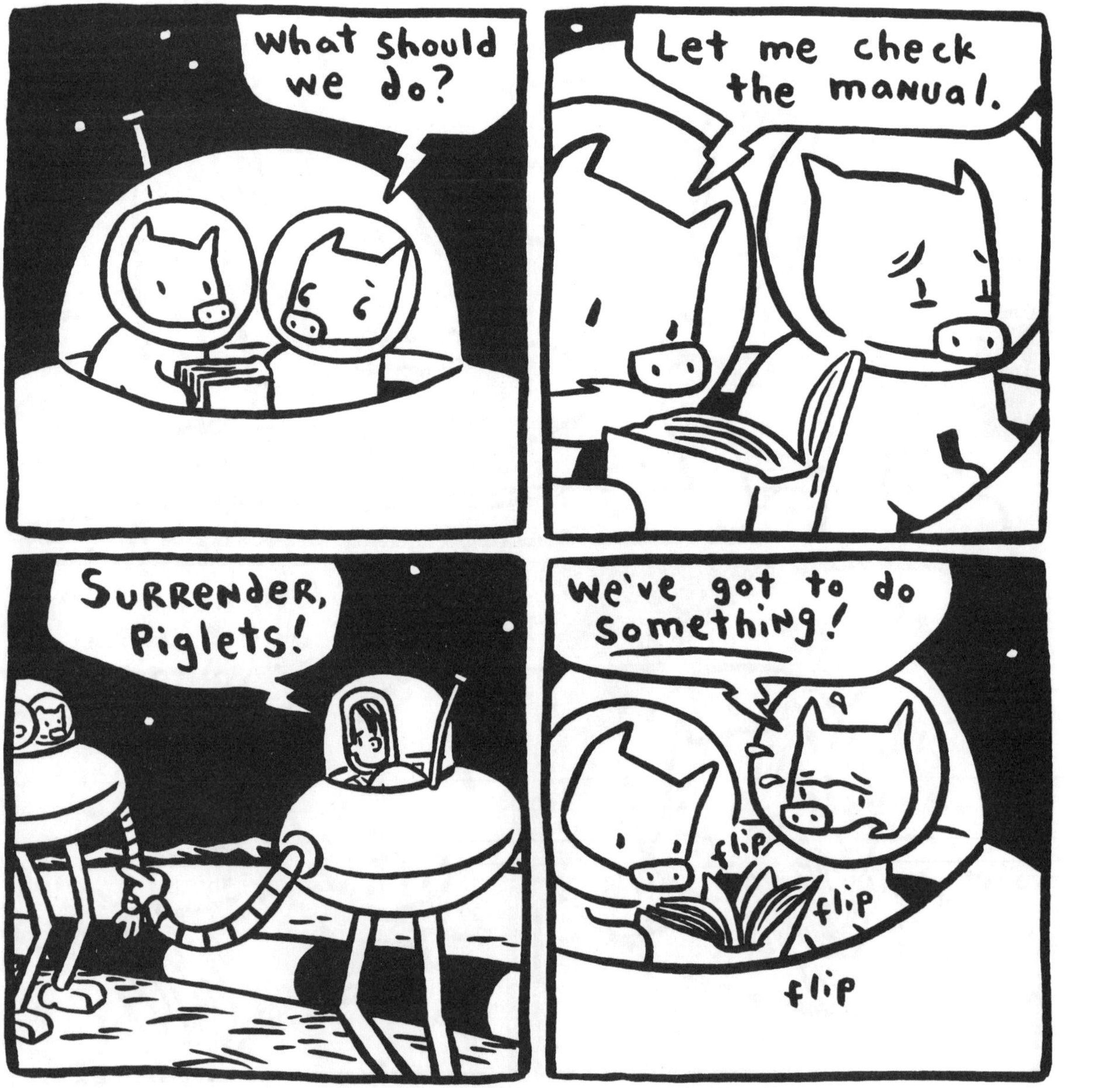
What should we do?
Let me check the manual.
SURRENDER, Piglets!
We've got to do something!
flip
flip
flip

I've got 'em
...steady...
flip flip
flip
flip
flip
flip
flip
flip
flip
flip
Oh, here's a good one... "jumping"!

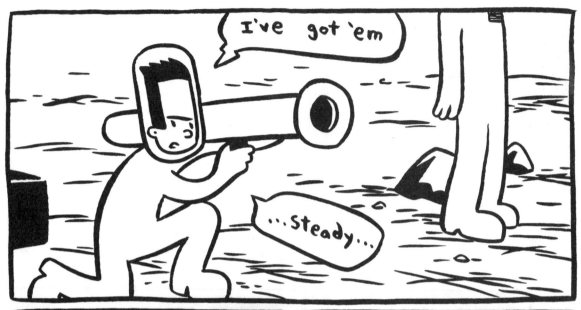

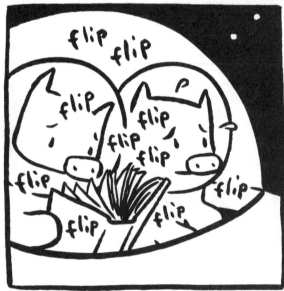

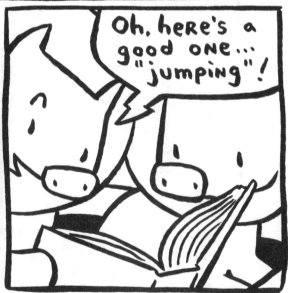

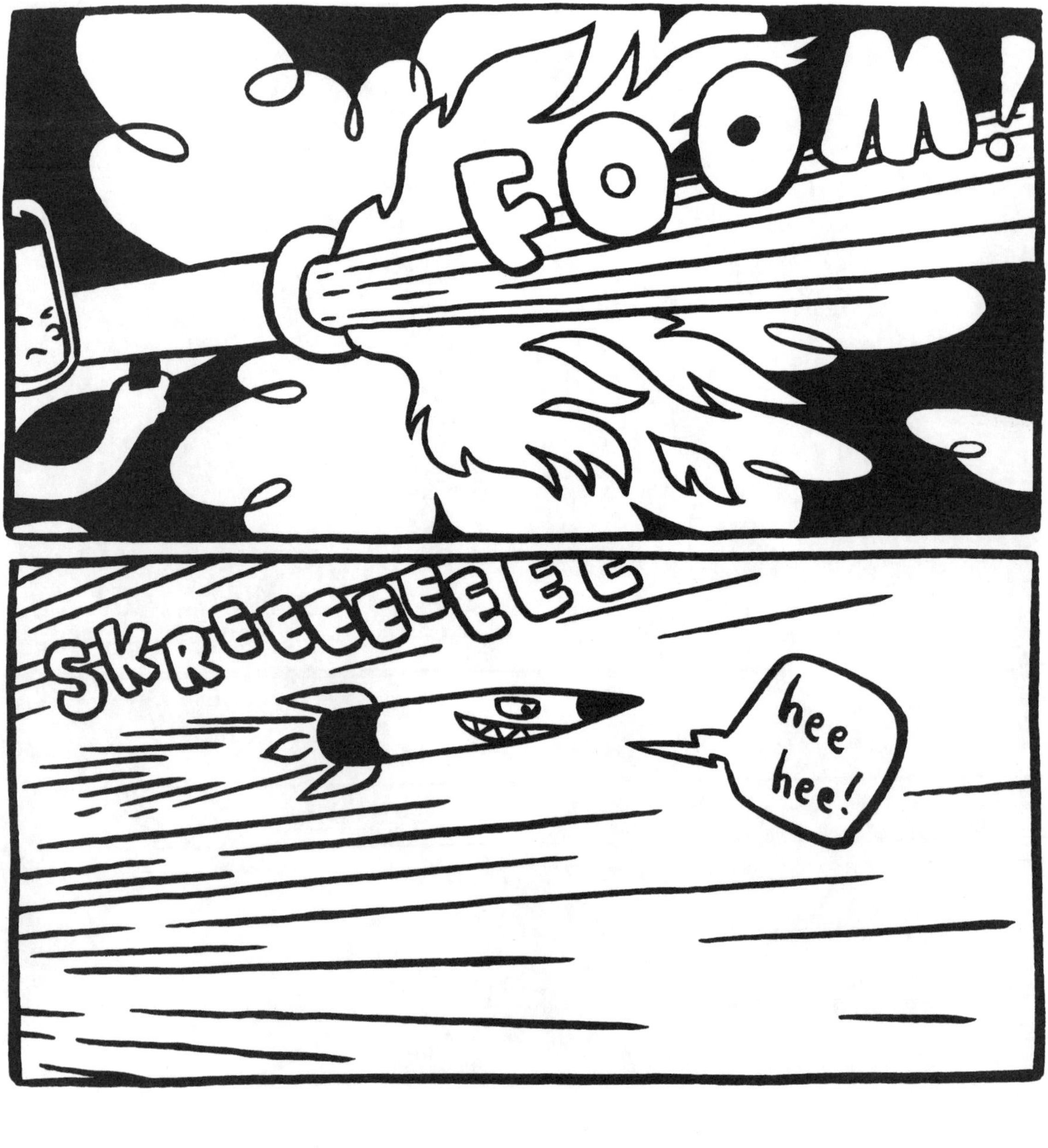
FOOM!
SKREEEEEEEL
hee hee!

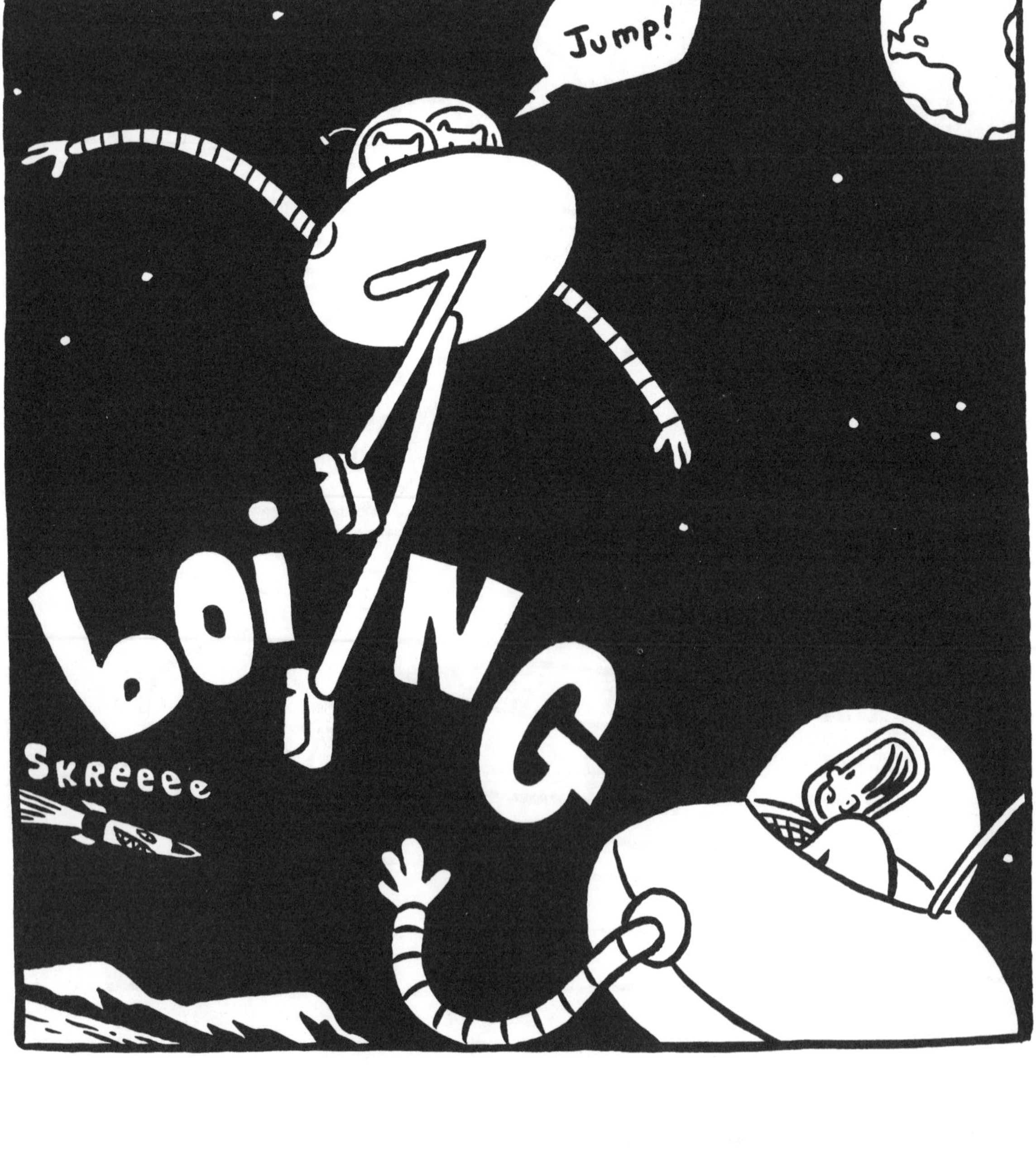
Jump!
boiNG
Skreeeee

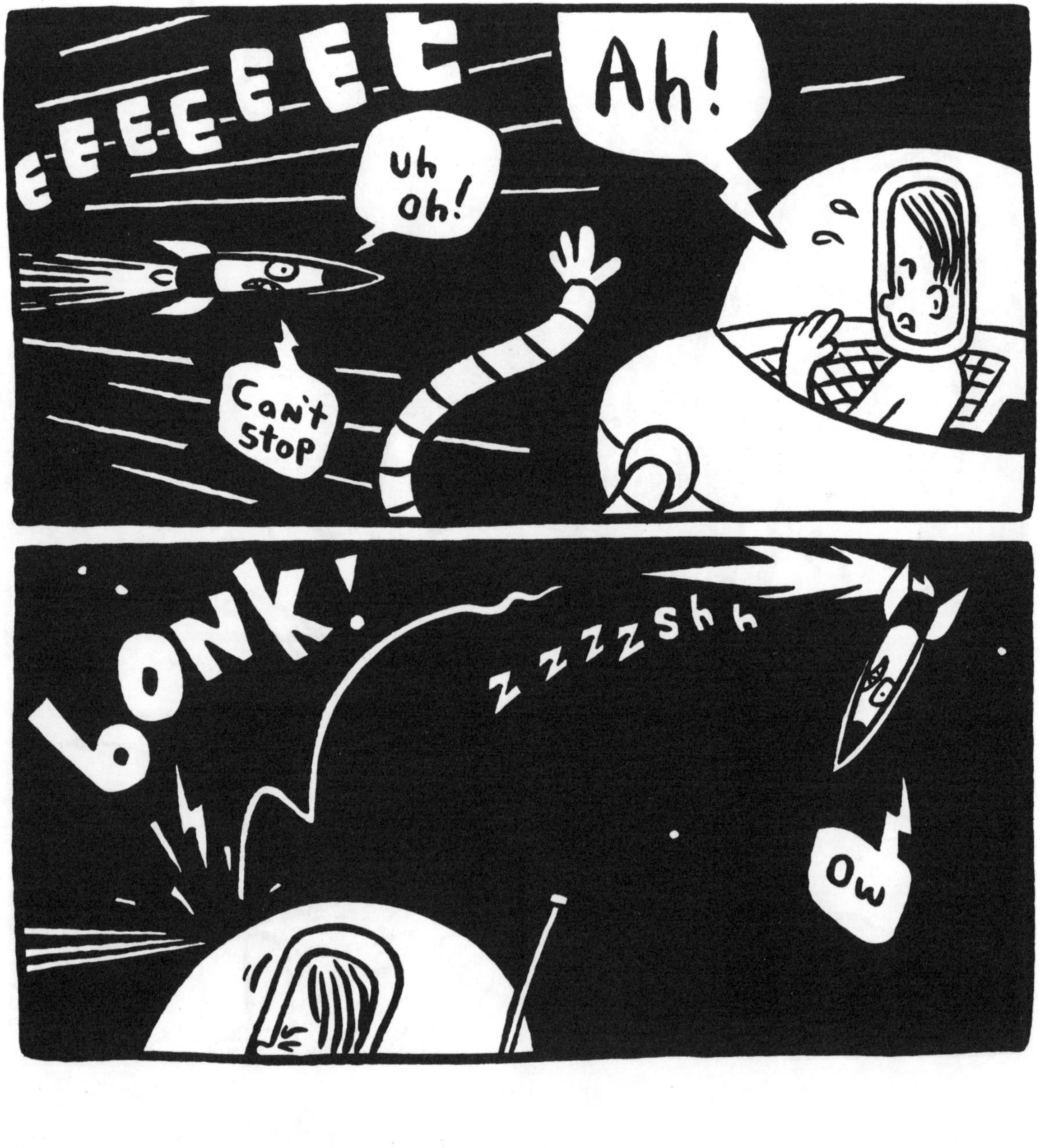
EEEEEEEEt
Ah!
Uh oh!
Can't stop
bONK!
zzzzzshhh
Ow

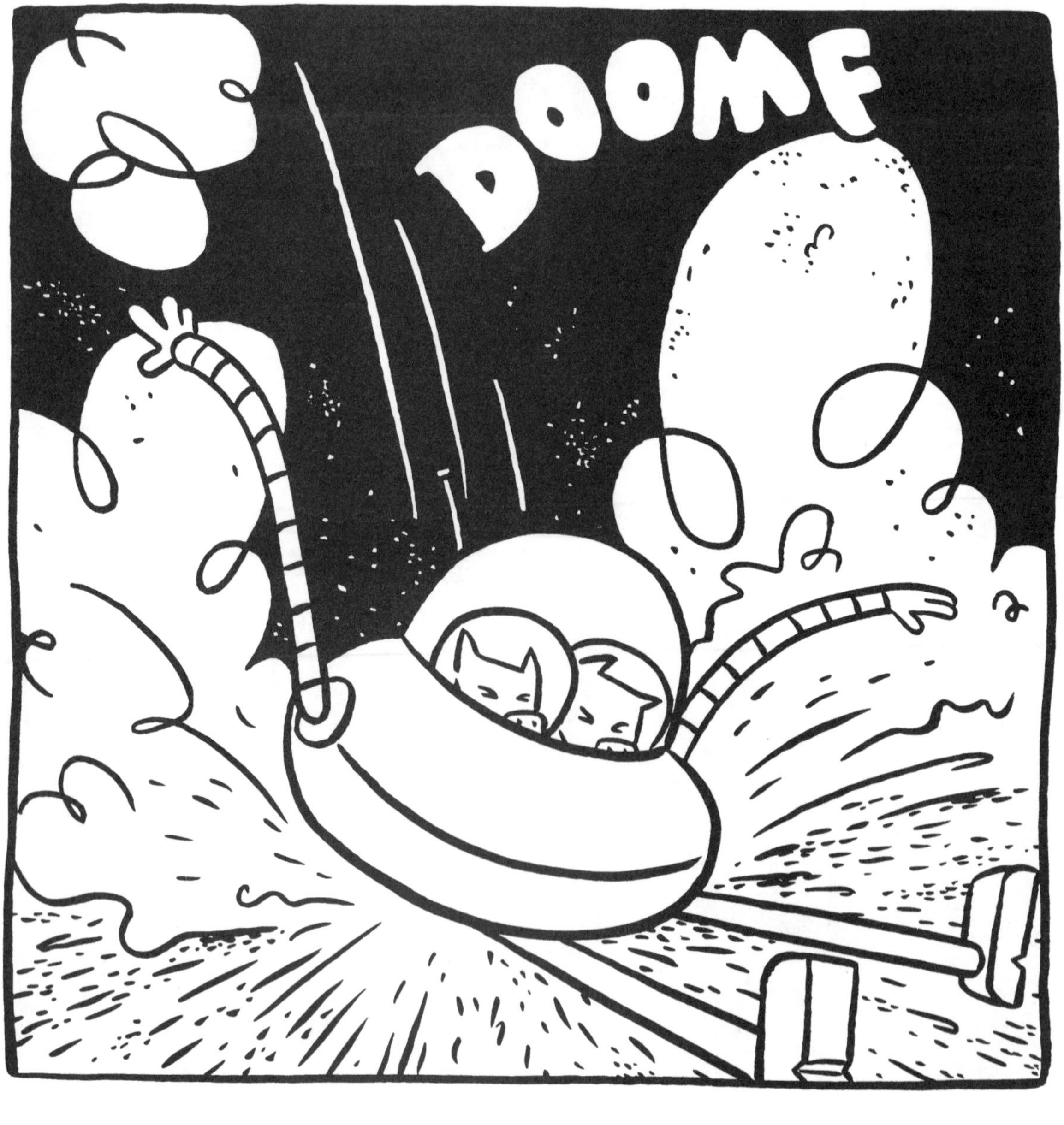
DOOMF

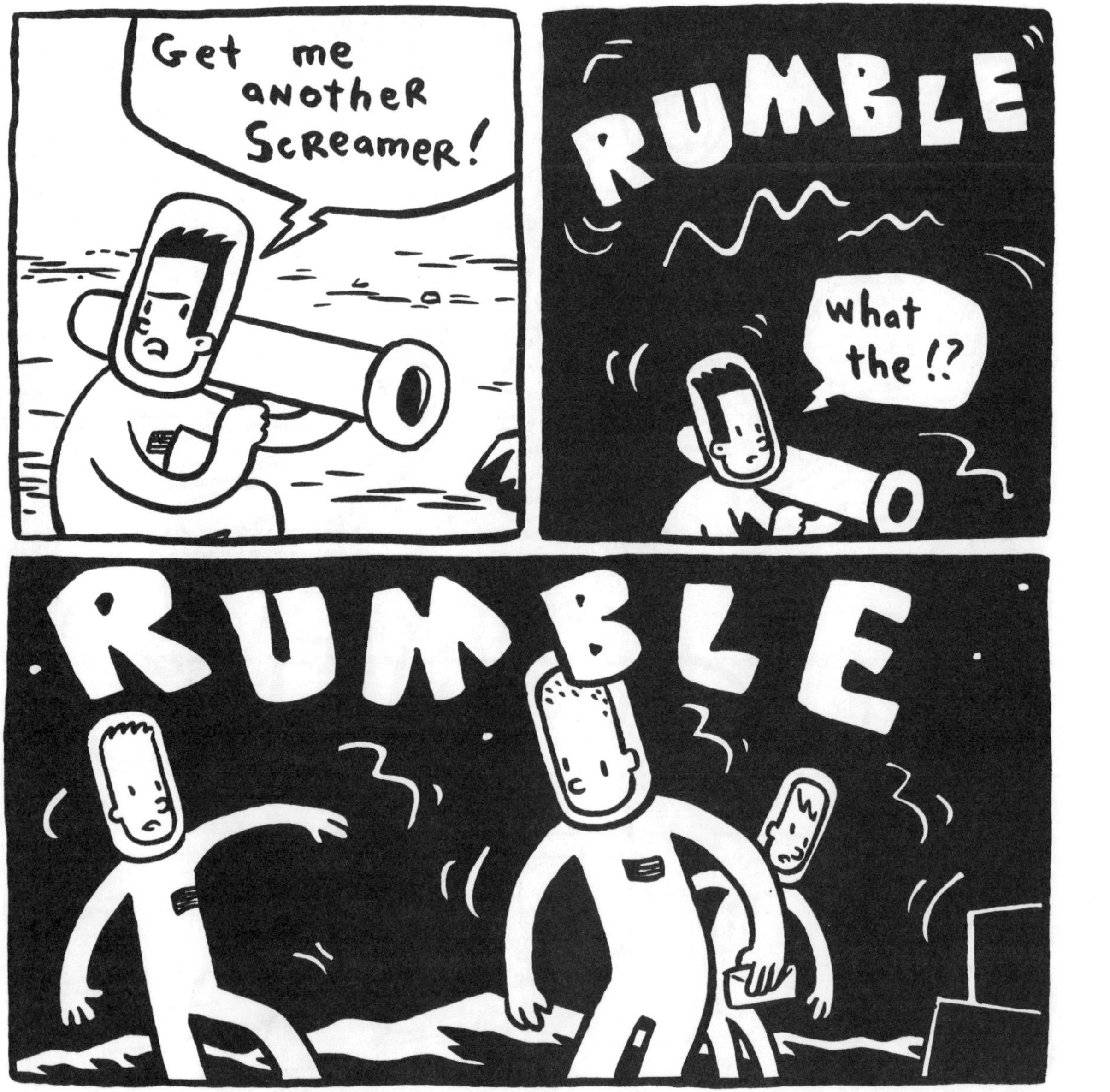
Get me another Screamer!
RUMBLE
what the!?
RUMBLE

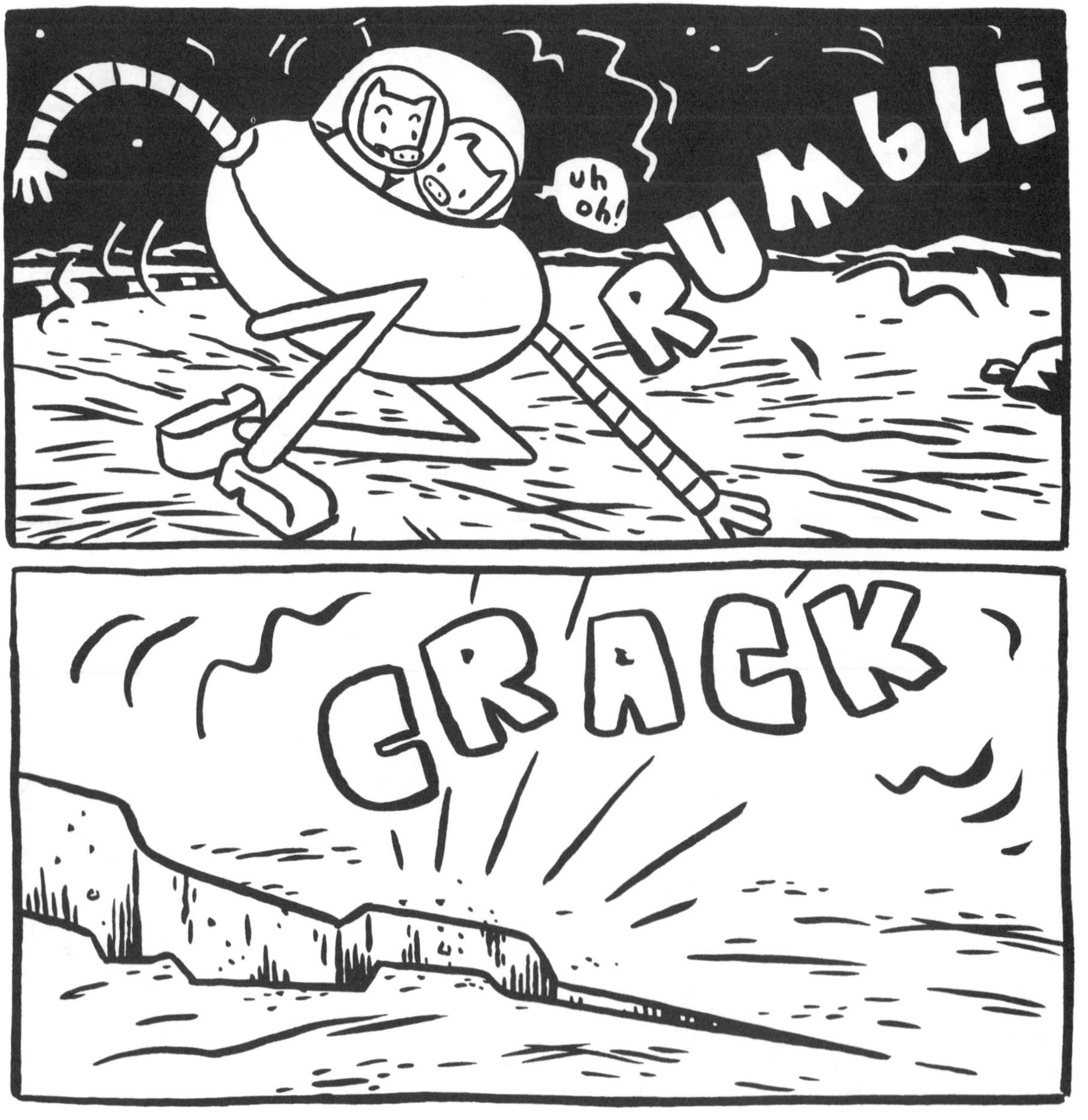
uh oh!
RUMBLE
CRACK

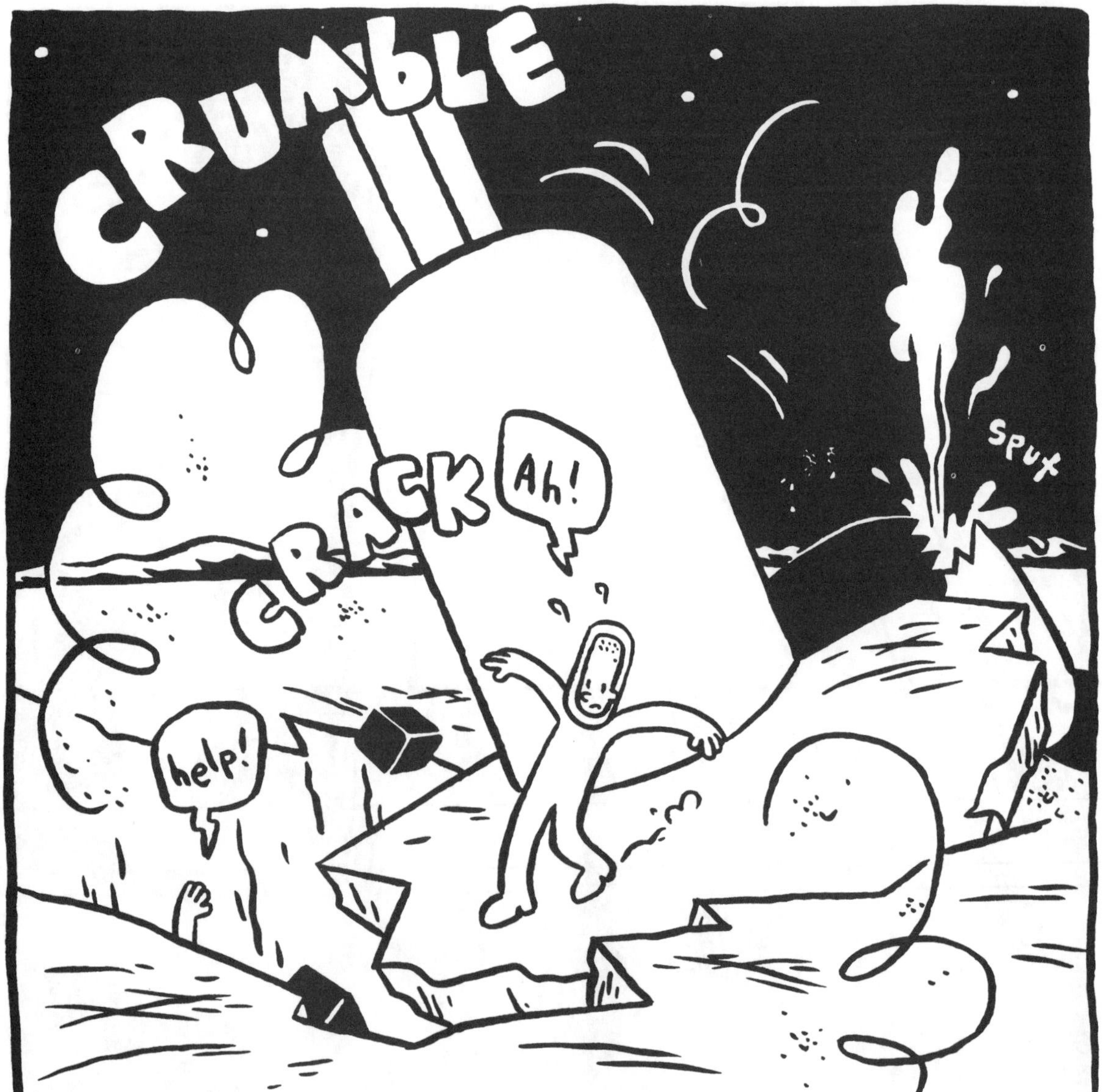

CRUMBLE
CRACK
Ah!
sput
help!

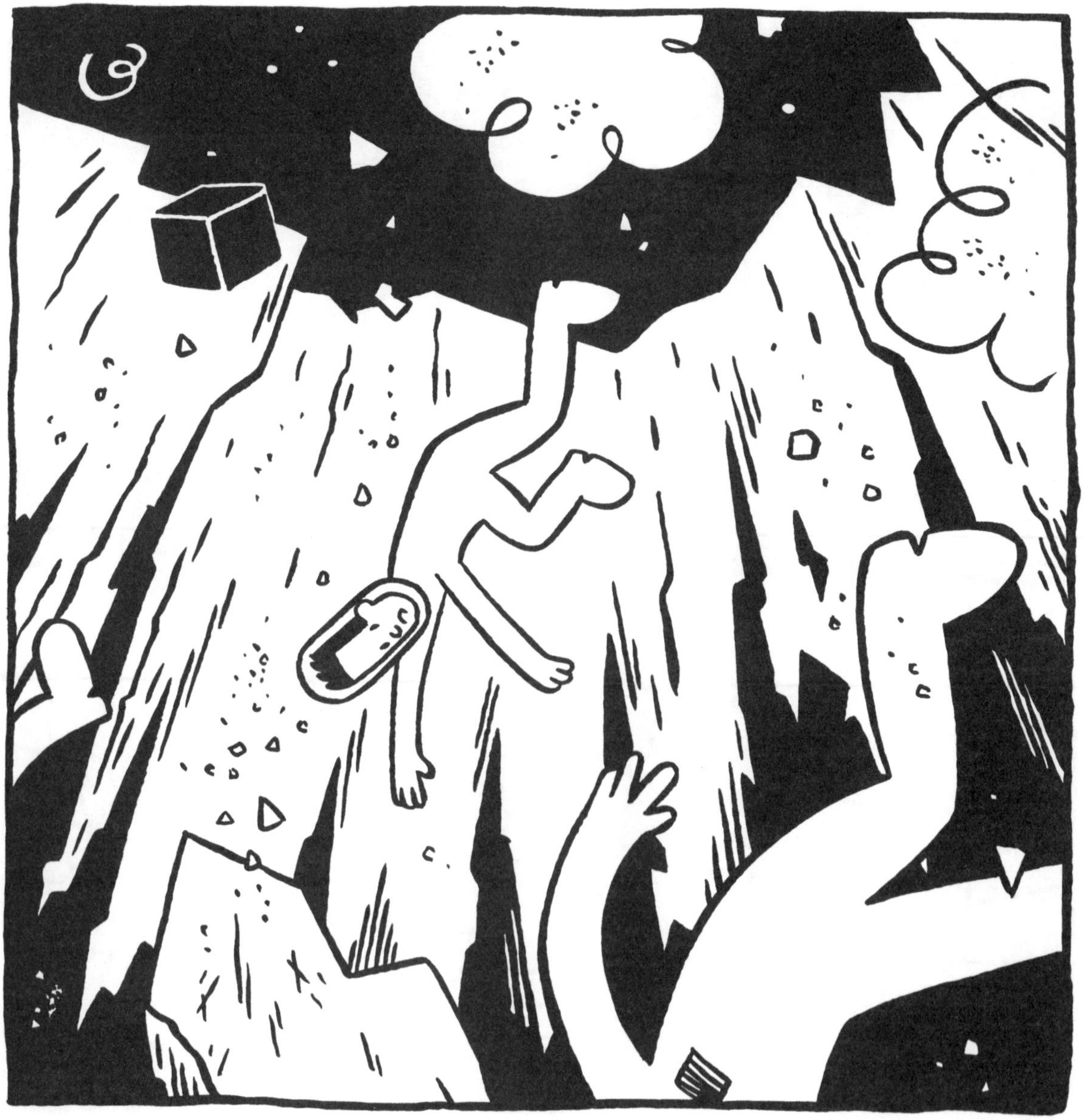

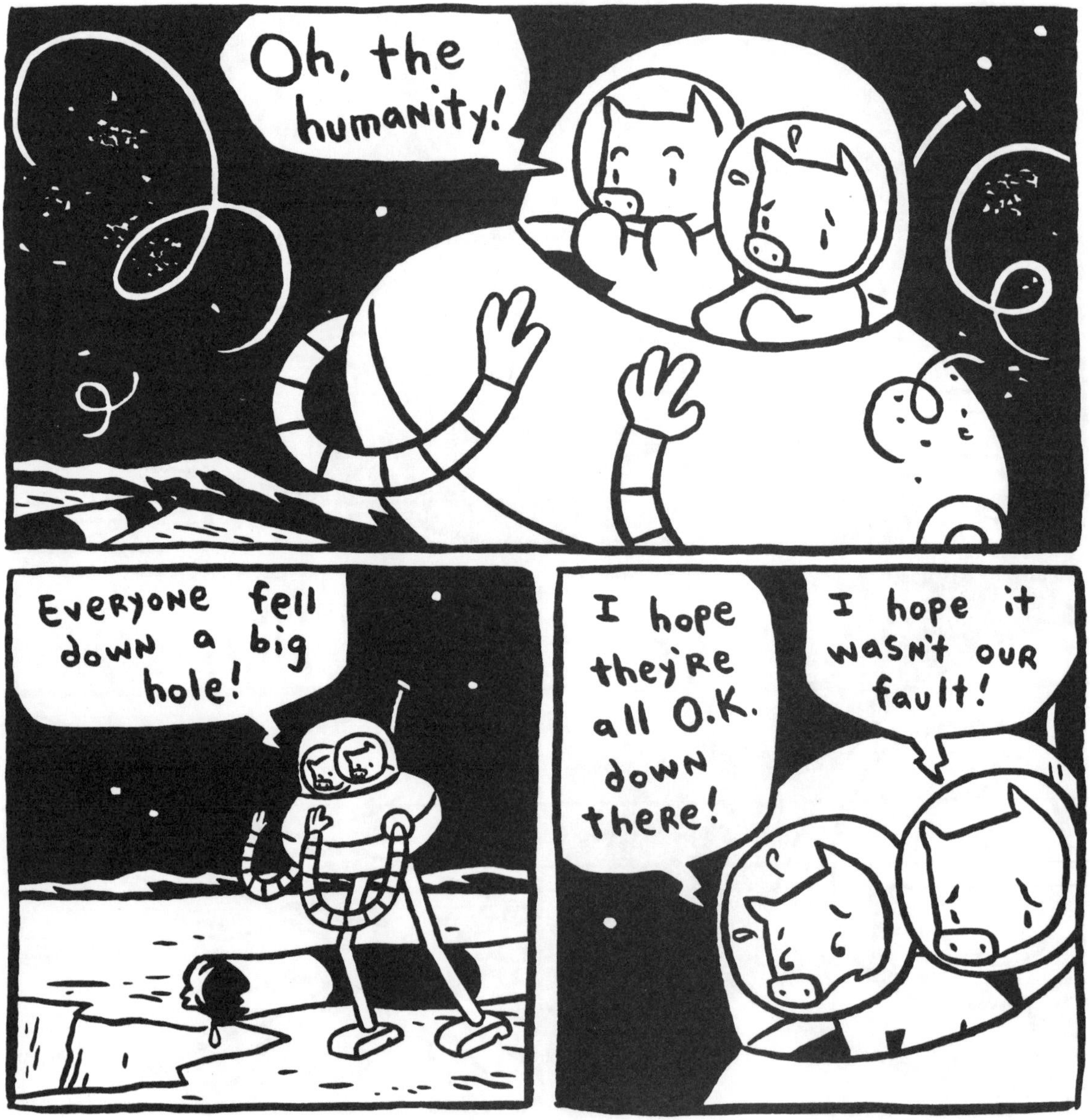
Oh, the humanity!
Everyone fell down a big hole!
I hope they're all O.K. down there!
I hope it wasn't our fault!

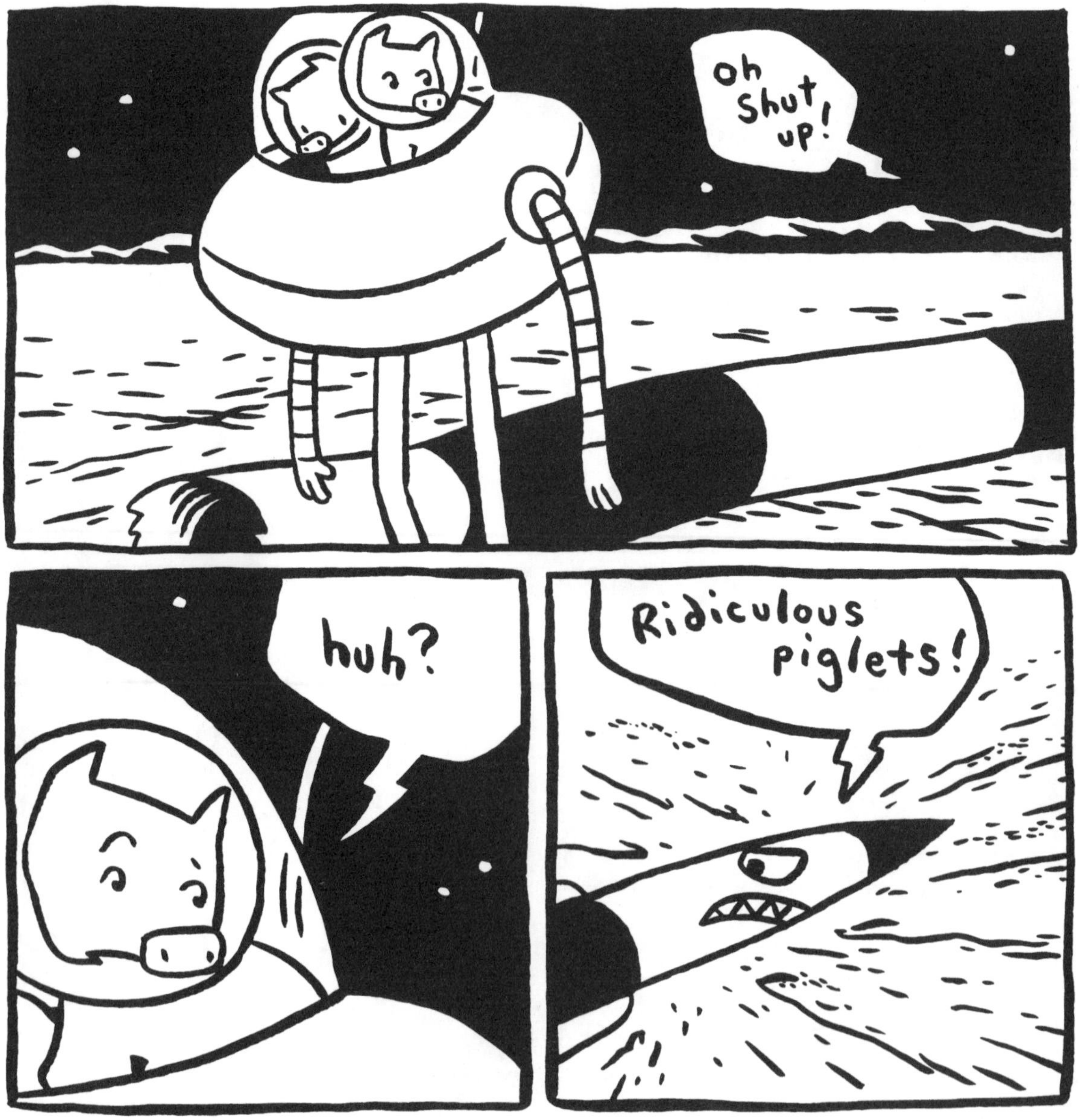
Oh Shut up!
huh?
Ridiculous piglets!

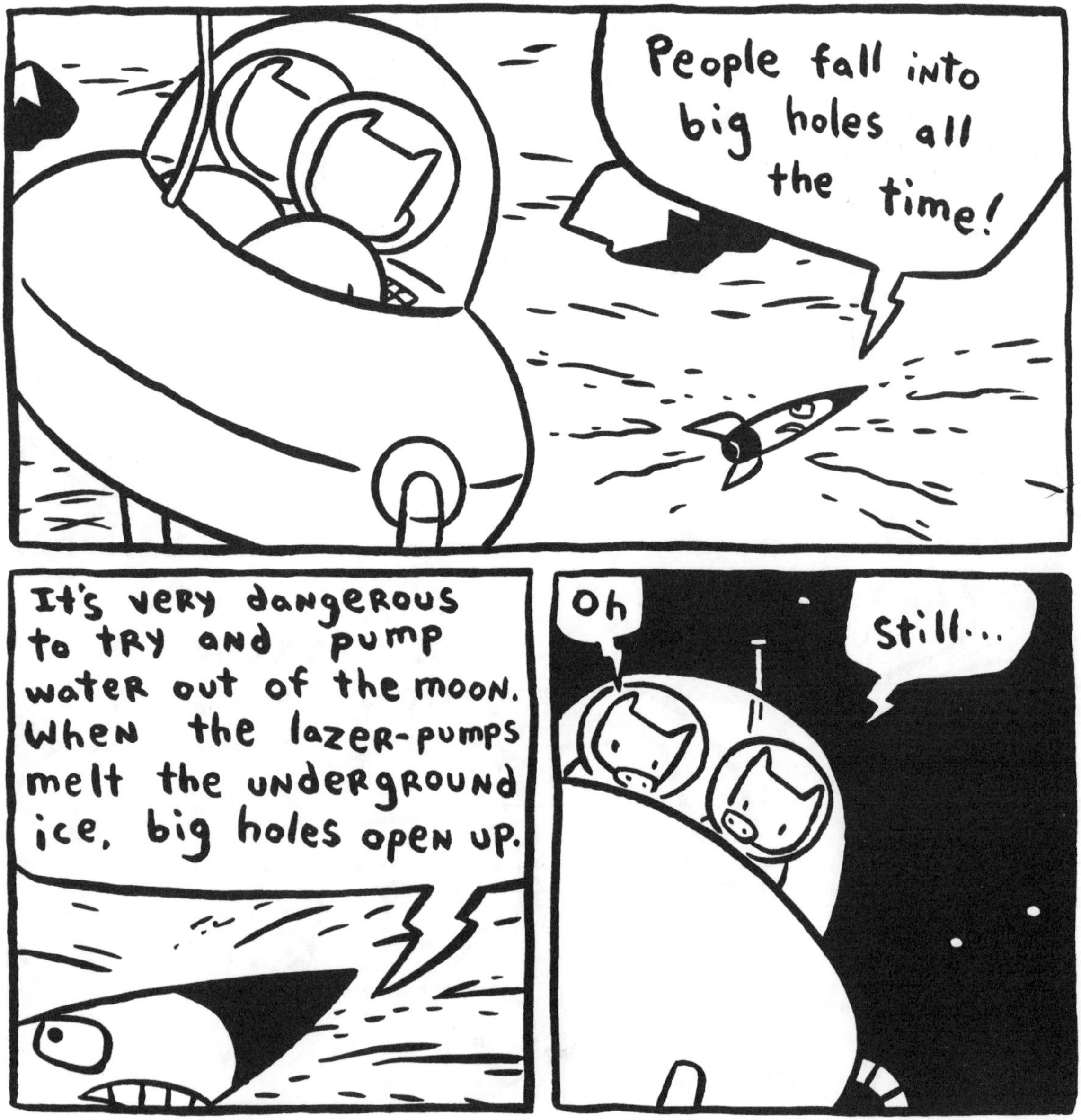
People fall into big holes all the time!
It's very dangerous to try and pump water out of the moon. When the lazer-pumps melt the underground ice, big holes open up.
Oh
Still...

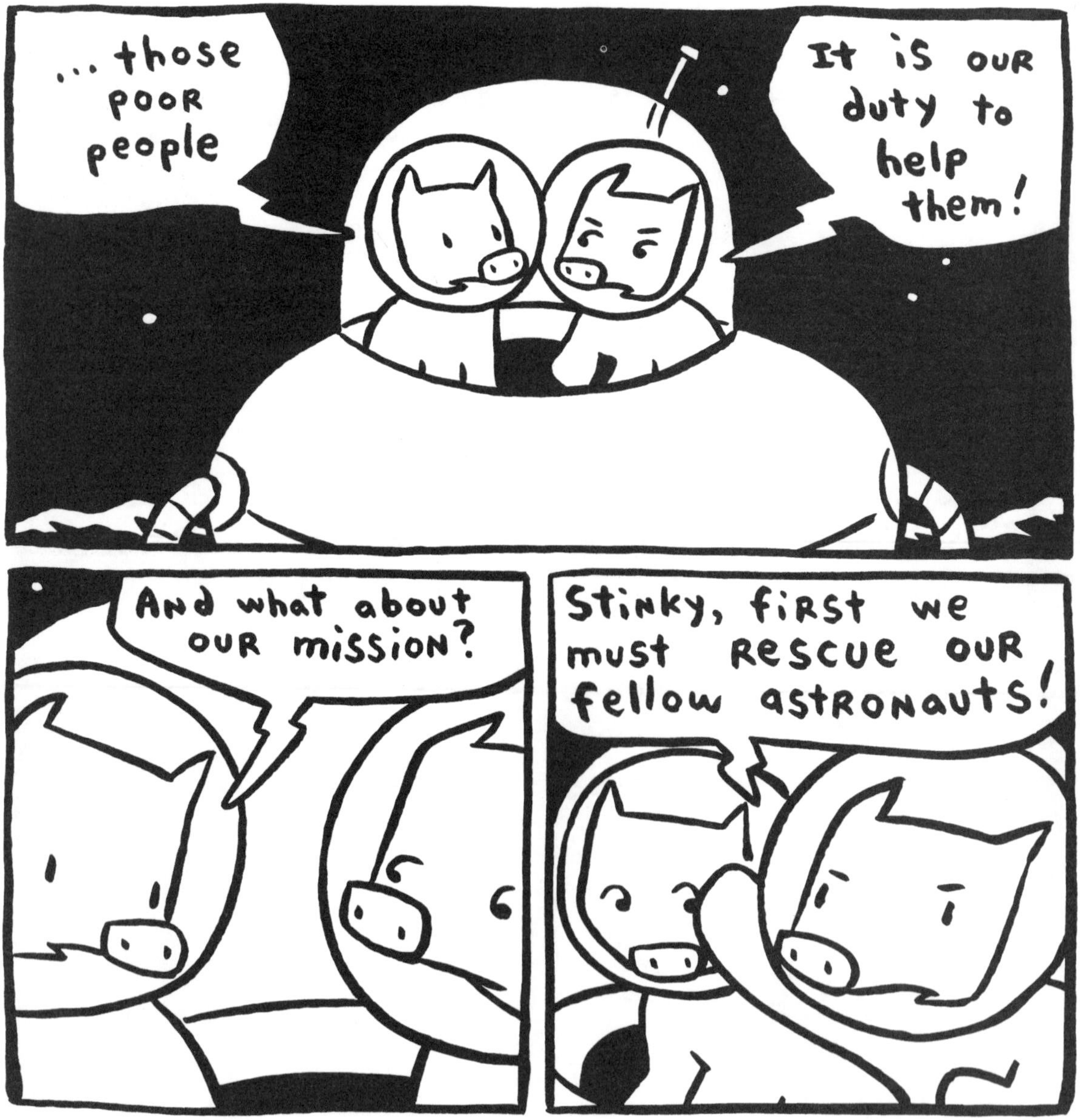
...those poor people
It is our duty to help them!
And what about our mission?
Stinky, first we must rescue our fellow astronauts!

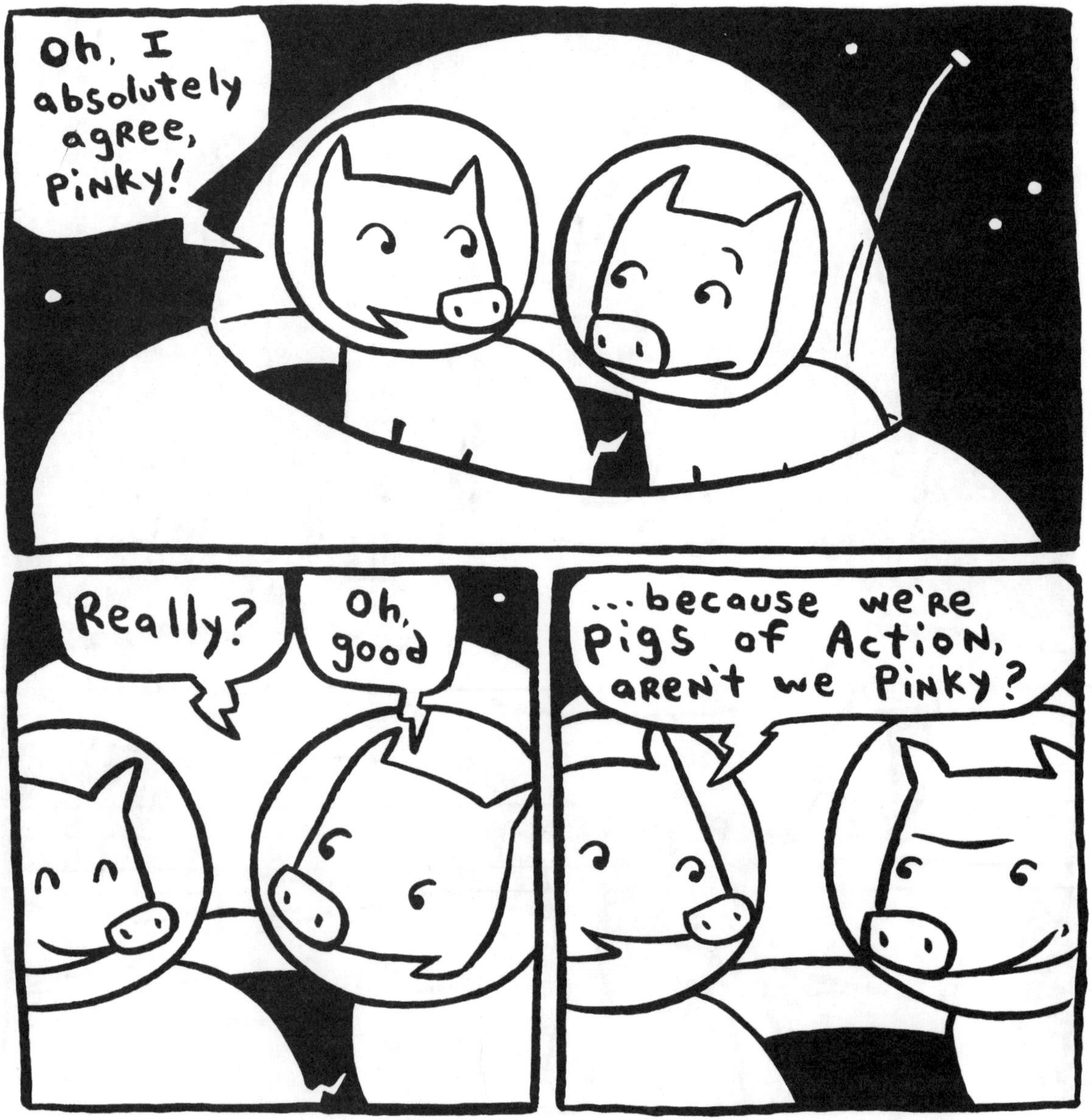
Oh, I absolutely agree, Pinky!
Really?
Oh, good
...because we're Pigs of Action, aren't we Pinky?

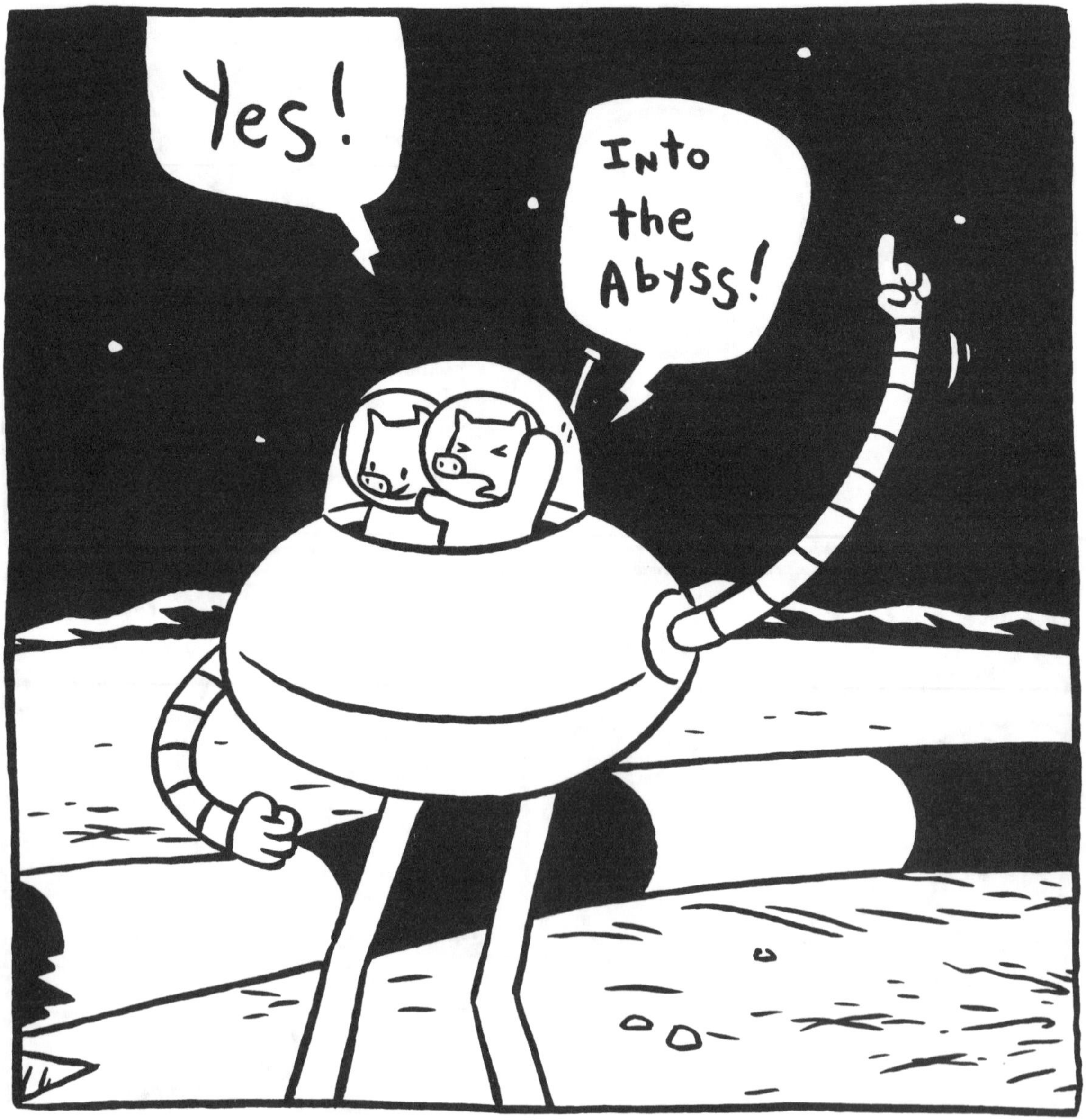
Yes!
Into the Abyss!

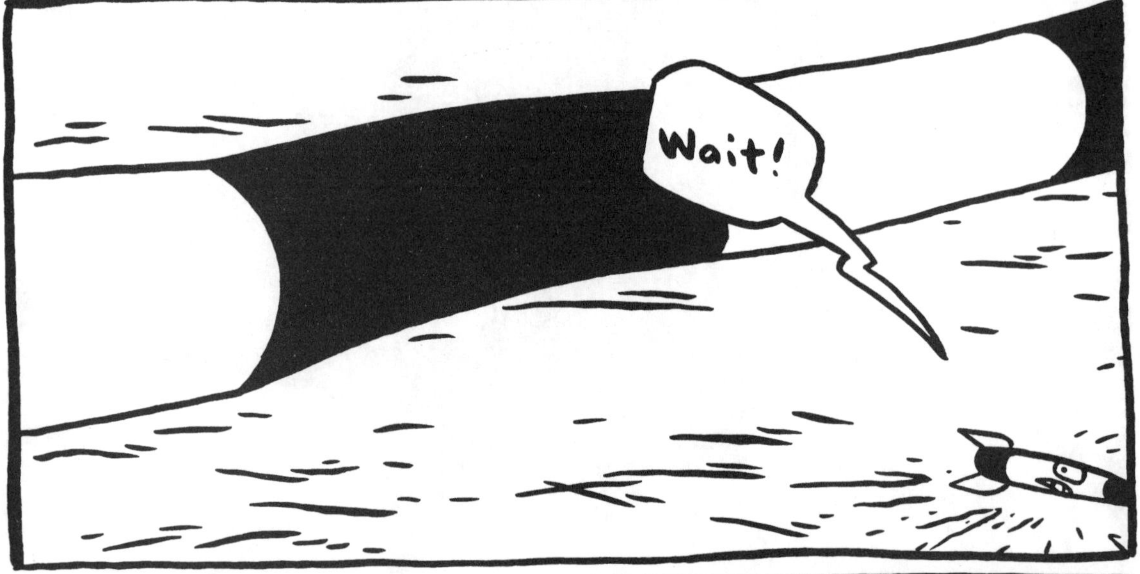
Wait!

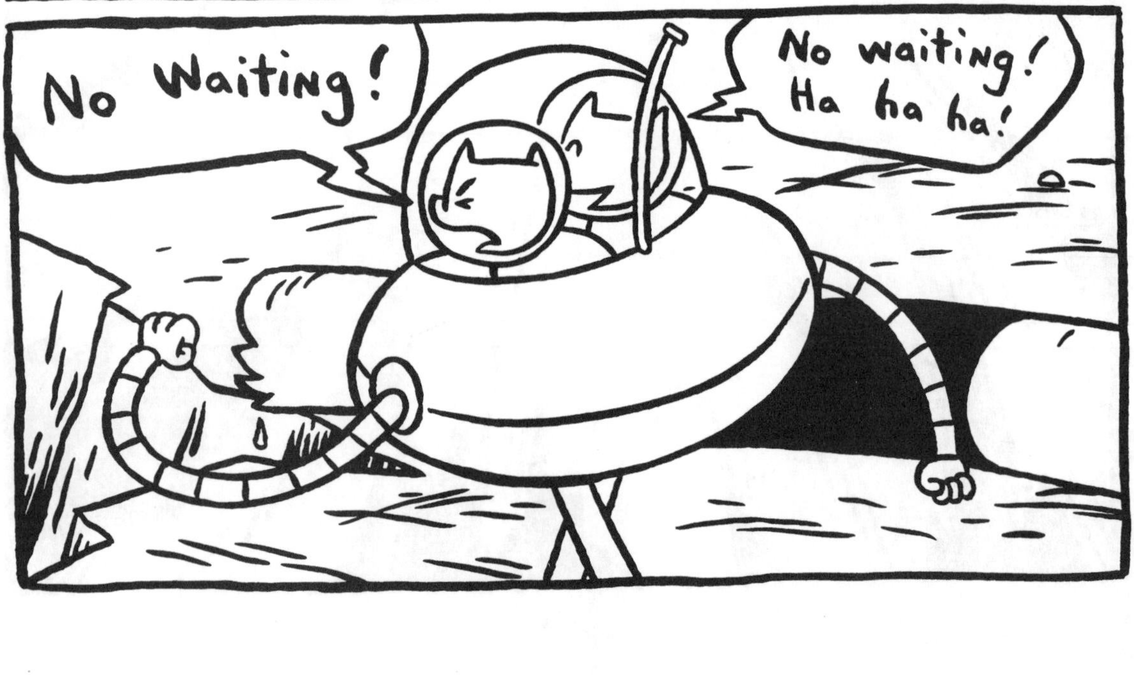
No Waiting!
No waiting! Ha ha ha!

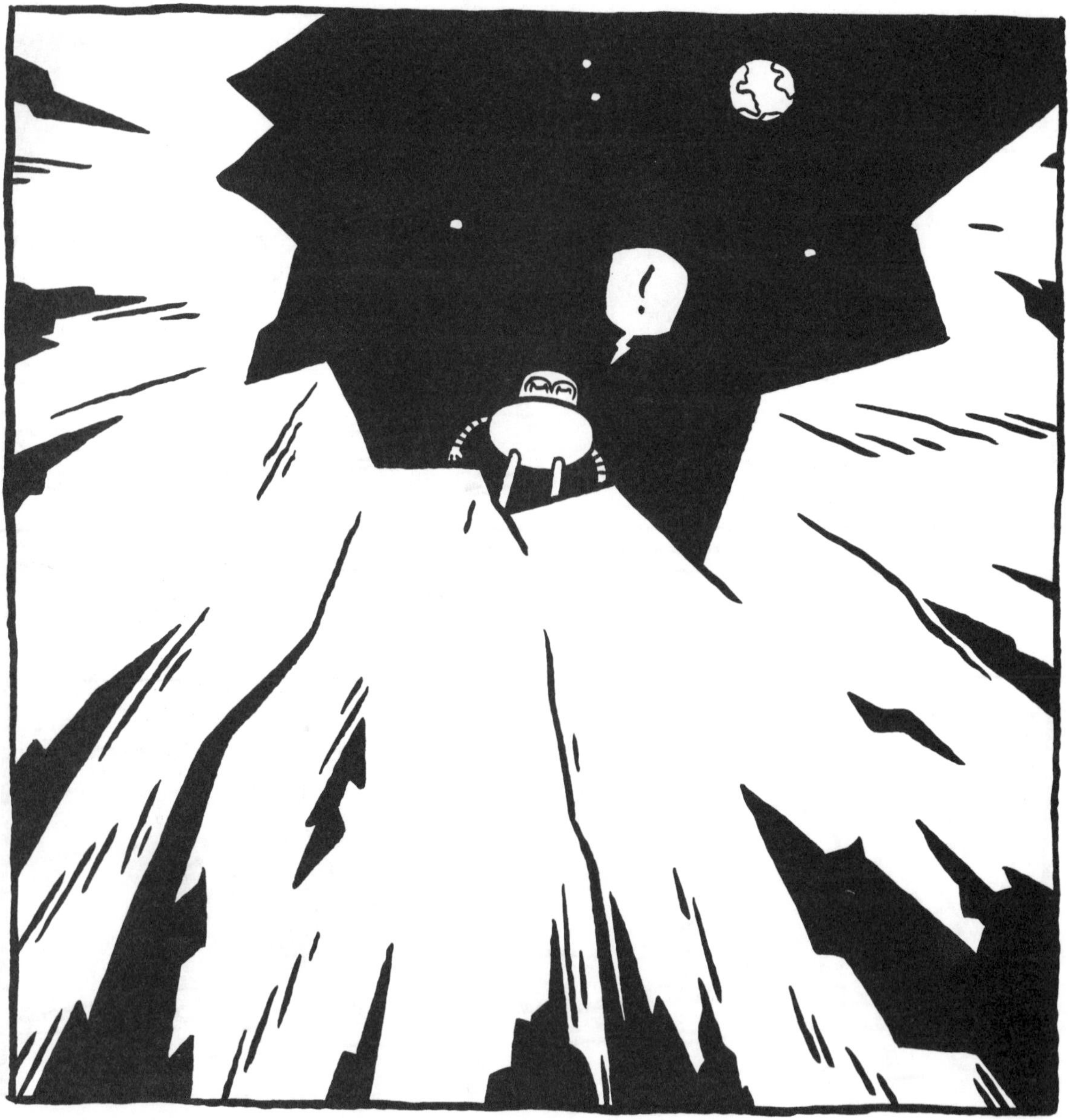
!

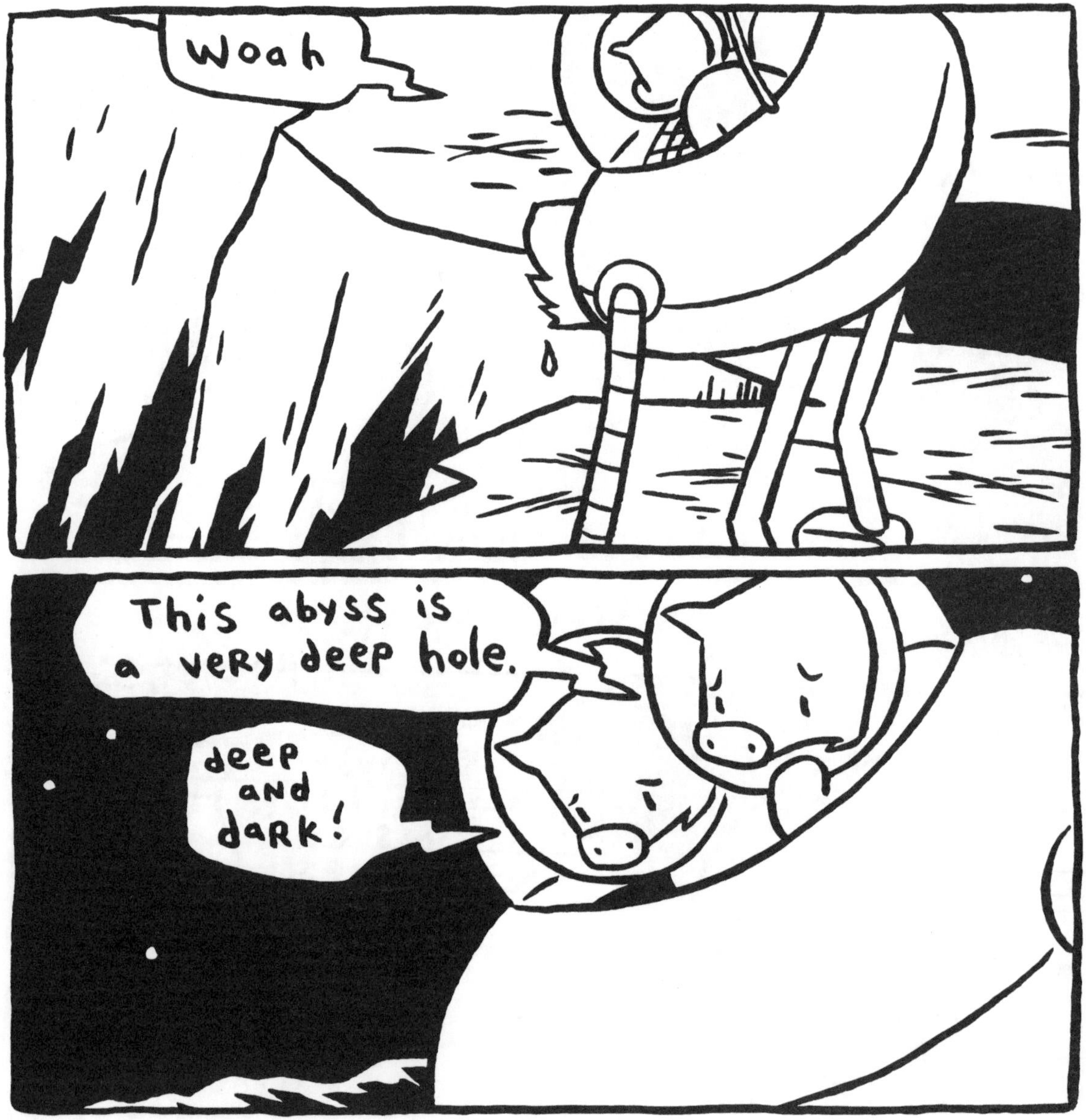
Woah
This abyss is a very deep hole.
deep and dark!

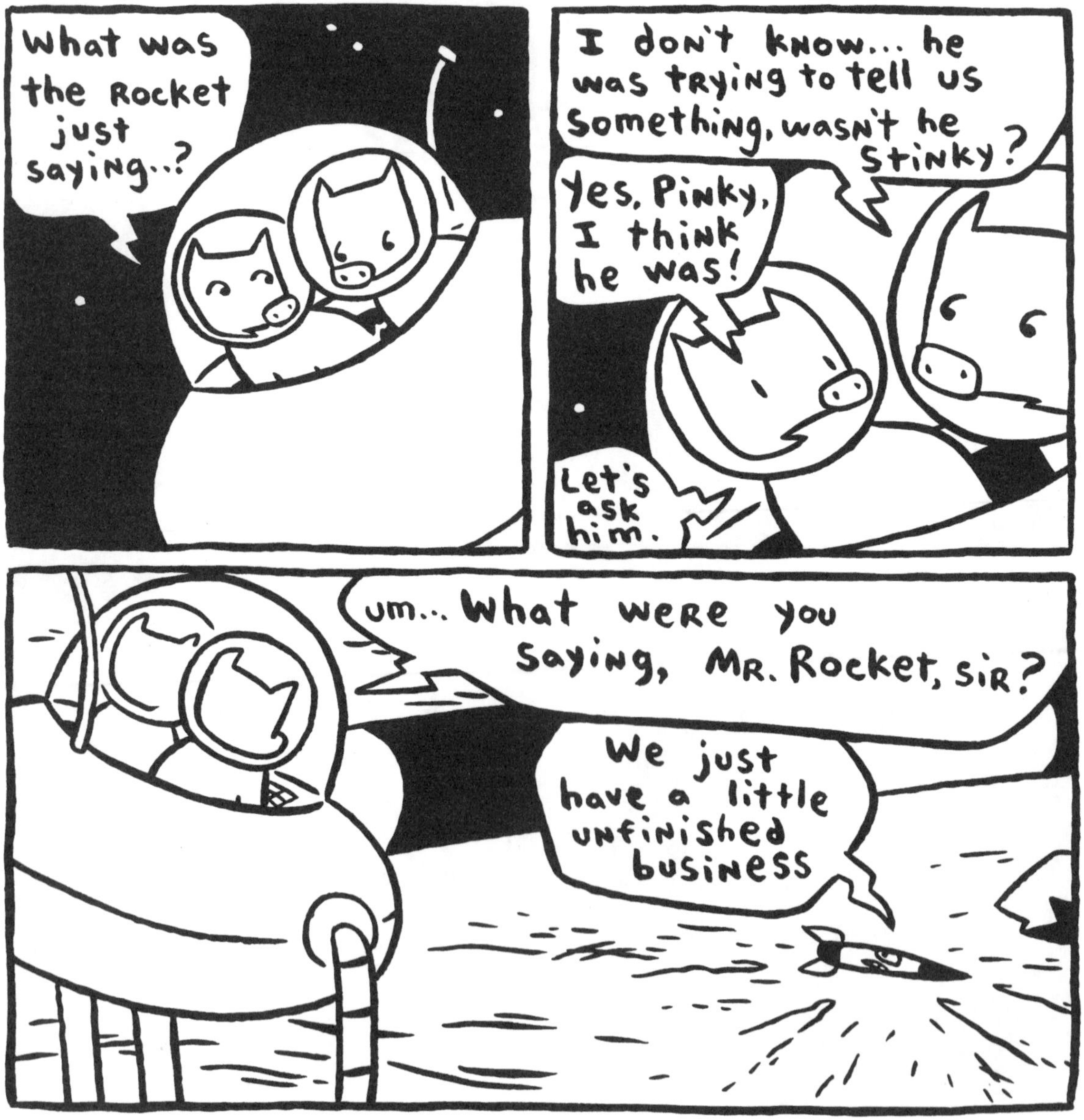
What was the Rocket just saying..?
I don't know... he was trying to tell us something, wasn't he Stinky?
Yes, Pinky, I think he was!
Let's ask him.
um... What were you saying, Mr. Rocket, sir?
We just have a little unfinished business

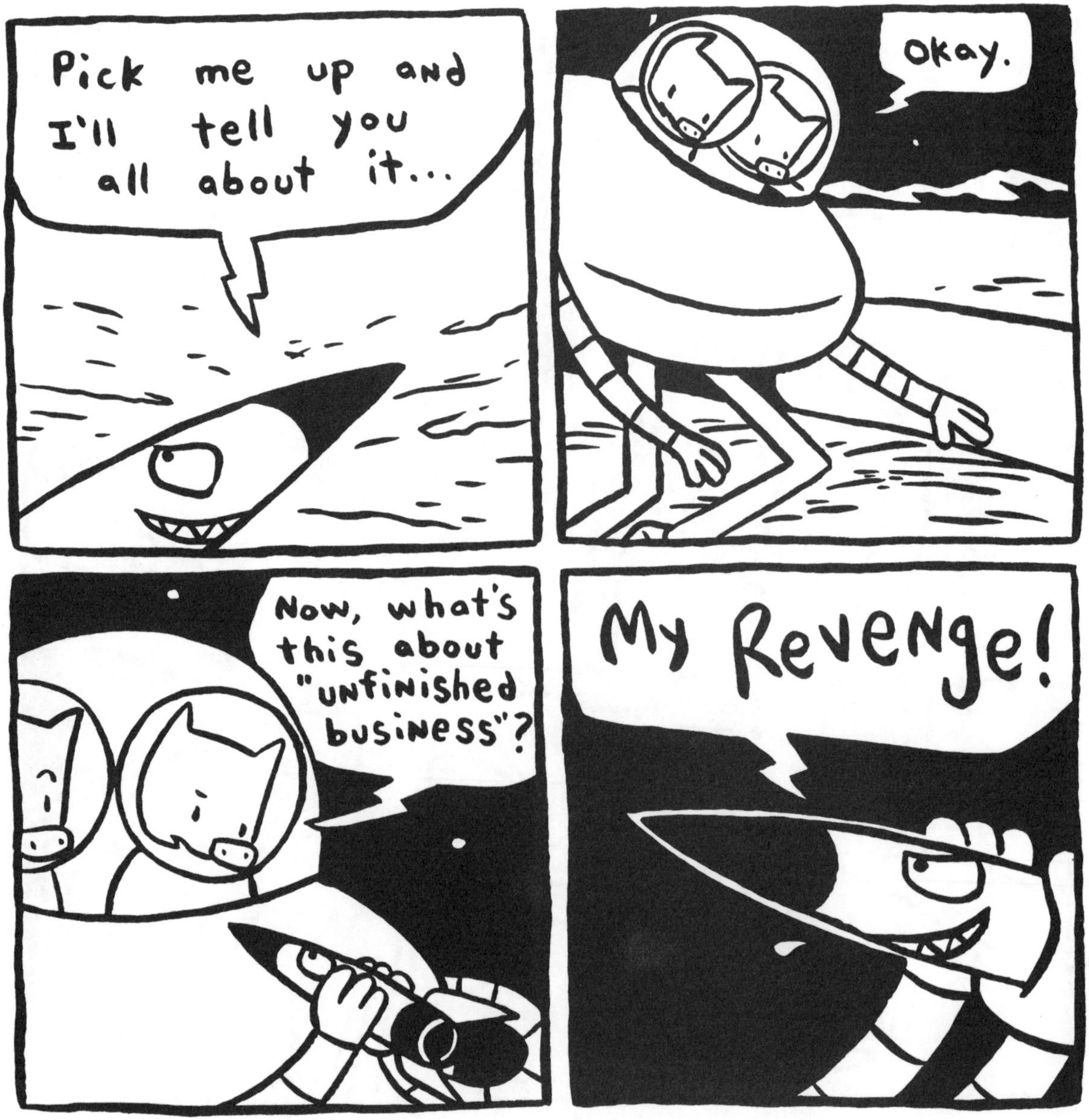
Pick me up and I'll tell you all about it...
Okay.
Now, what's this about "unfinished business"?
My Revenge!

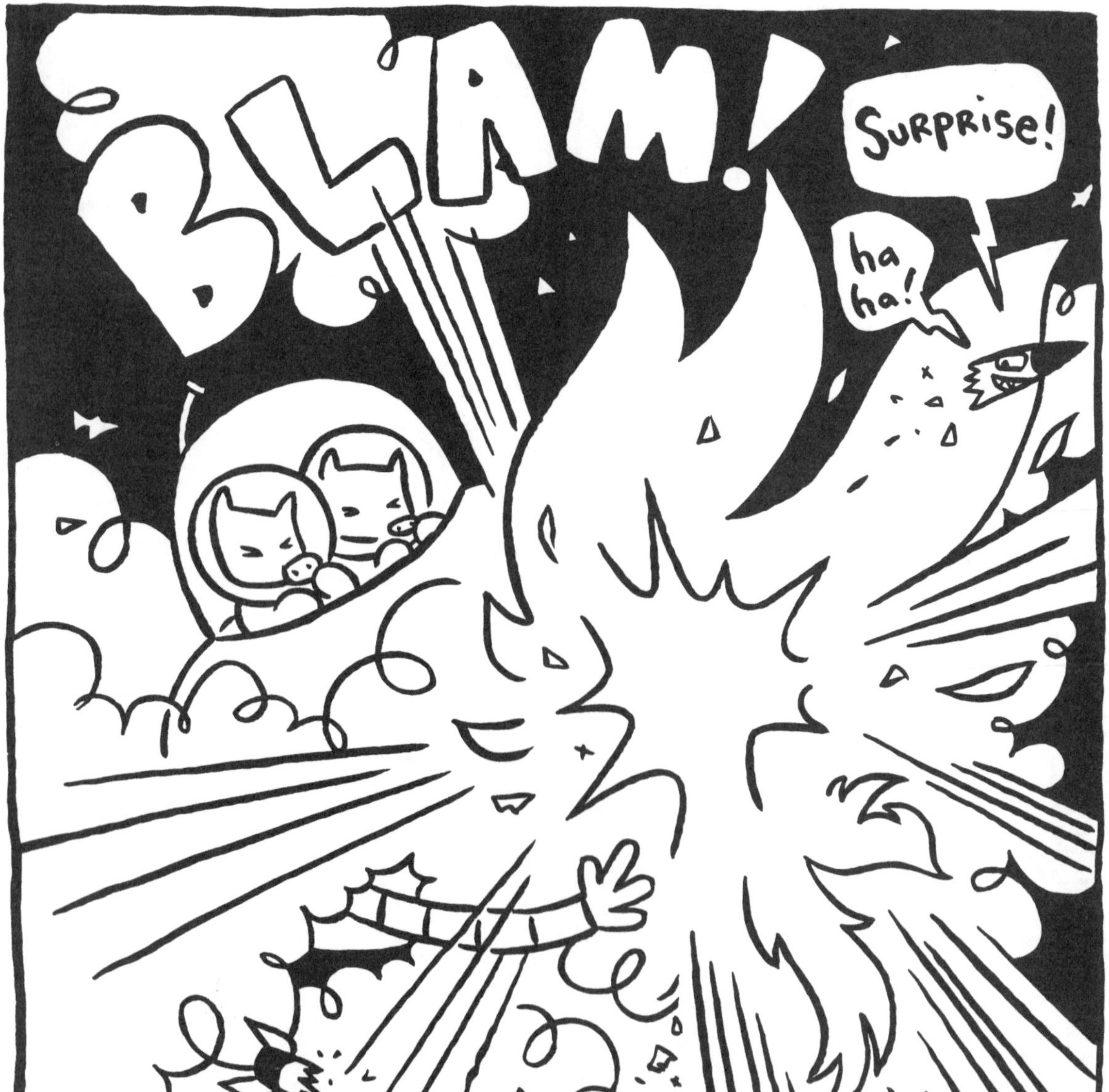
BLAM!
Surprise!
ha ha!

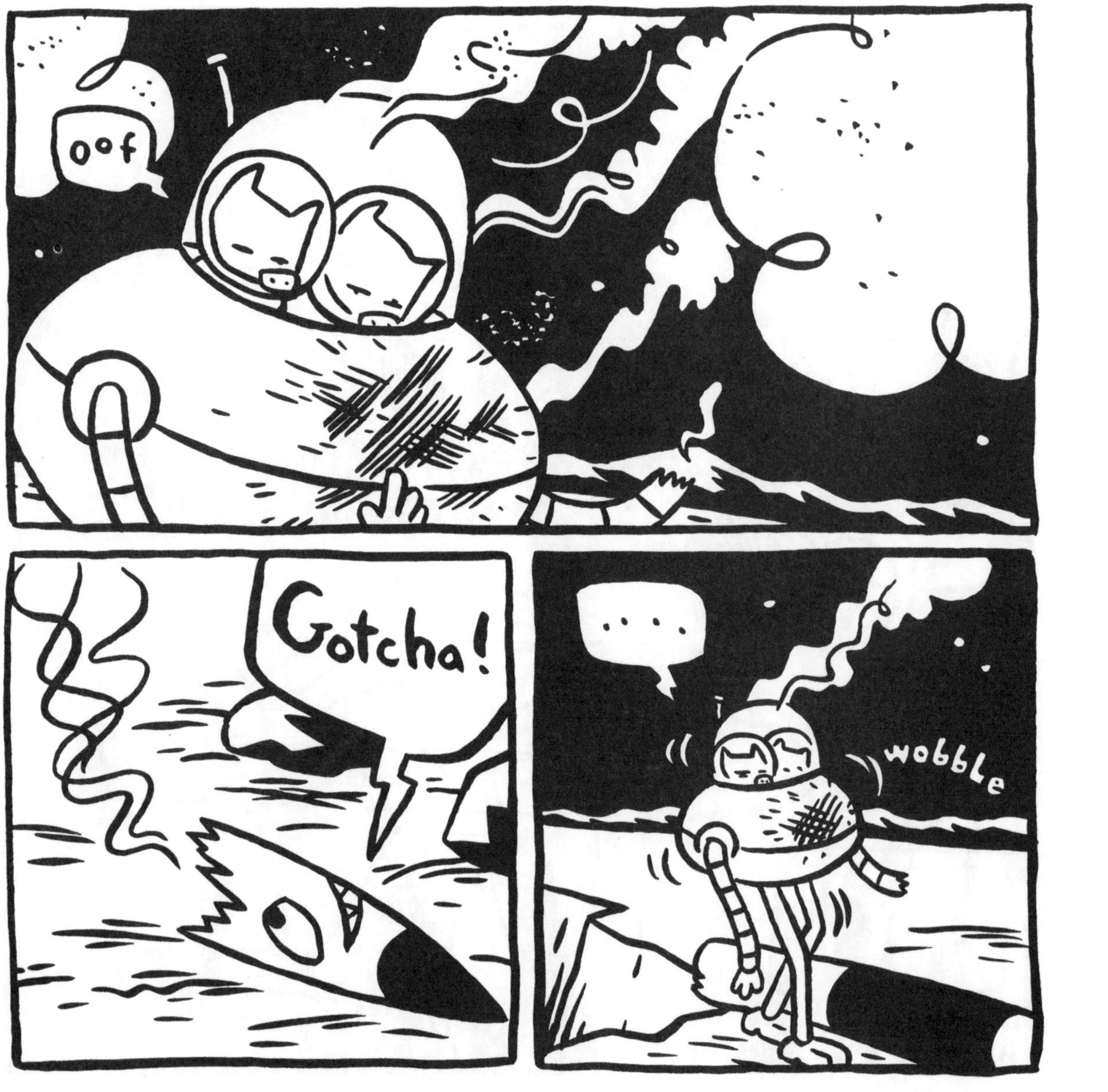
oof
Gotcha!
. . . .
wobble

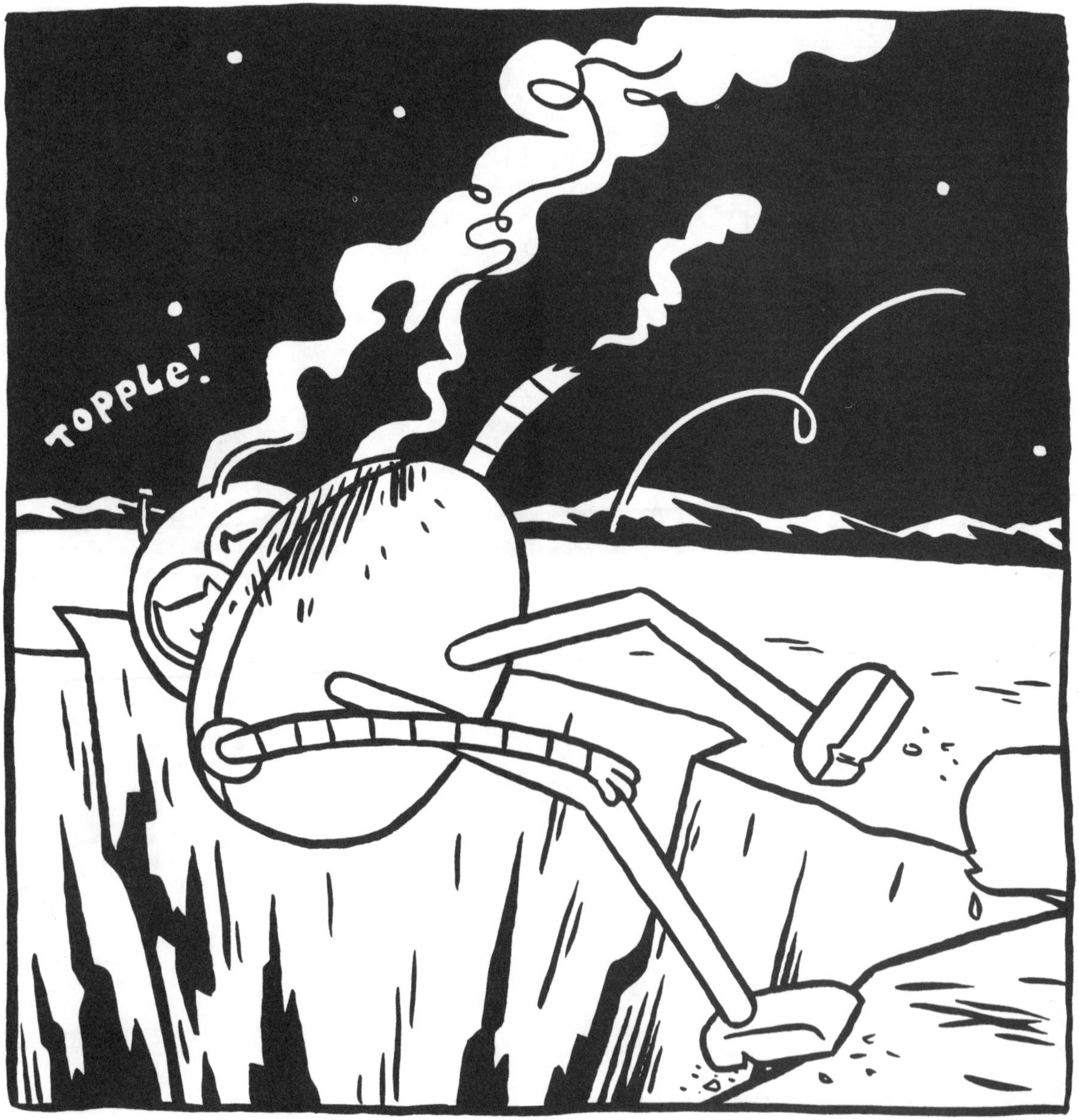
TOPPLE!

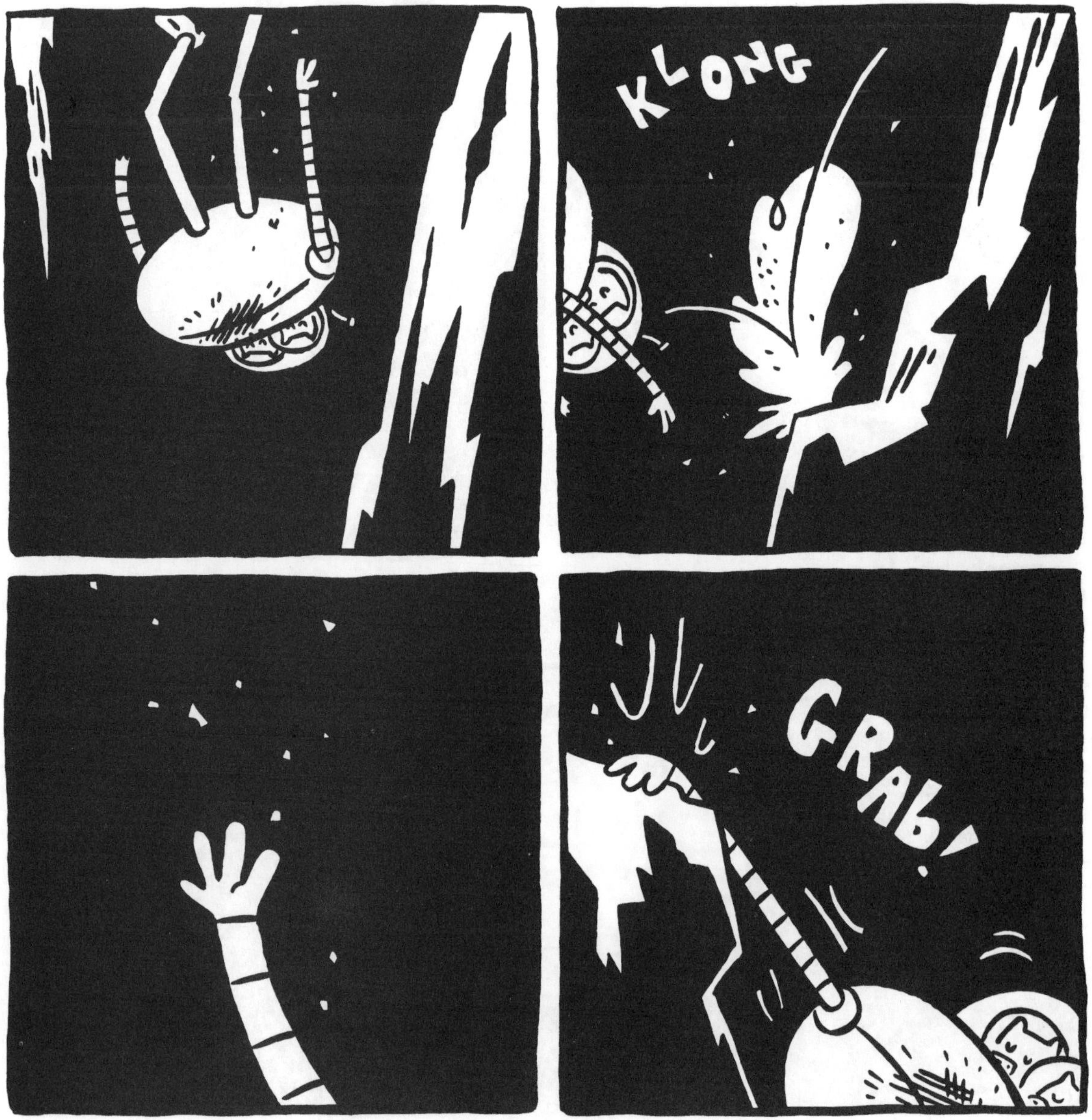
KLONG
GRAB!

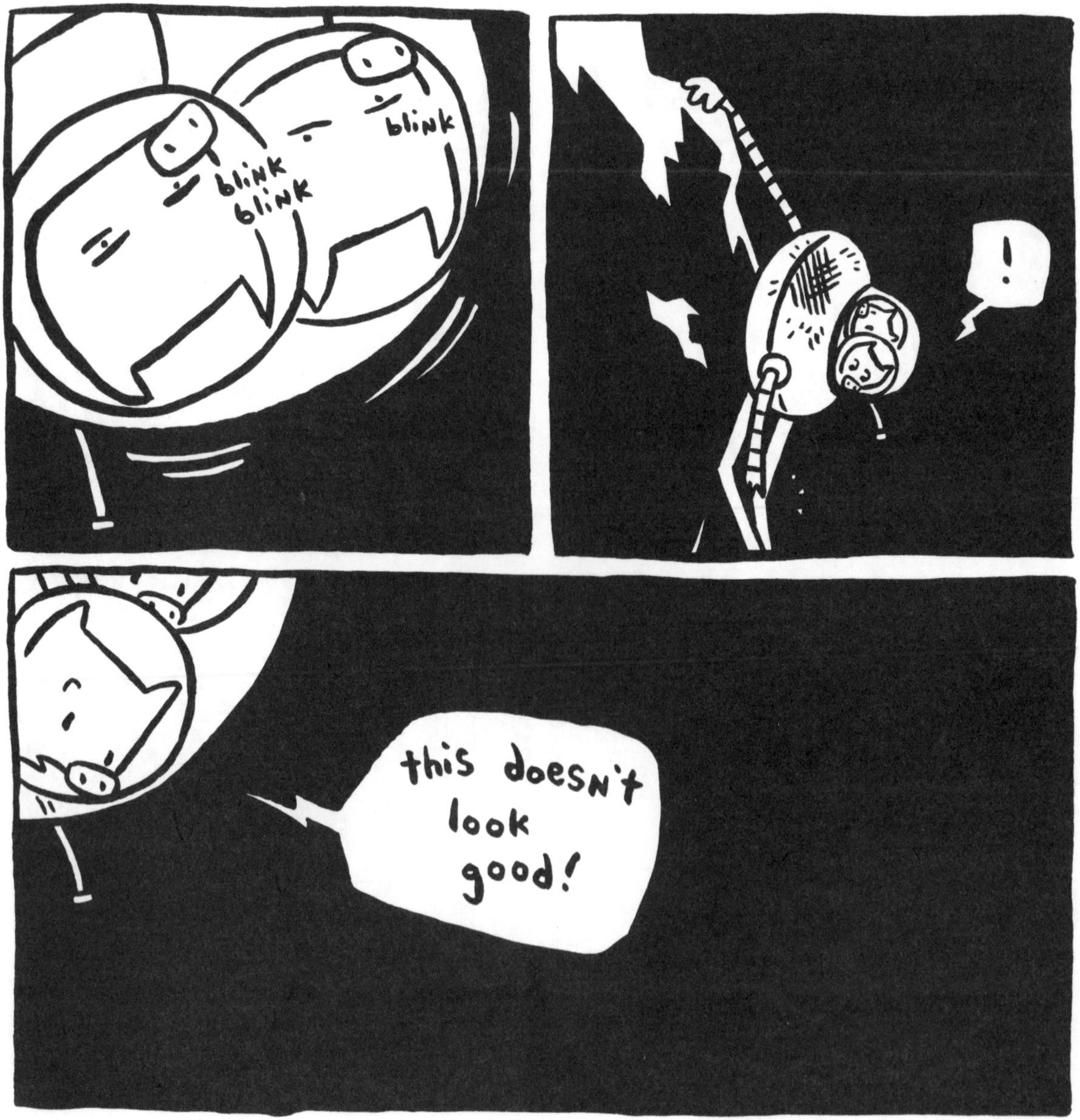
blink blink
blink
!
this doesn't look good!

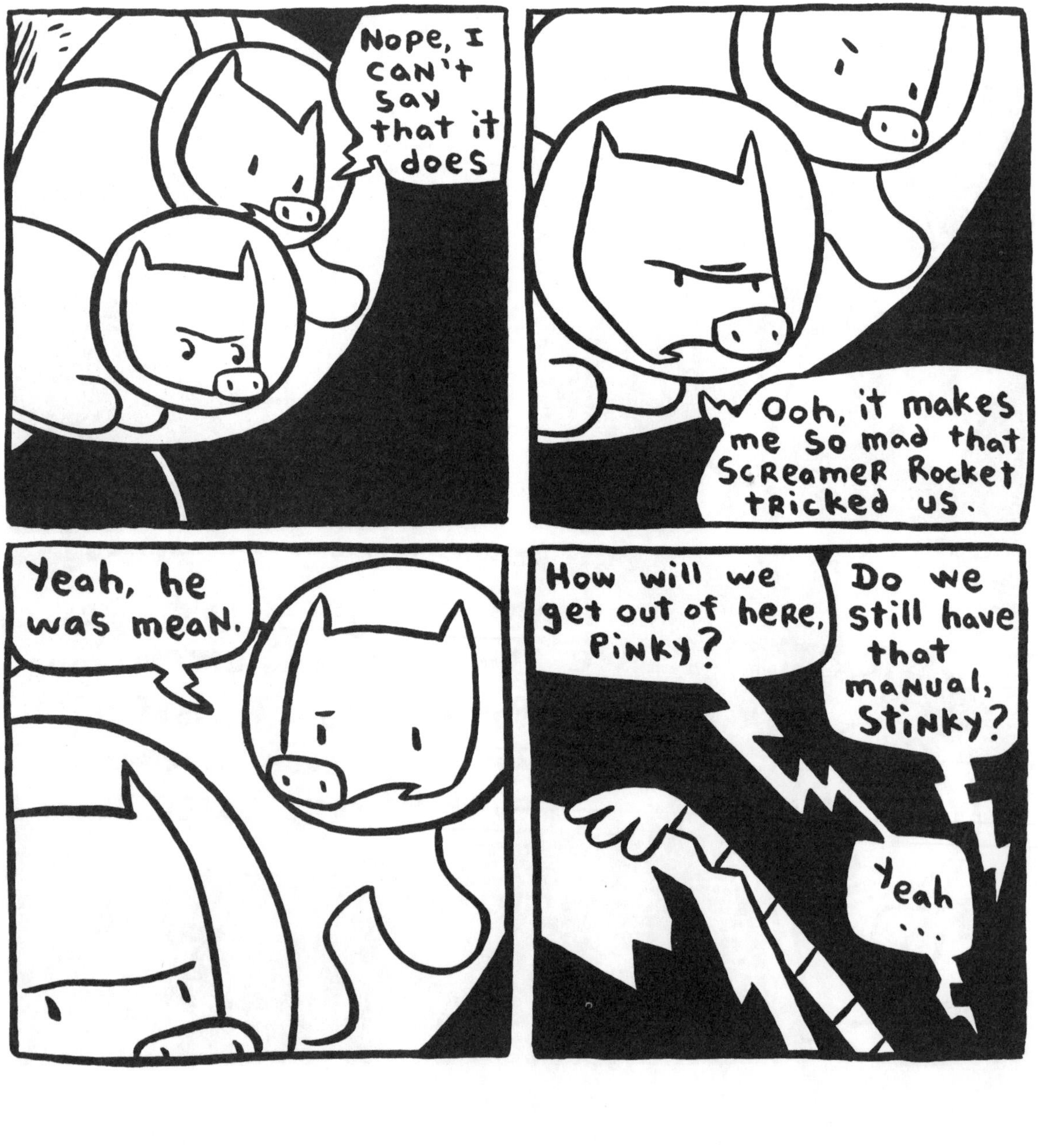
Nope, I can't say that it does
Ooh, it makes me so mad that Screamer Rocket tricked us.
Yeah, he was mean.
How will we get out of here, Pinky?
Do we still have that manual, Stinky?
Yeah ...

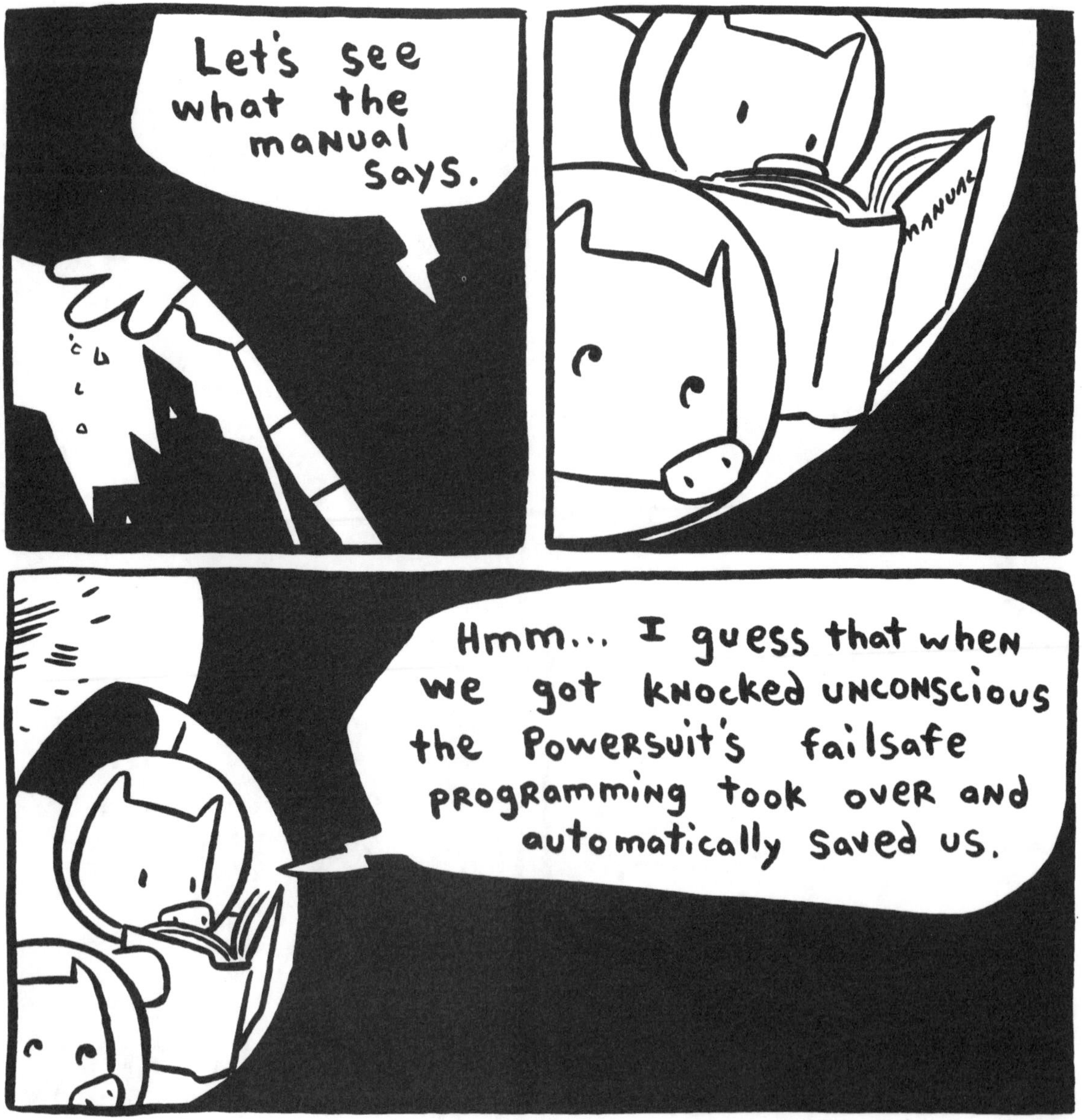
Let's see what the manual says.
MANUAL
Hmm... I guess that when we got knocked unconscious the Powersuit's failsafe programming took over and automatically saved us.

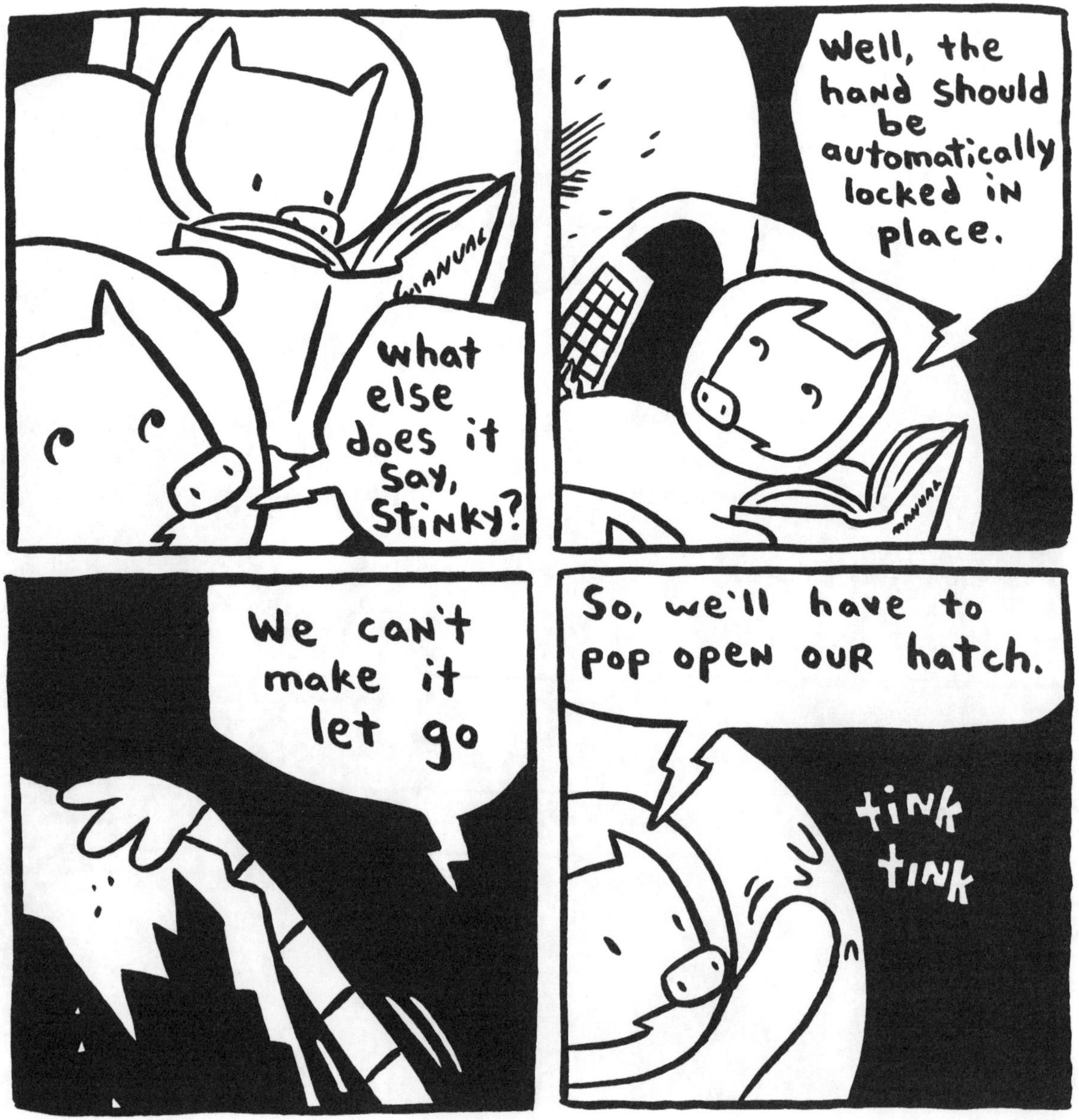
MANUAL
What else does it say, Stinky?
Well, the hand should be automatically locked in place.
MANUAL
We can't make it let go
So, we'll have to pop open our hatch.
tink tink

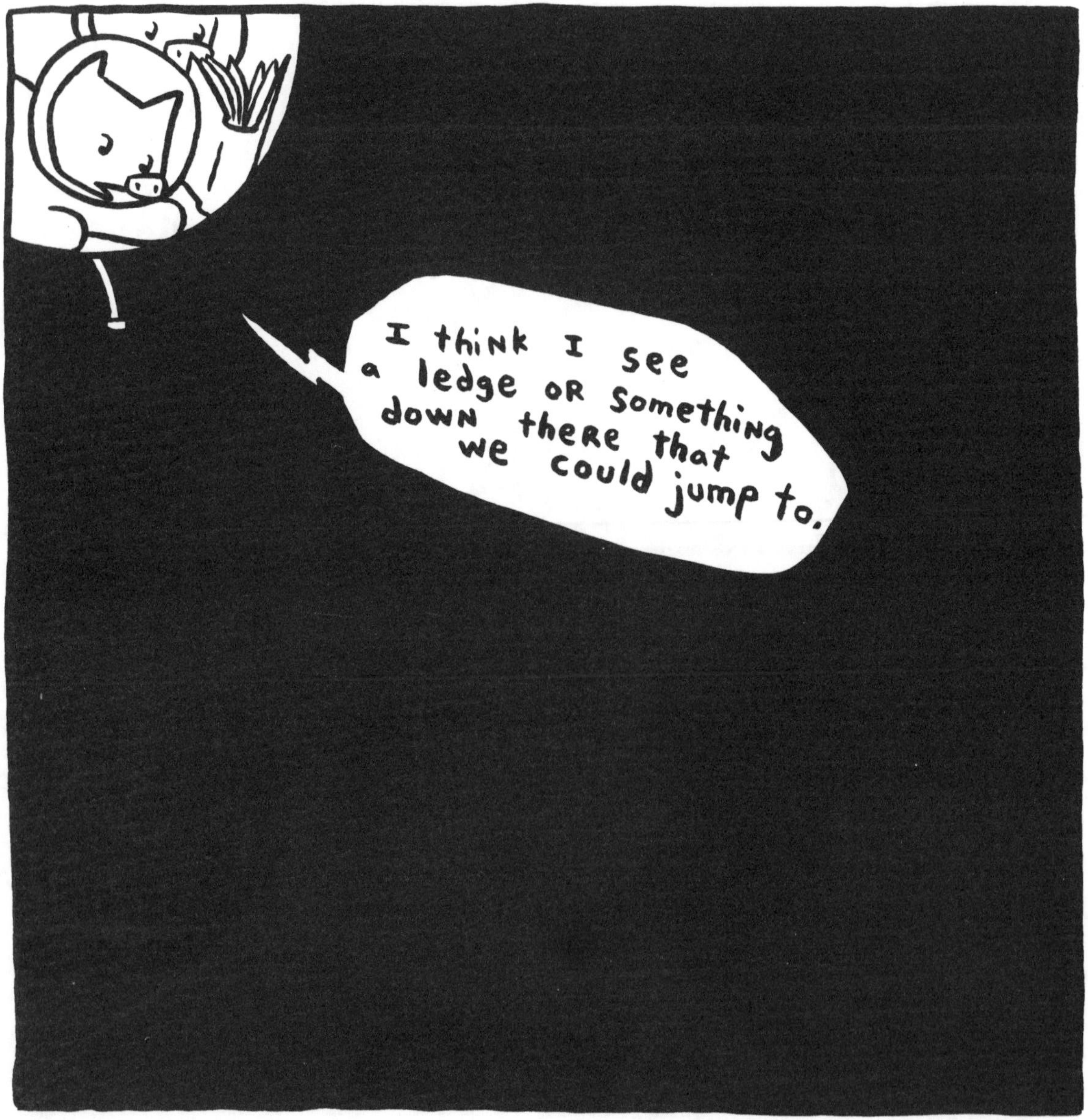
I think I see a ledge or something down there that we could jump to.

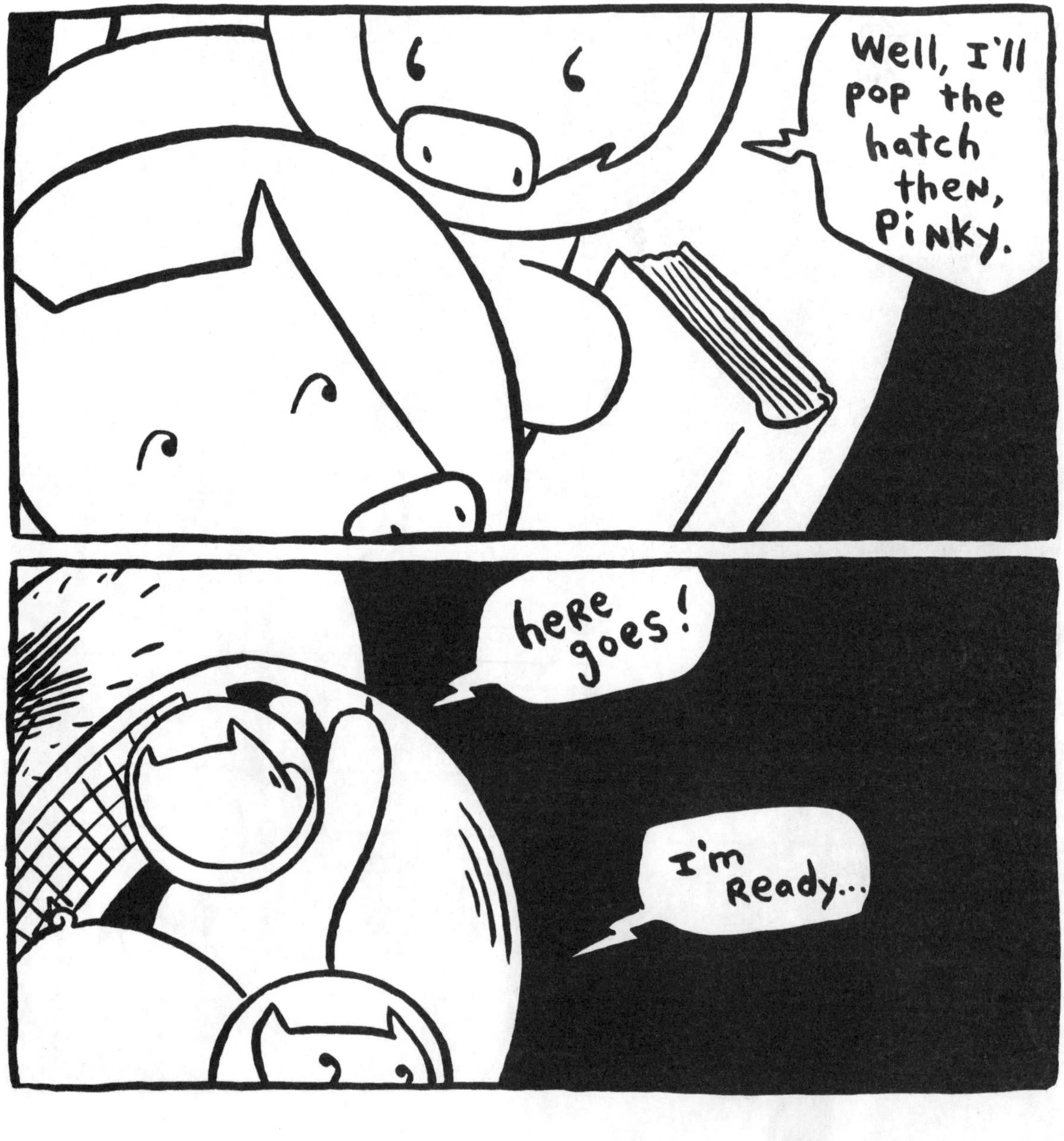
Well, I'll pop the hatch then, Pinky.
here goes!
I'm Ready...

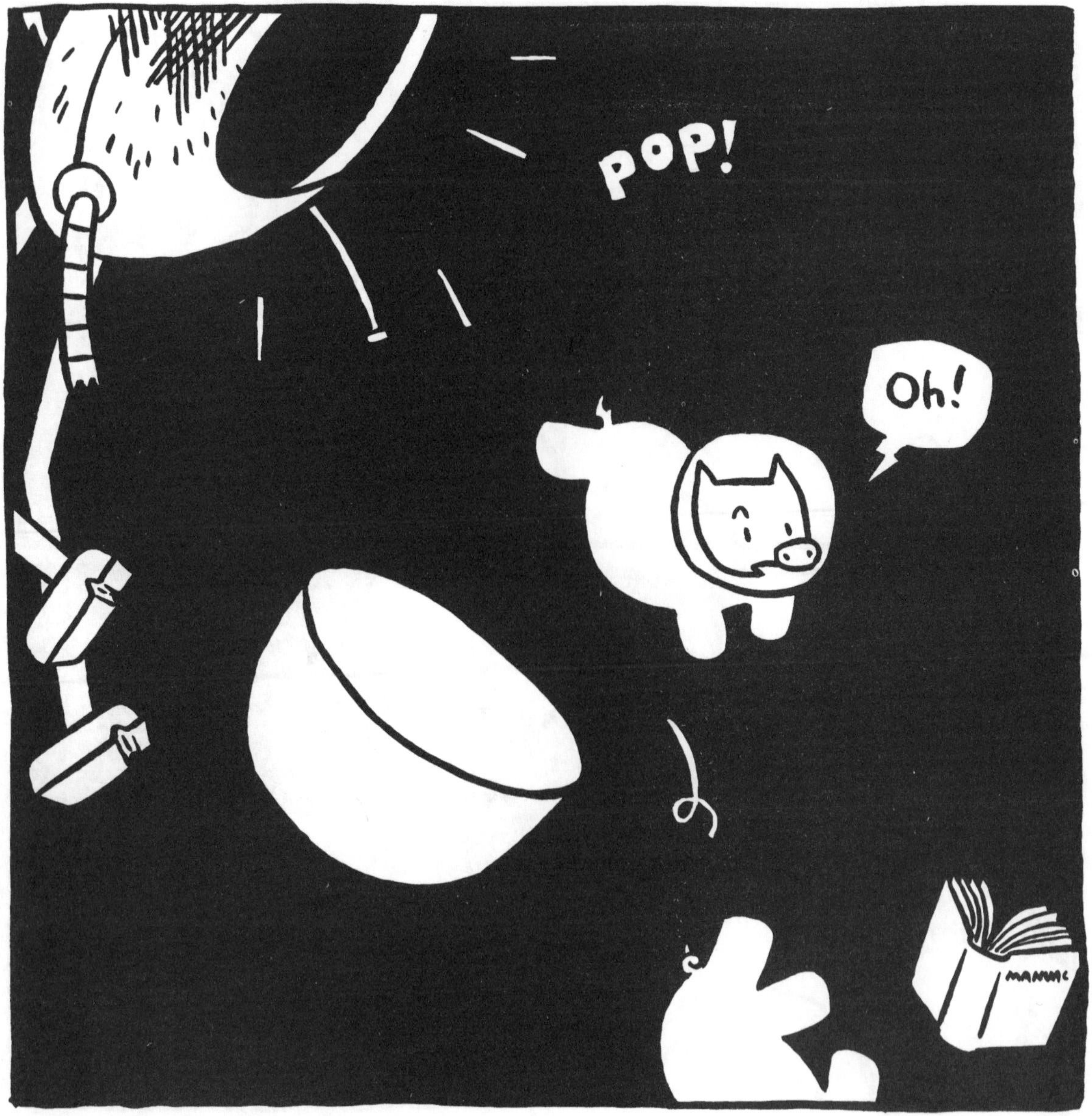
POP!
Oh!
MANUAL

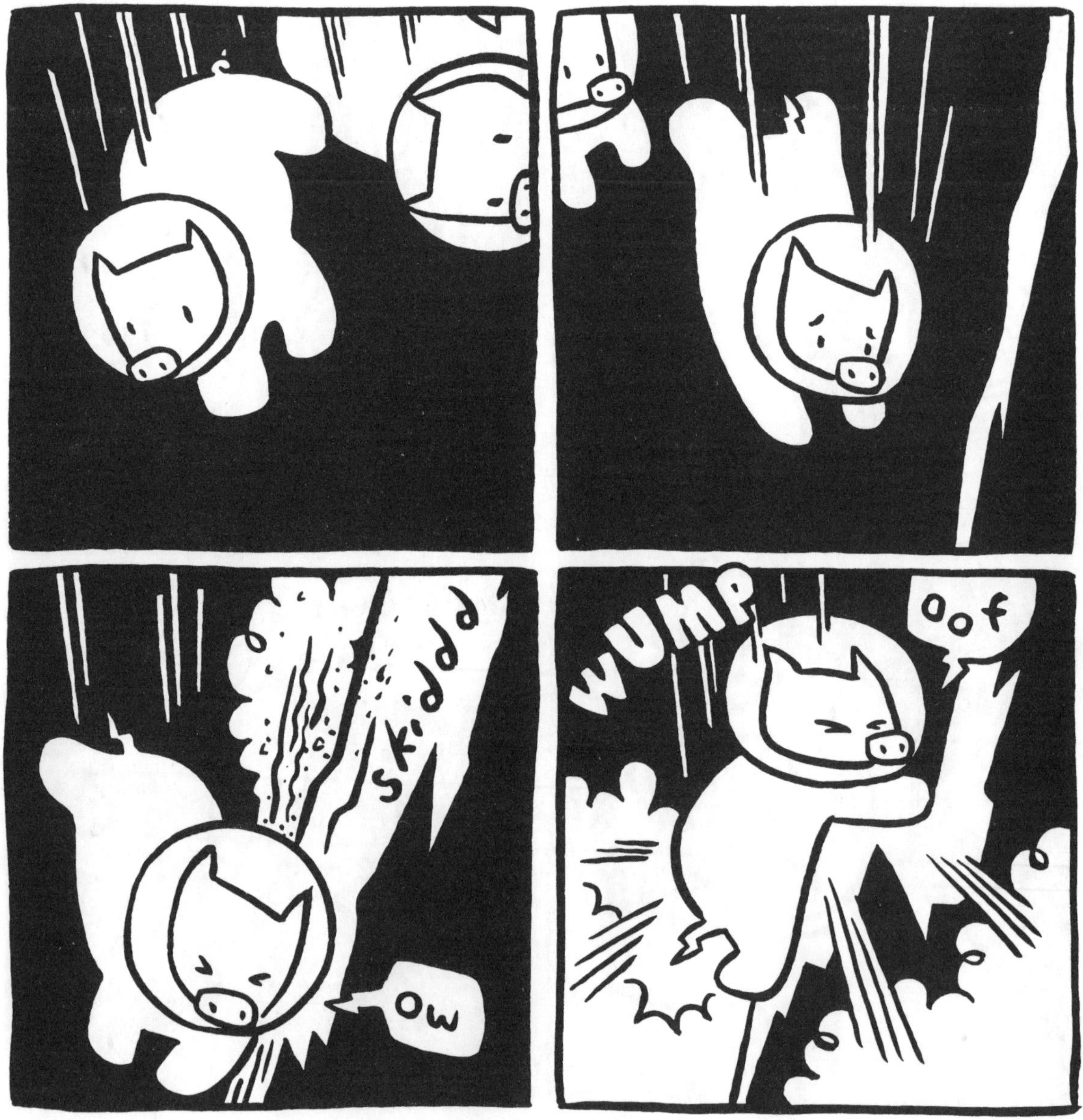
Skiddd
ow
WUMP
oof

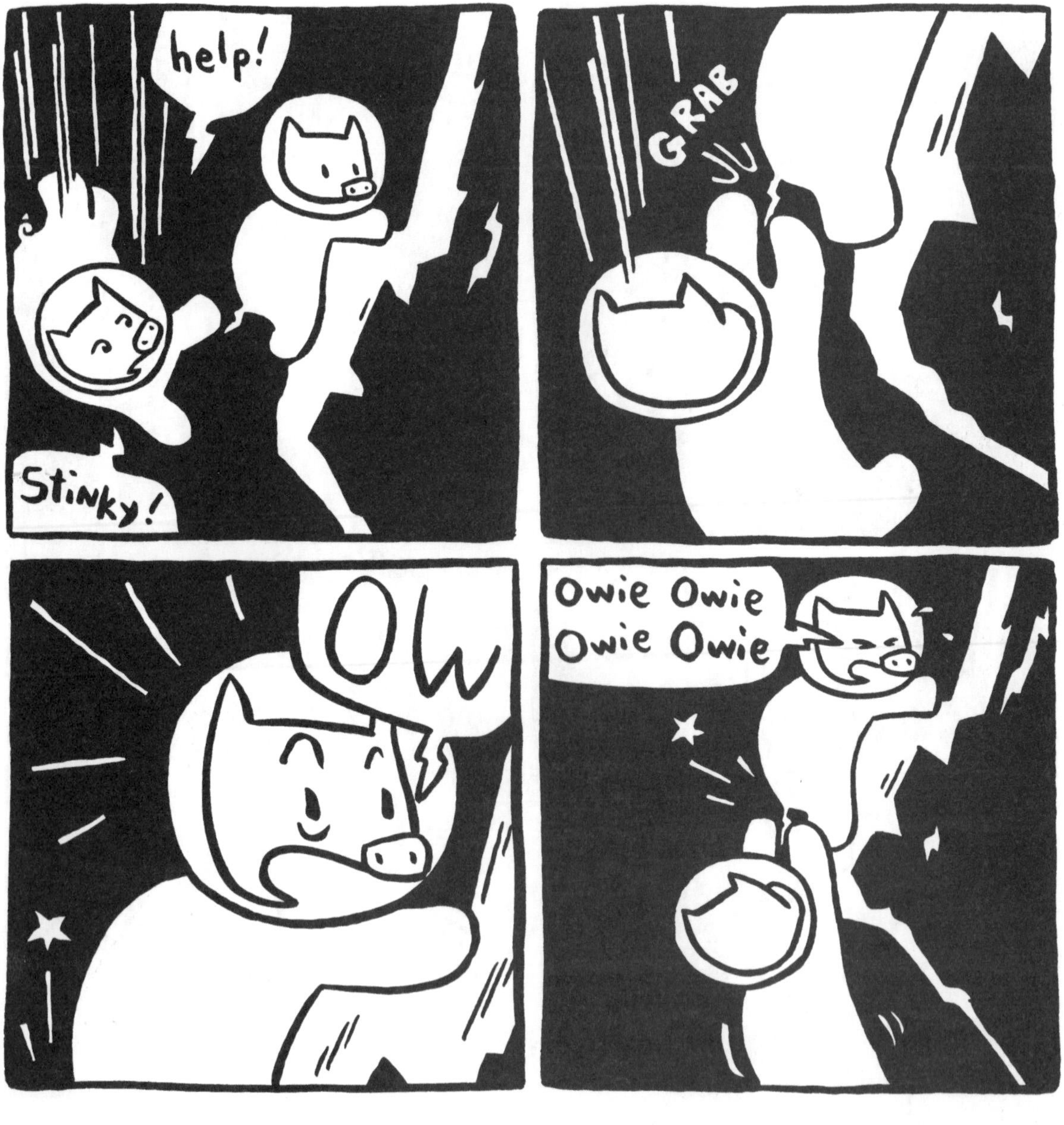
help!
Stinky!
GRAB
OW
Owie Owie
Owie Owie

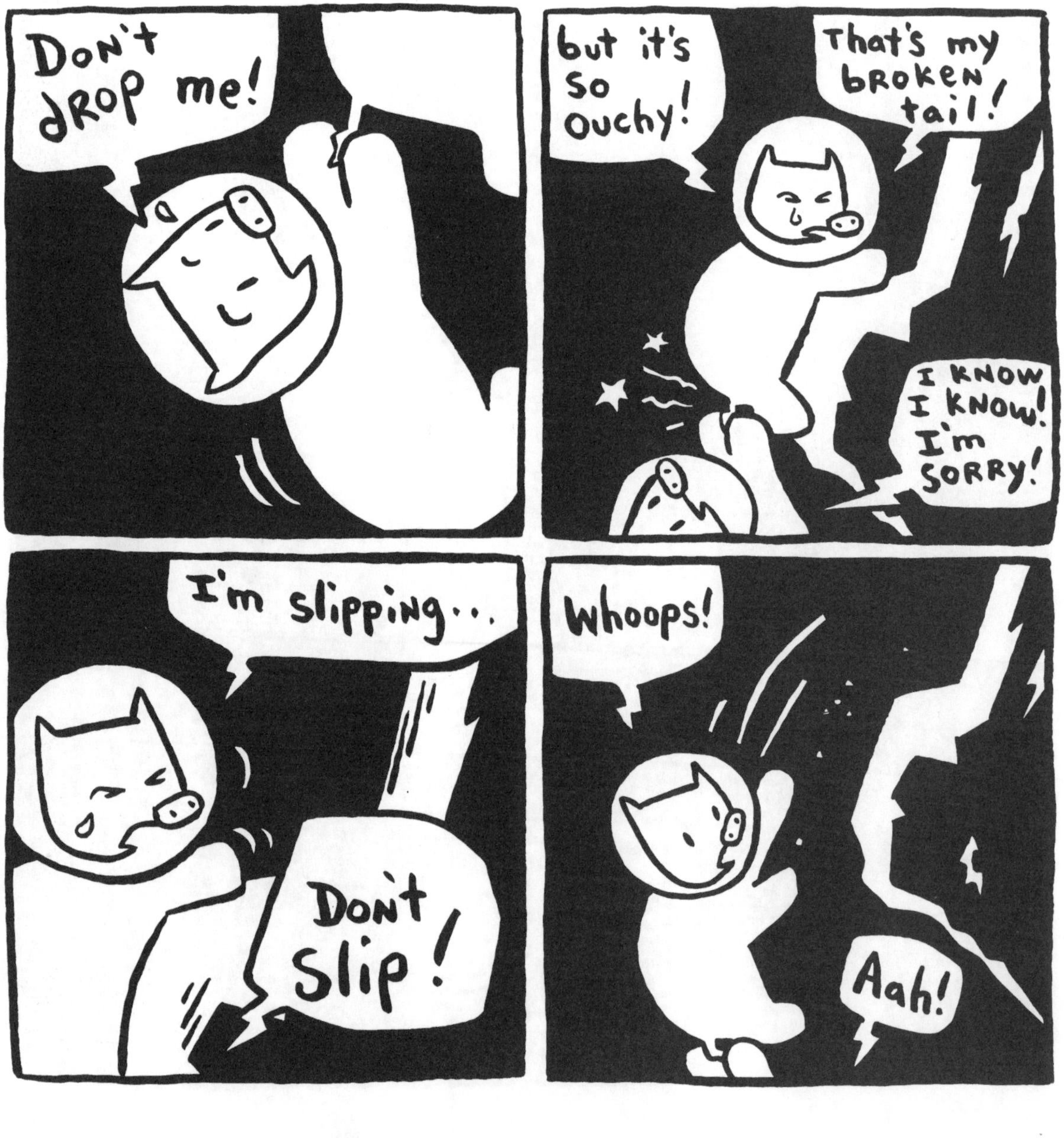

Don't drop me!
but it's so ouchy!
That's my broken tail!
I know I know! I'm sorry!
I'm slipping...
Don't slip!
Whoops!
Aah!

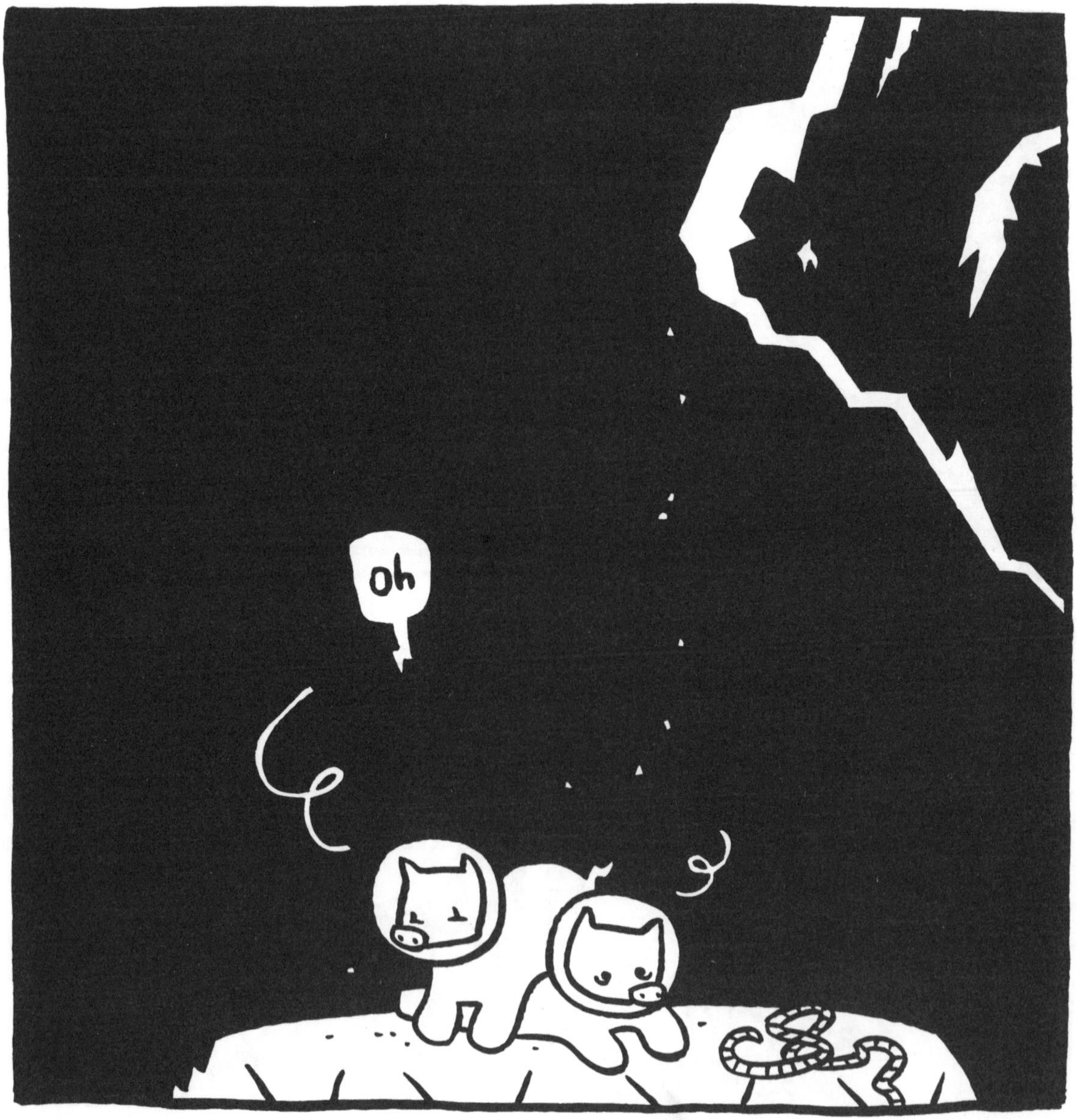
Oh

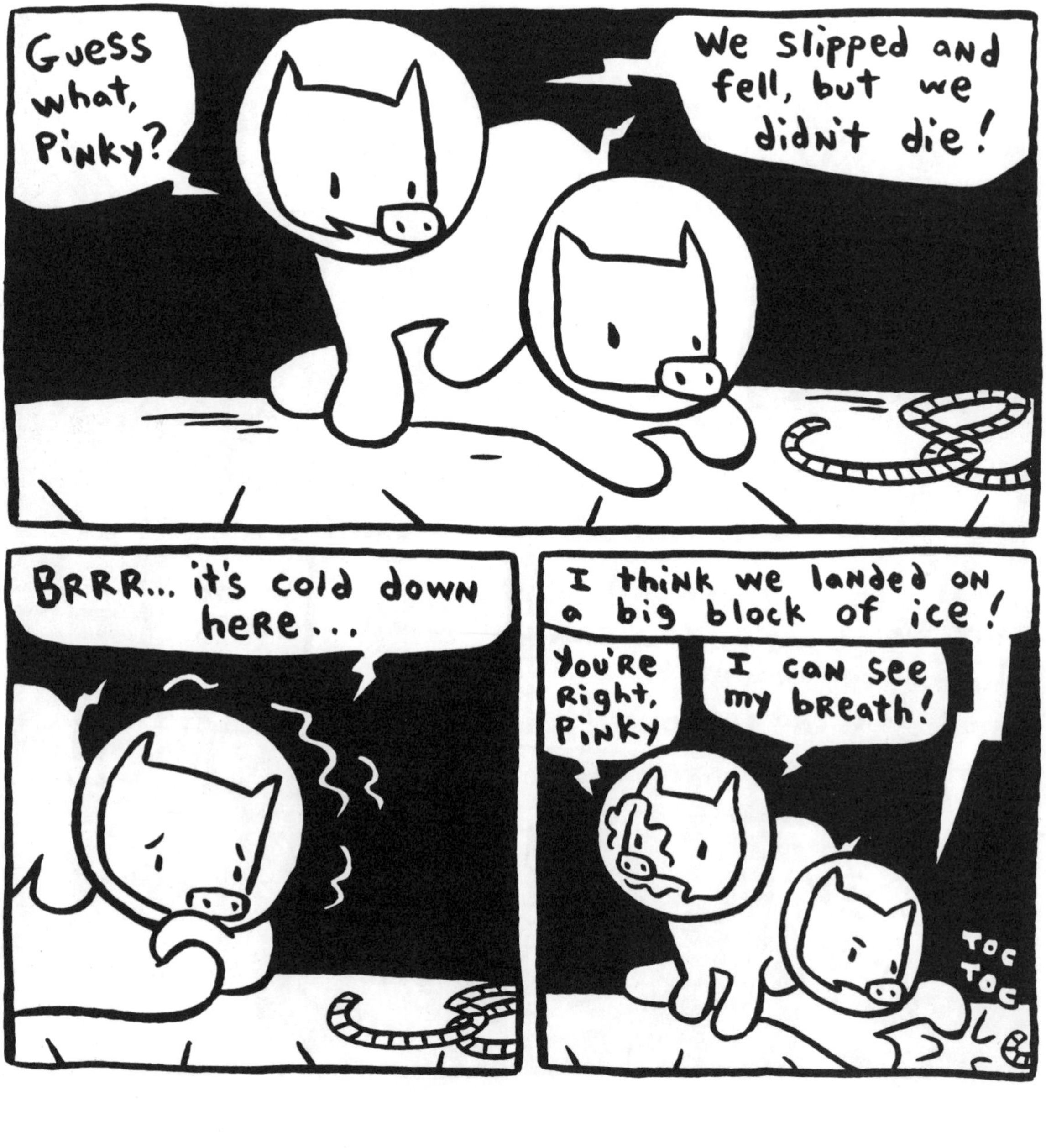
Guess what, Pinky?
We slipped and fell, but we didn't die!
BRRR... it's cold down here...
I think we landed on a big block of ice!
You're right, Pinky
I can see my breath!
TOC TOC

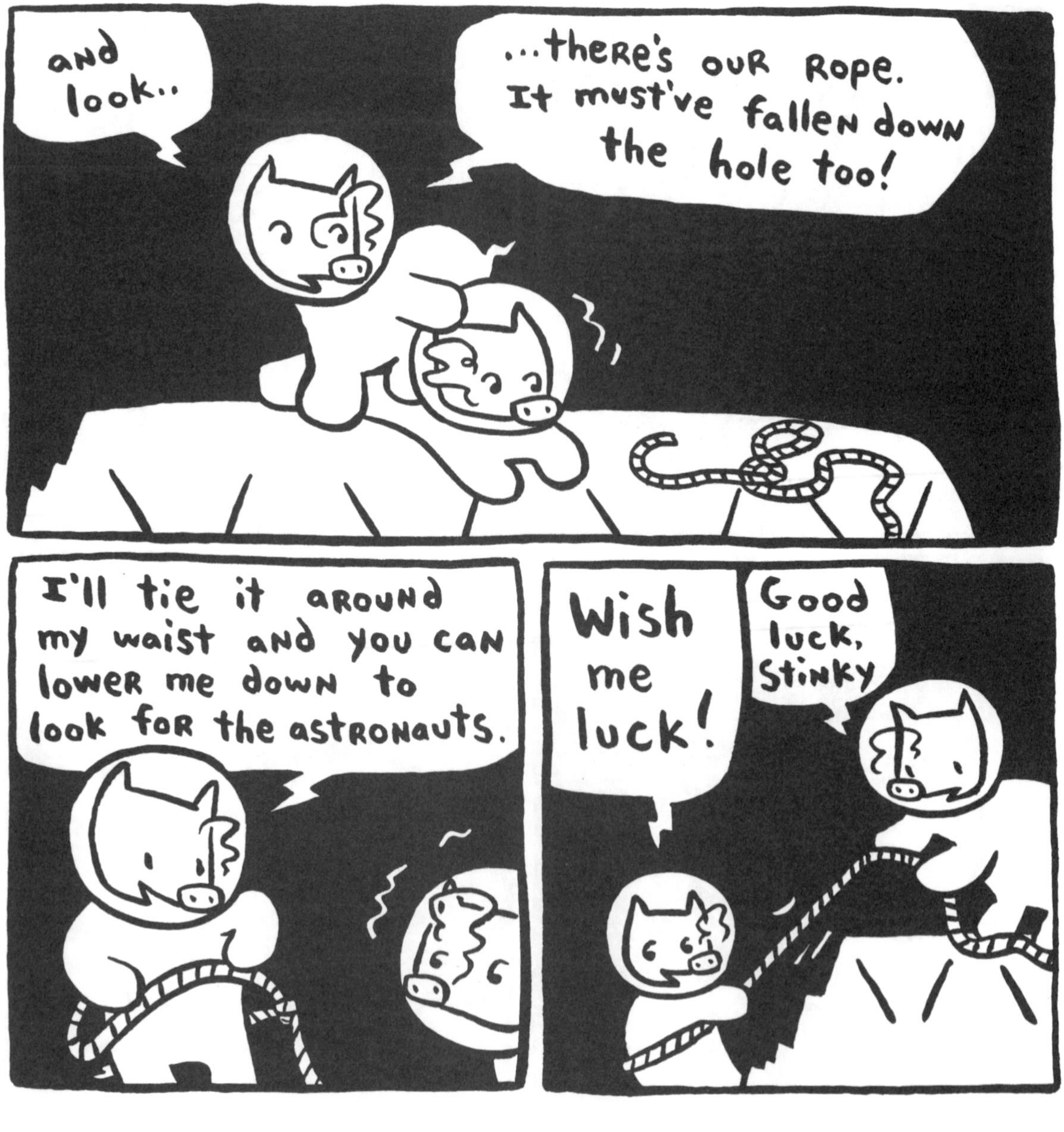
and look..
...there's our rope. It must've fallen down the hole too!
I'll tie it around my waist and you can lower me down to look for the astronauts.
Wish me luck!
Good luck, Stinky

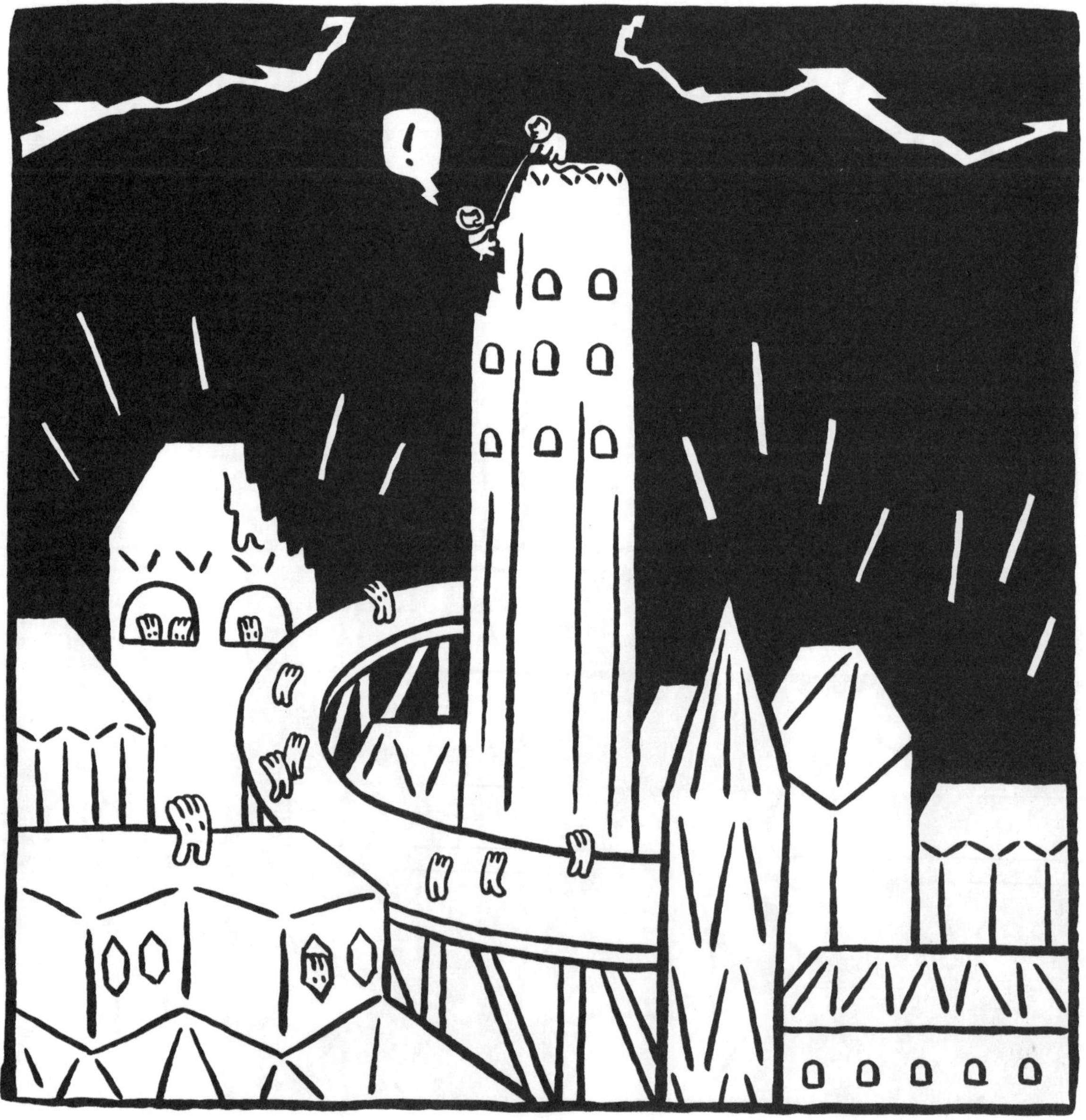
!

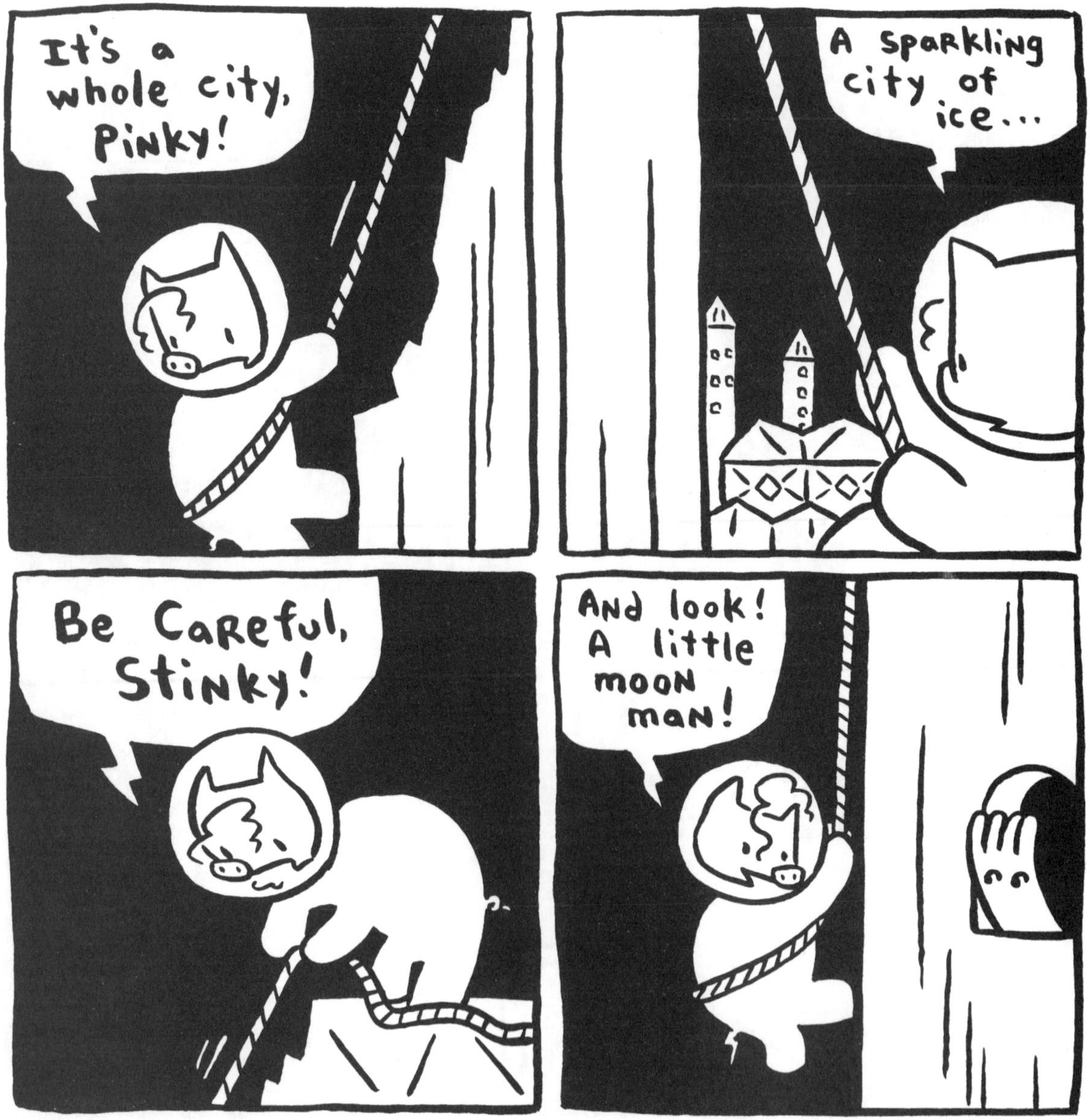
It's a whole city, Pinky!
A sparkling city of ice...
Be Careful, Stinky!
And look! A little moon man!

Ha ha! I think he wants to be friends!
Careful Stinky...
Eek! That's Cold!
Stinky!
help!
Uh oh!

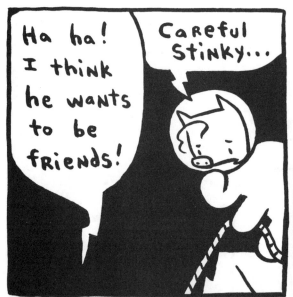

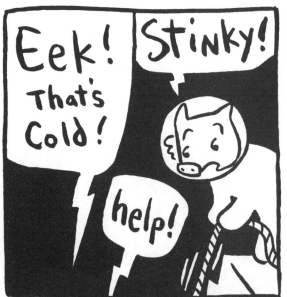

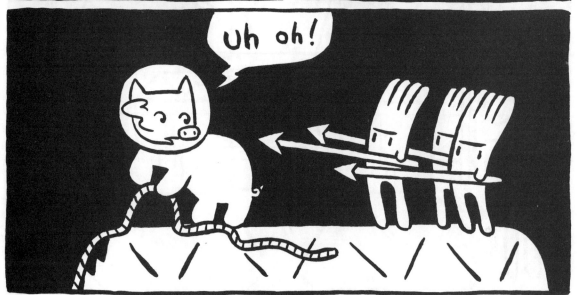

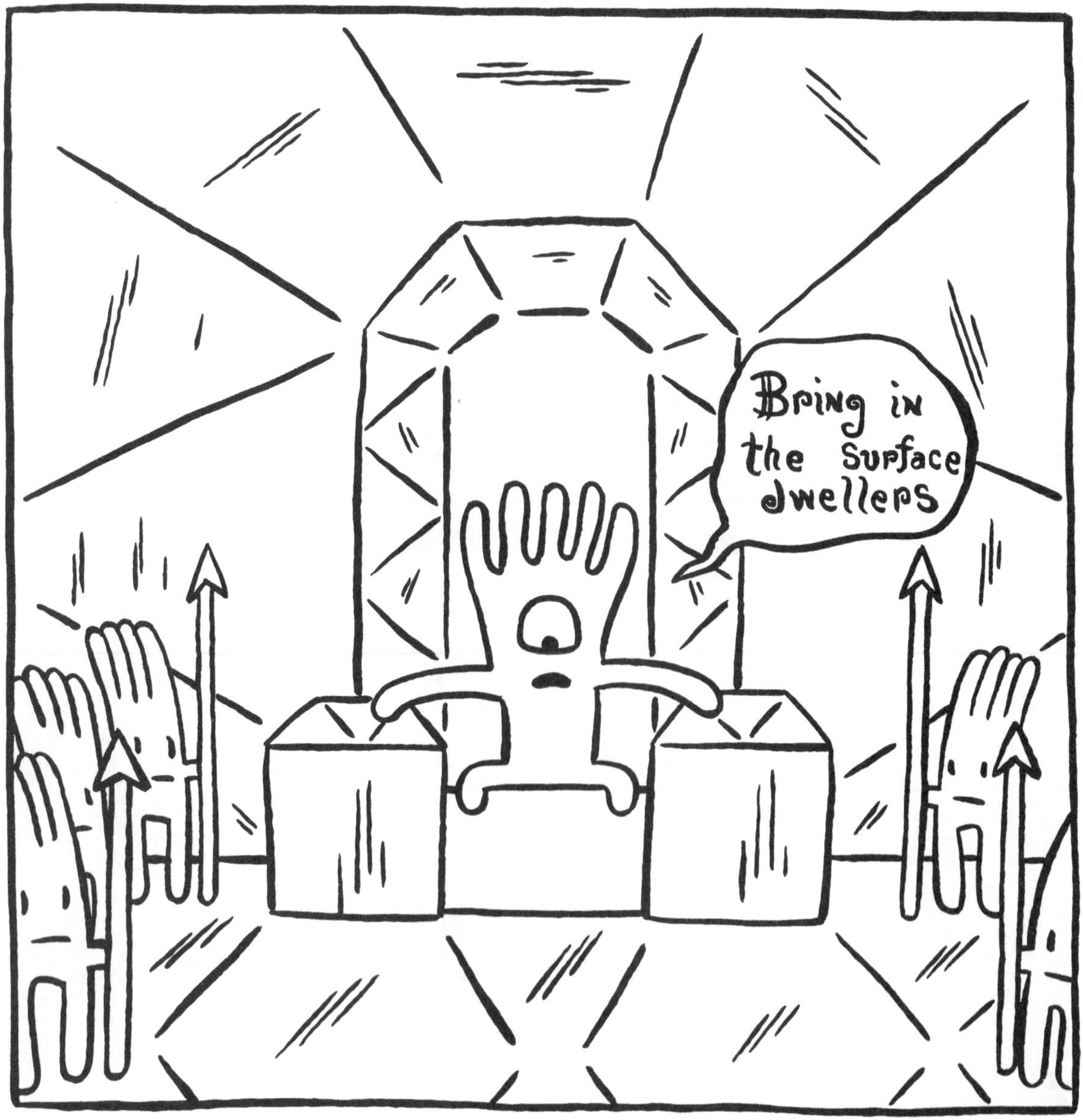
Bring in the surface dwellers

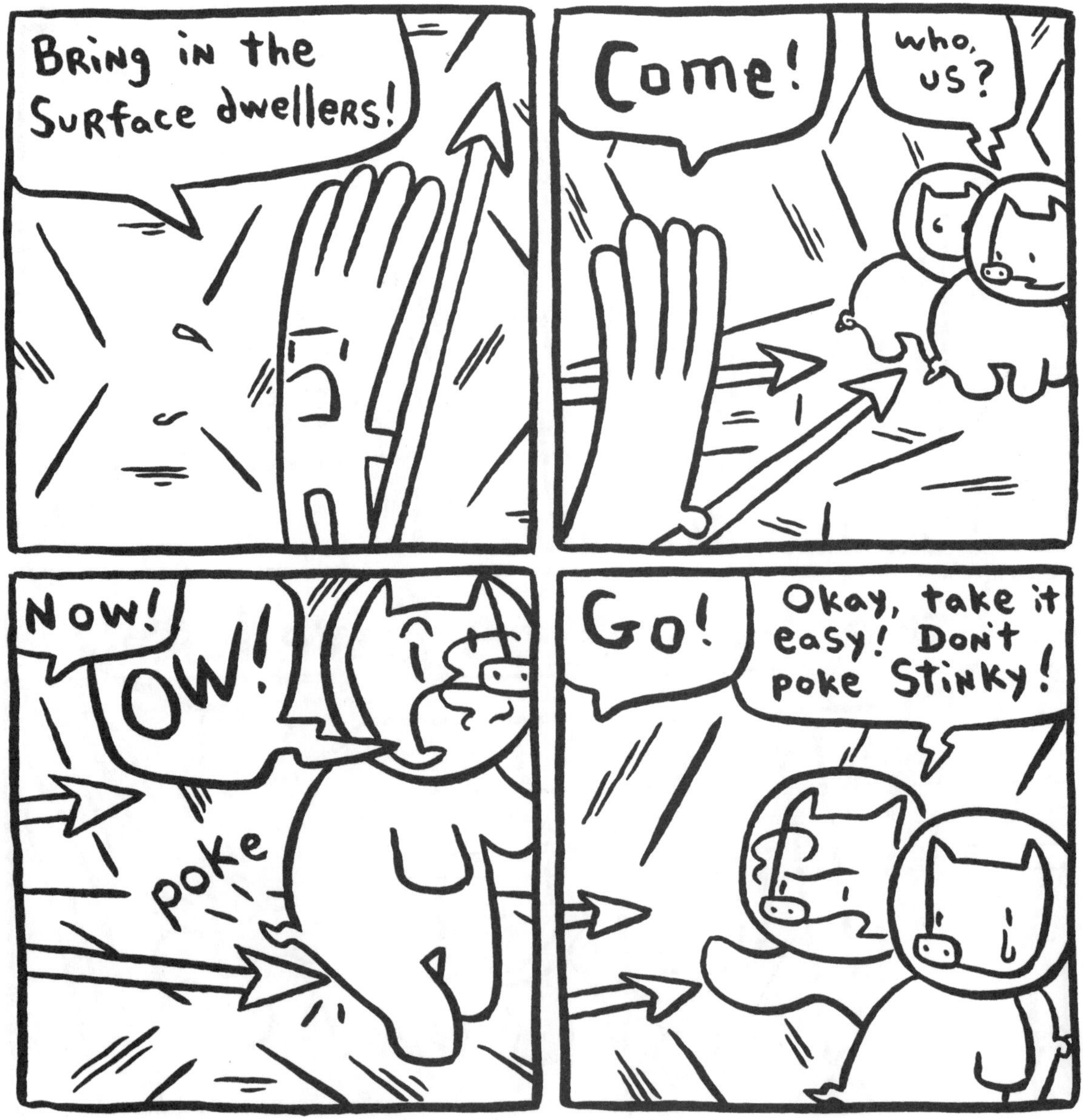
Bring in the Surface dwellers!
Come!
who, us?
Now!
OW!
poke
Go!
Okay, take it easy! Don't poke Stinky!

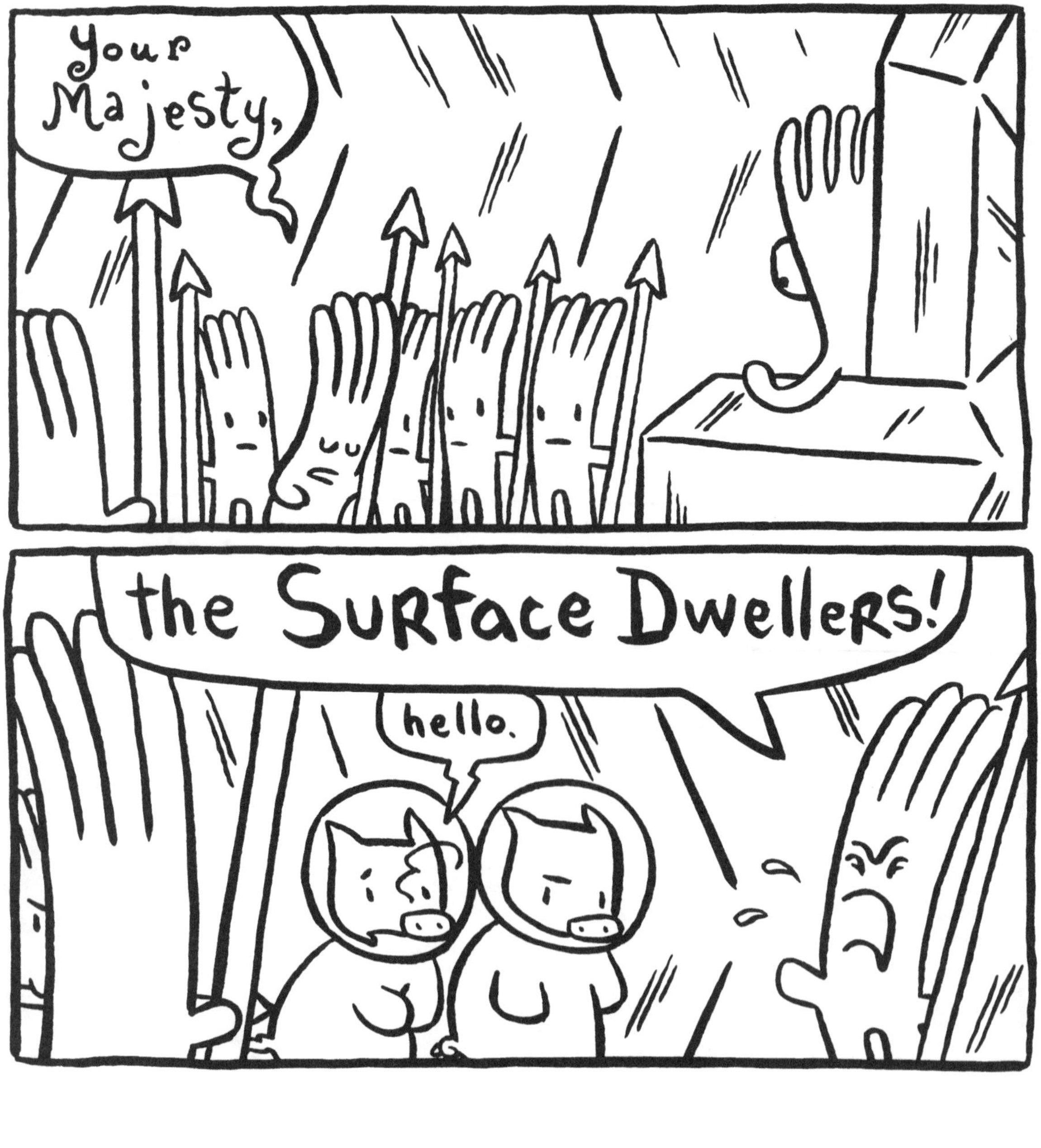
Your Majesty,
the Surface Dwellers!
hello.

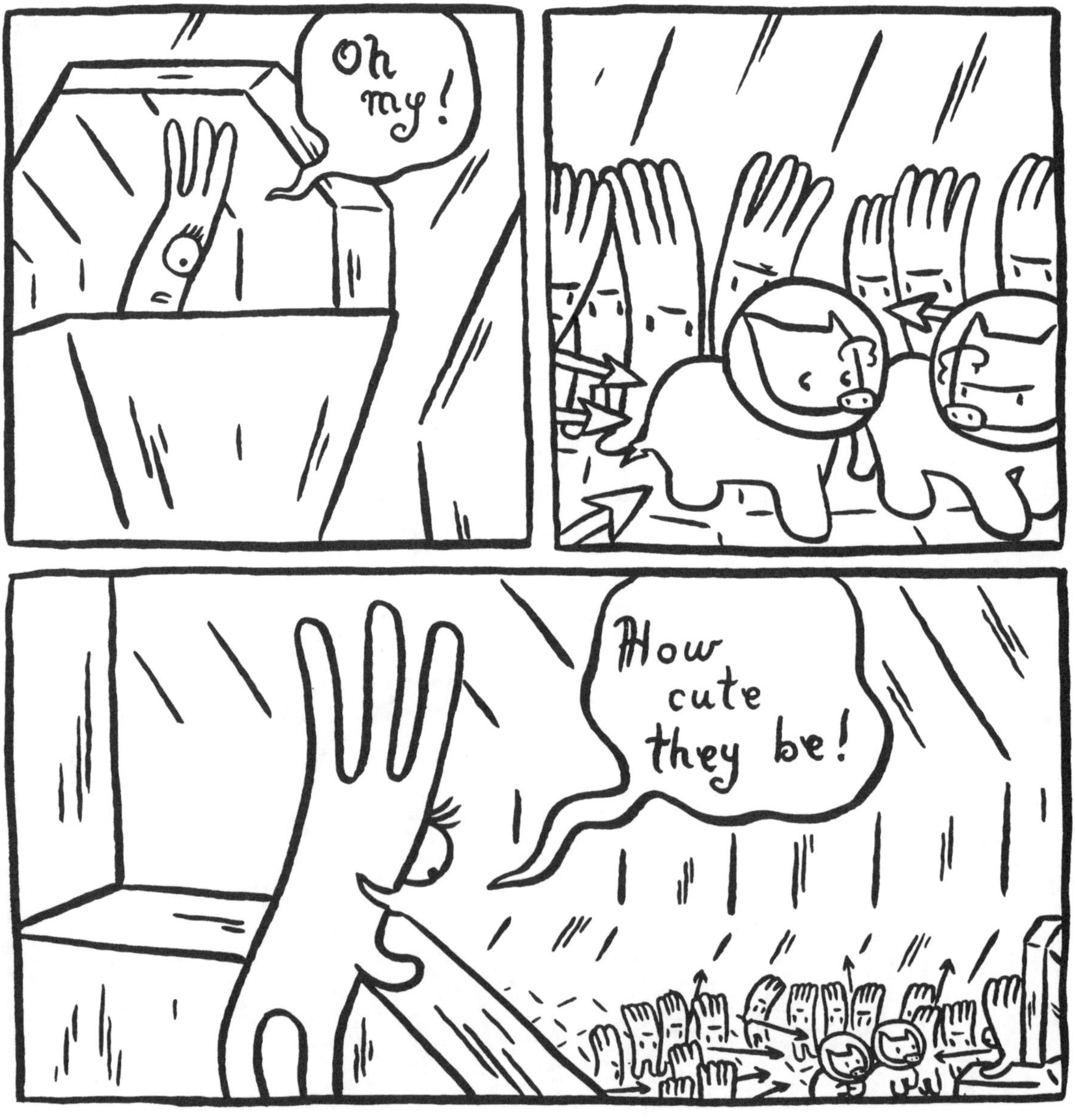
Oh my!
How cute they be!

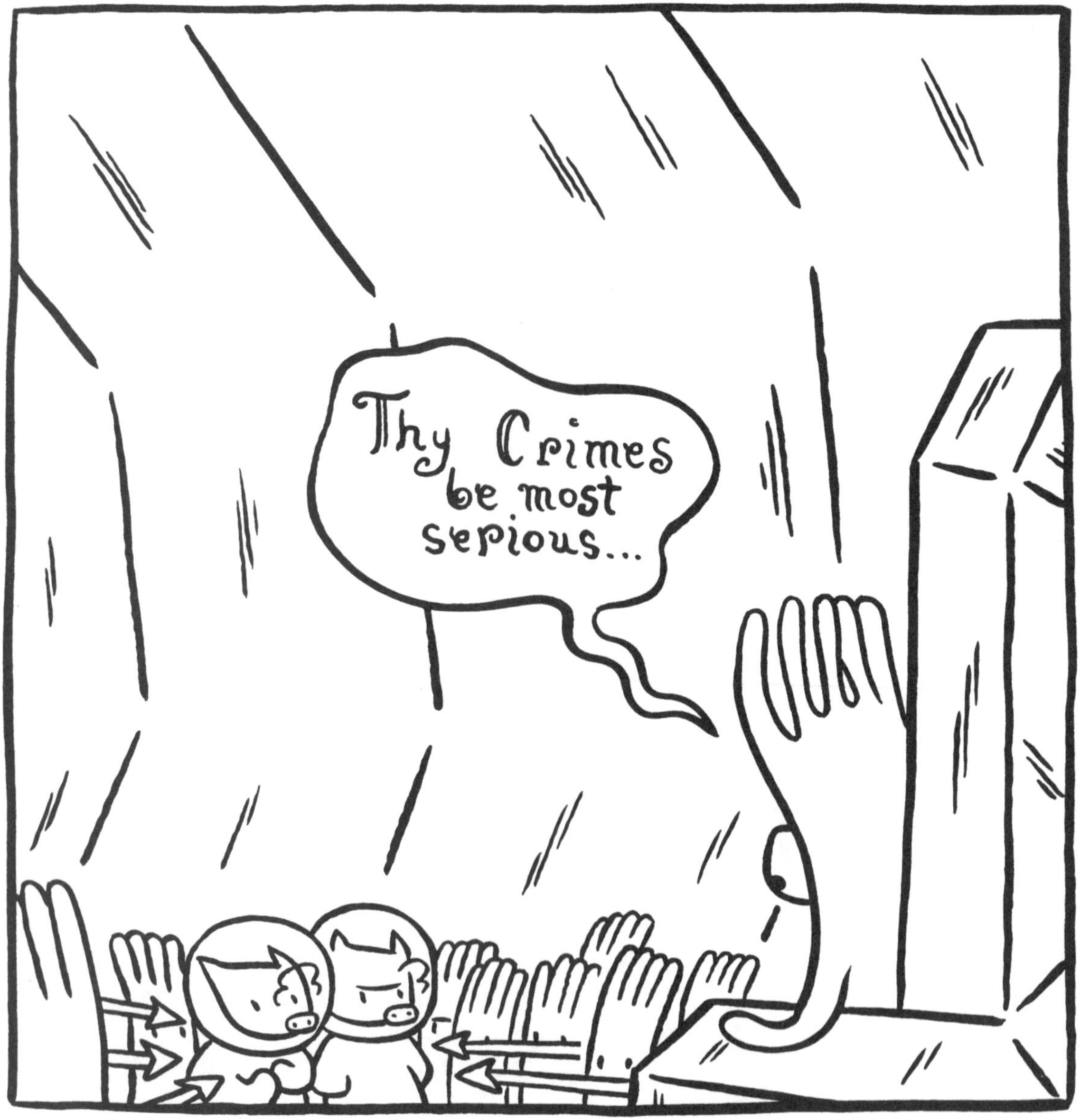
Thy Crimes be most serious...

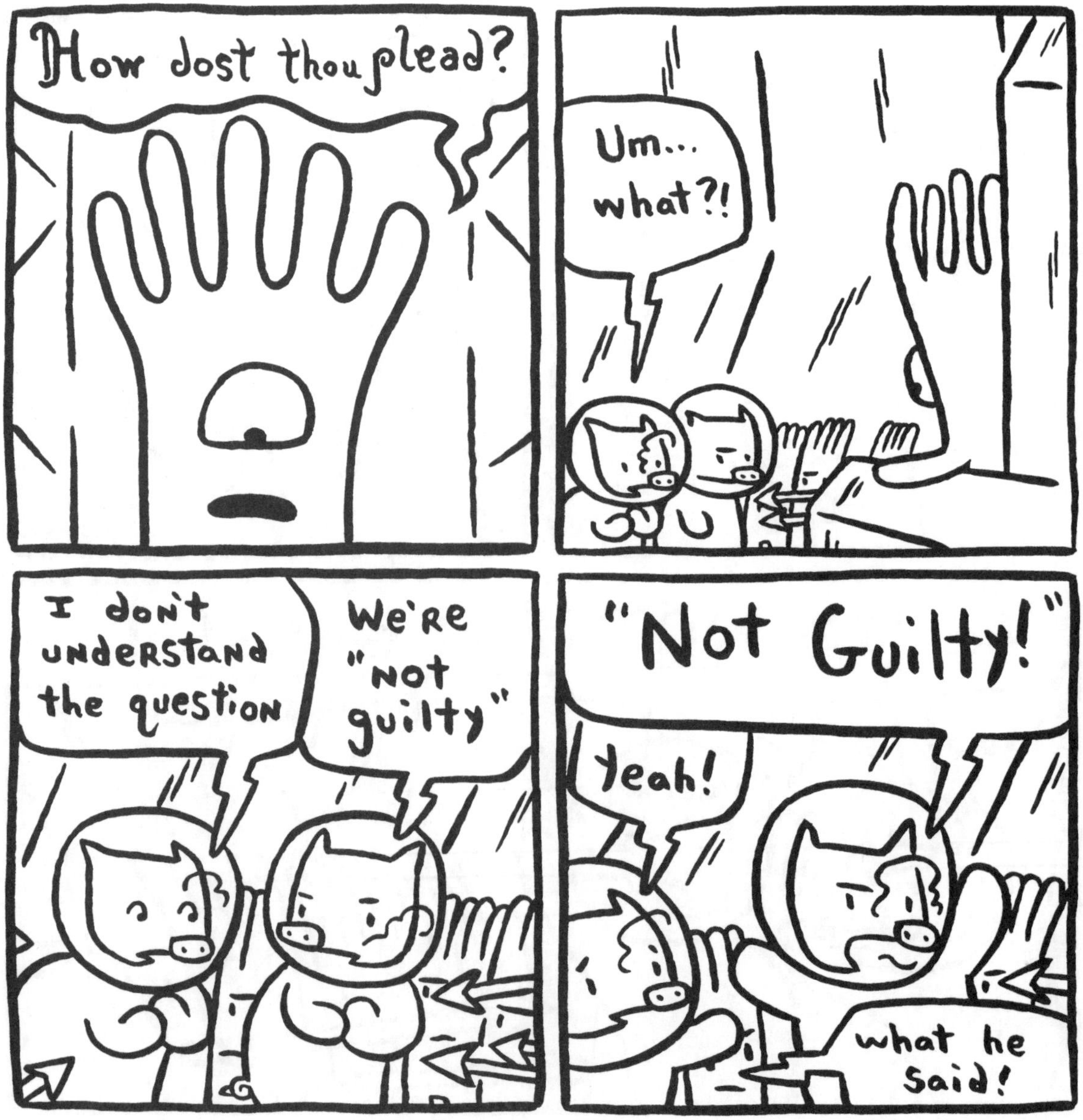
How dost thou plead?
Um... what?!
I don't understand the question
We're "not guilty"
"Not Guilty!"
Yeah!
what he said!

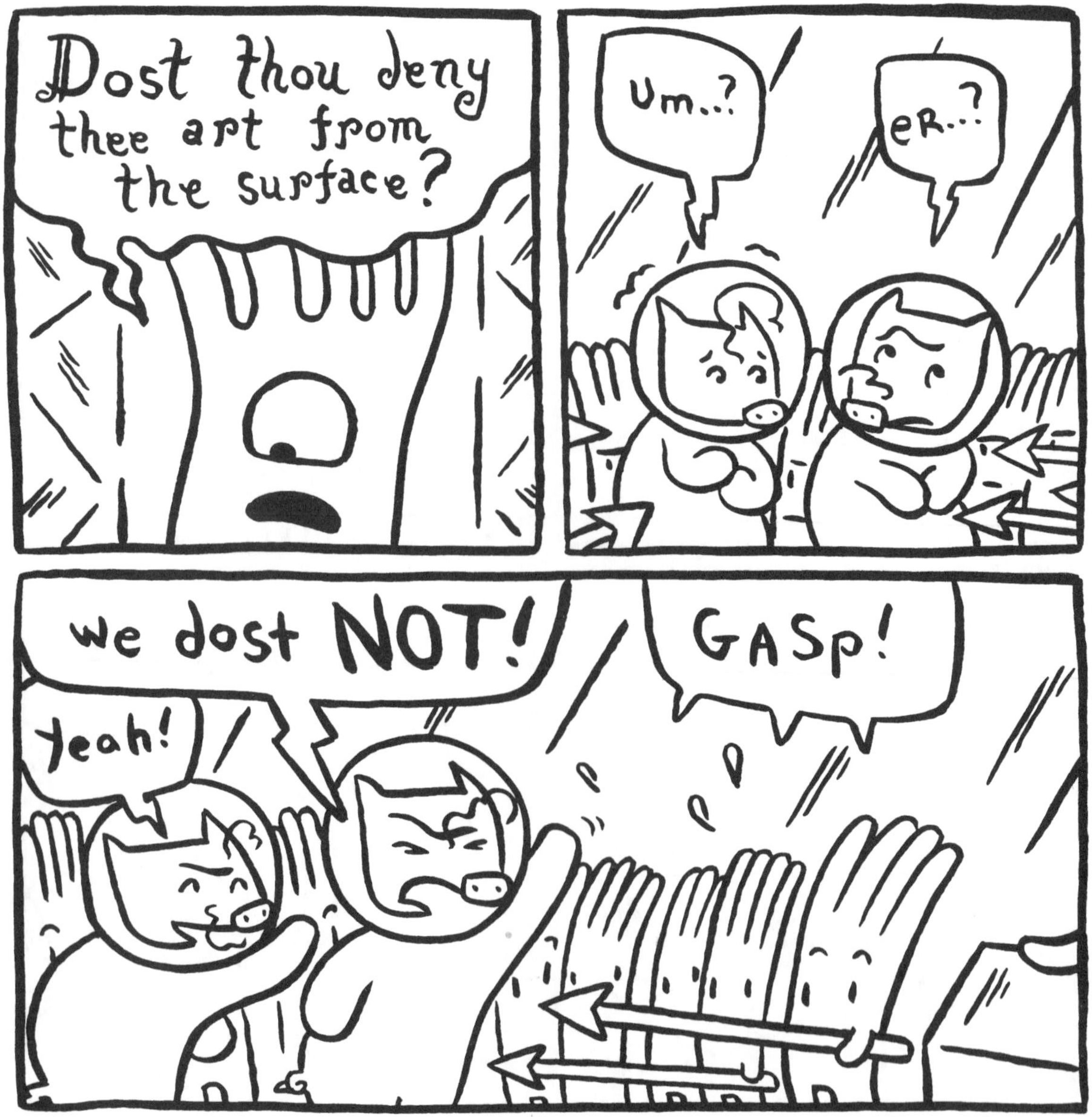
Dost thou deny thee art from the surface?
Um..?
eR..?
we dost NOT!
Yeah!
GASp!

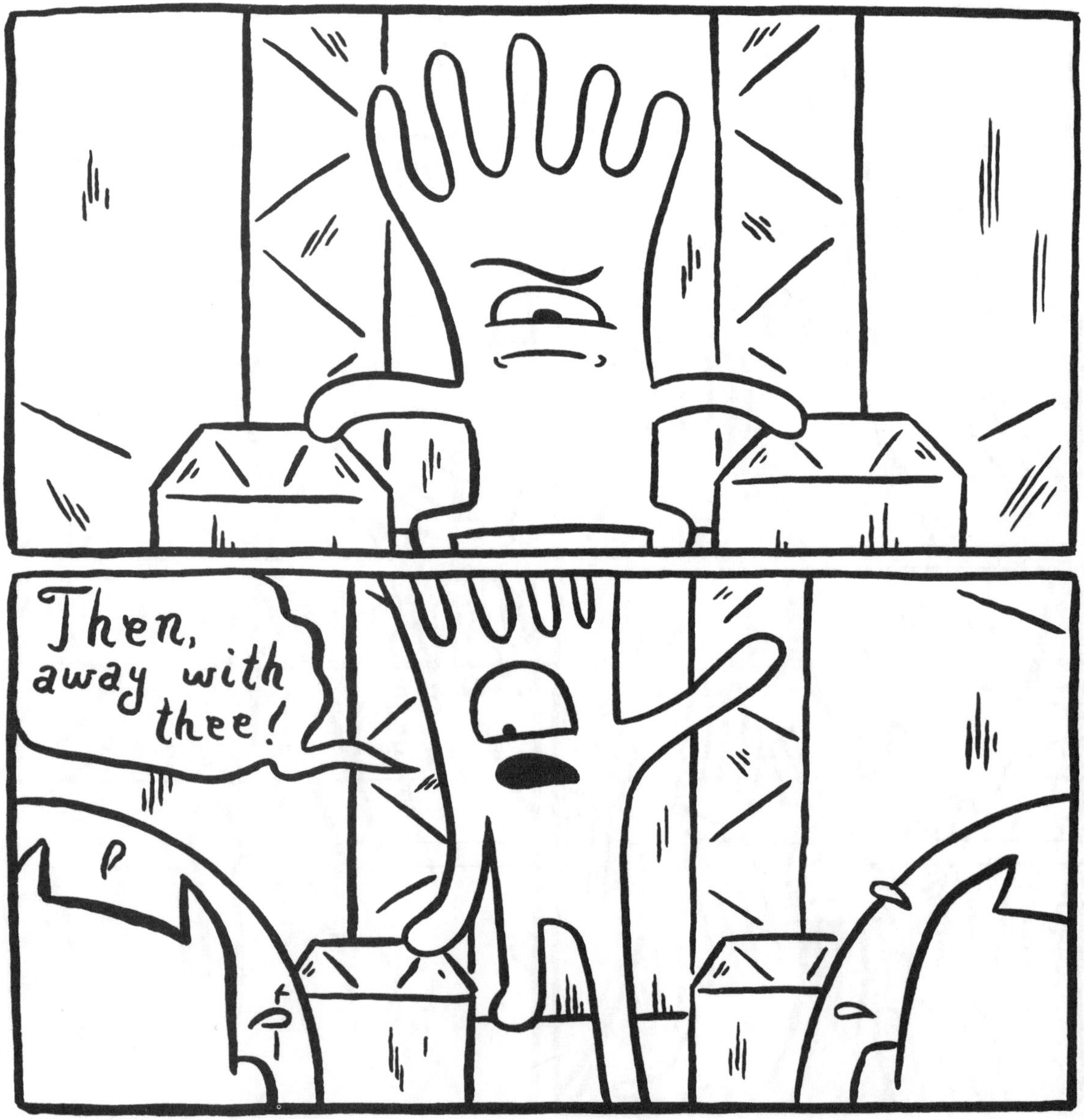
Then, away with thee!

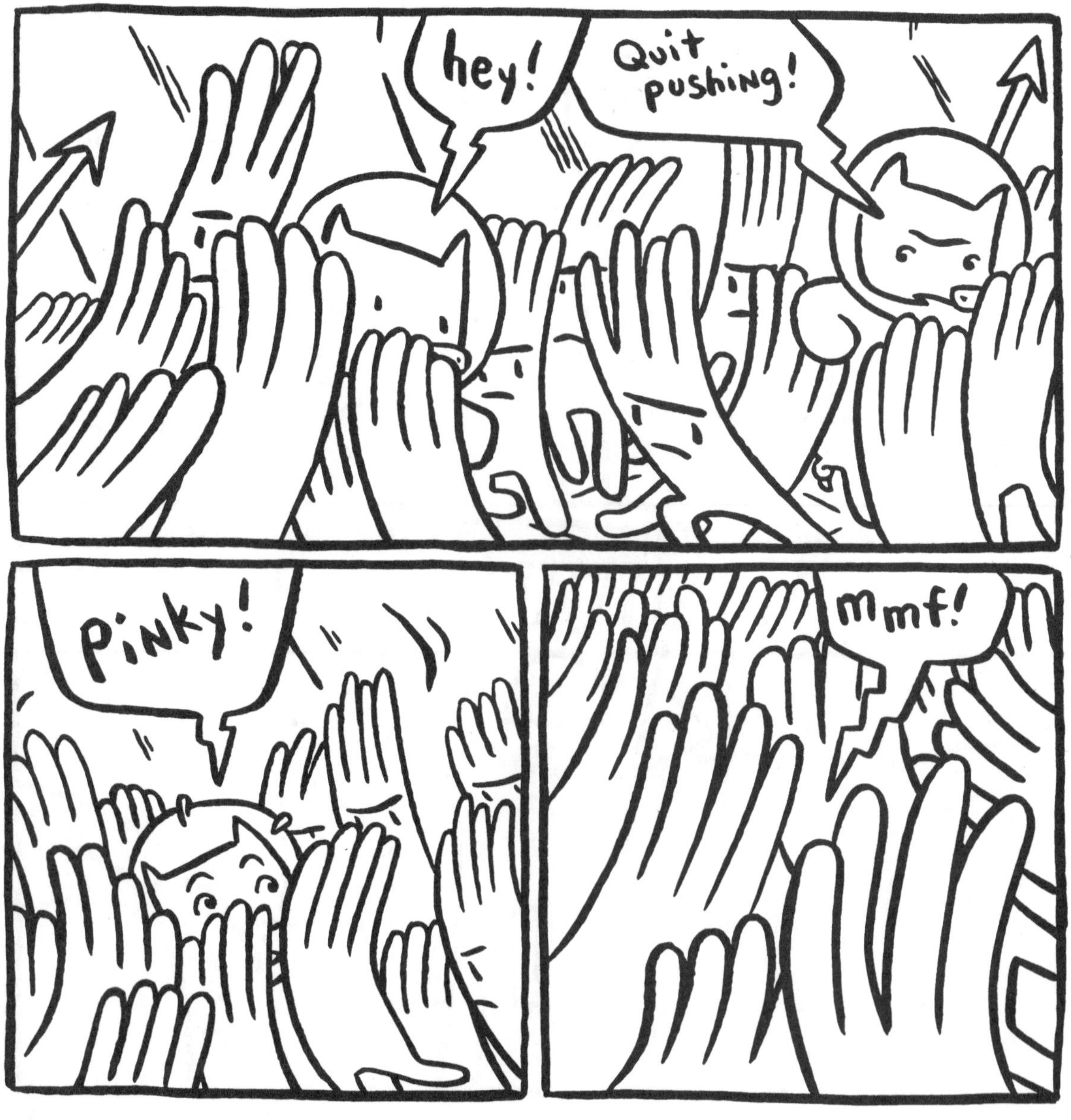
hey!
Quit pushing!
Pinky!
Mmf!

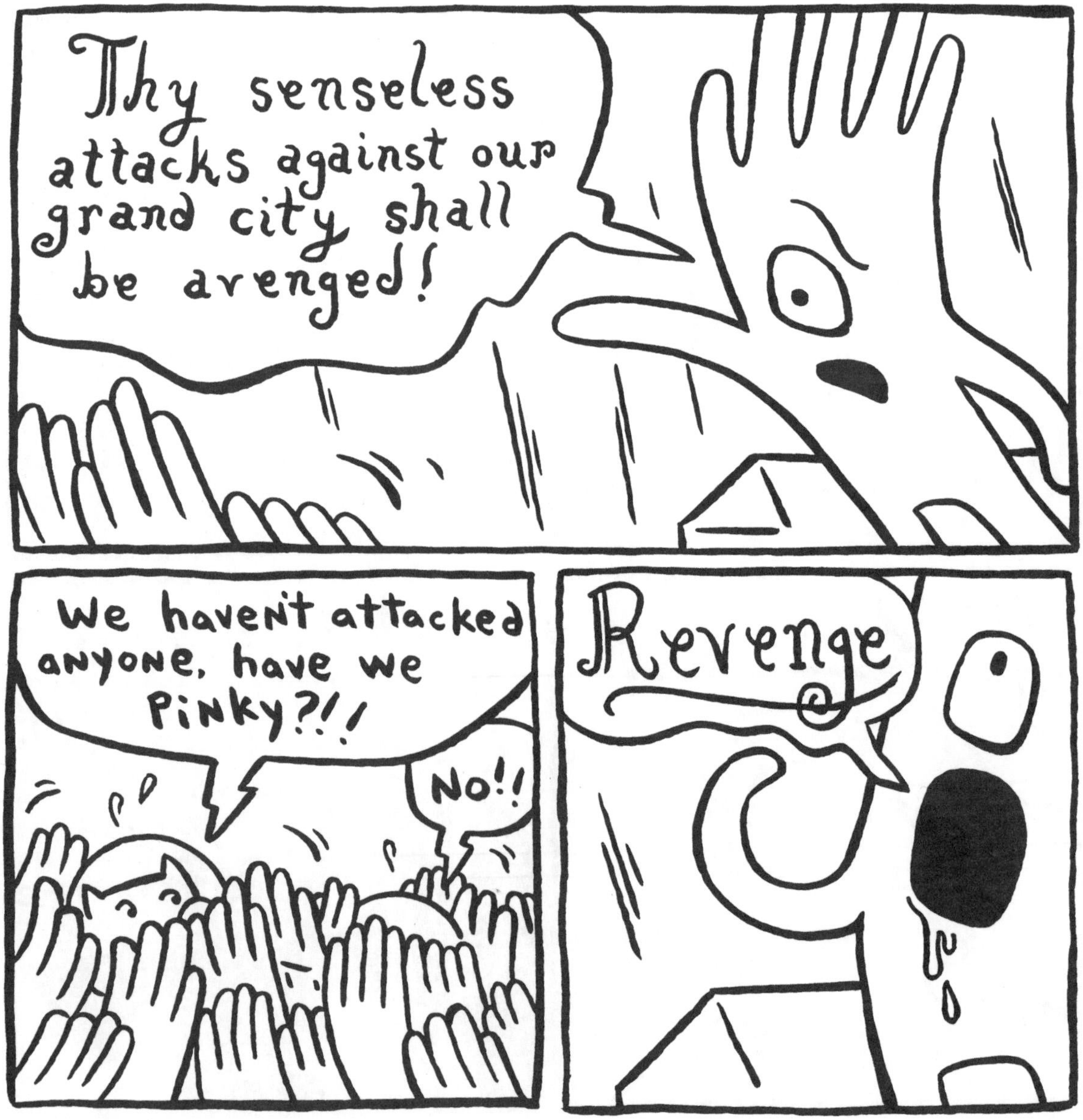
Thy senseless attacks against our grand city shall be avenged!
We haven't attacked anyone, have we Pinky?!!
No!!
Revenge

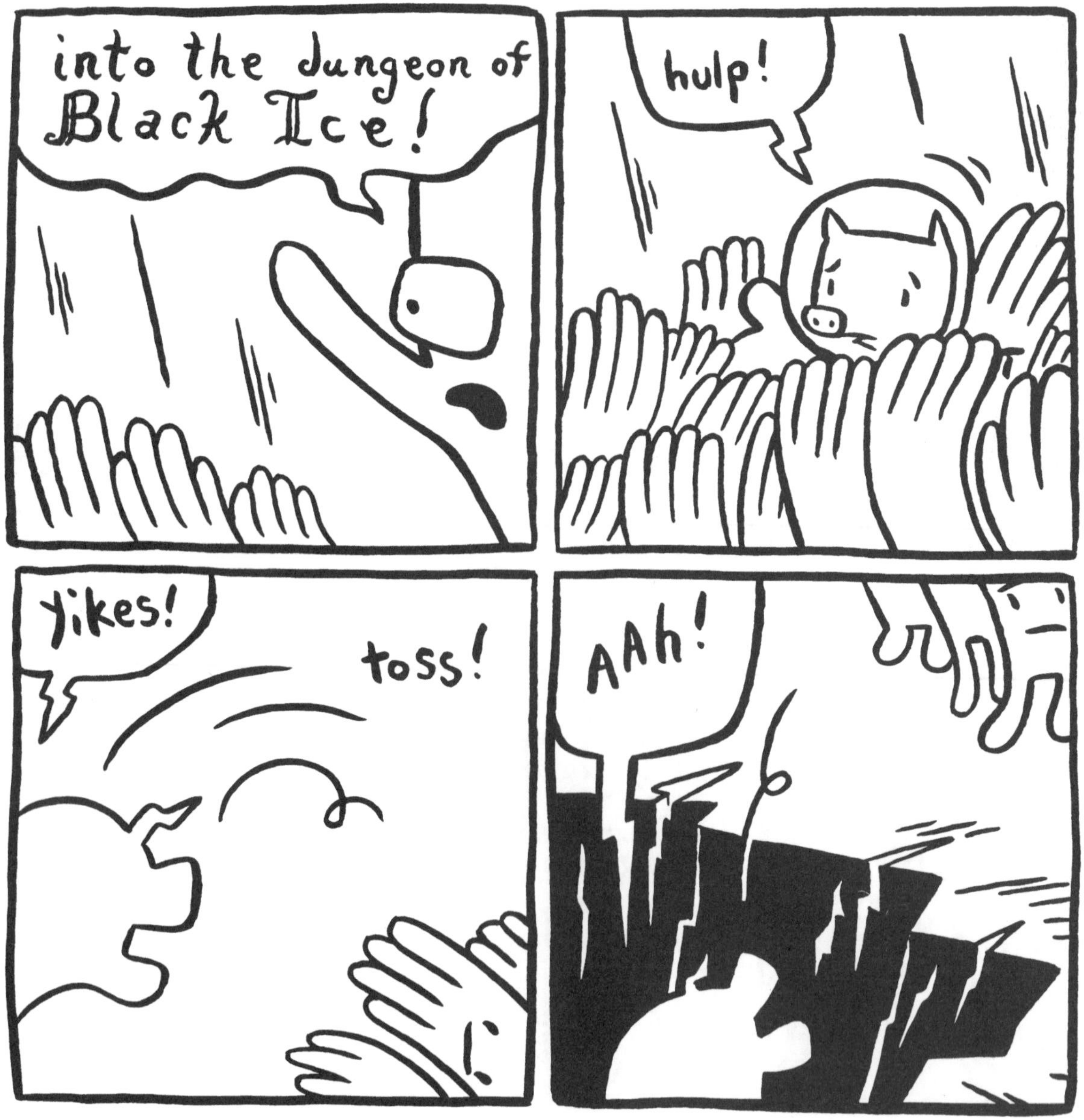
into the dungeon of Black Ice!
hulp!
yikes!
toss!
AAh!

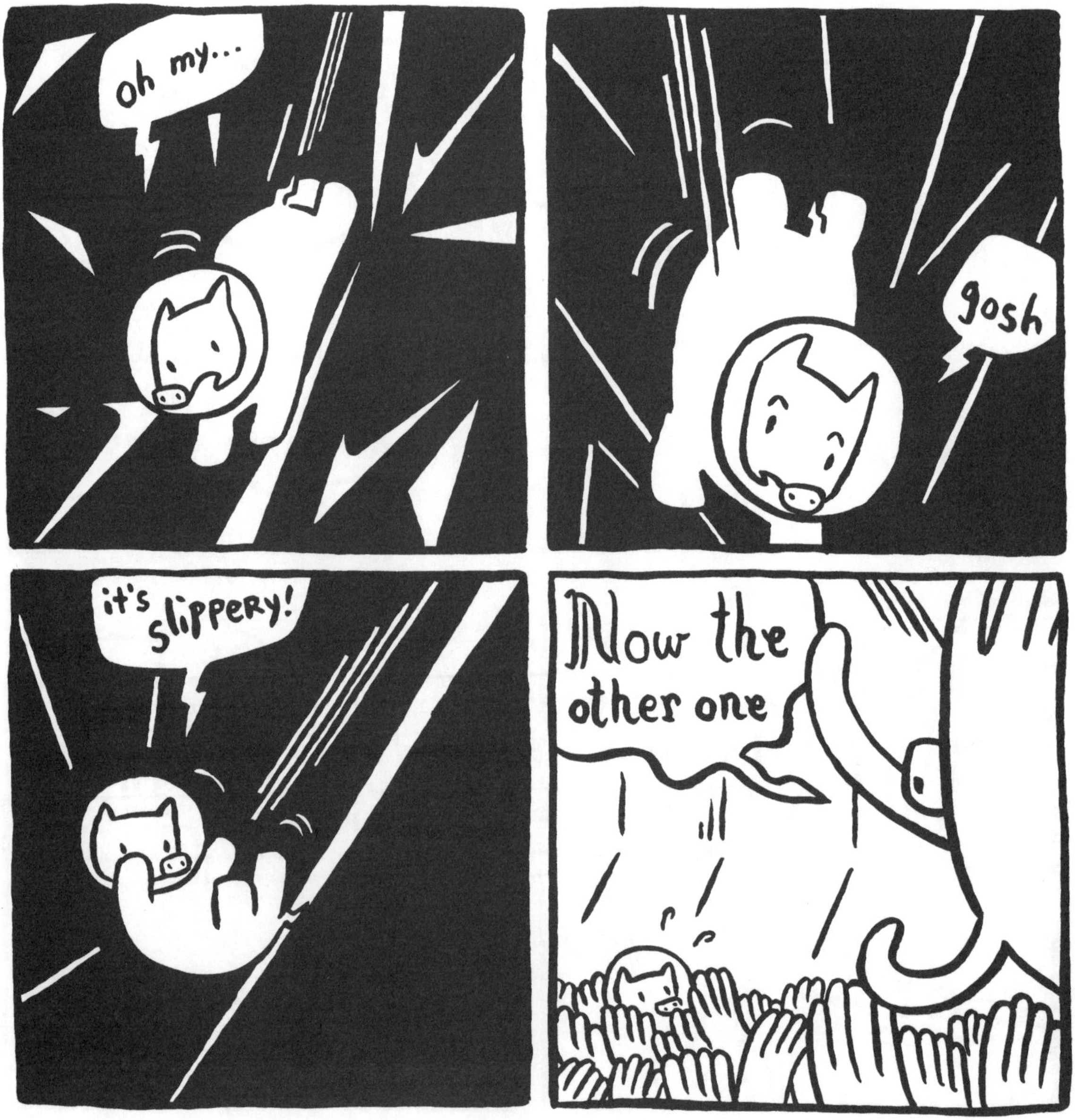
oh my...
gosh
it's slippery!
Now the other one

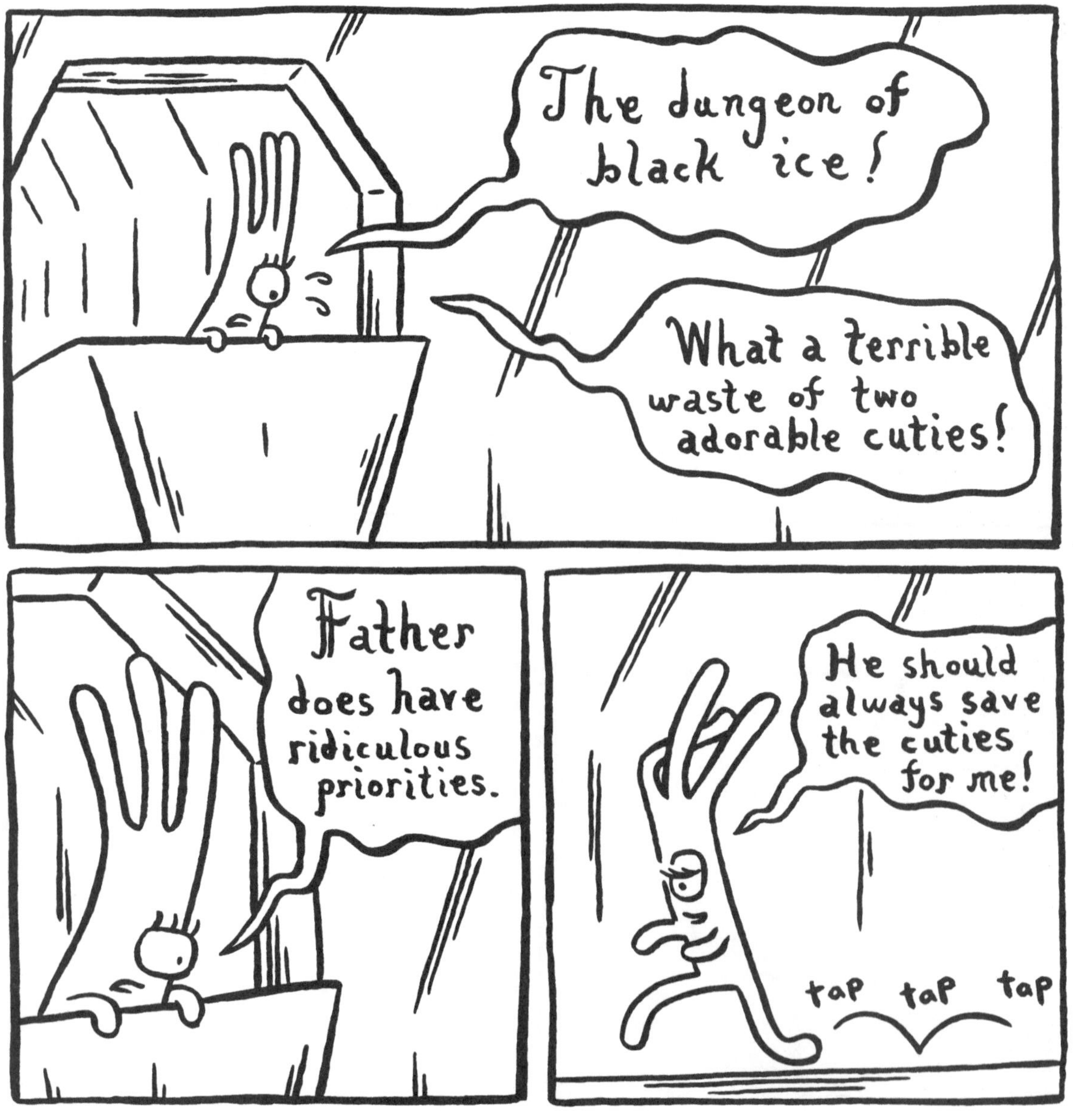
The dungeon of black ice!
What a terrible waste of two adorable cuties!
Father does have ridiculous priorities.
He should always save the cuties for me!
tap tap tap

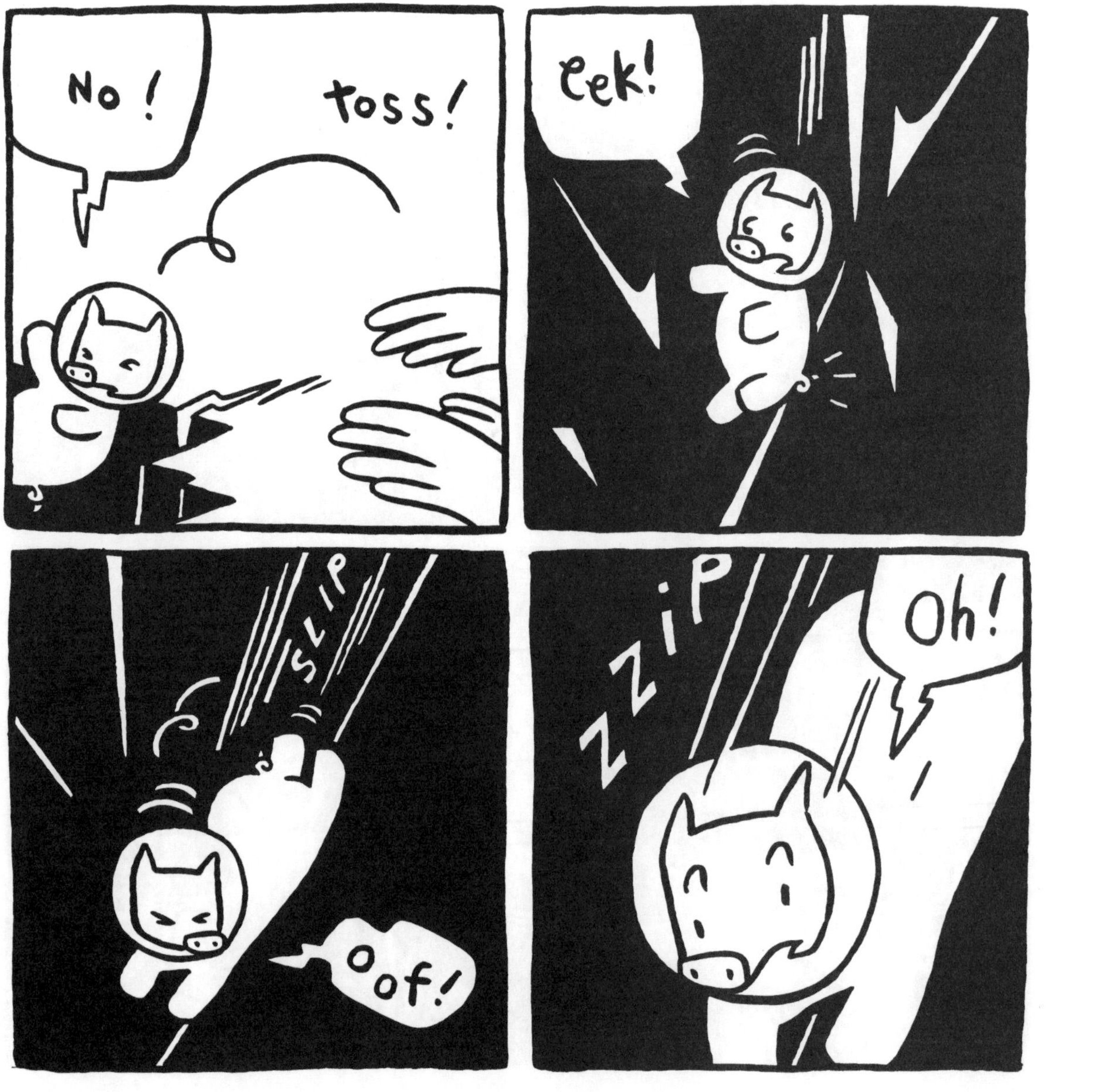
No!
toss!
eek!
SLIP
Oof!
zzip
Oh!

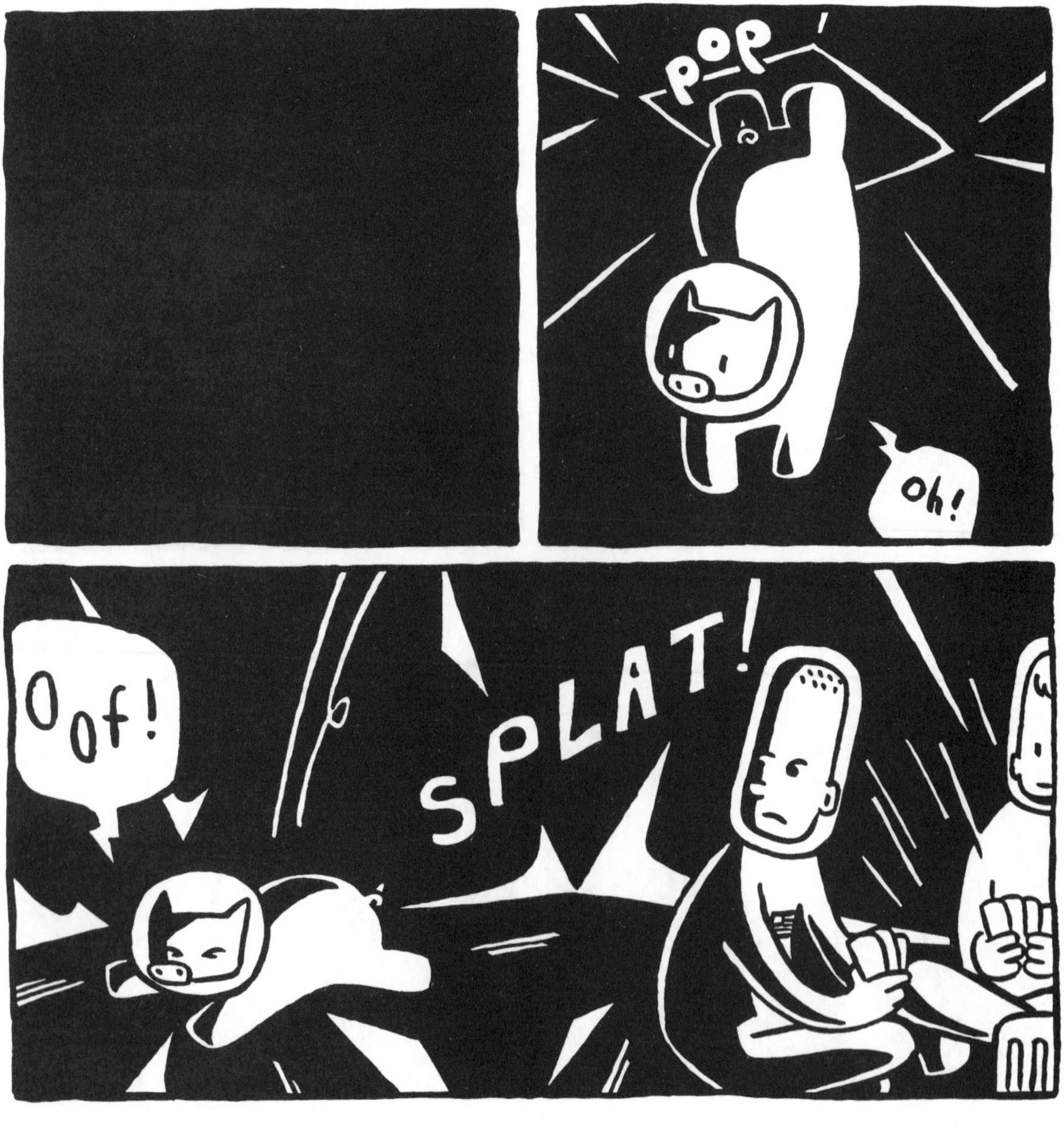
POP
Oh!
Oof!
SPLAT!

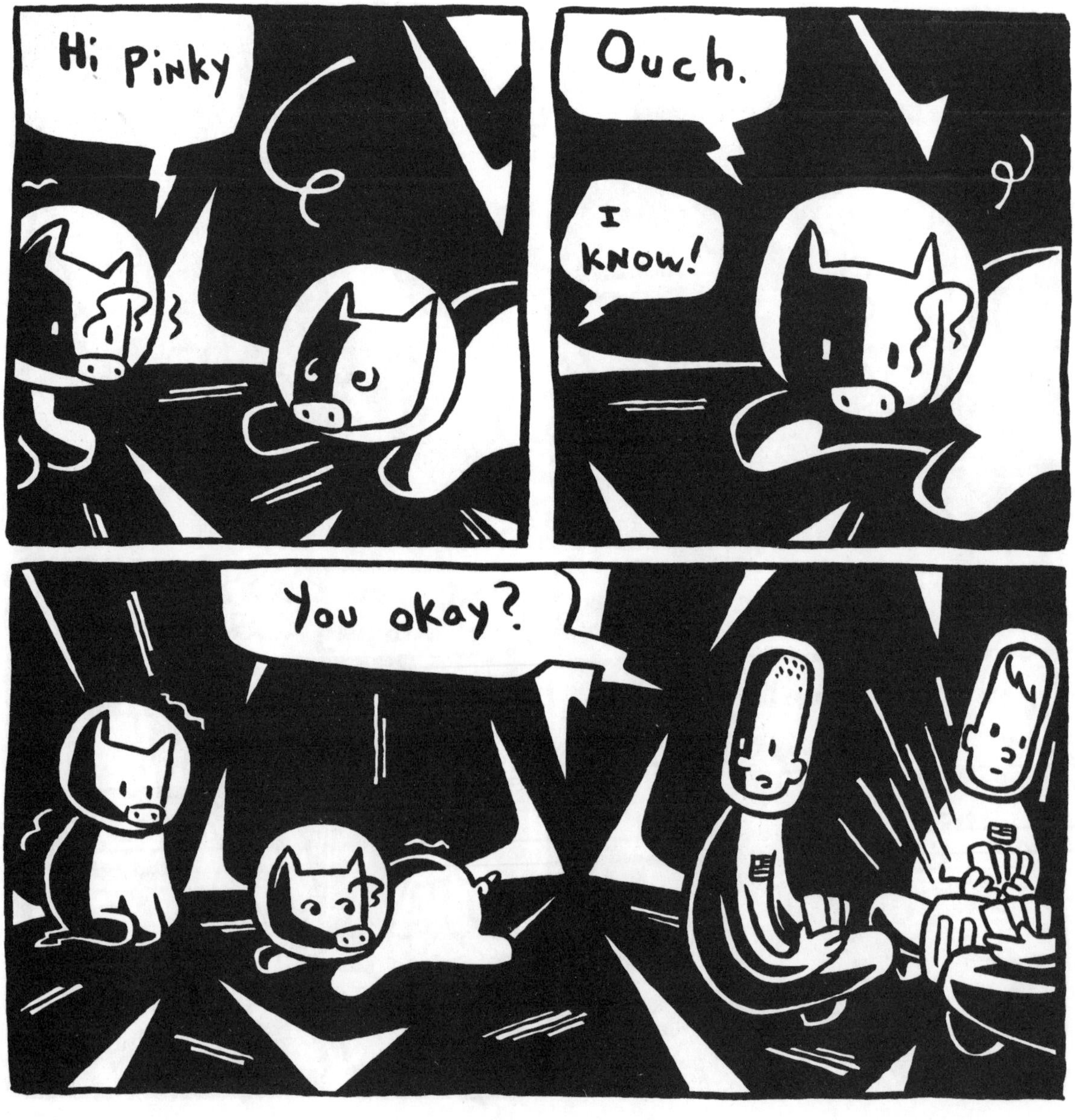
Hi Pinky
Ouch.
I KNOW!
You okay?

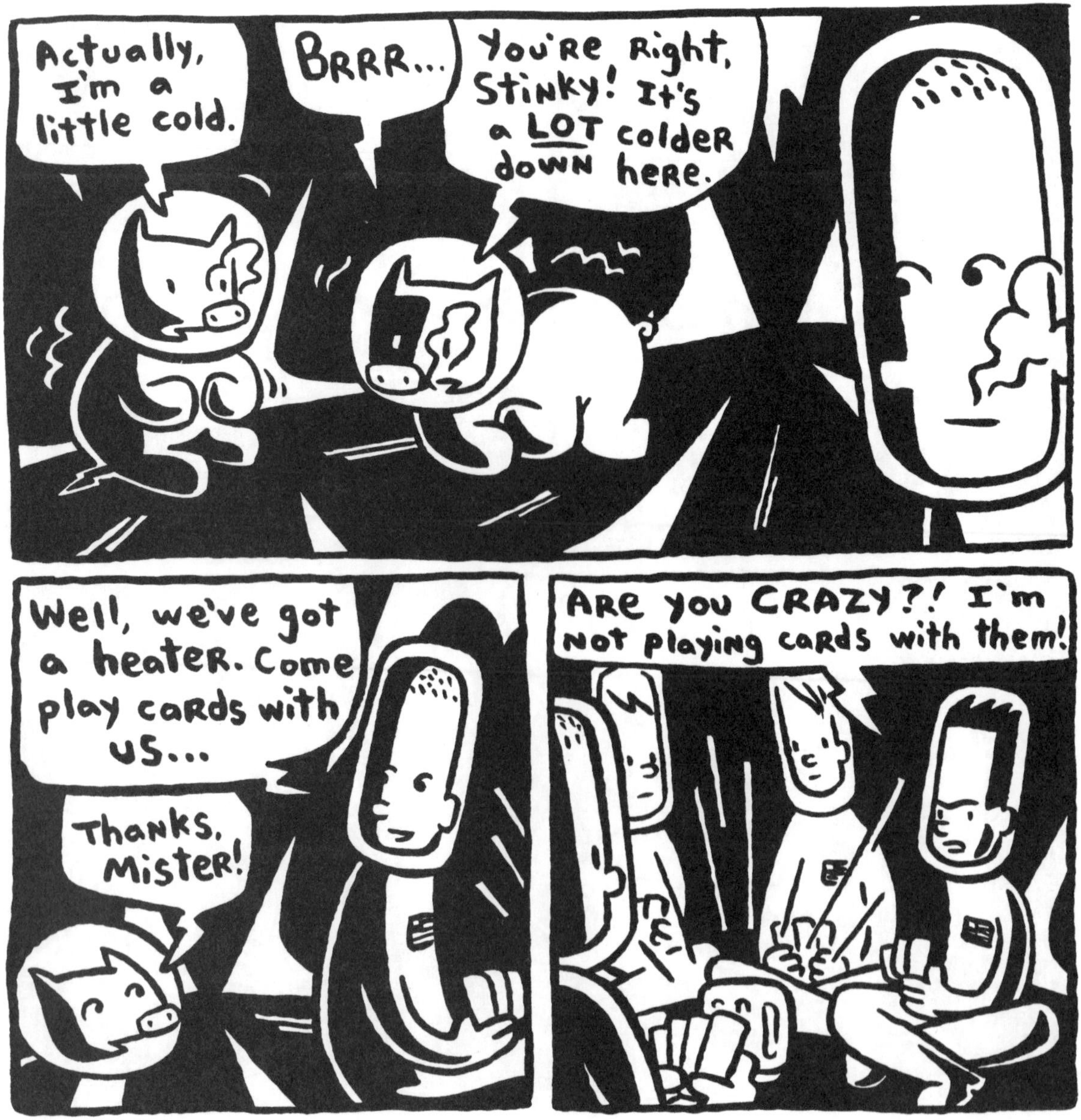
Actually, I'm a little cold.
BRRR...
You're right, Stinky! It's a LOT colder down here.
Well, we've got a heater. Come play cards with us...
Thanks, Mister!
ARE you CRAZY?! I'm not playing cards with them!

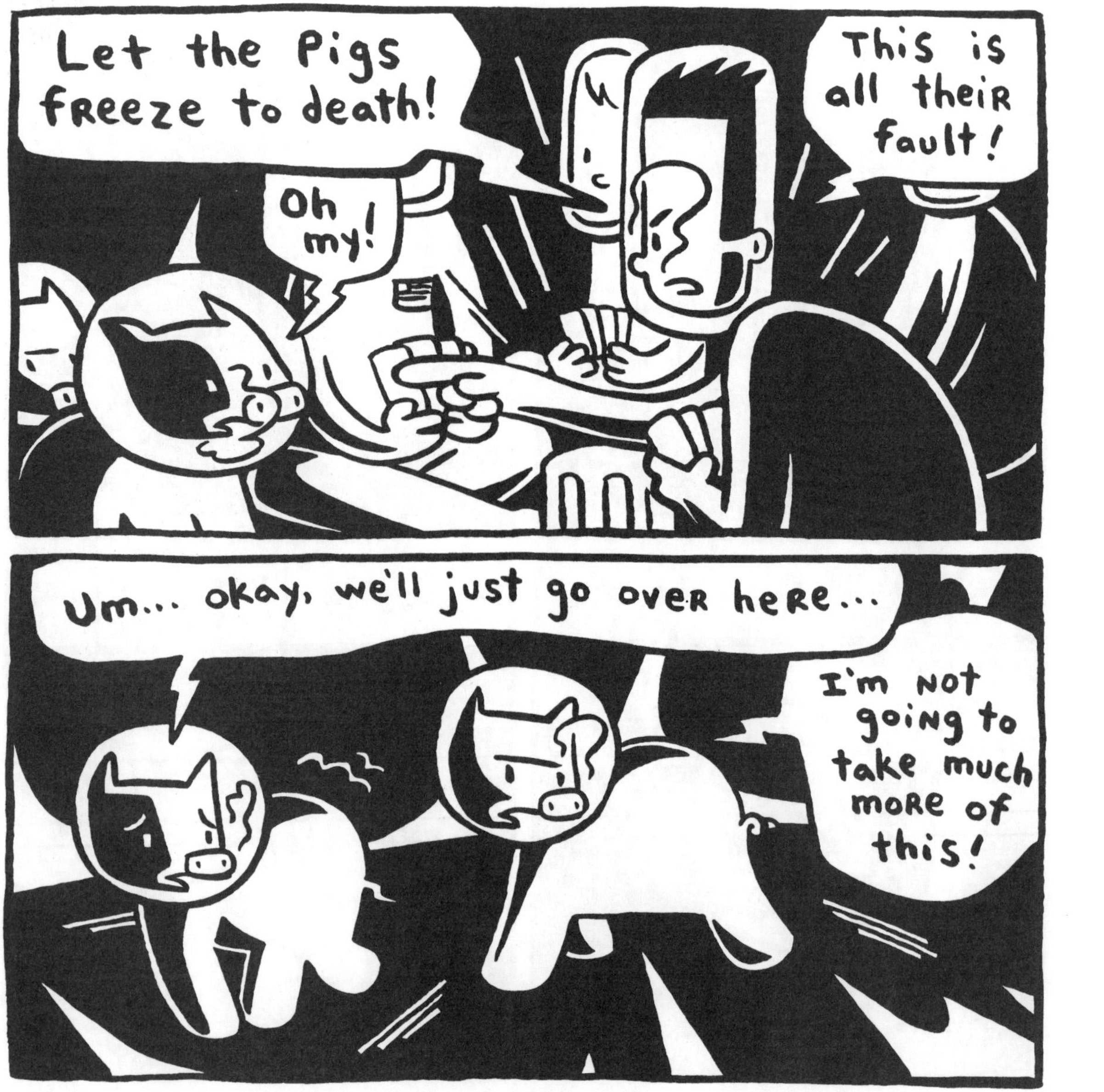
Let the Pigs freeze to death!
This is all their fault!
Oh my!
Um... okay, we'll just go over here...
I'm not going to take much more of this!

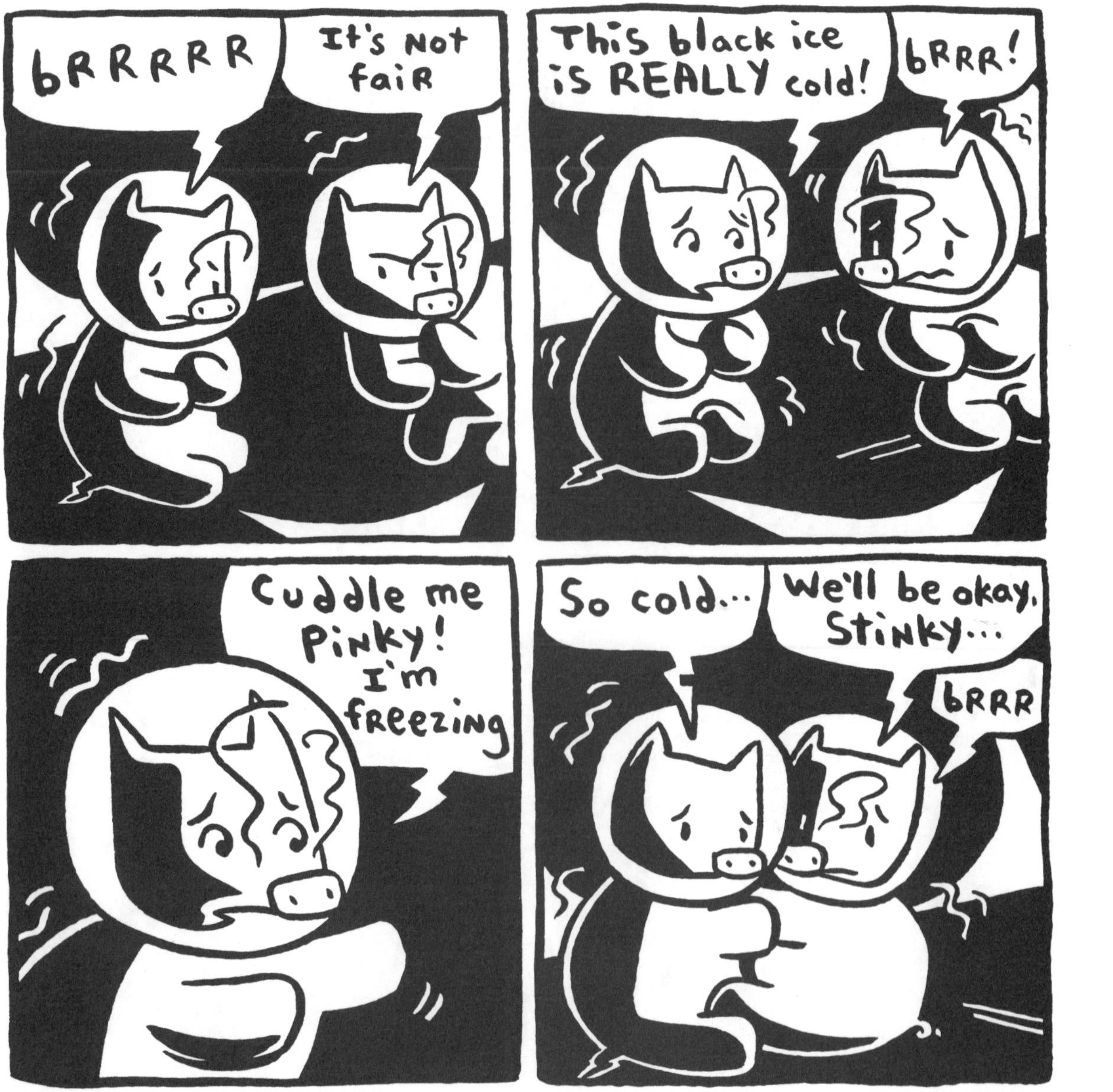
bRRRRRR
It's Not fair
This black ice is REALLY cold!
bRRR!
Cuddle me Pinky! I'm freezing
So cold...
We'll be okay, Stinky...
bRRR

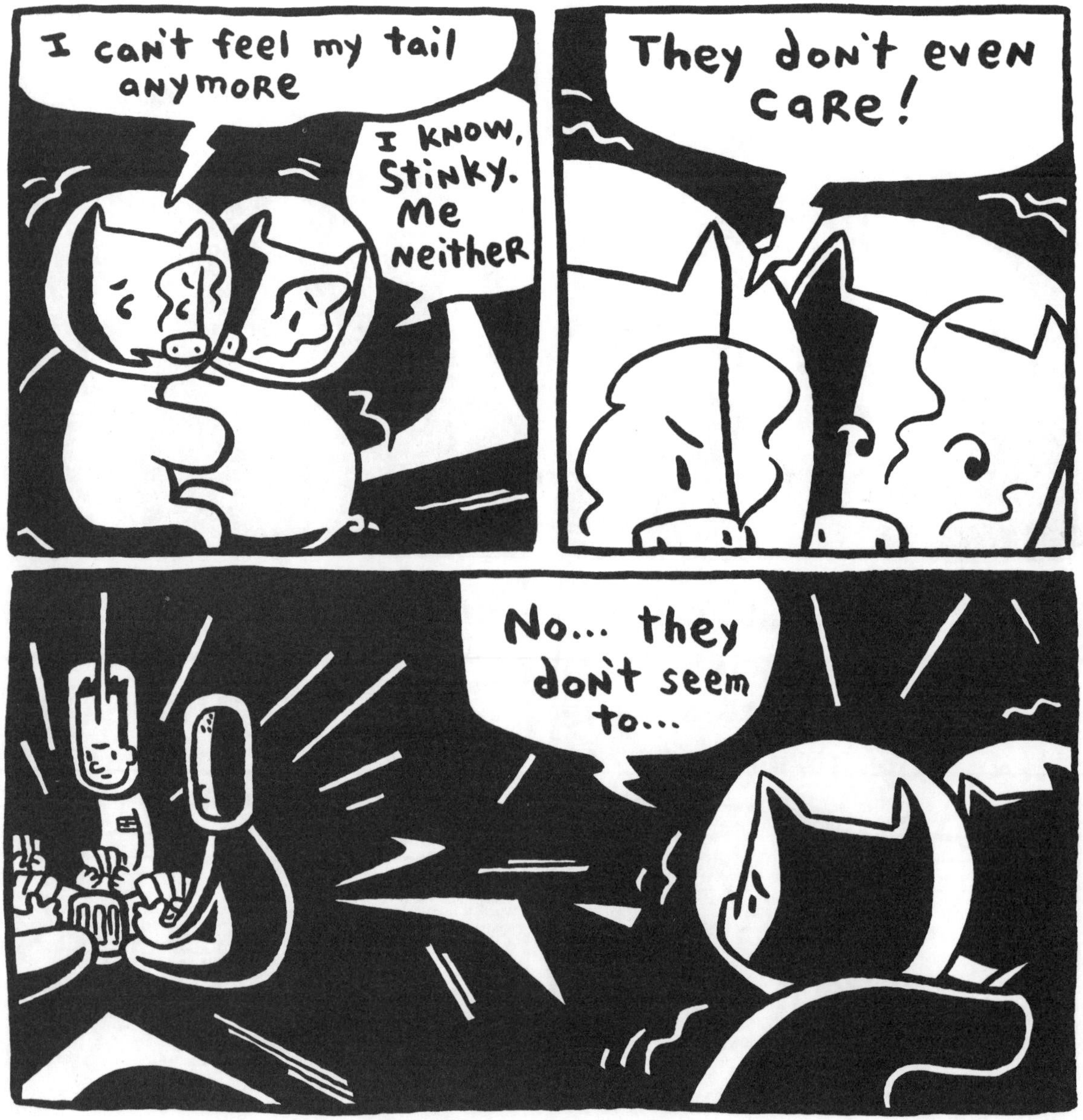
I can't feel my tail anymore
I KNOW, Stinky. Me neither
They don't even care!
No... they don't seem to...

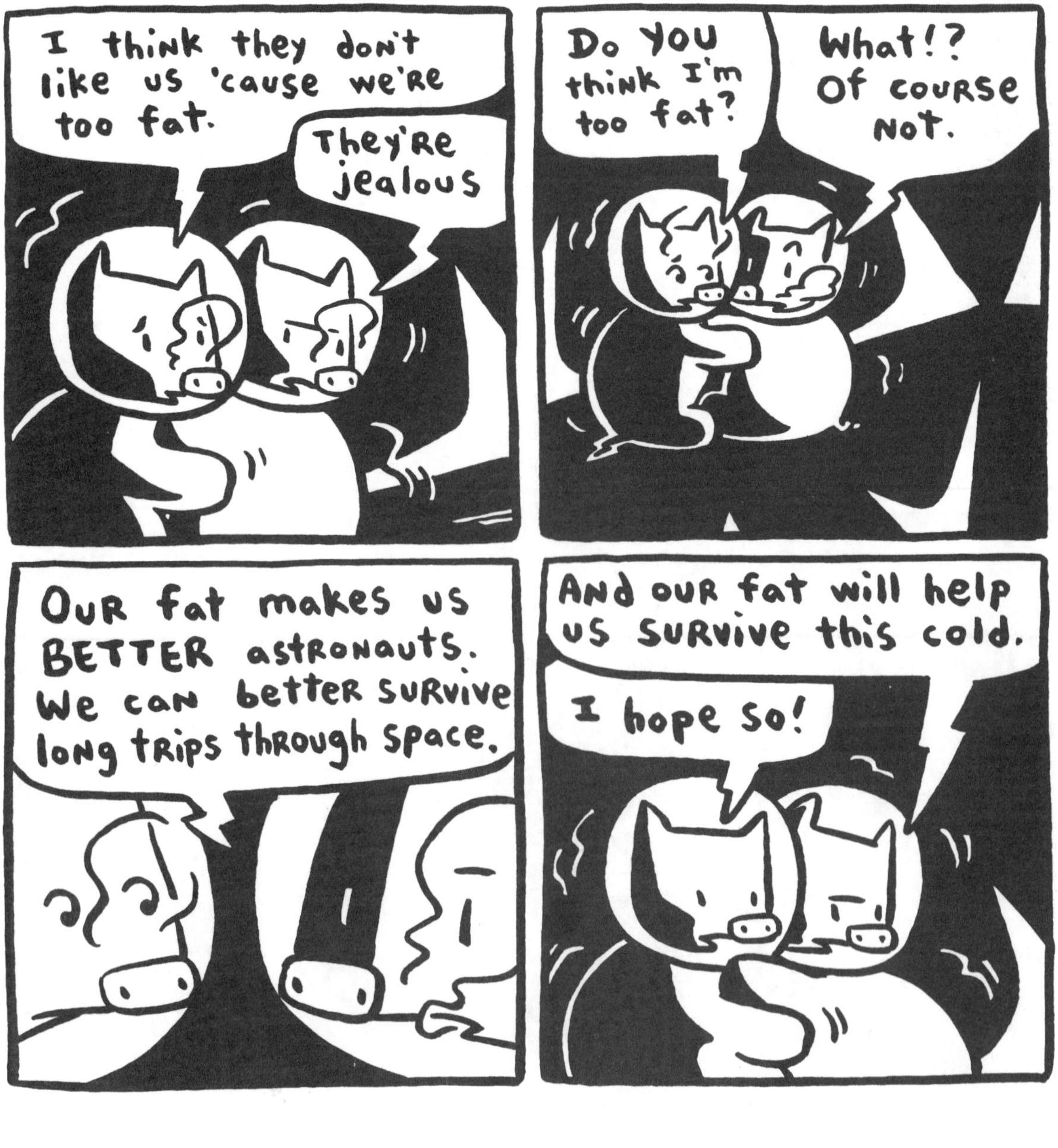
I think they don't like us 'cause we're too fat.
They're jealous
Do YOU think I'm too fat?
What!? Of course not.
Our fat makes us BETTER astronauts. We can better survive long trips through space.
And our fat will help us survive this cold.
I hope so!

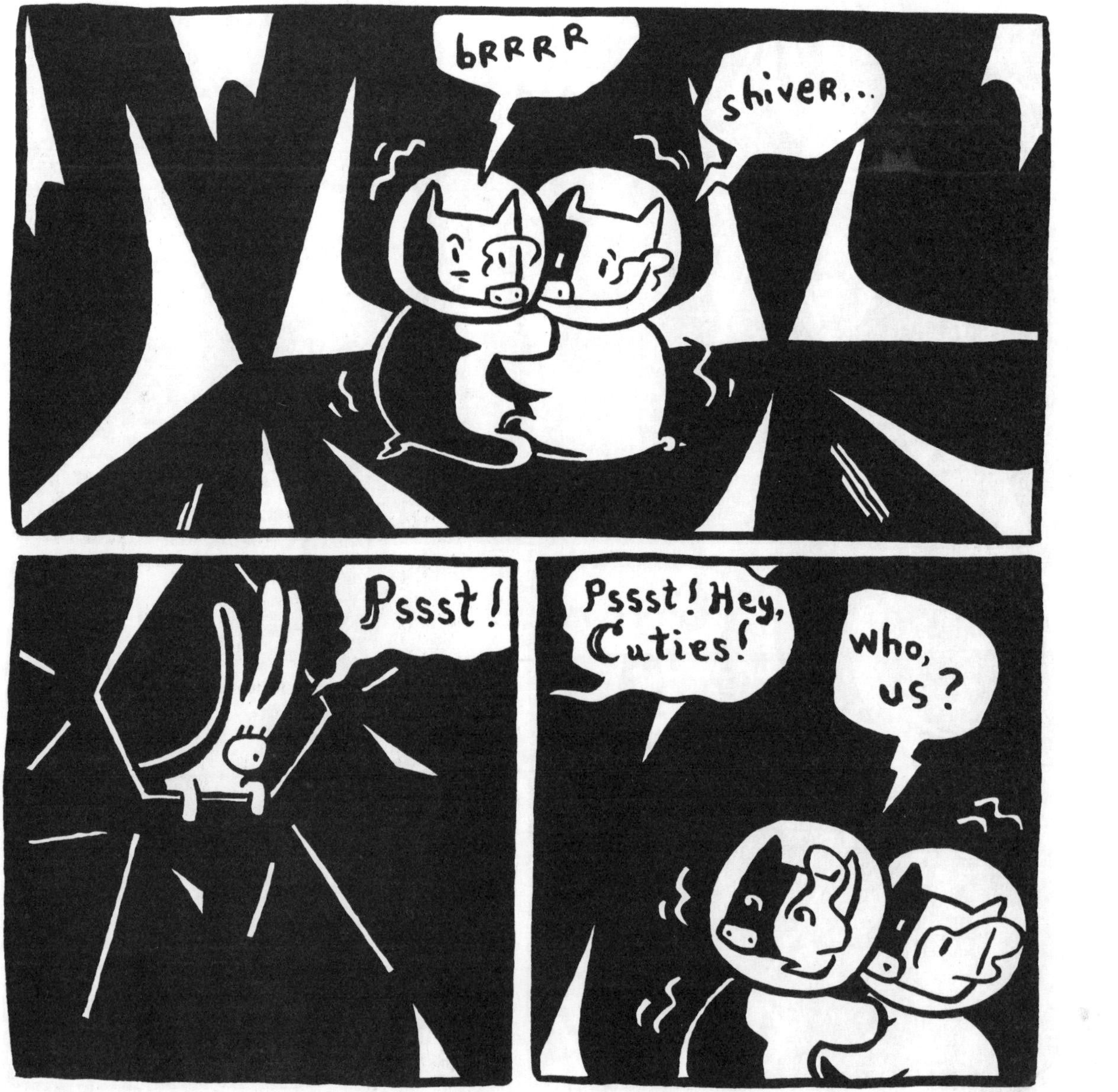
bRRRR
shiver...
Pssst!
Pssst! Hey, Cuties!
who, us?

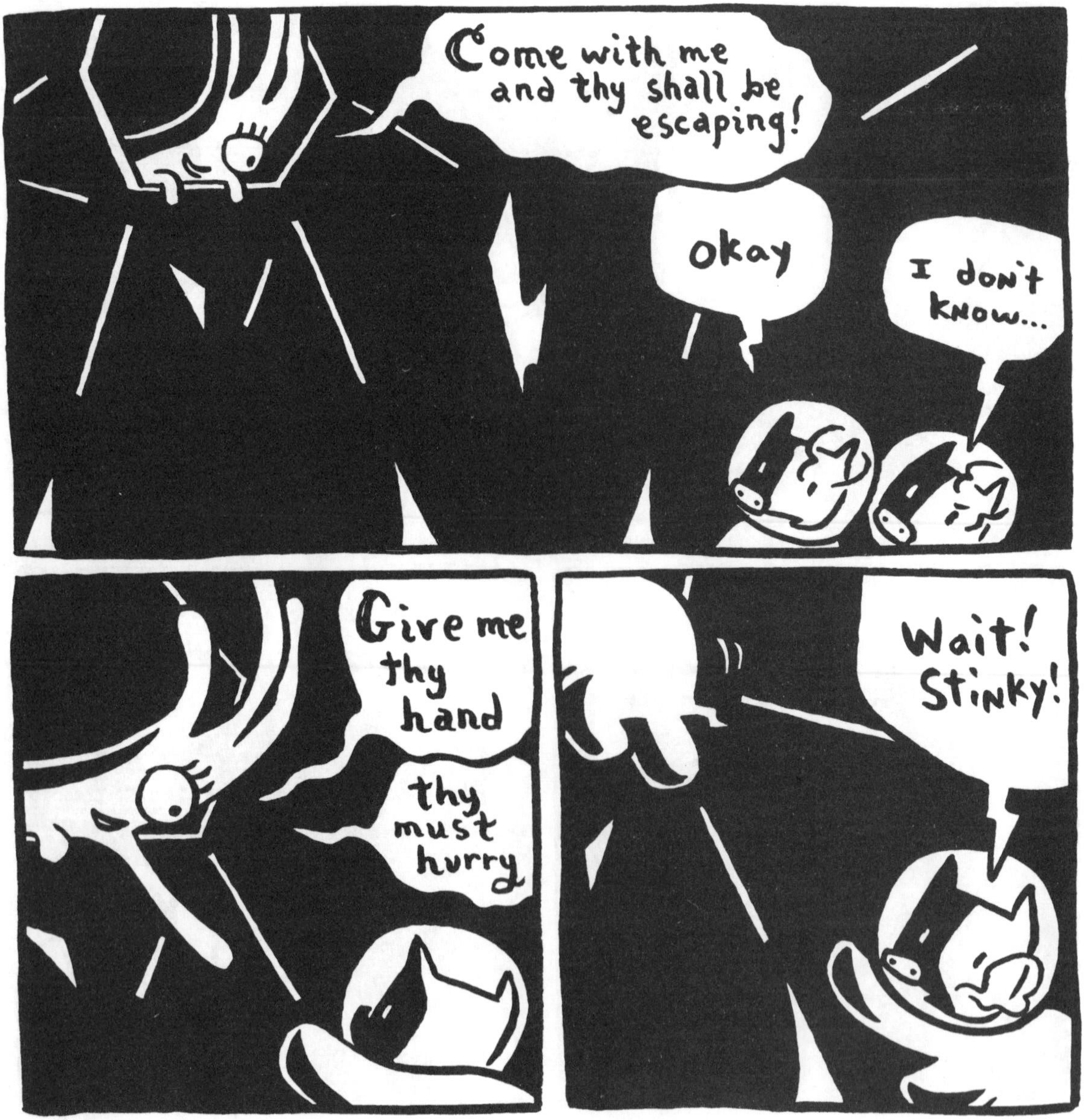
Come with me and thy shall be escaping!
Okay
I don't know...
Give me thy hand
thy must hurry
Wait! Stinky!

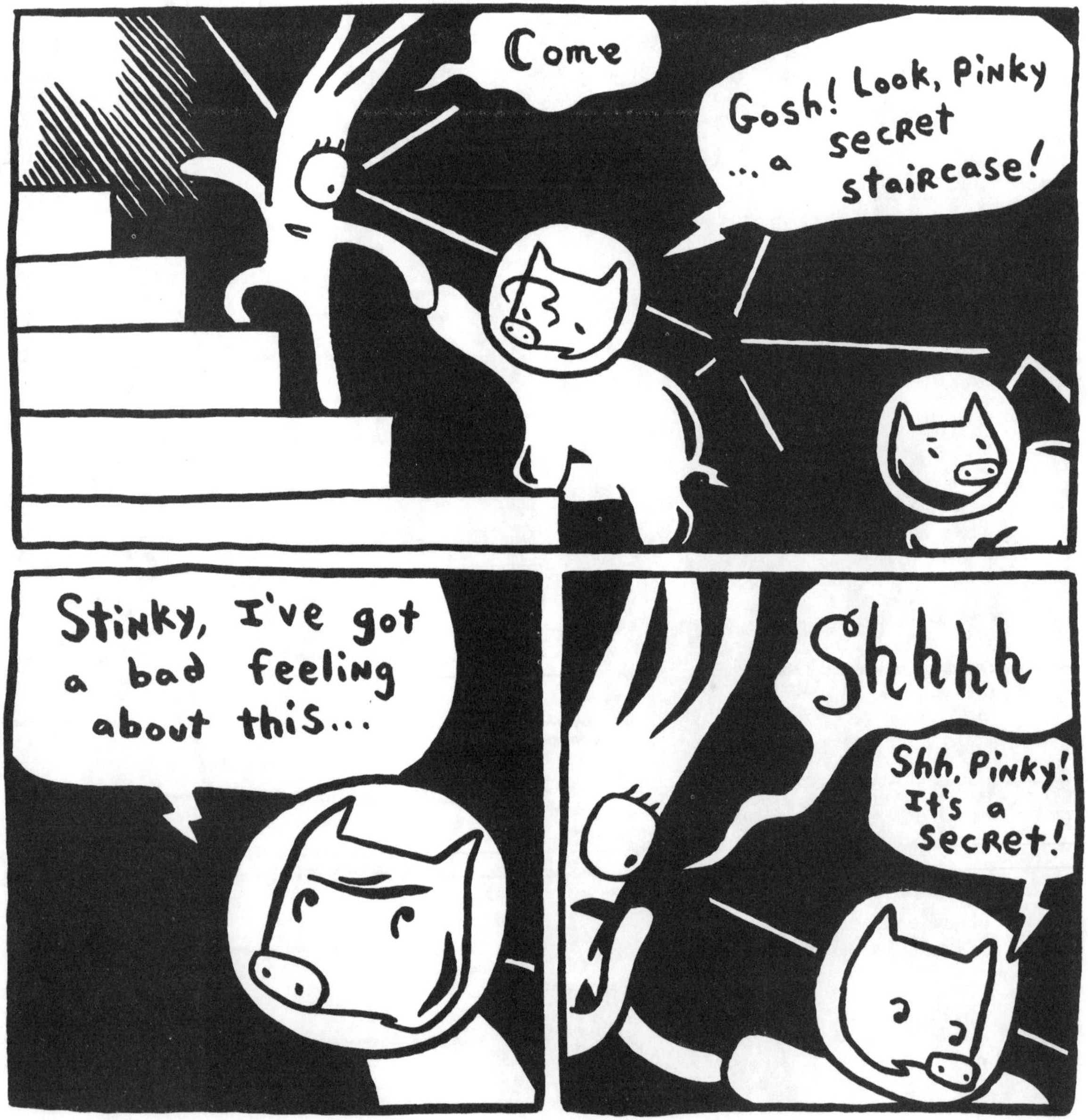
Come
Gosh! Look, Pinky ...a secret secret staircase!
Stinky, I've got a bad feeling about this...
Shhhh
Shh, Pinky! It's a secret!

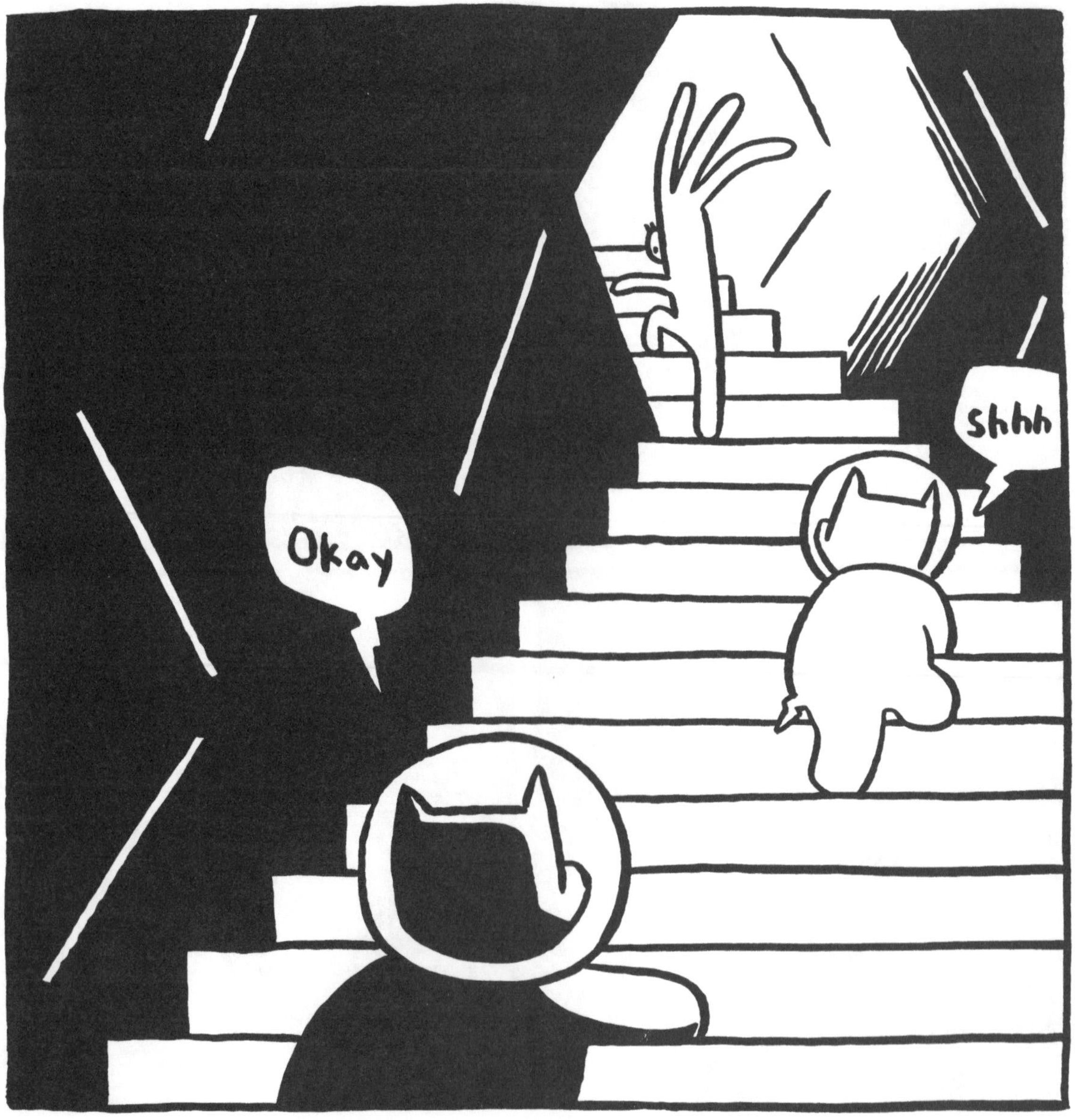
shhh
Okay

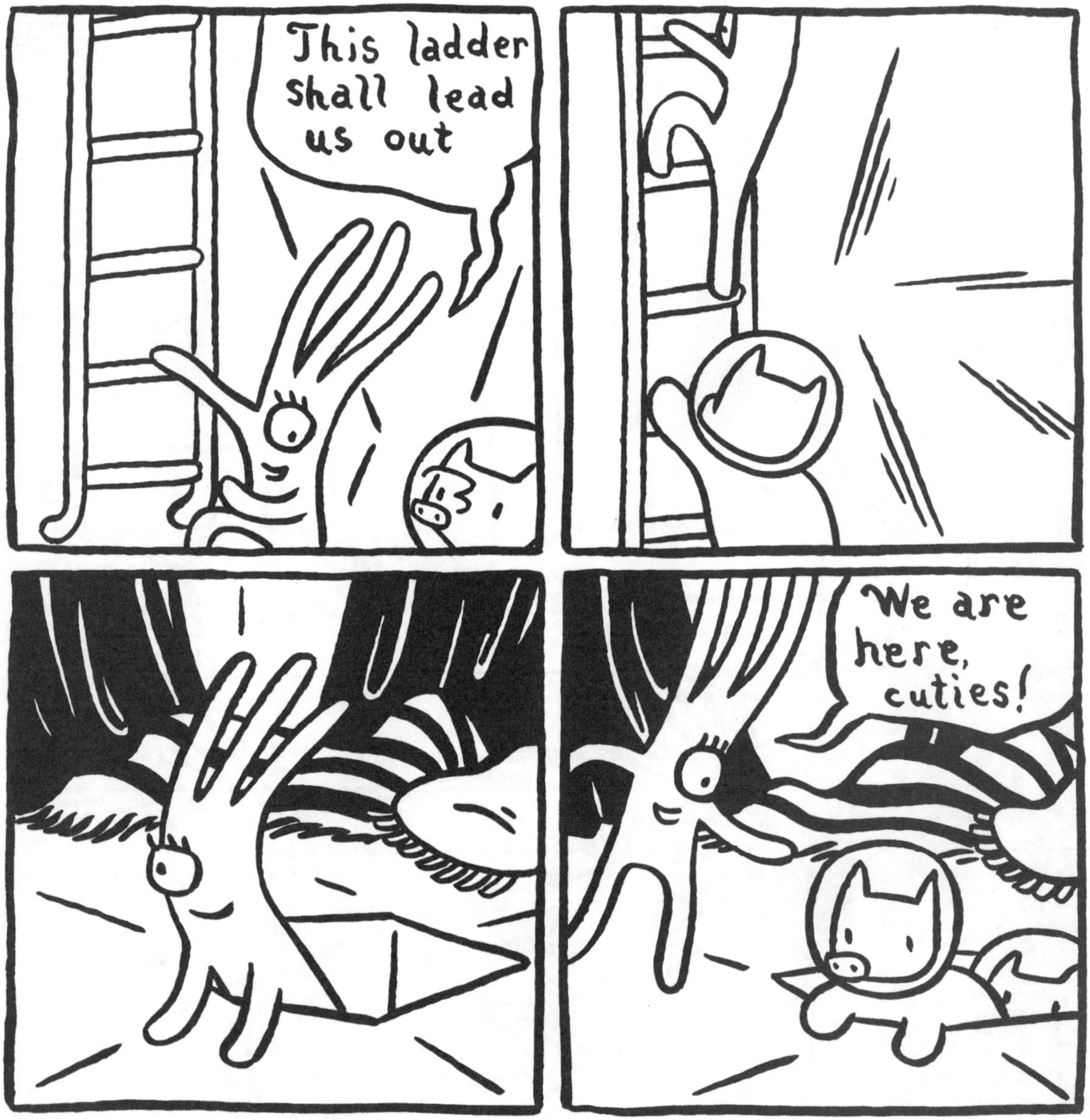
This ladder shall lead us out
We are here, cuties!

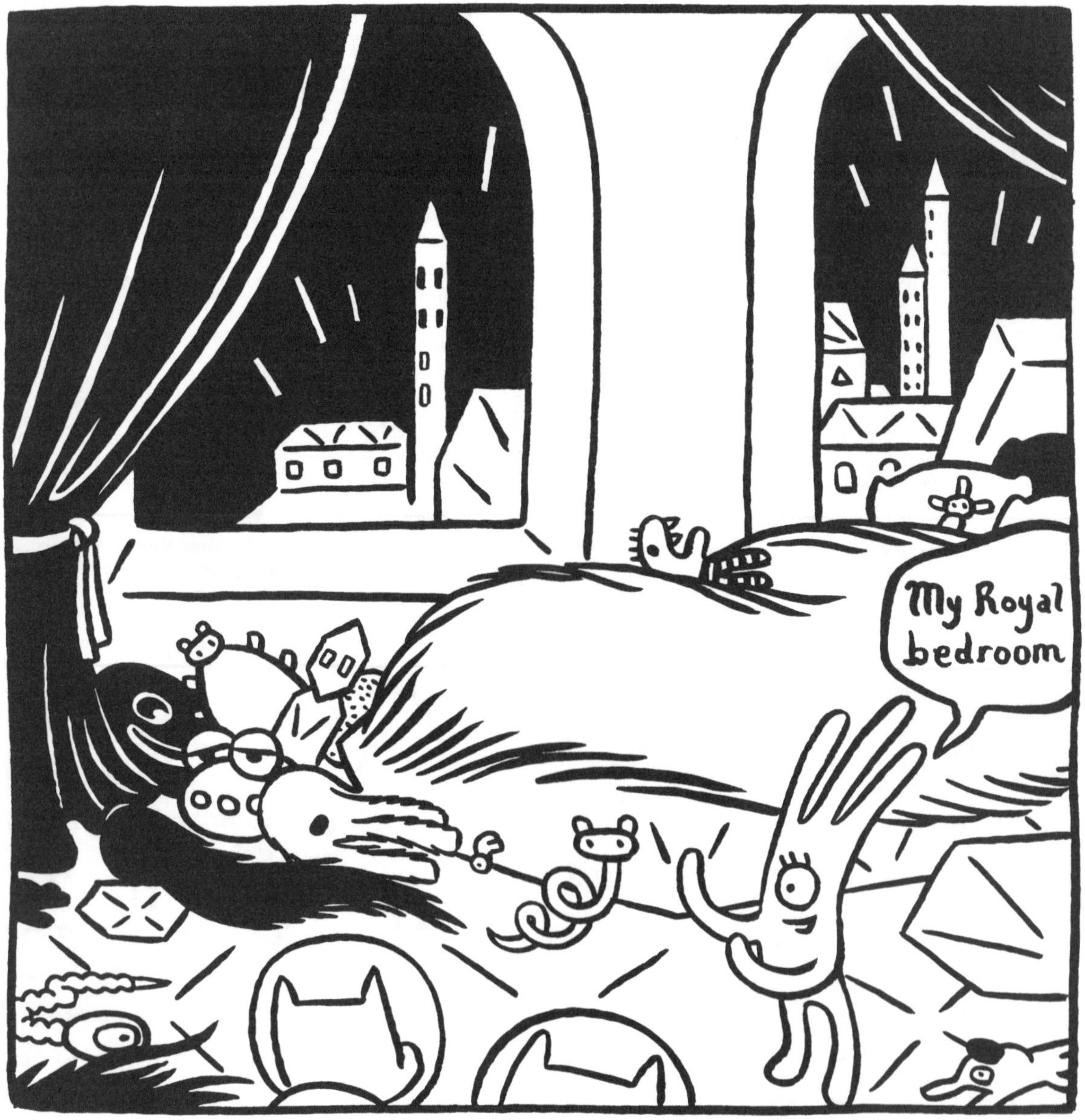
My Royal bedroom

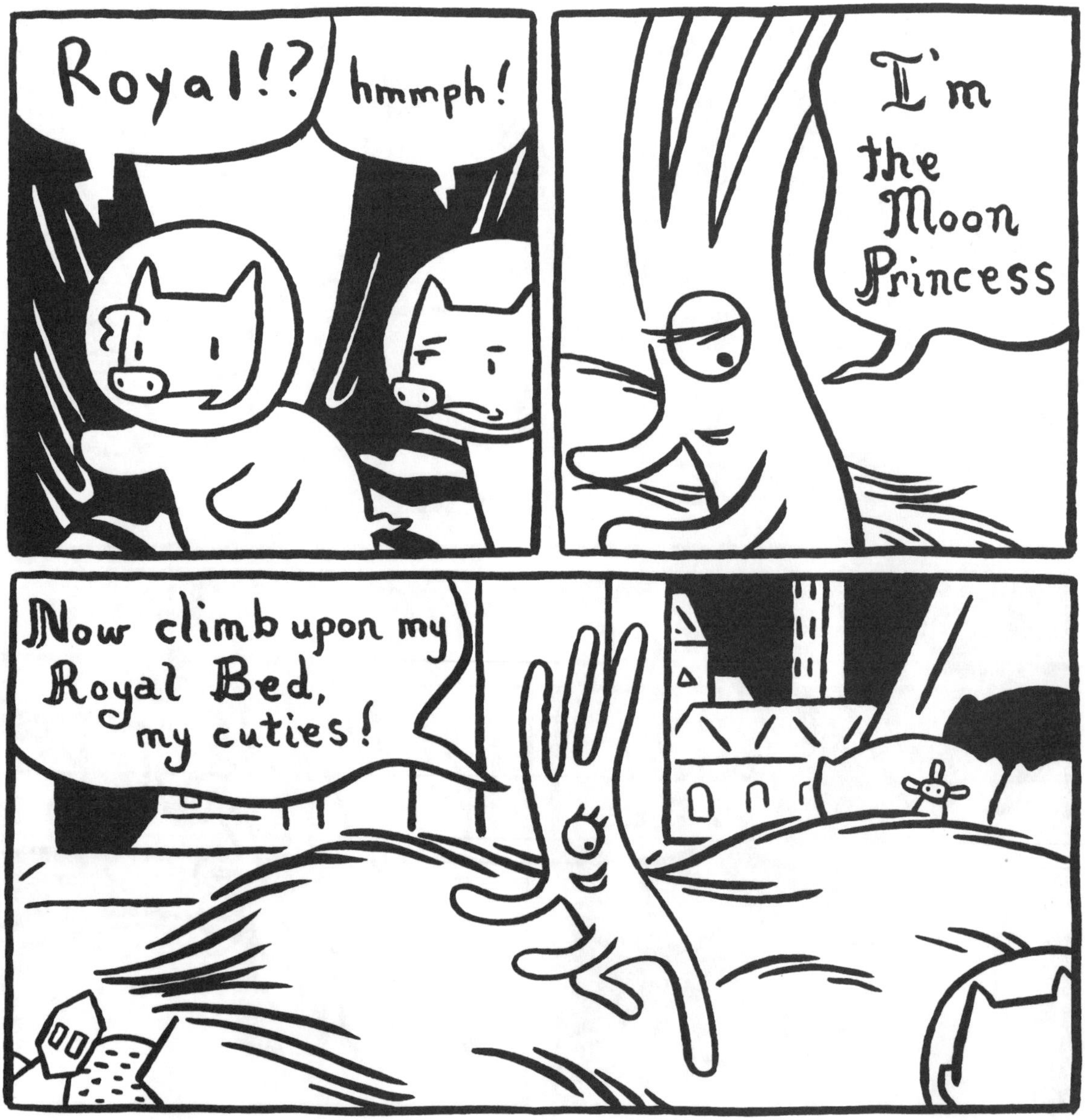
Royal!?
hmmph!
I'm the Moon Princess
Now climb upon my Royal Bed, my cuties!

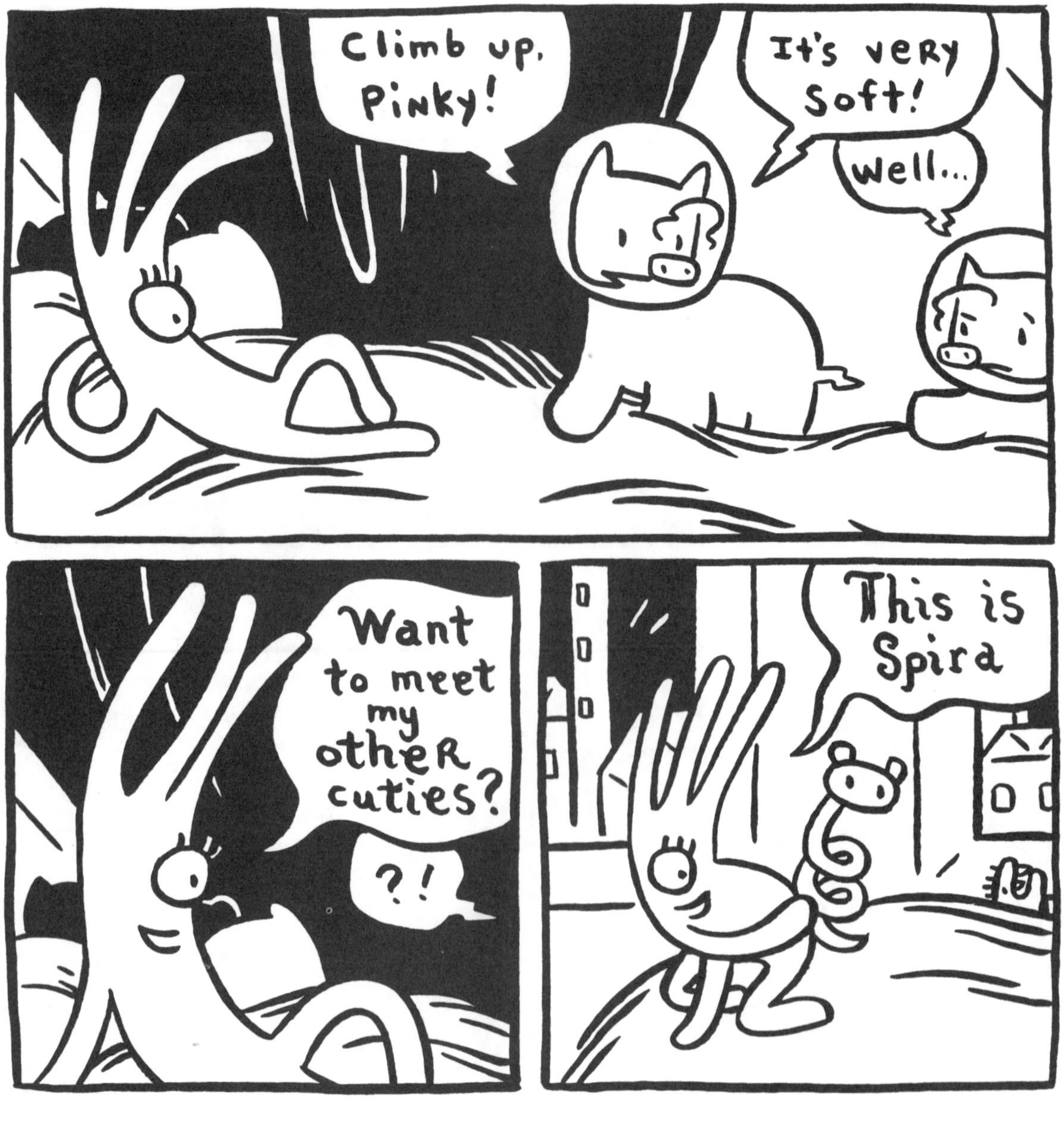
Climb up, Pinky!
It's very Soft!
well...
Want to meet my other cuties?
?!
This is Spira

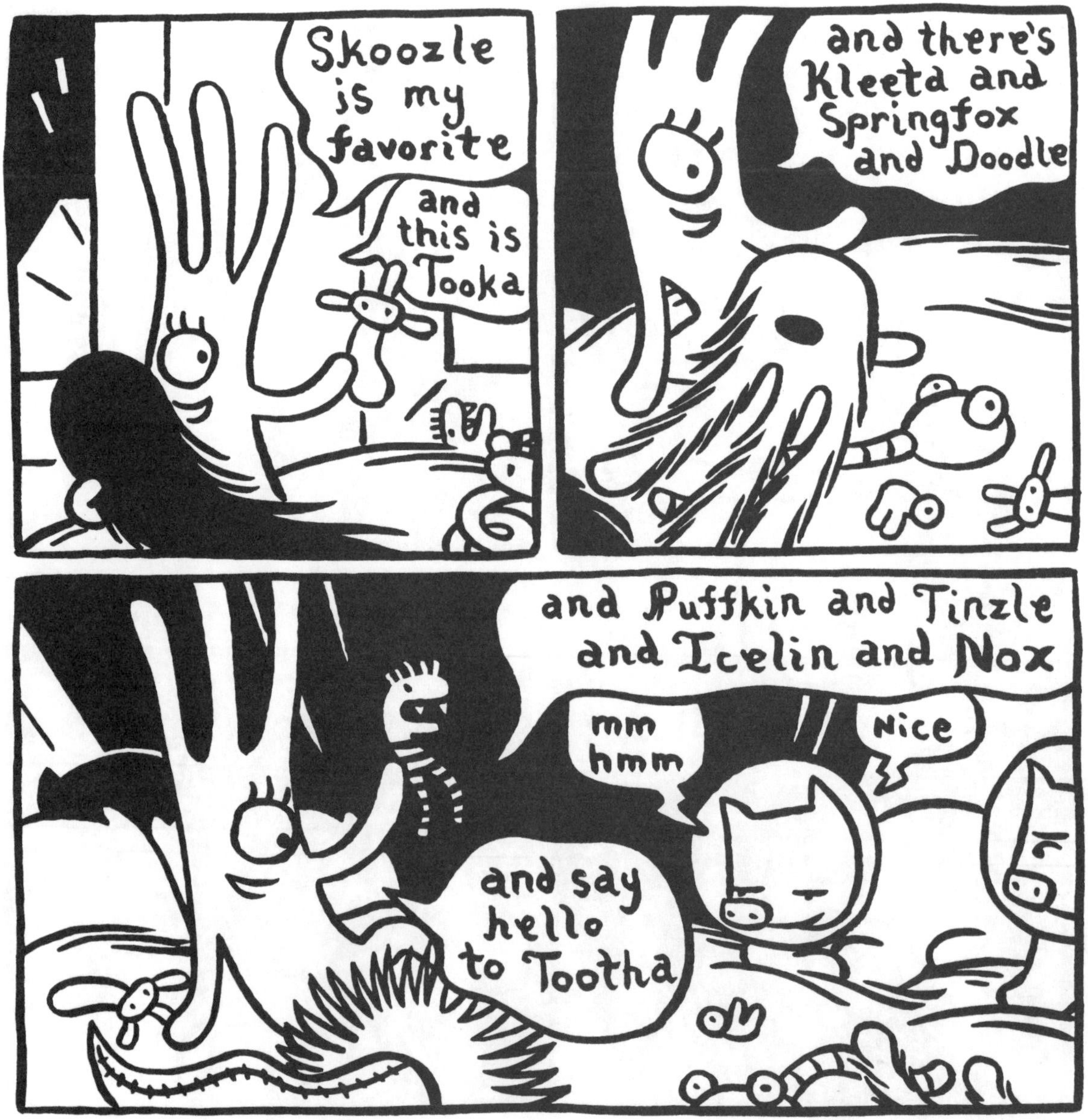
Skoozle is my favorite
and this is Tooka
and there's Kleeta and Springfox and Doodle
and Puffkin and Tinzle and Icelin and Nox
mm hmm
Nice
and say hello to Tootha

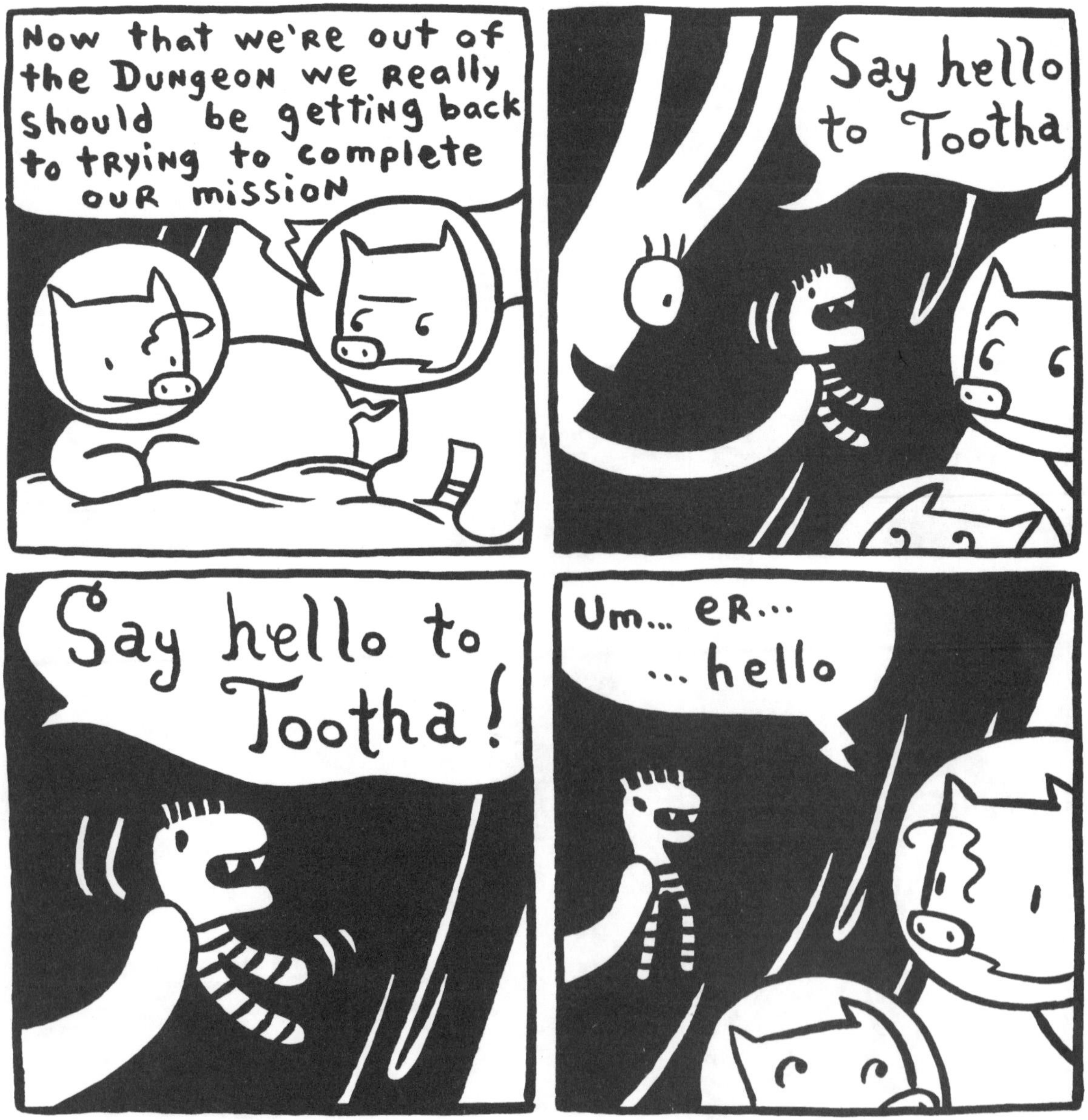
Now that we're out of the Dungeon we really should be getting back to trying to complete our mission
Say hello to Tootha
Say hello to Tootha!
Um... er...
... hello

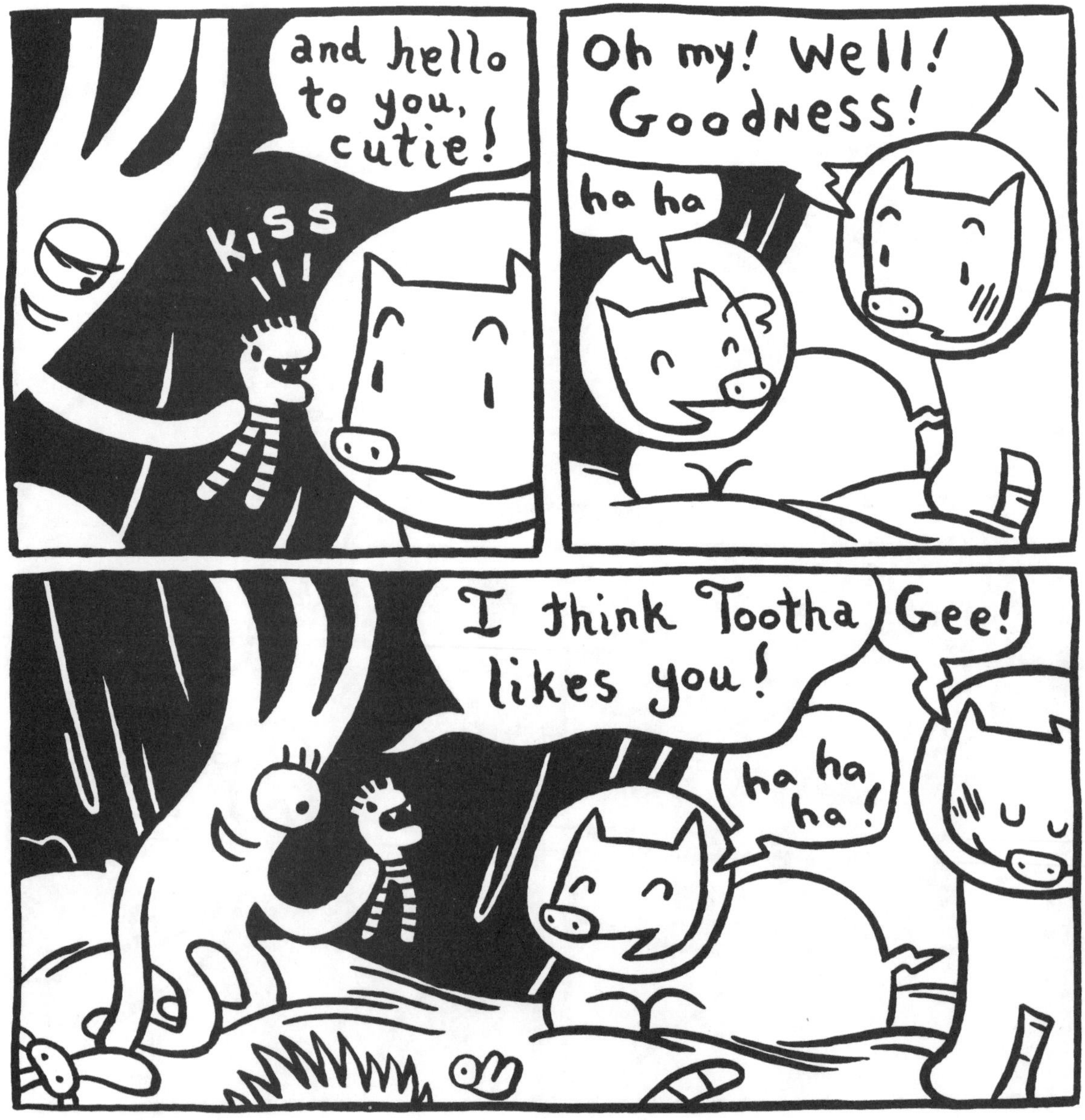
and hello to you, cutie!
KISS
Oh my! Well! Goodness!
ha ha
I think Tootha likes you!
Gee!
ha ha, ha!

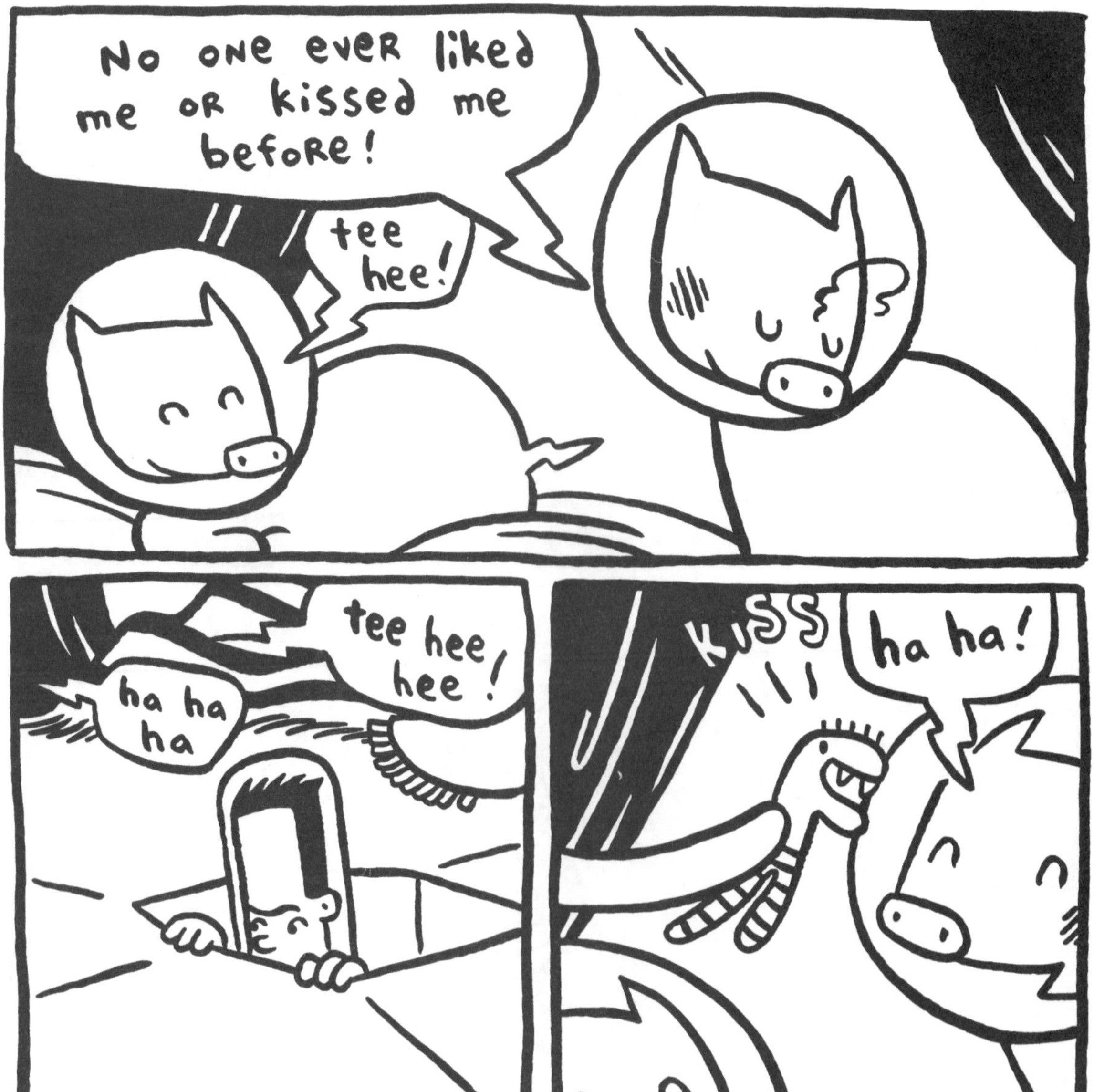
No one ever liked me or kissed me before!
tee hee!
tee hee, hee!
ha ha ha
KISS
ha ha!

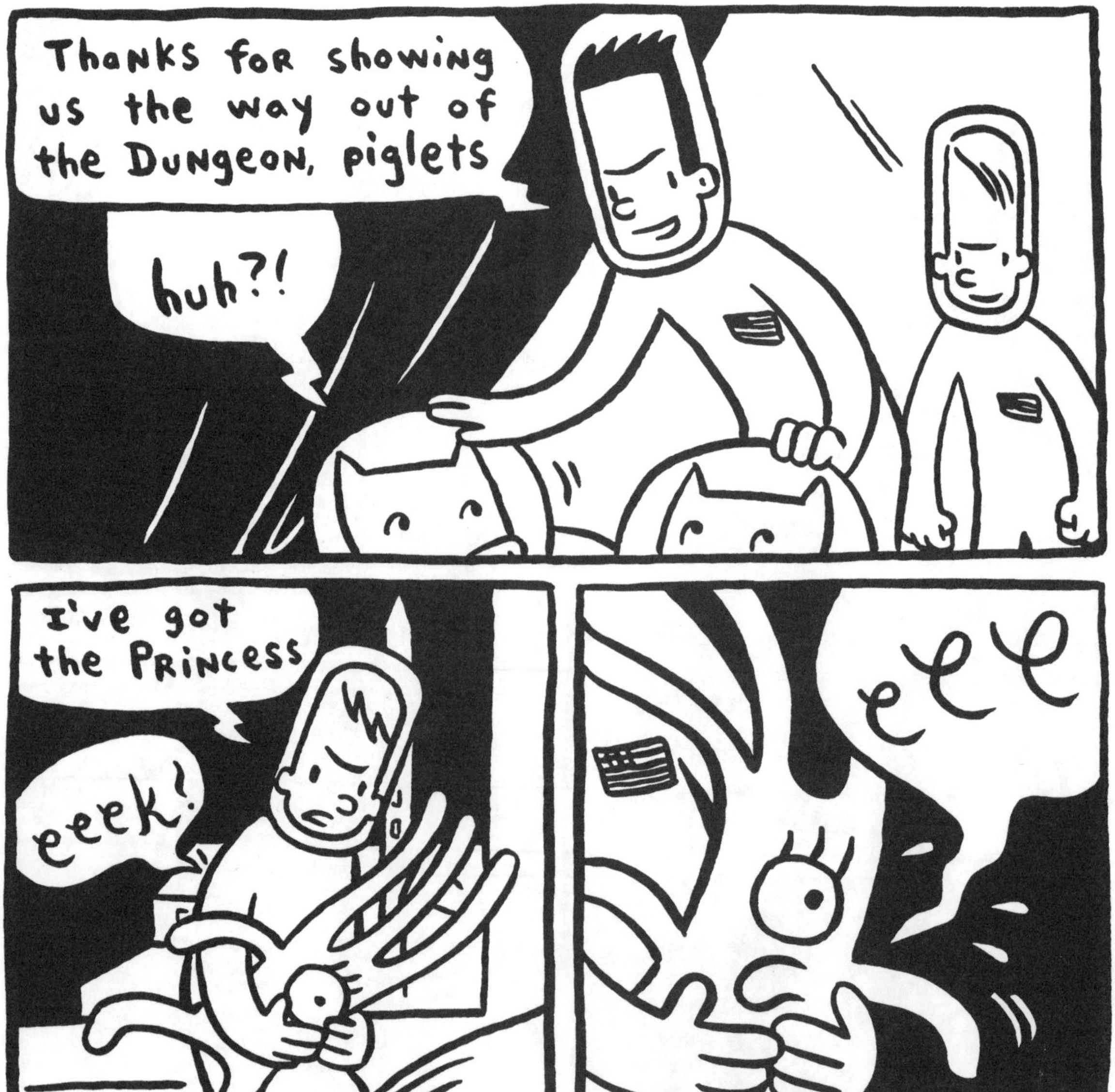
Thanks for showing us the way out of the Dungeon, piglets
huh?!
I've got the Princess
eeek!
eee

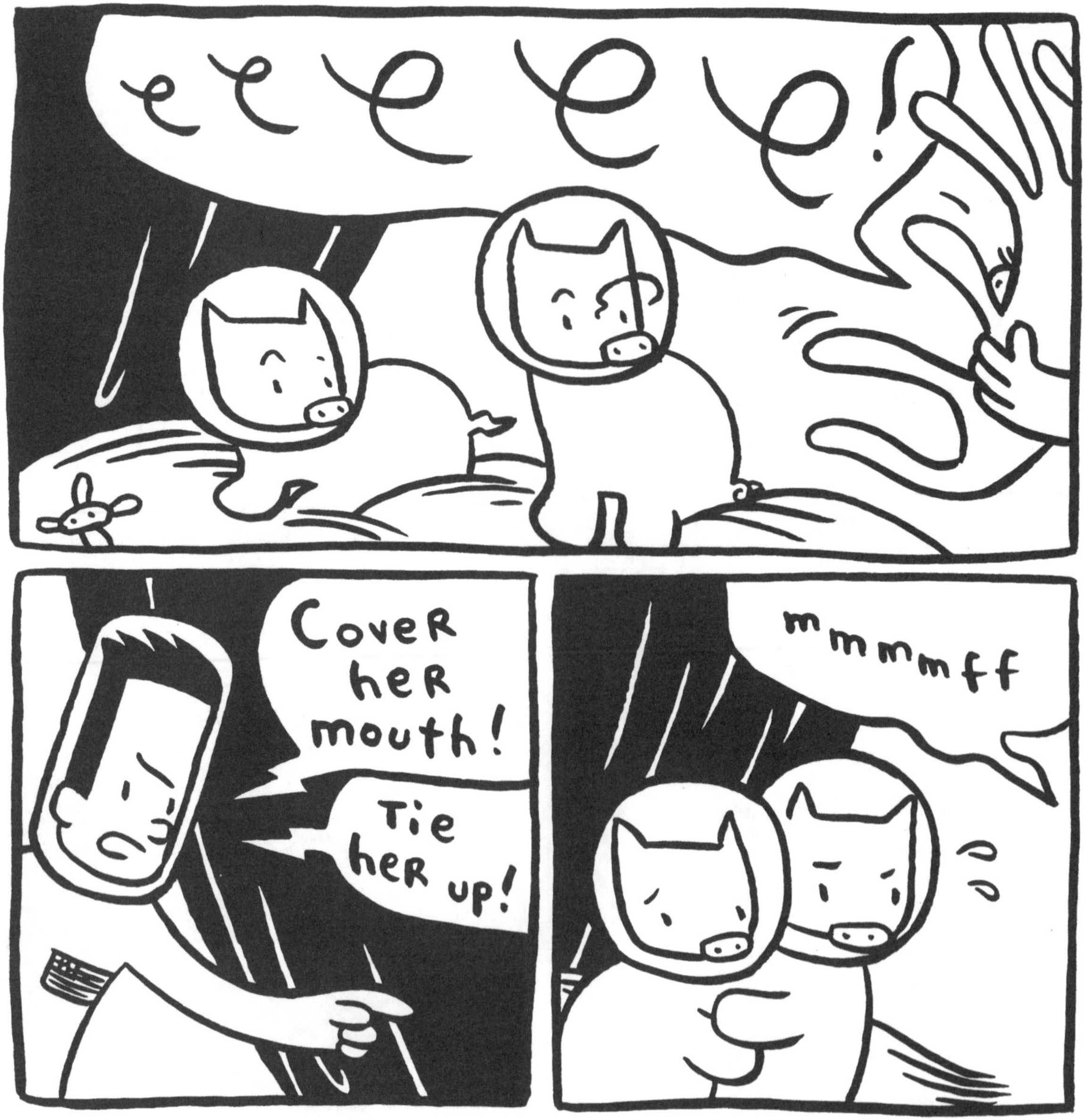
eeeeee!
Cover her mouth!
Tie her up!
mmmmff

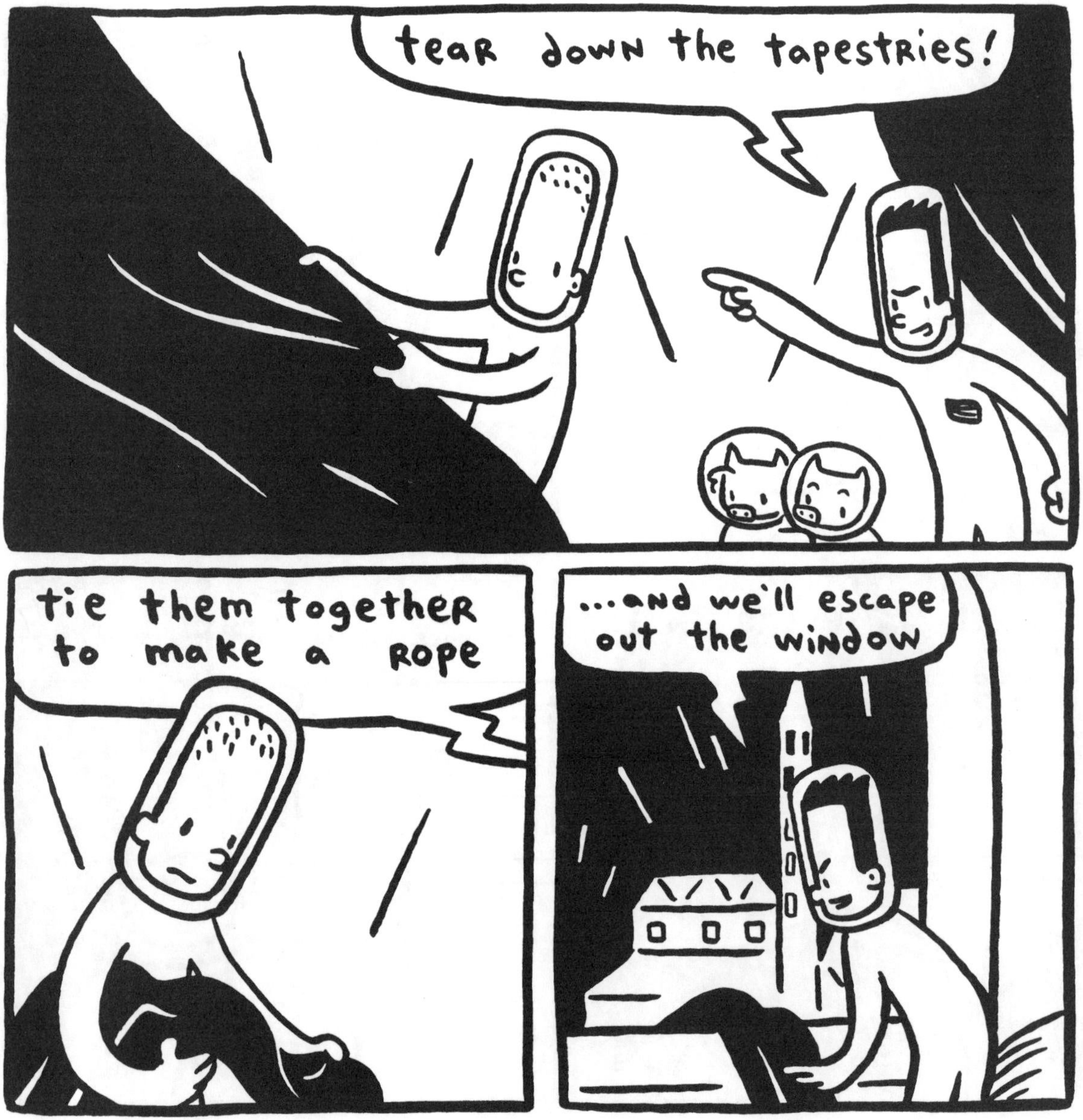
tear down the tapestries!
tie them together to make a rope
...and we'll escape out the window

Mmff!
Come in, Drilling Station 3, do you read me?
Mmf
LOUD AND CLEAR, ASTRONAUT TEN...
We're in the Moon King's Palace. Set the lazer drill for our location and fire in 5 minutes
WILL DO, ASTRONAUT TEN!
Over and out

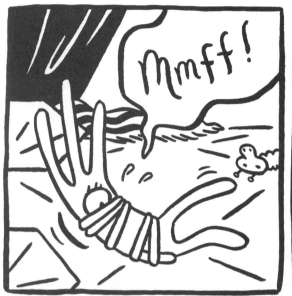

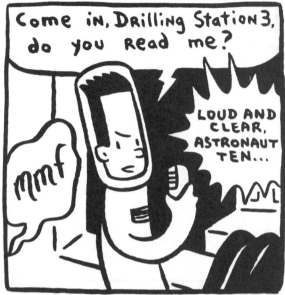

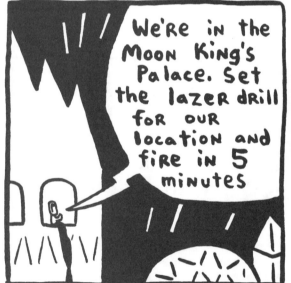

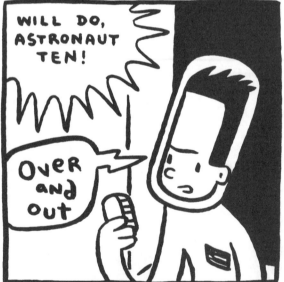

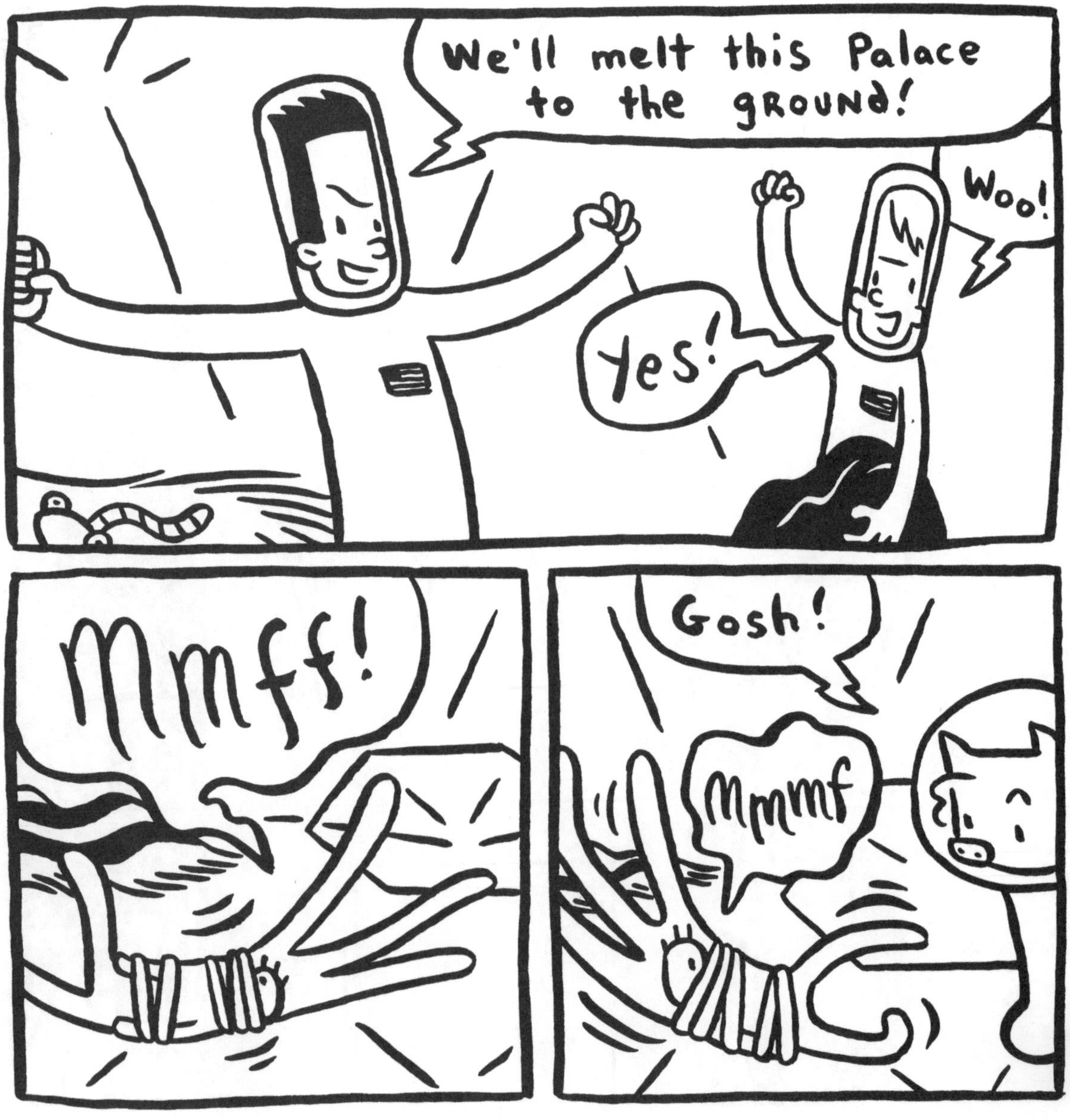
We'll melt this Palace to the GROUND!
Yes!
Woo!
Mmff!
Gosh!
Mmmf

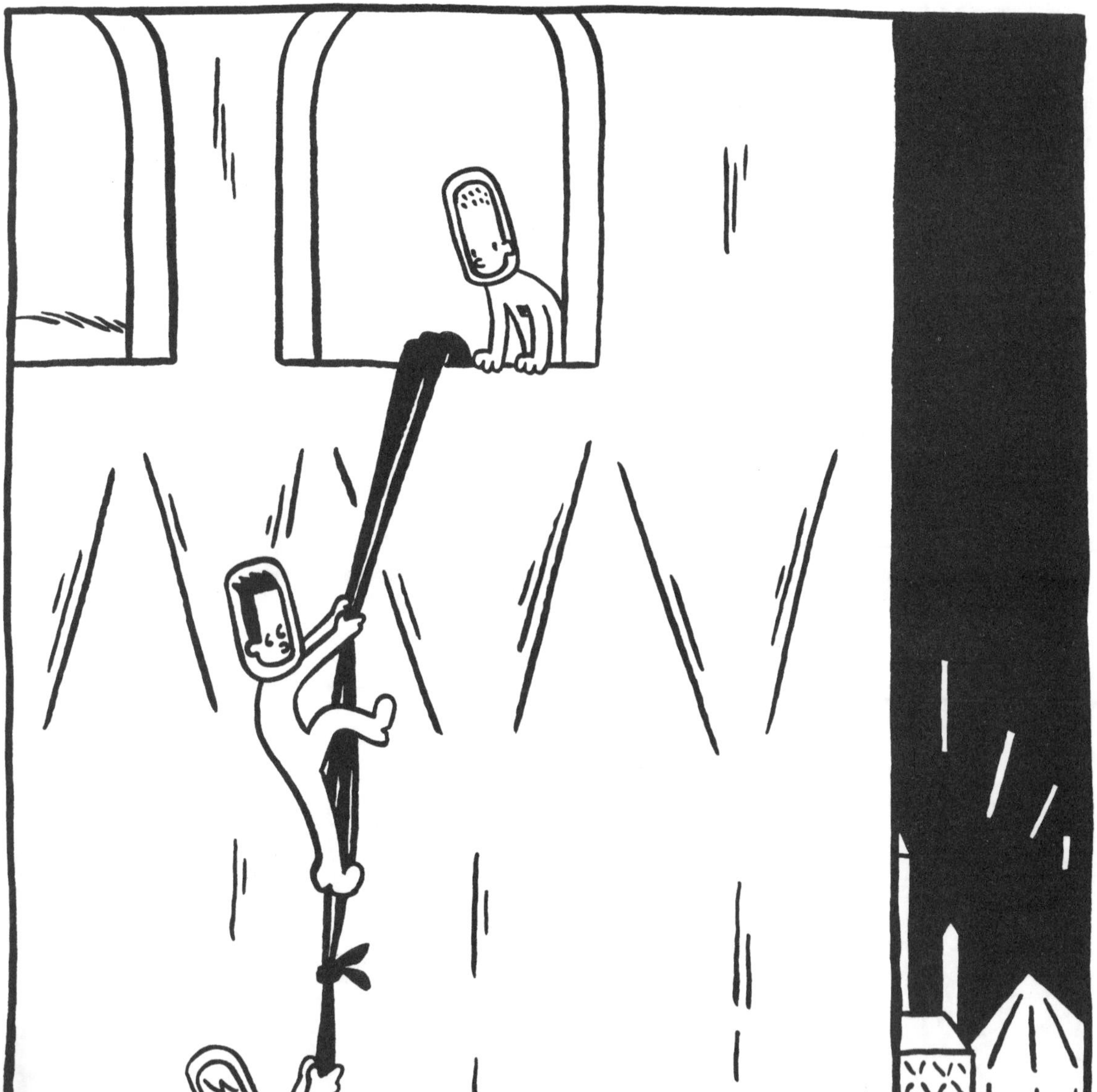

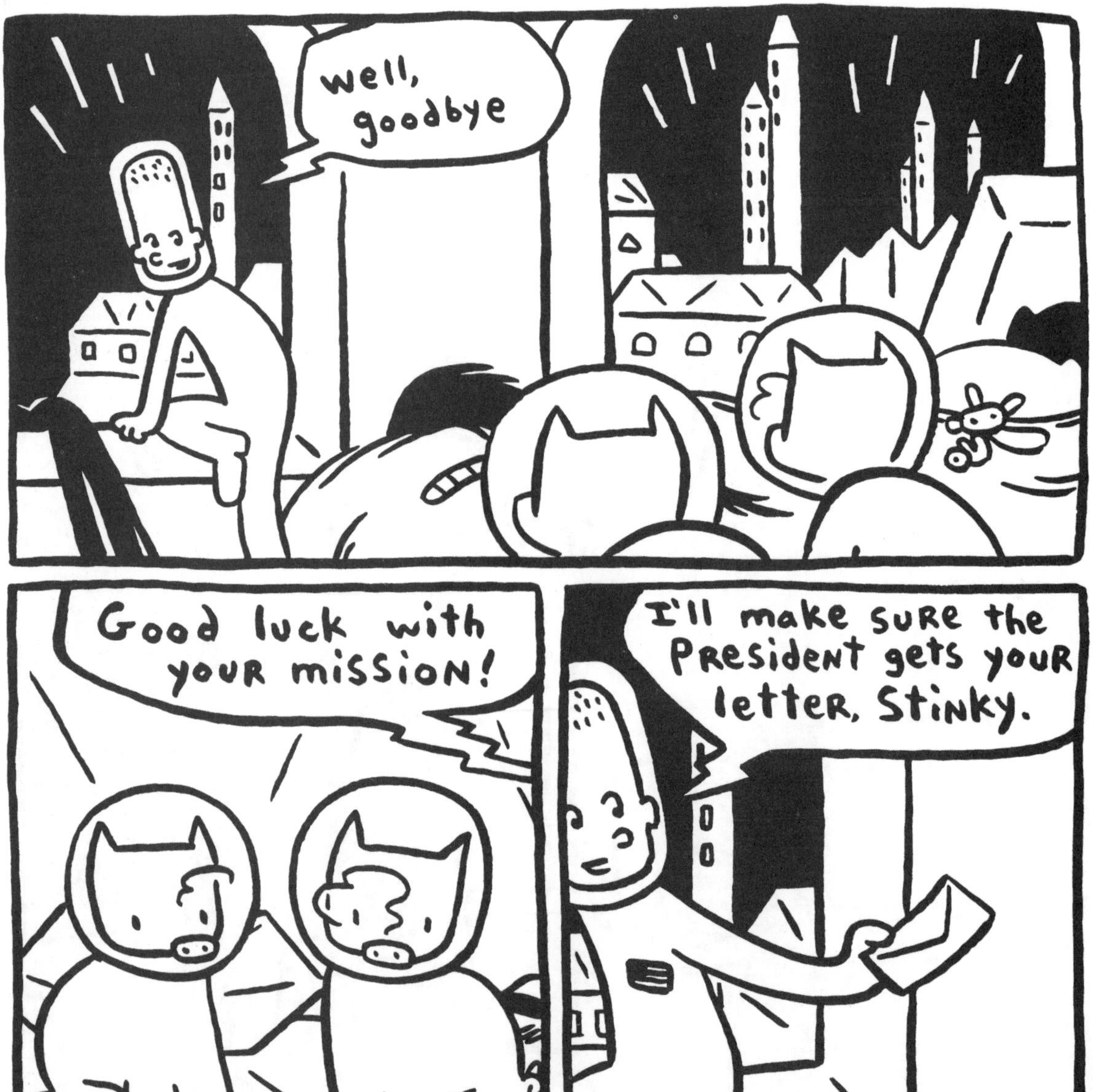
well, goodbye
Good luck with your mission!
I'll make sure the President gets your letter, Stinky.

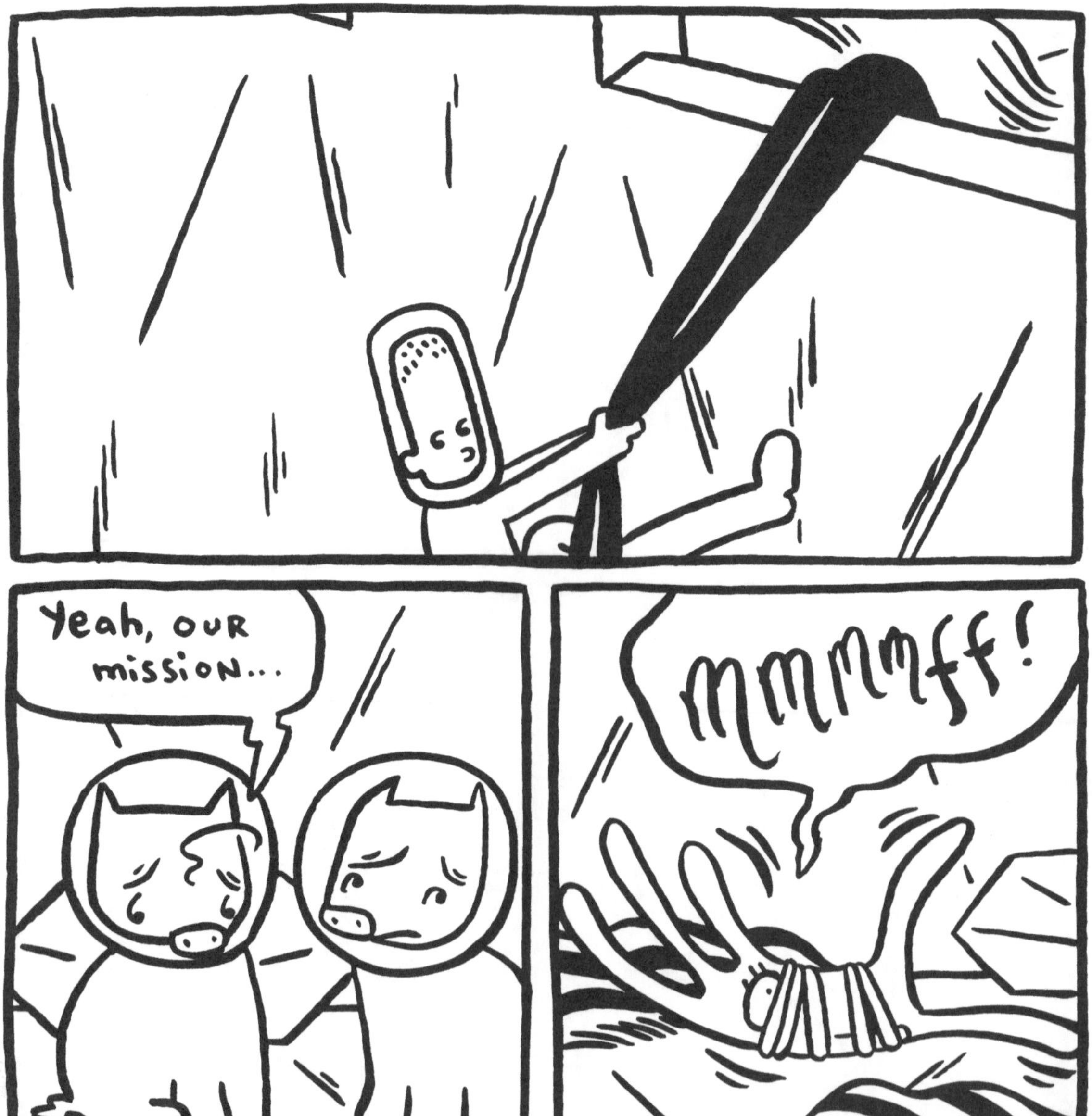
Yeah, our mission...
mmmmff!

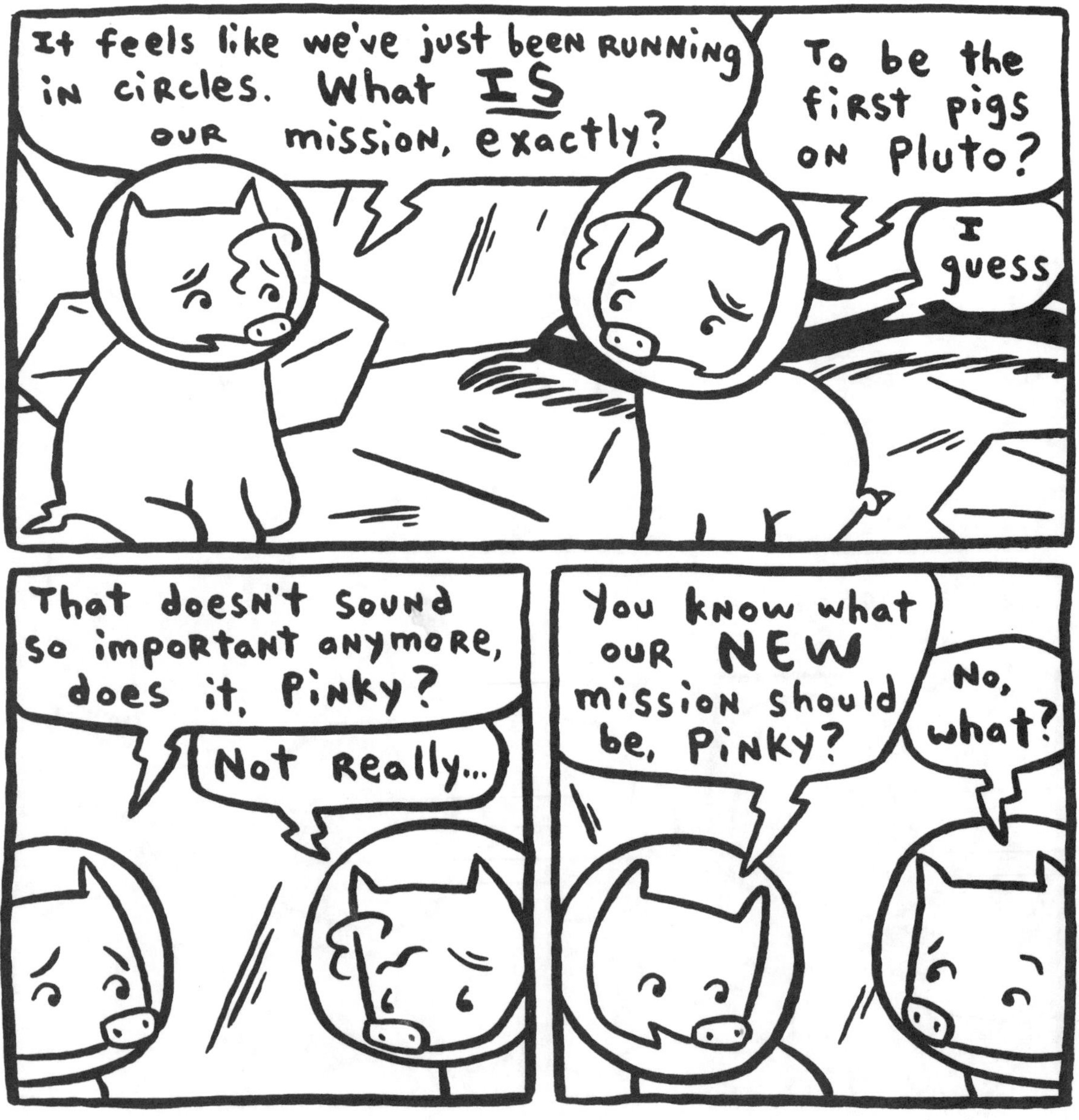
It feels like we've just been RUNNING in circles. What IS our mission, exactly?
To be the first pigs on Pluto?
I guess
That doesn't sound so important anymore, does it, Pinky?
Not Really...
You know what our NEW mission should be, Pinky?
No, what?

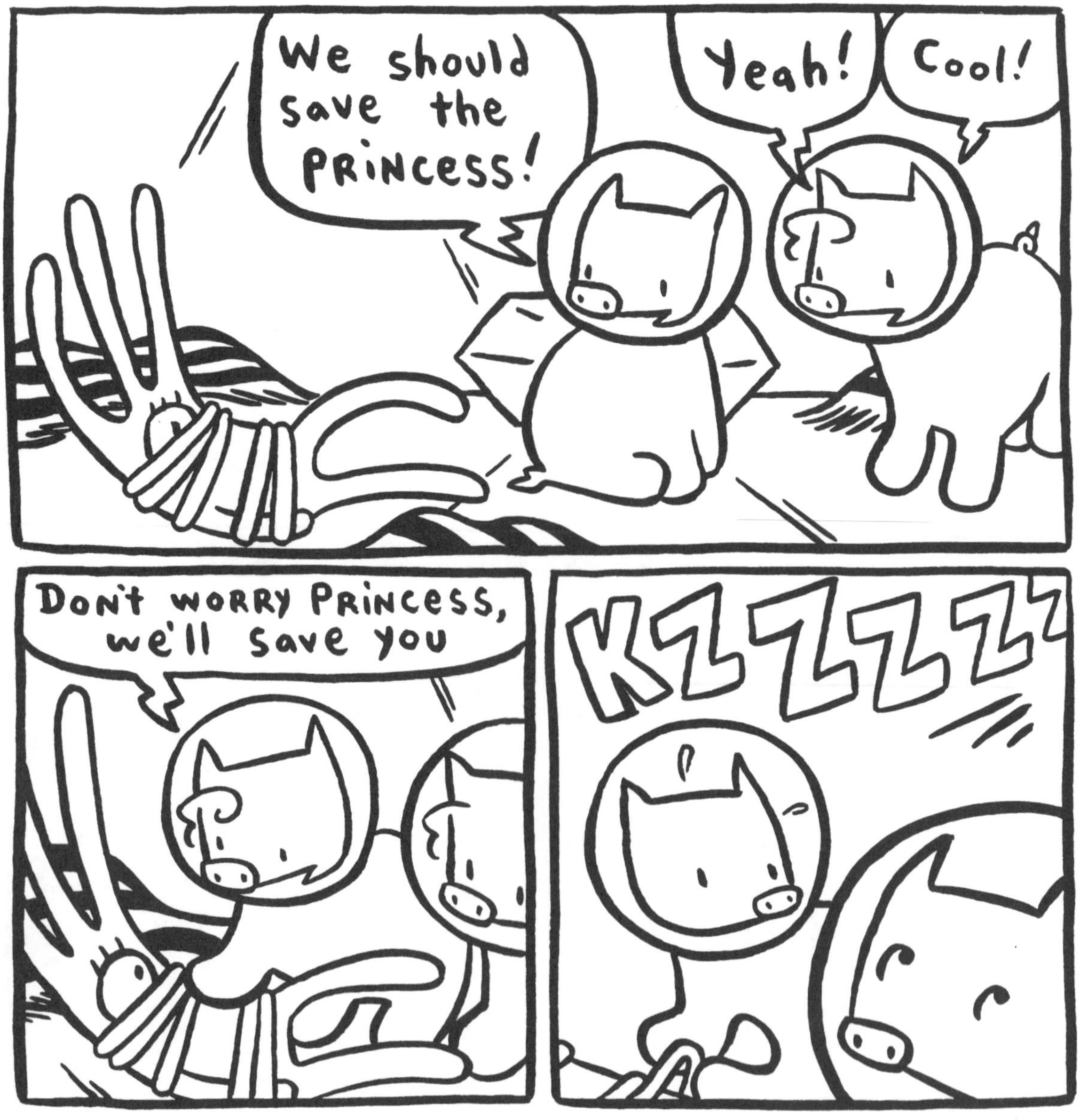
We should save the PRINCESS!
Yeah!
Cool!
DON'T WORRY PRINCESS, we'll save you
KZZZZZZ

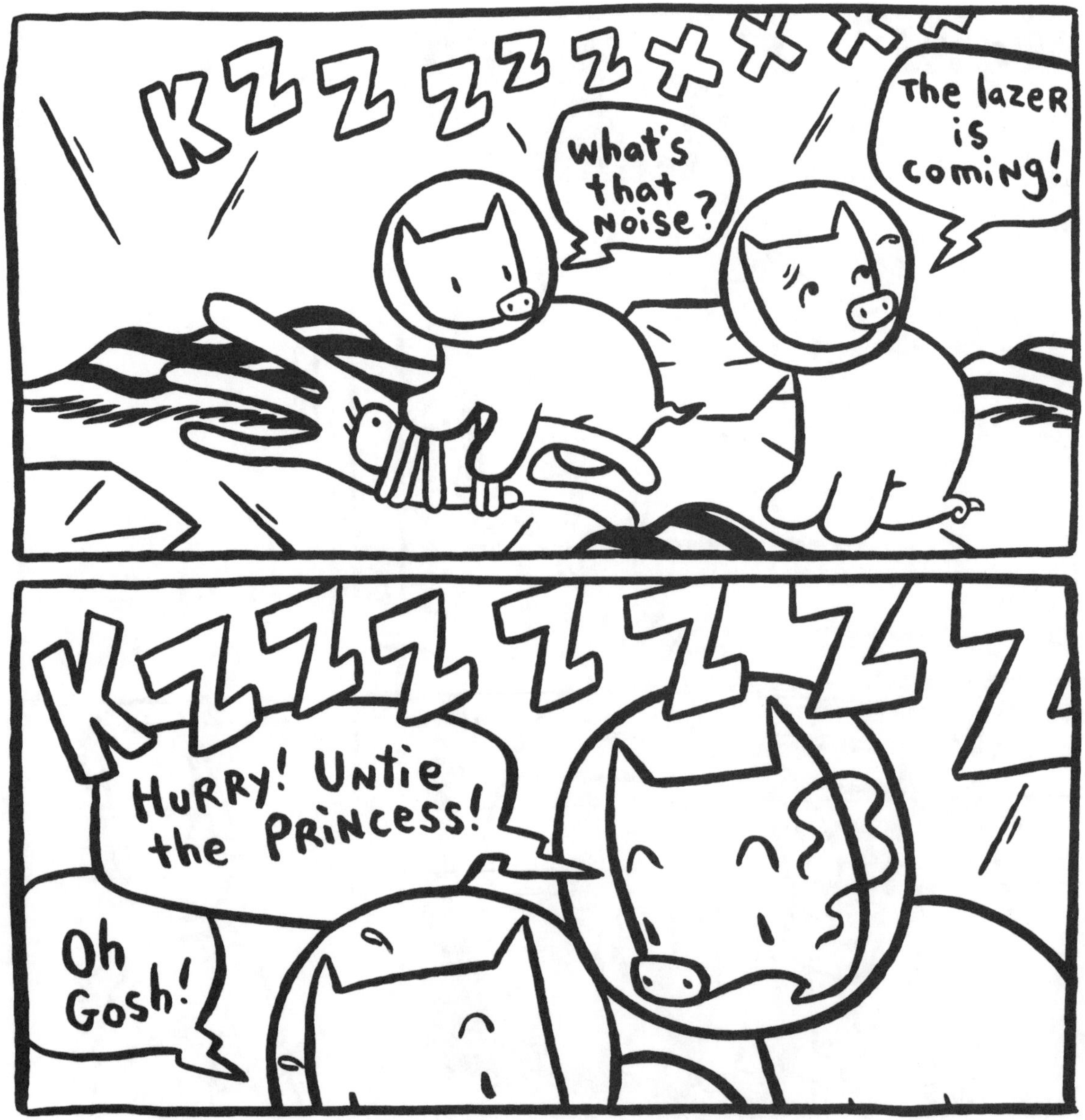
KZZZZZZXXX
what's that noise?
The lazer is coming!
KZZZZZZZZZ
HURRY! Untie the PRINCESS!
Oh Gosh!

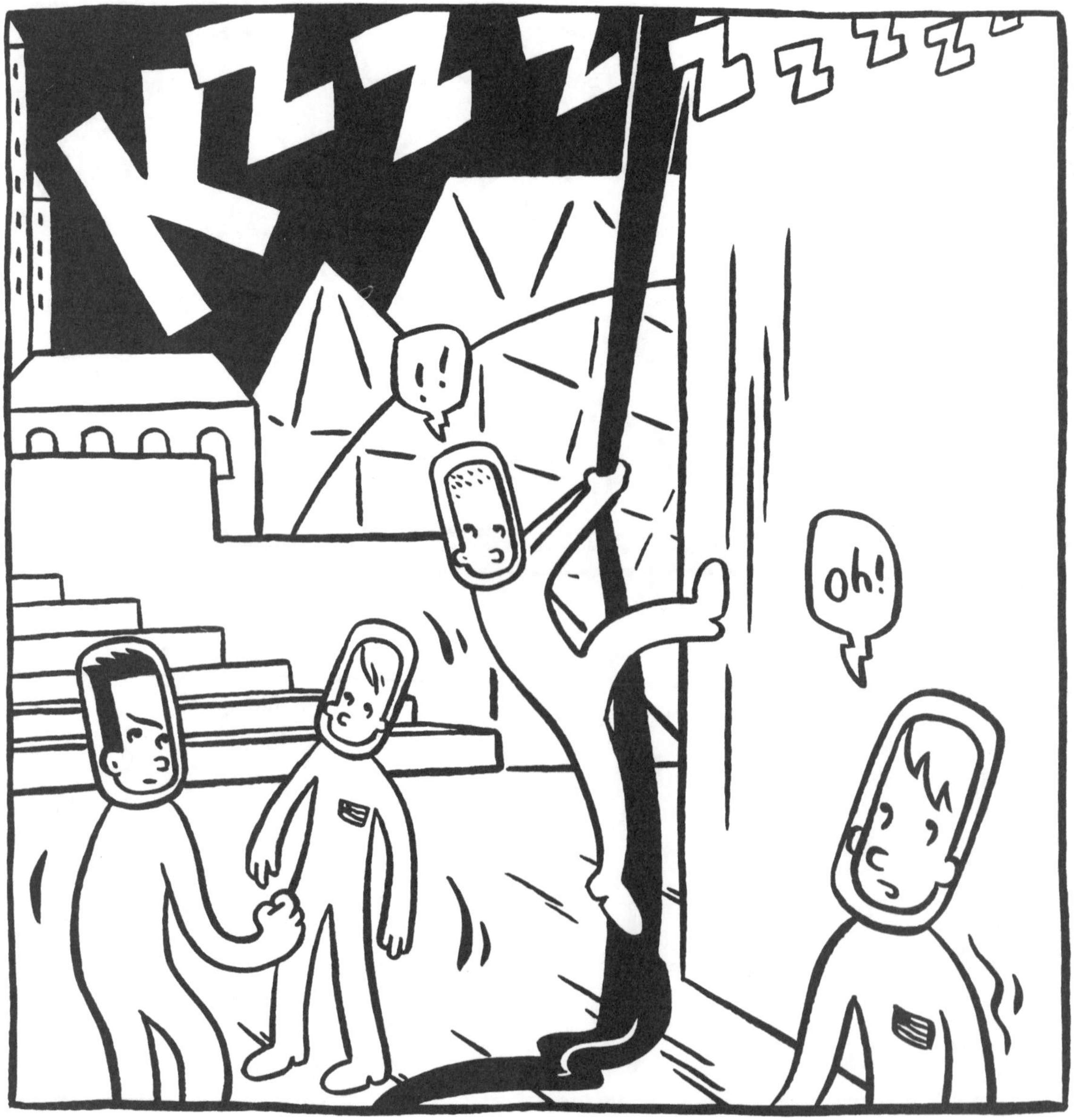
KZZZZZZZZZ
!!
oh!

that's it men!
Let's Go!
Move!
Now!

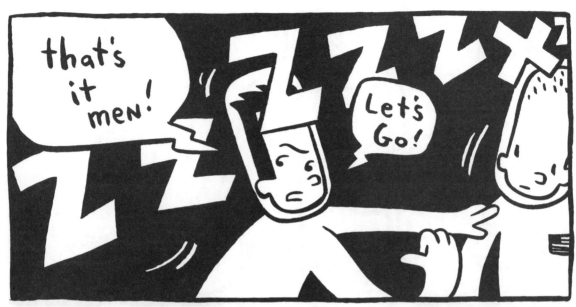

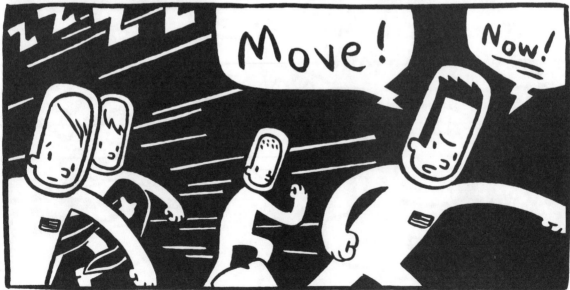

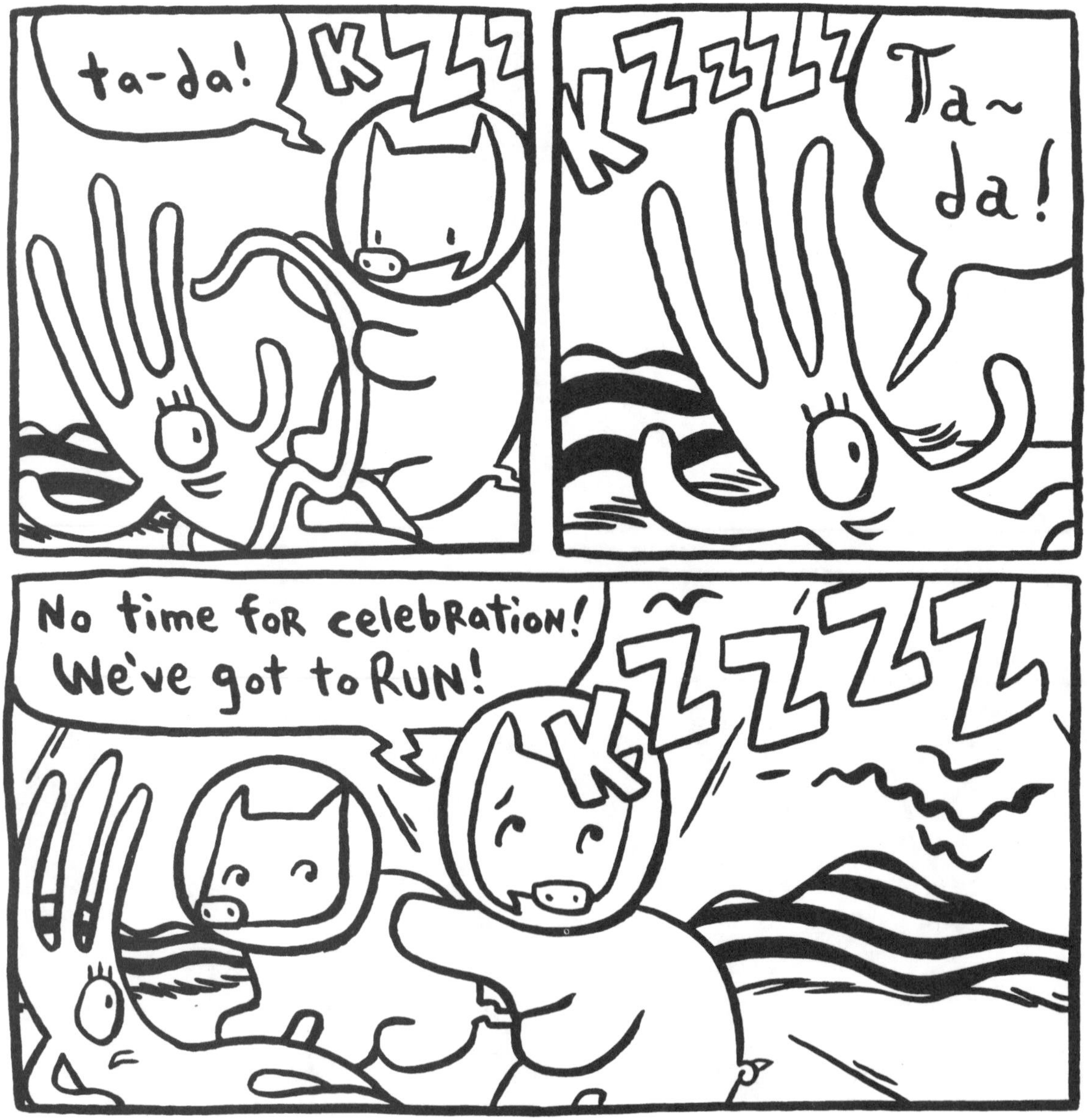
ta-da!
KZZZ
KZZZZZ
Ta~ da!
No time for celebration! We've got to RUN!
KZZZZZ

KZZZZ
Get on my back!
KZZZZ
Uh oh!
here it comes
ZANG!
the lazer!

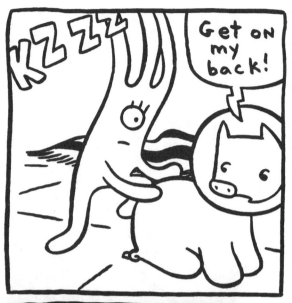

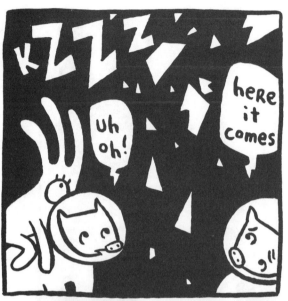

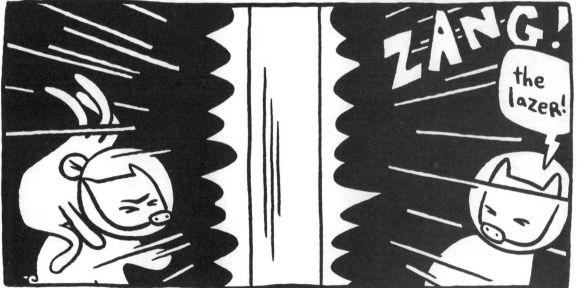

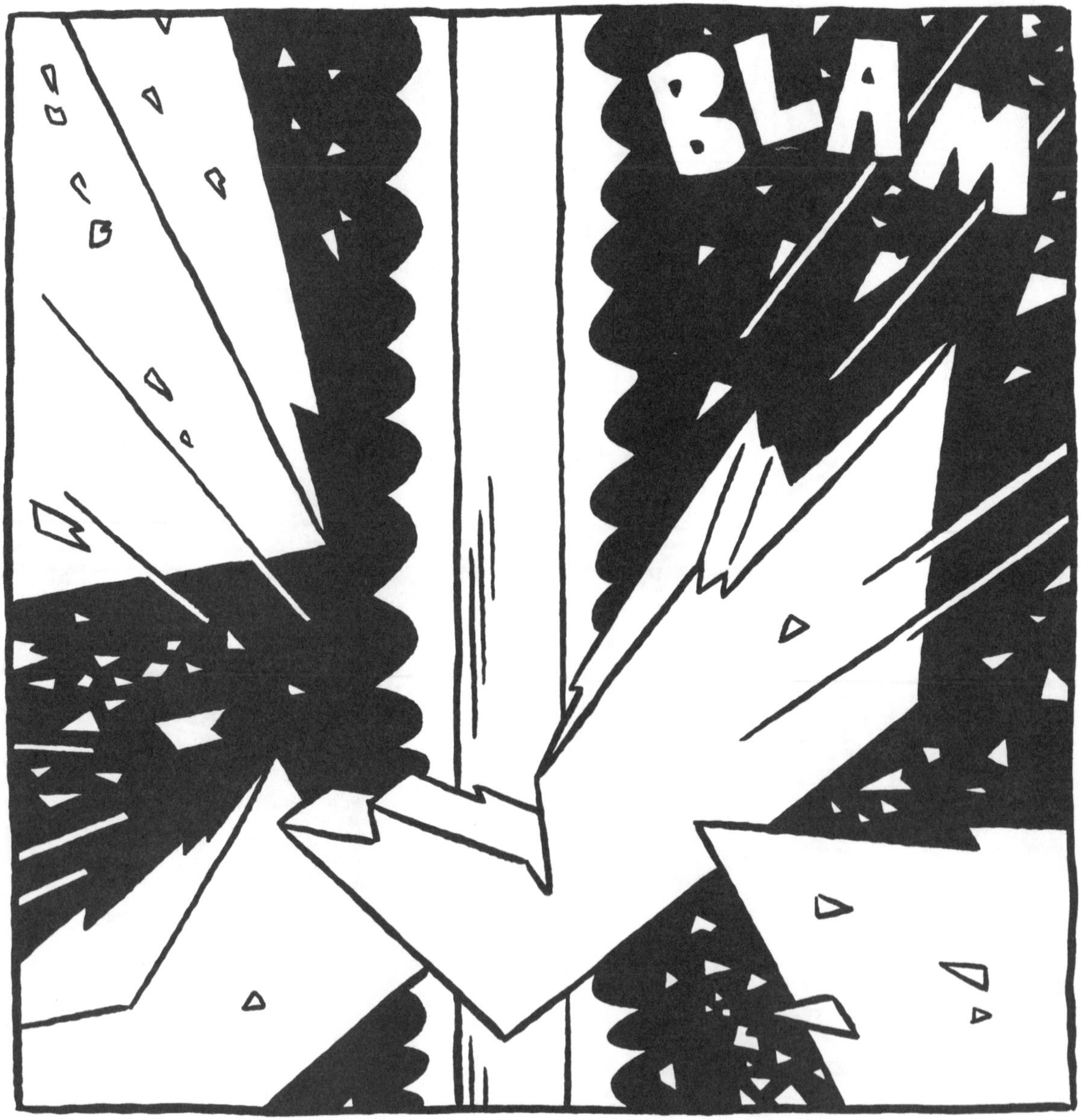
BLAM

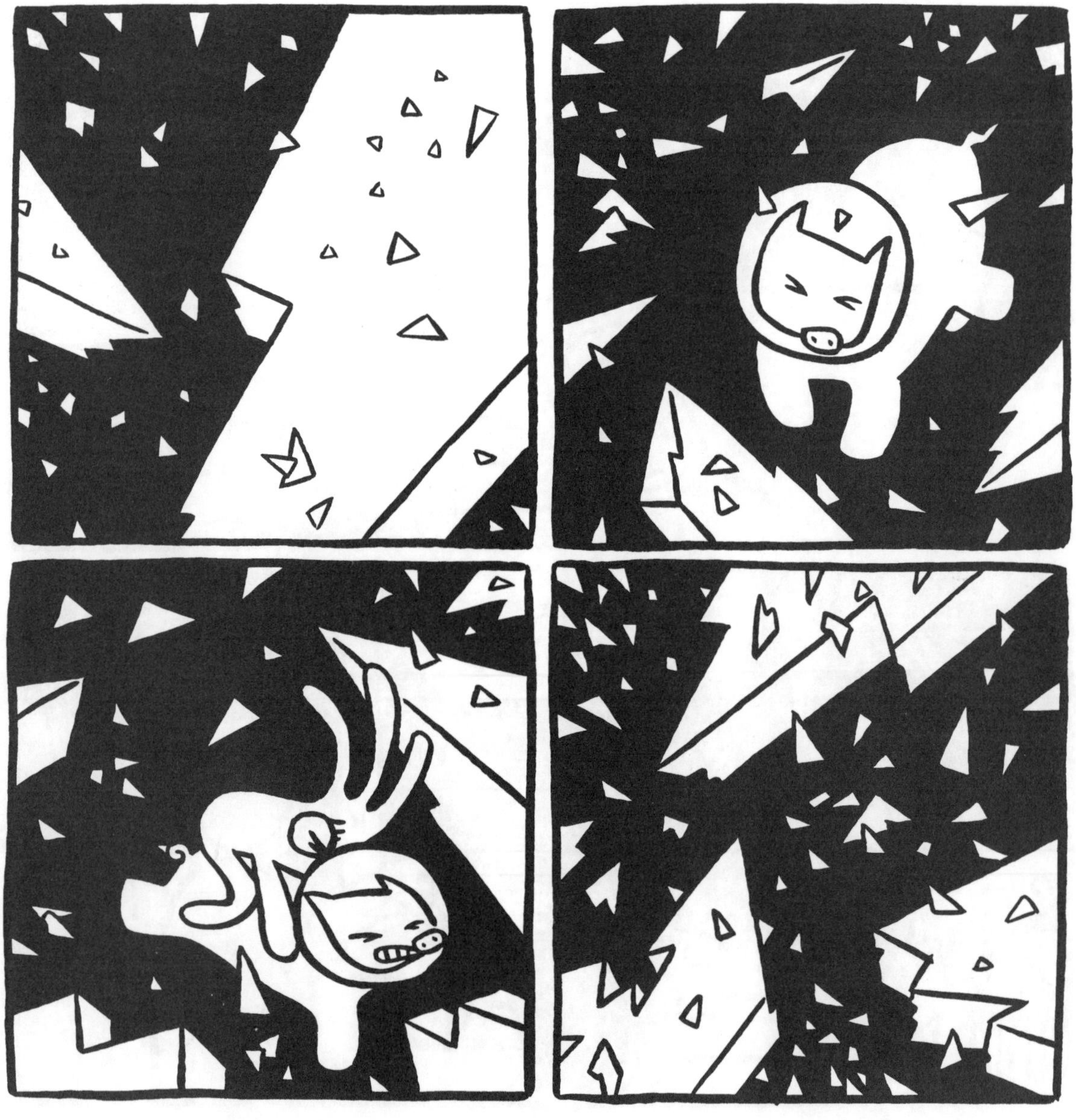

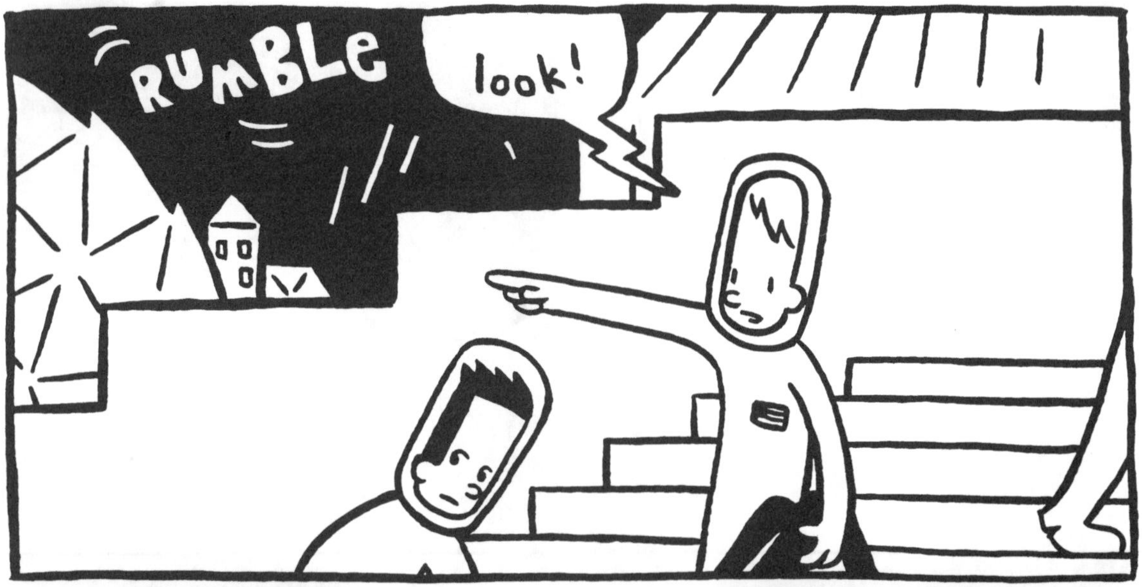
RUMBLE
look!

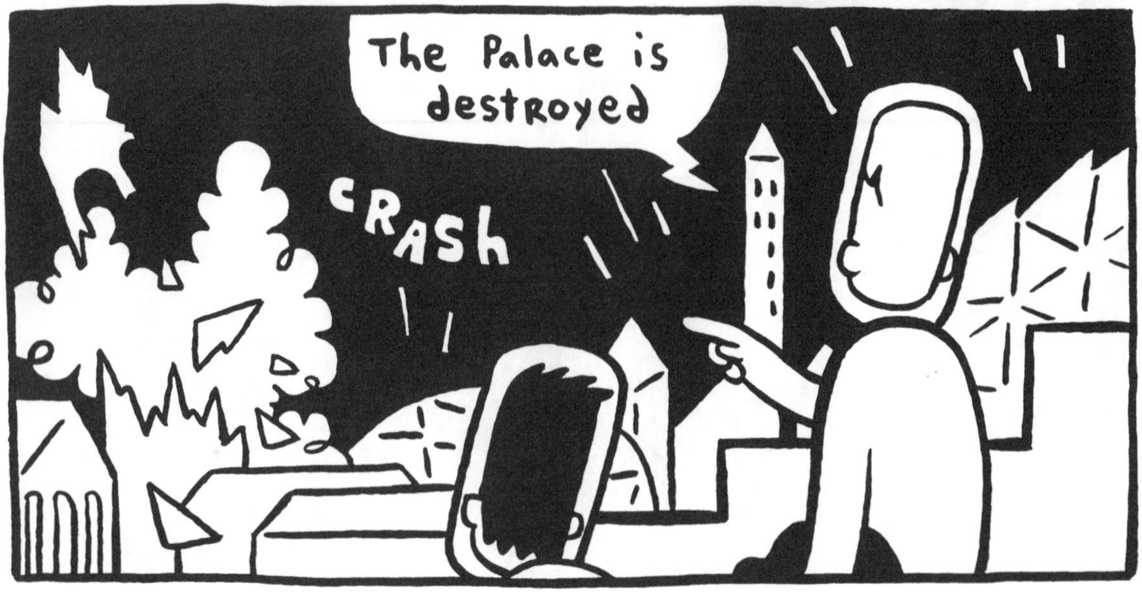
The Palace is destroyed
CRASH

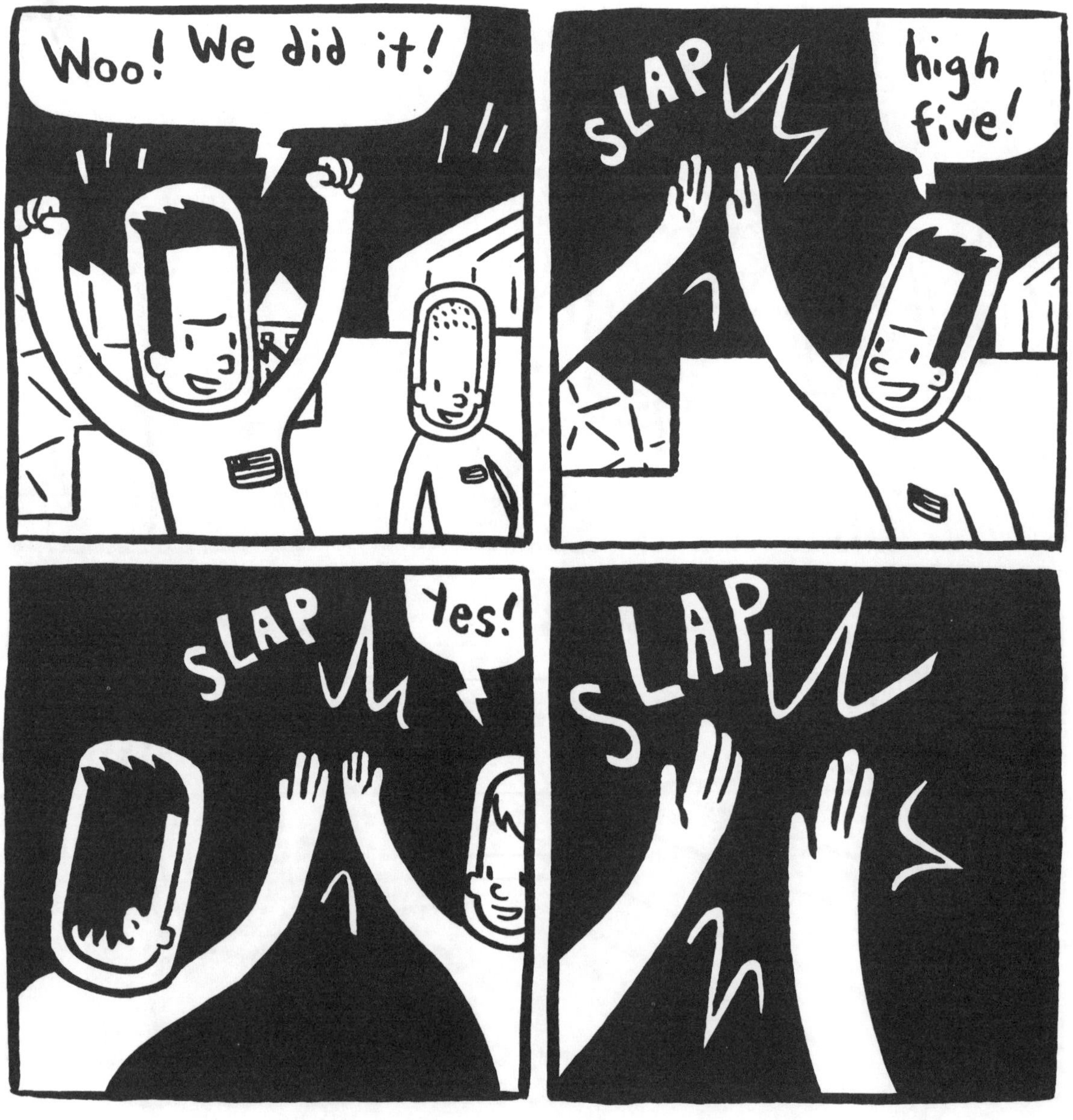
Woo! We did it!
SLAP
high five!
SLAP
Yes!
SLAP

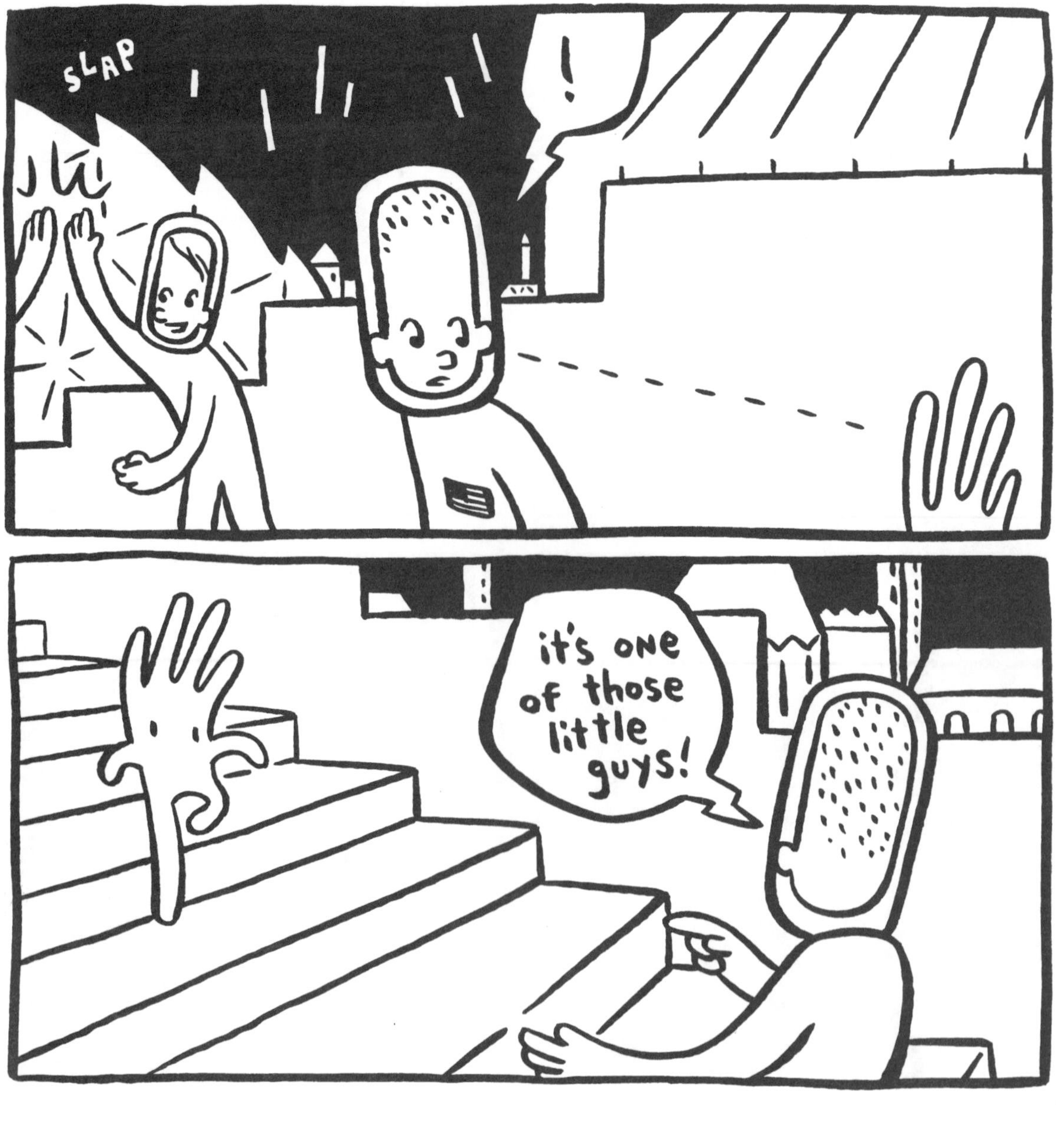
SLAP
!
it's one of those little guys!

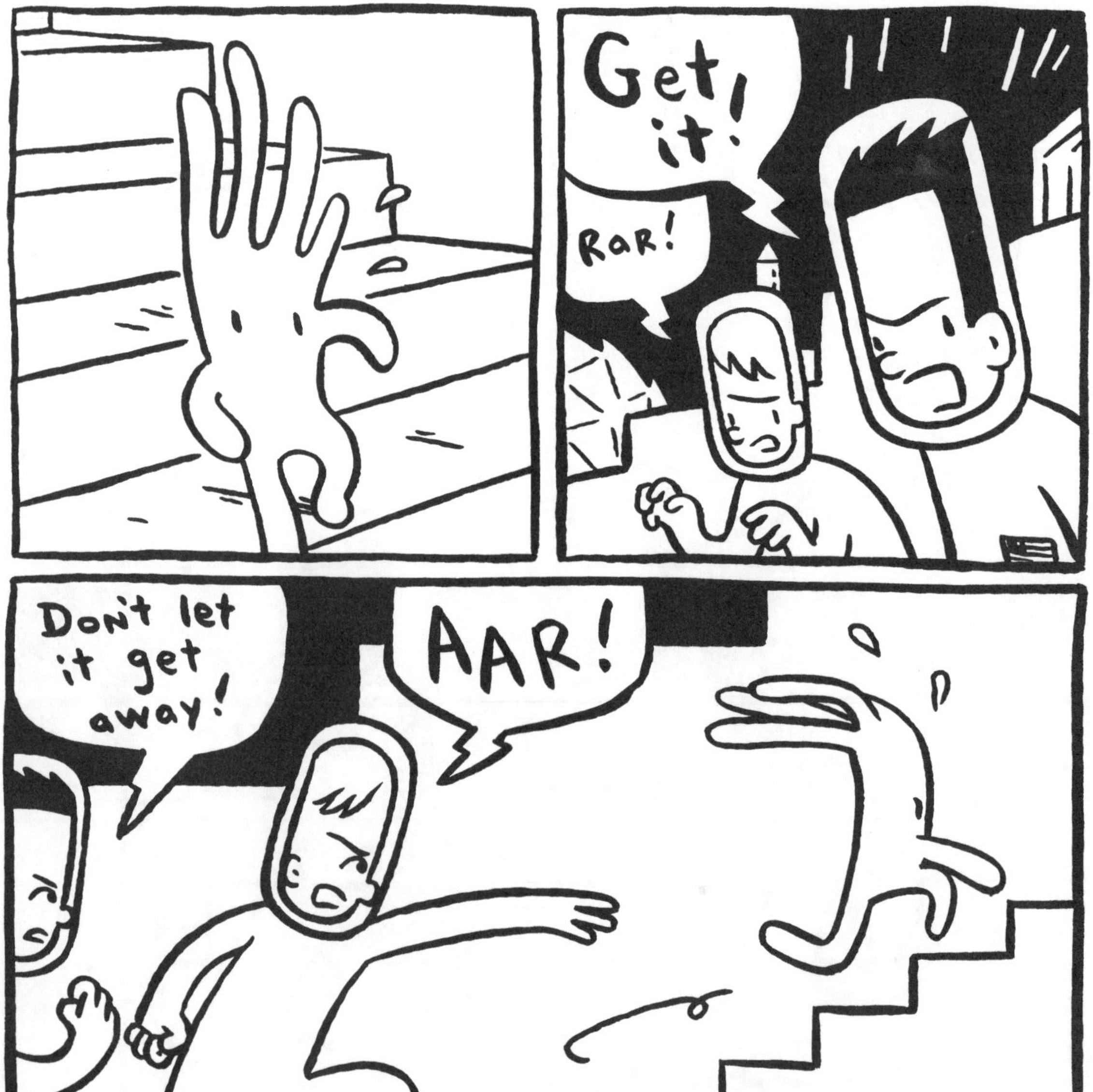
Get it!
RaR!
Don't let it get away!
AAR!

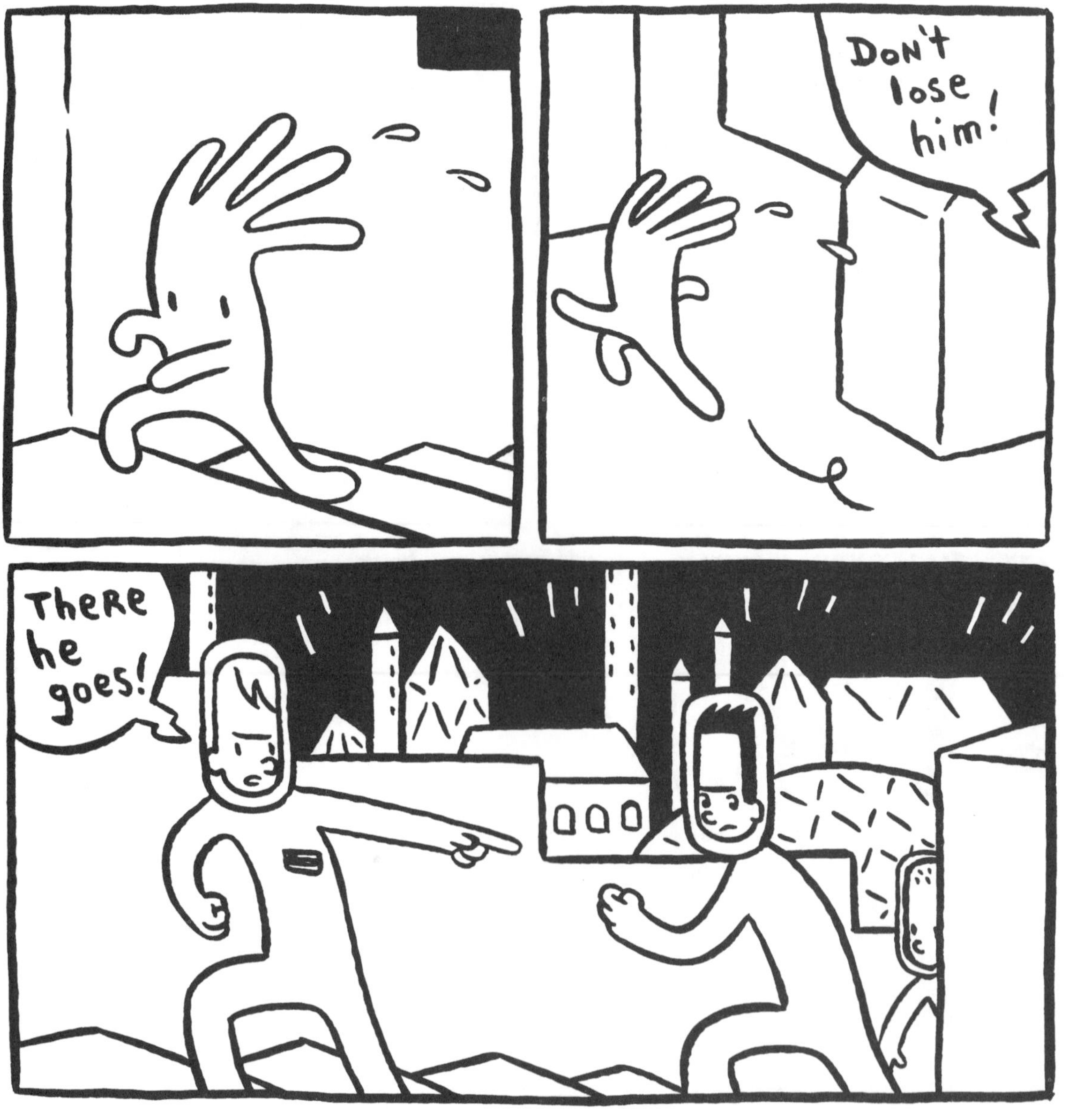

Don't lose him!
There he goes!

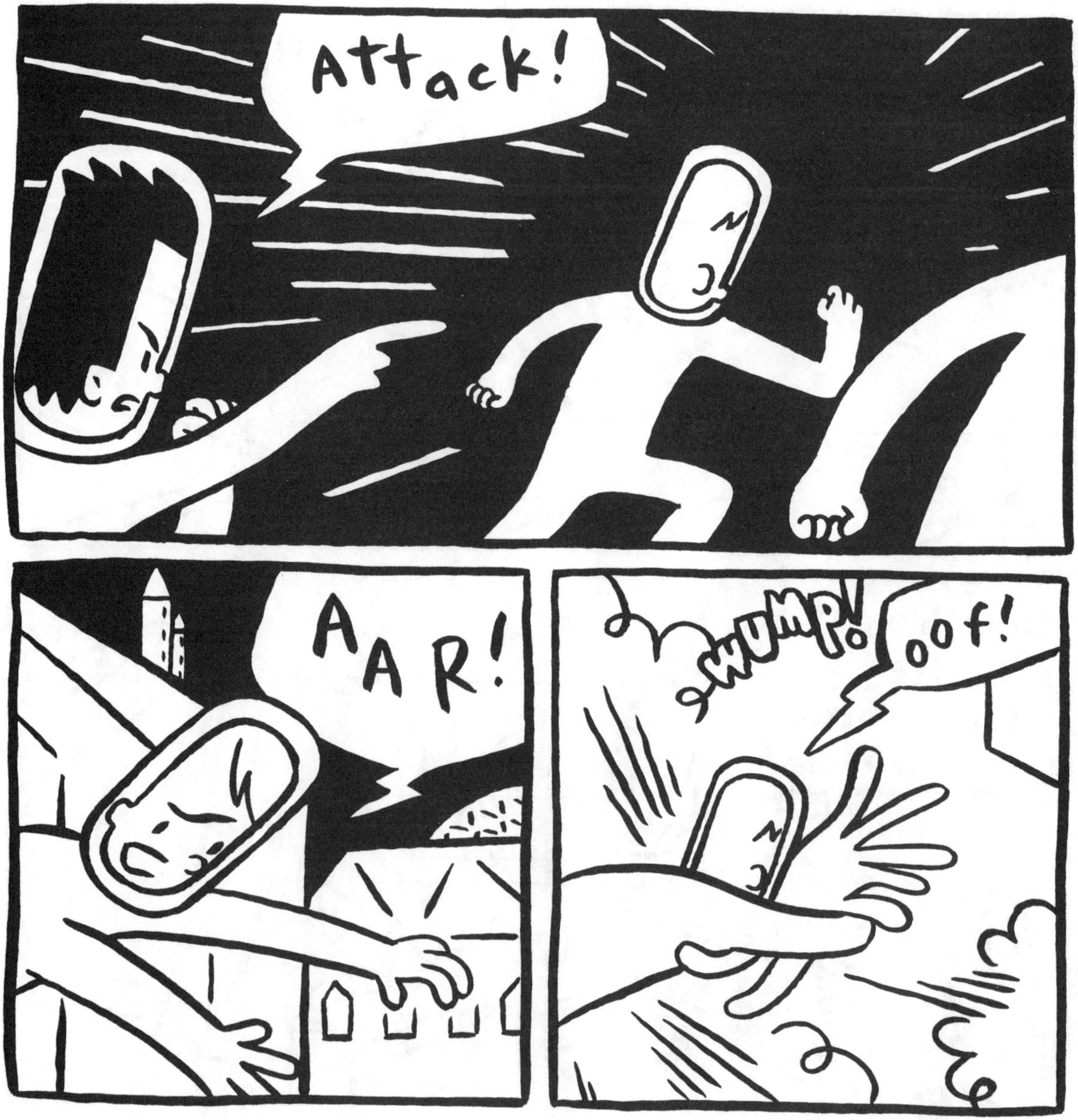
Attack!
AAR!
WUMP!
oof!

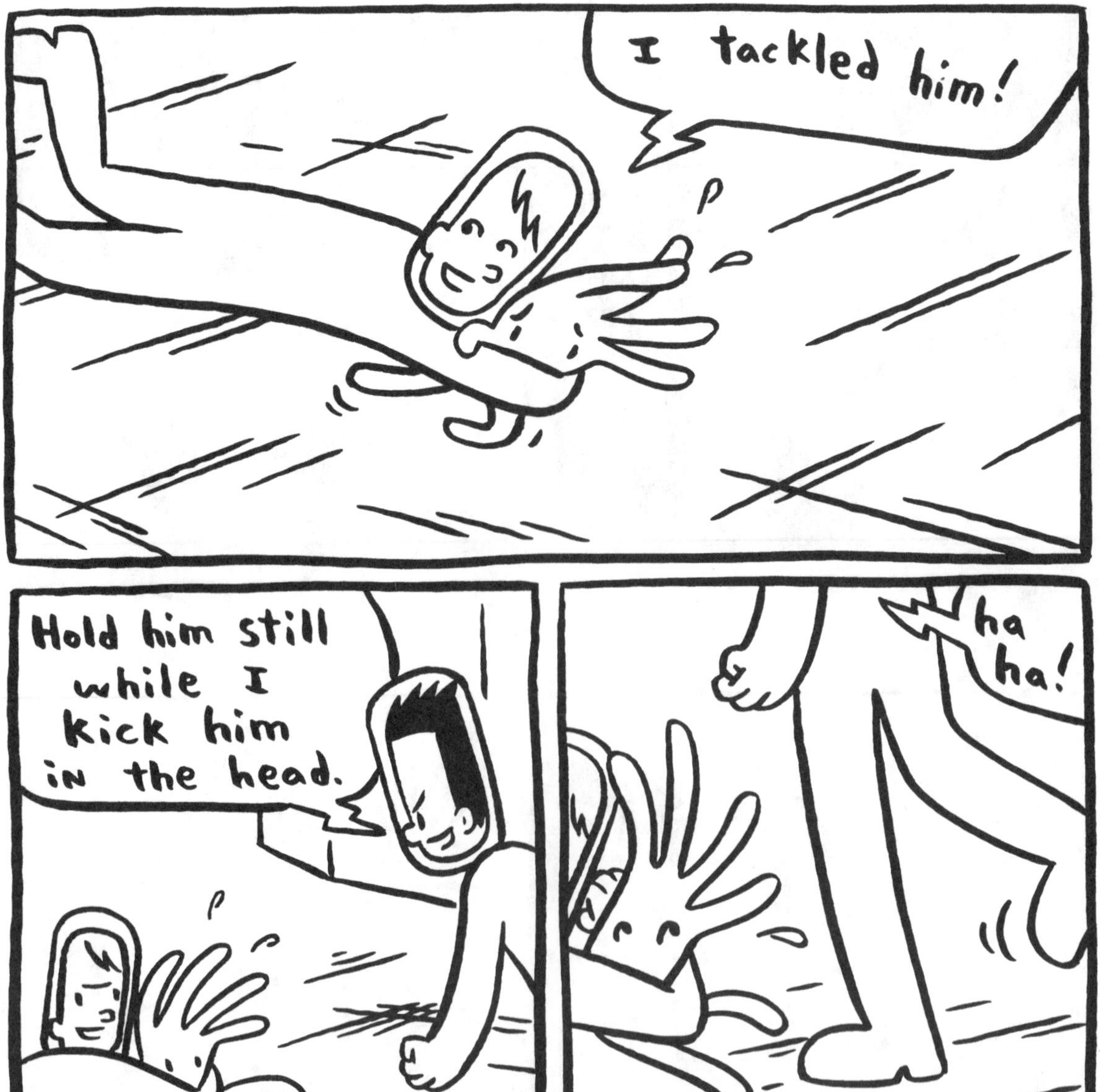
I tackled him!
Hold him still while I kick him in the head.
ha ha!

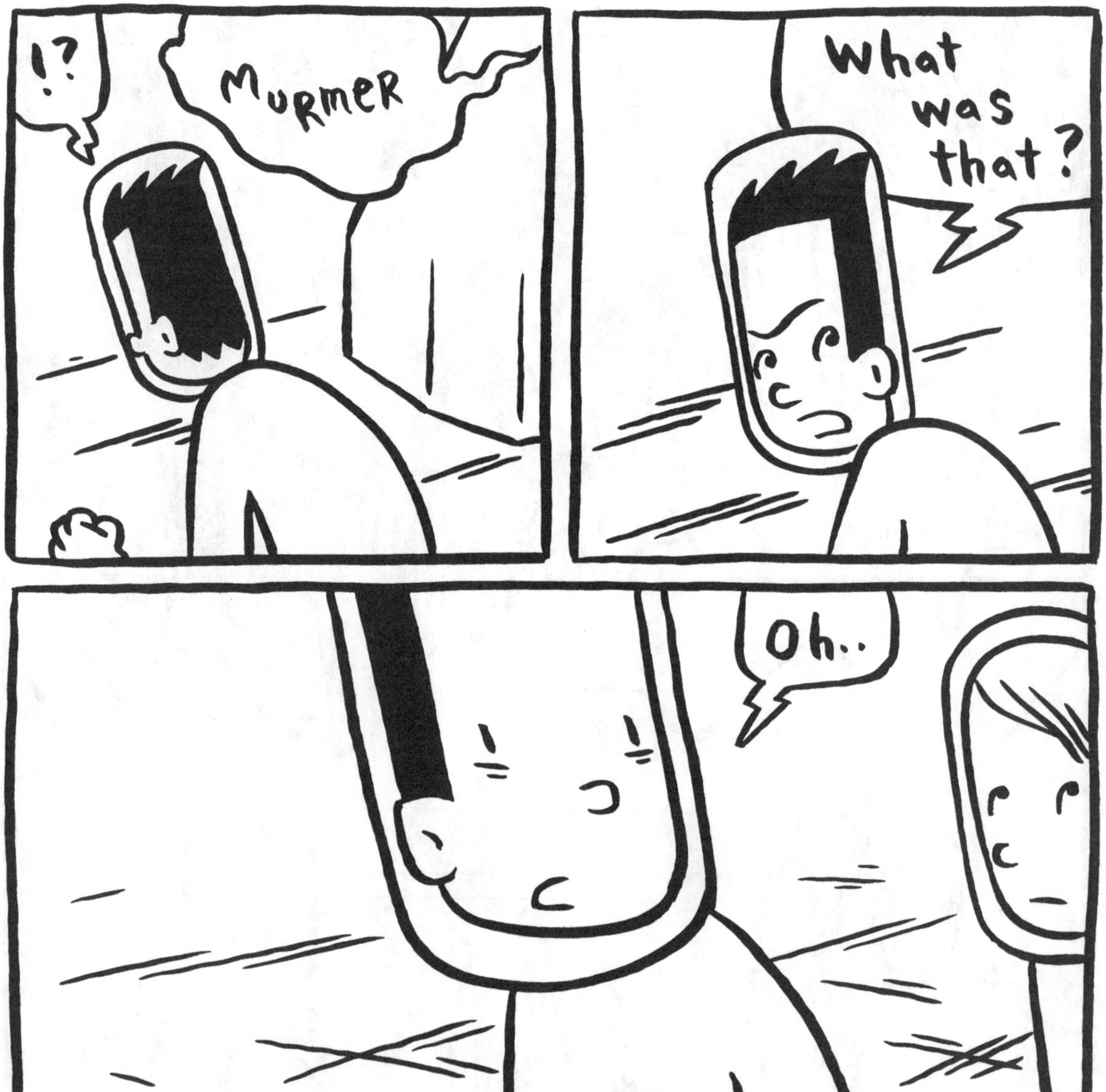
!?
Murmer
What was that?
Oh..

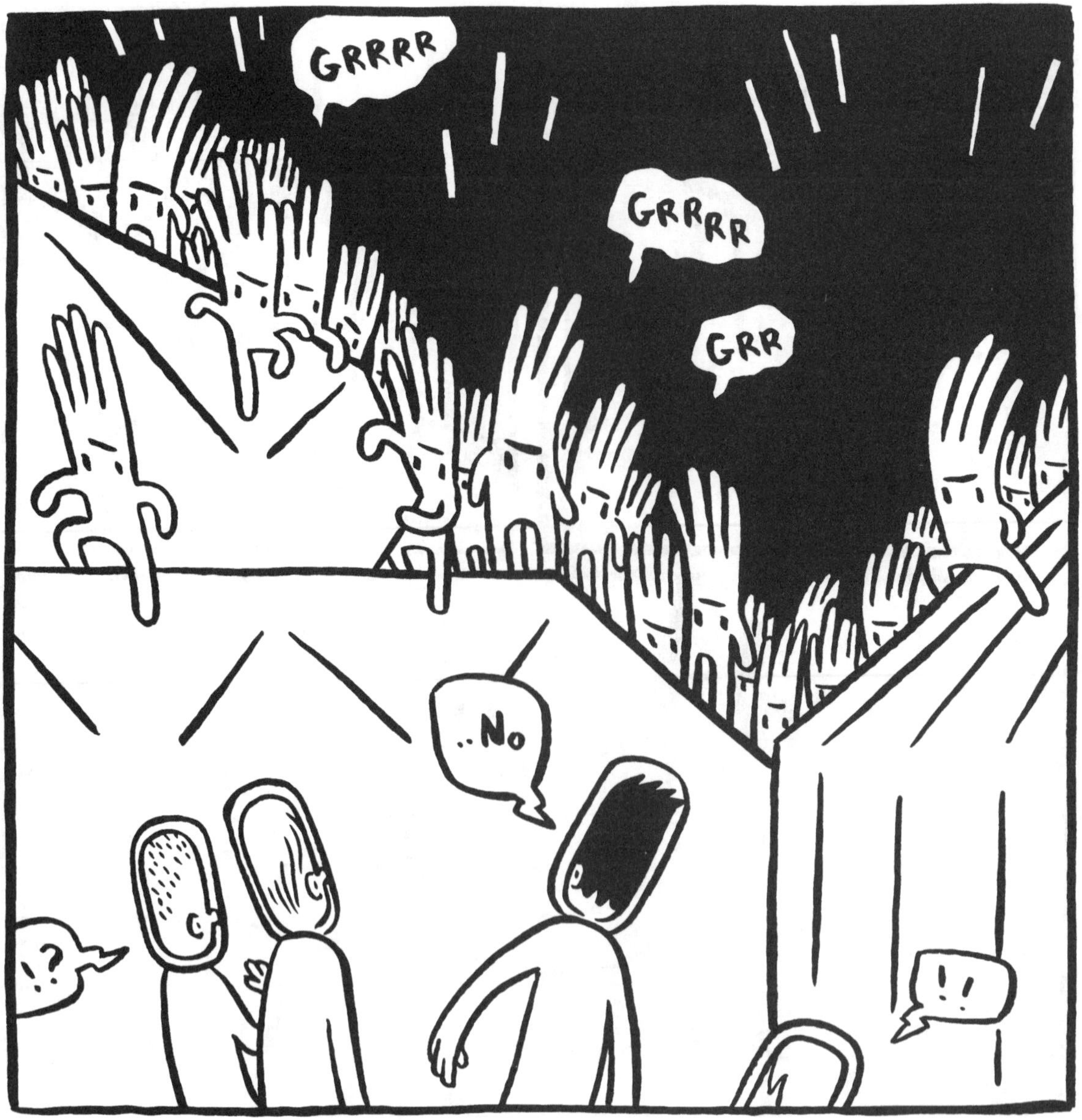
GRRRR
GRRRRR
GRR
..No
!?
!!

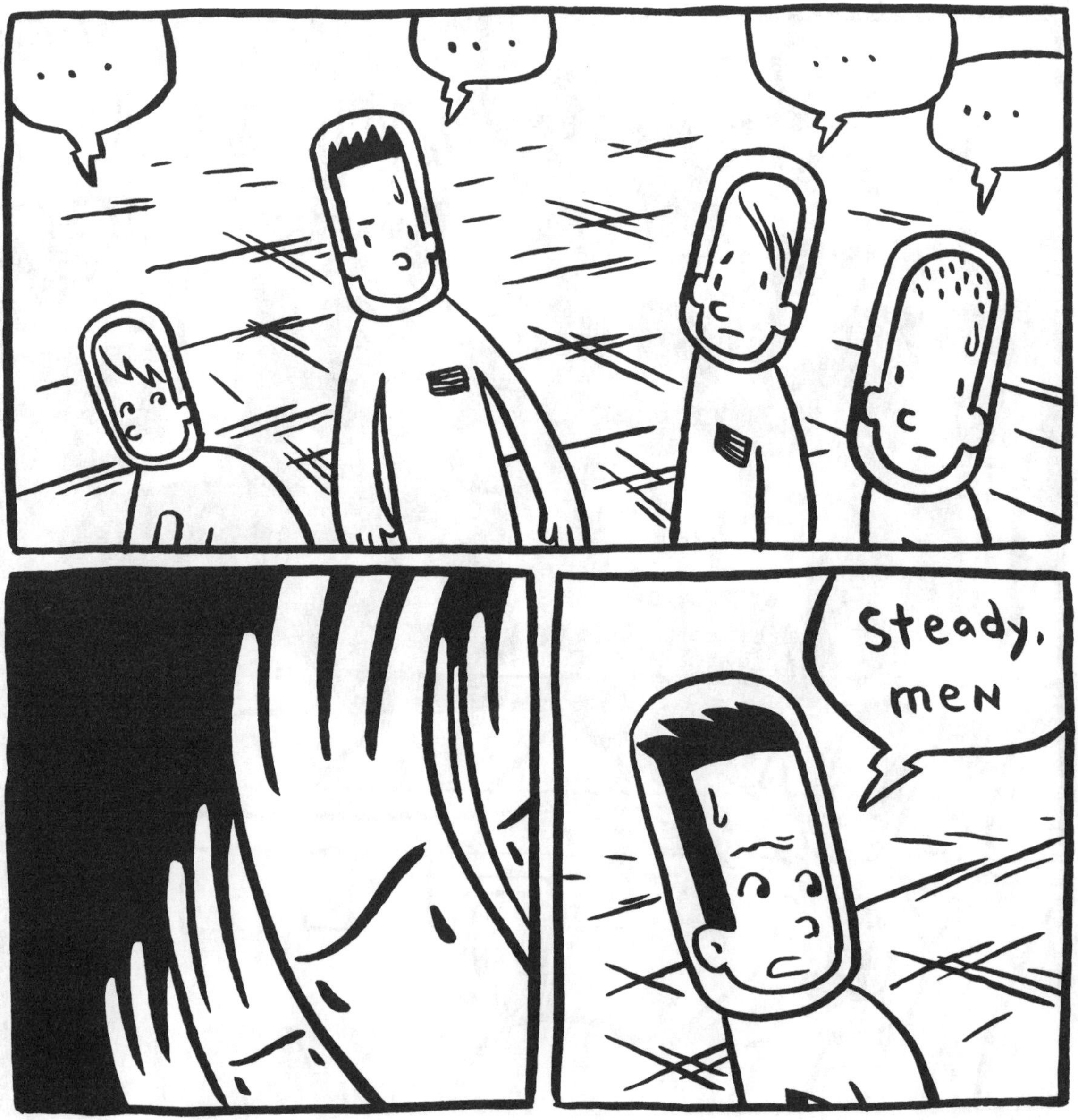
...
...
...
...
Steady, men

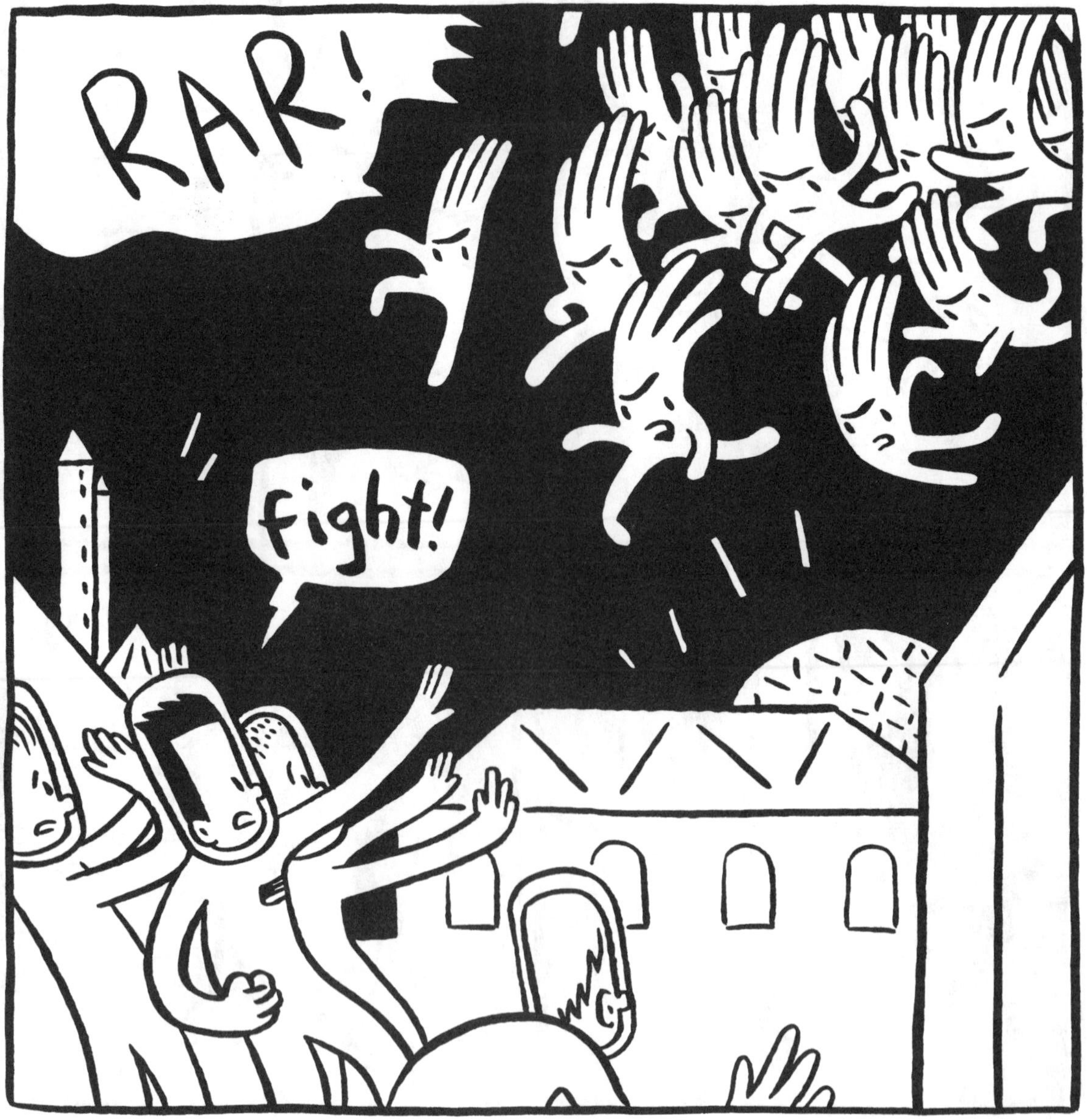
RAR!
fight!

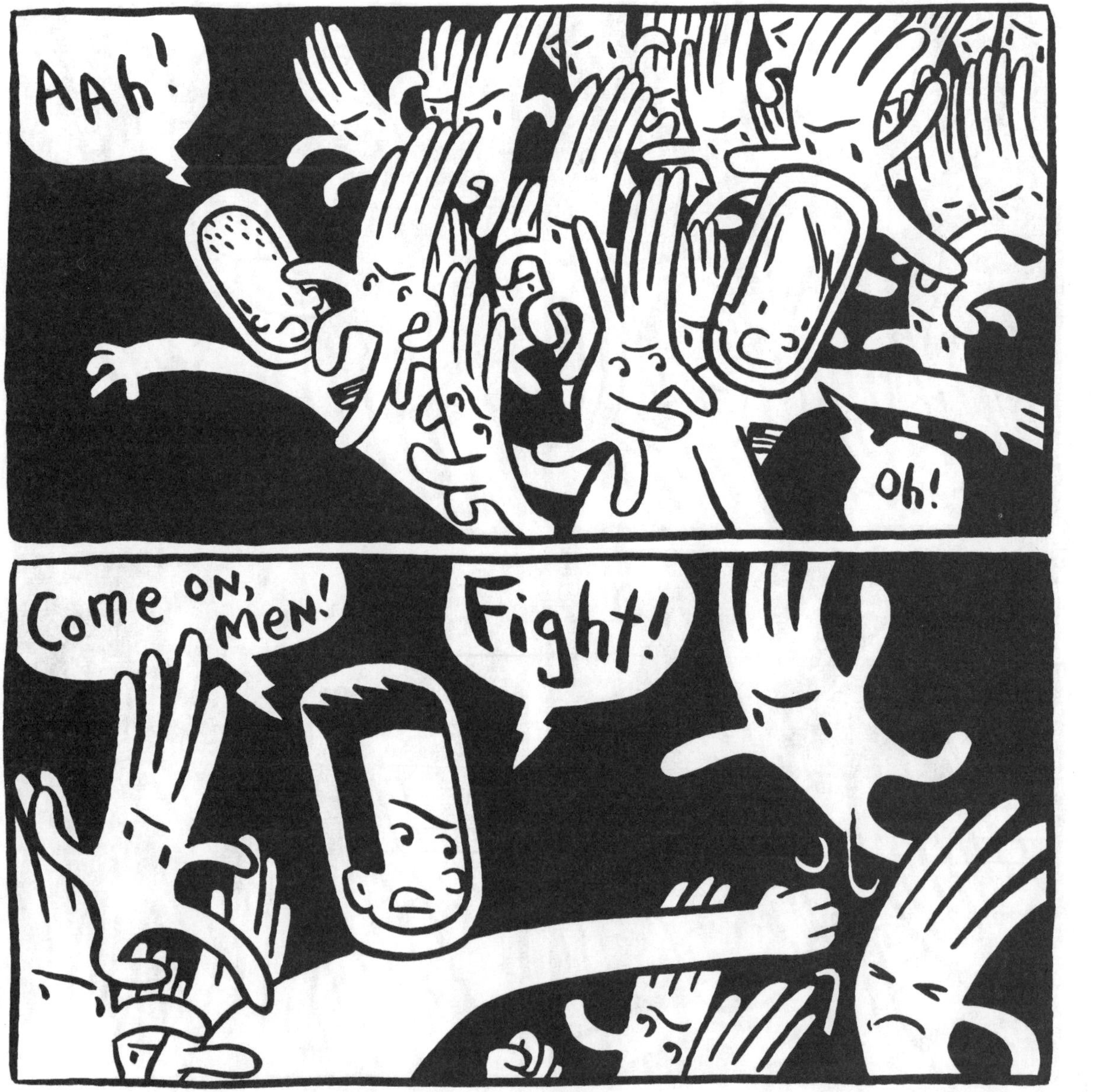
Aah!
Oh!
Come on, men!
Fight!

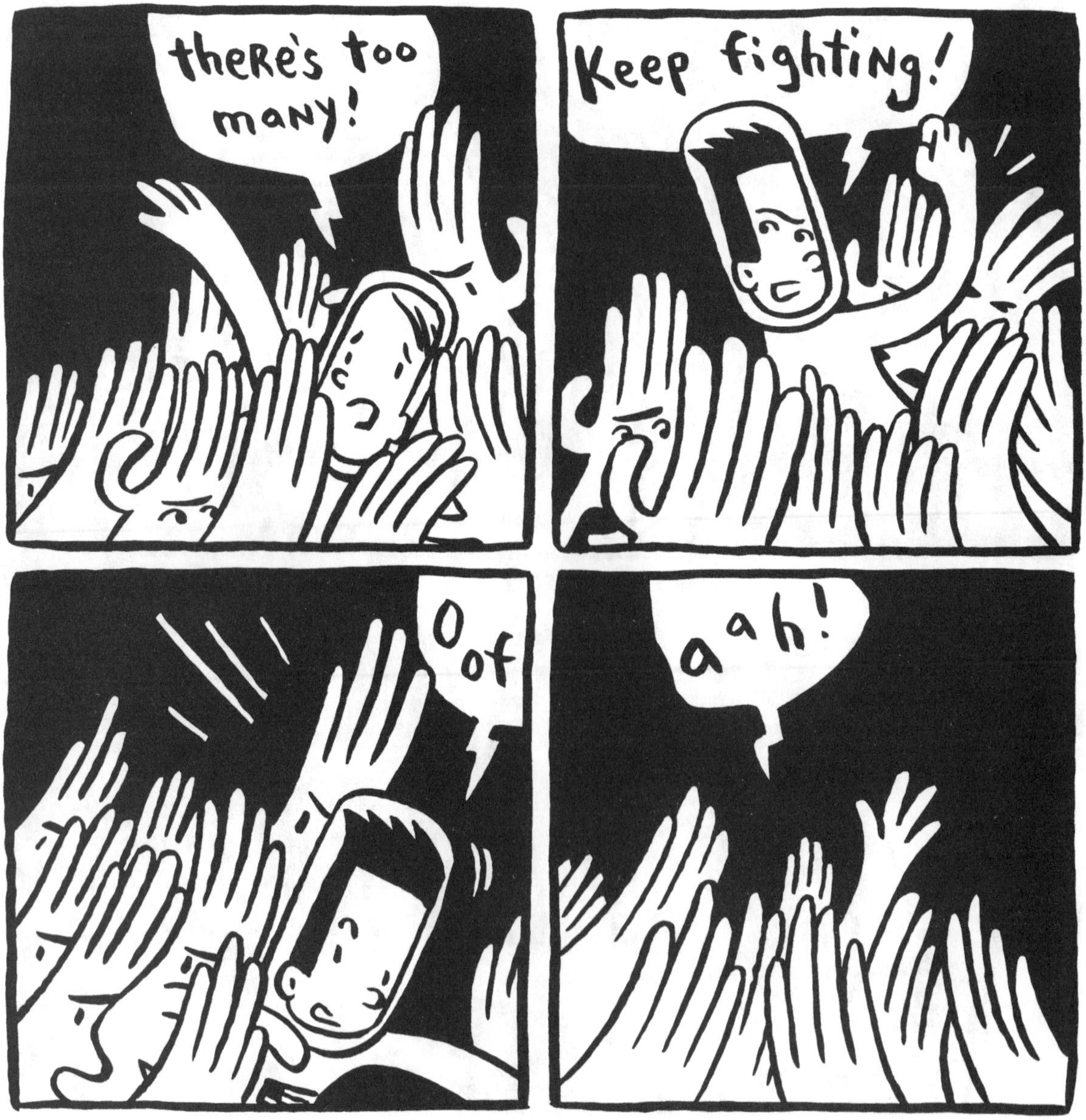
there's too many!
Keep fighting!
Oof
aah!

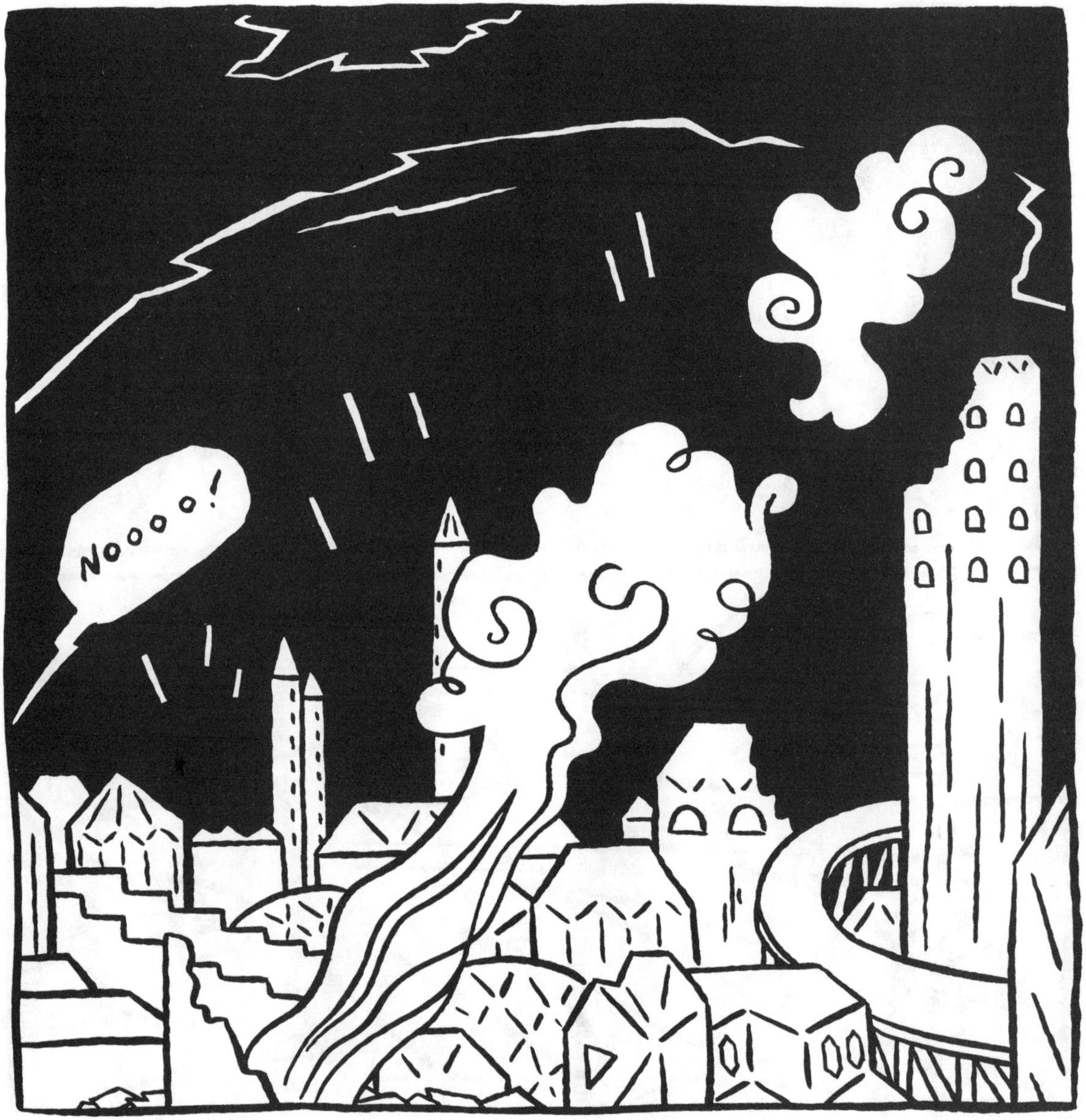
Noooo!

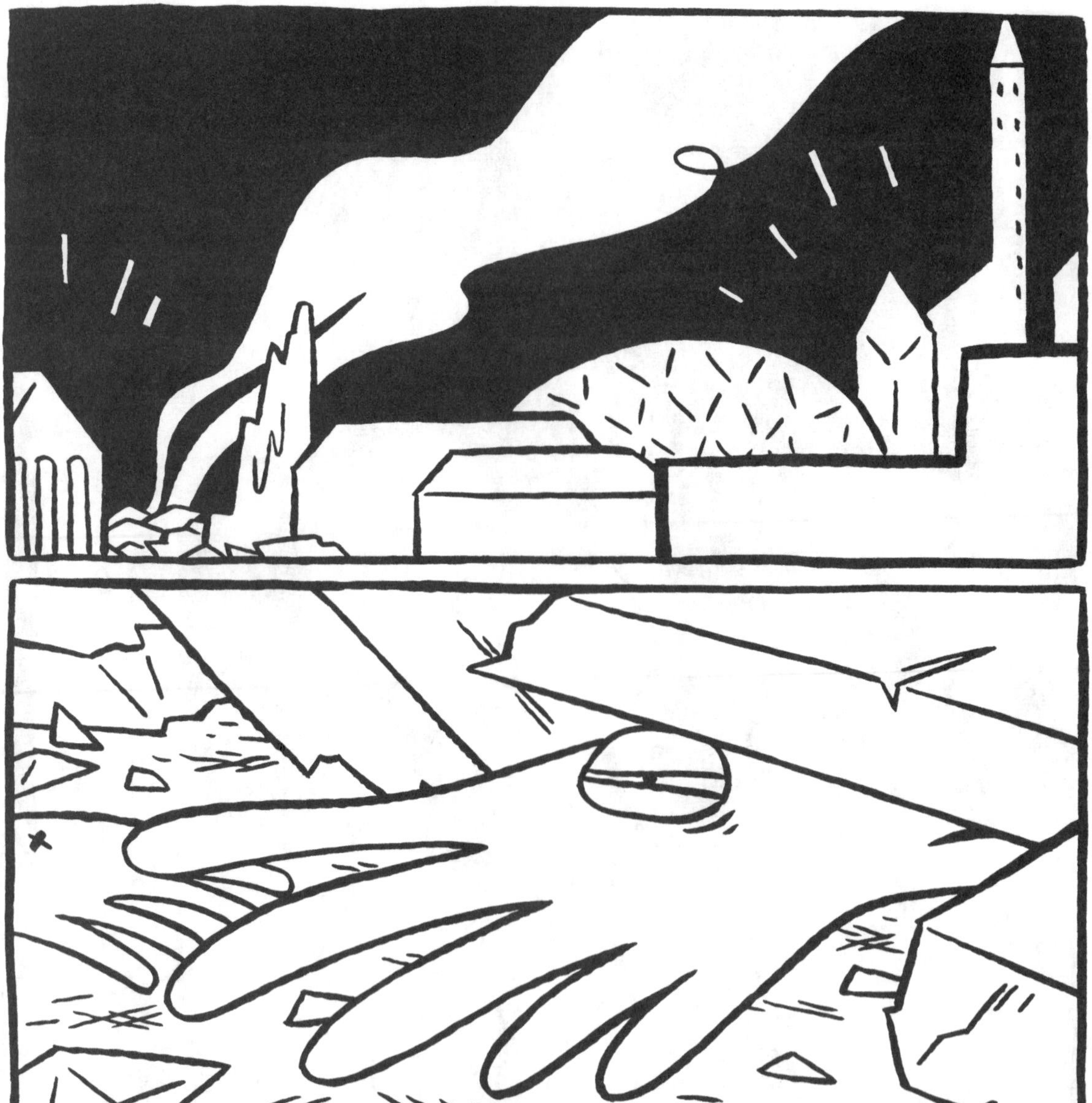

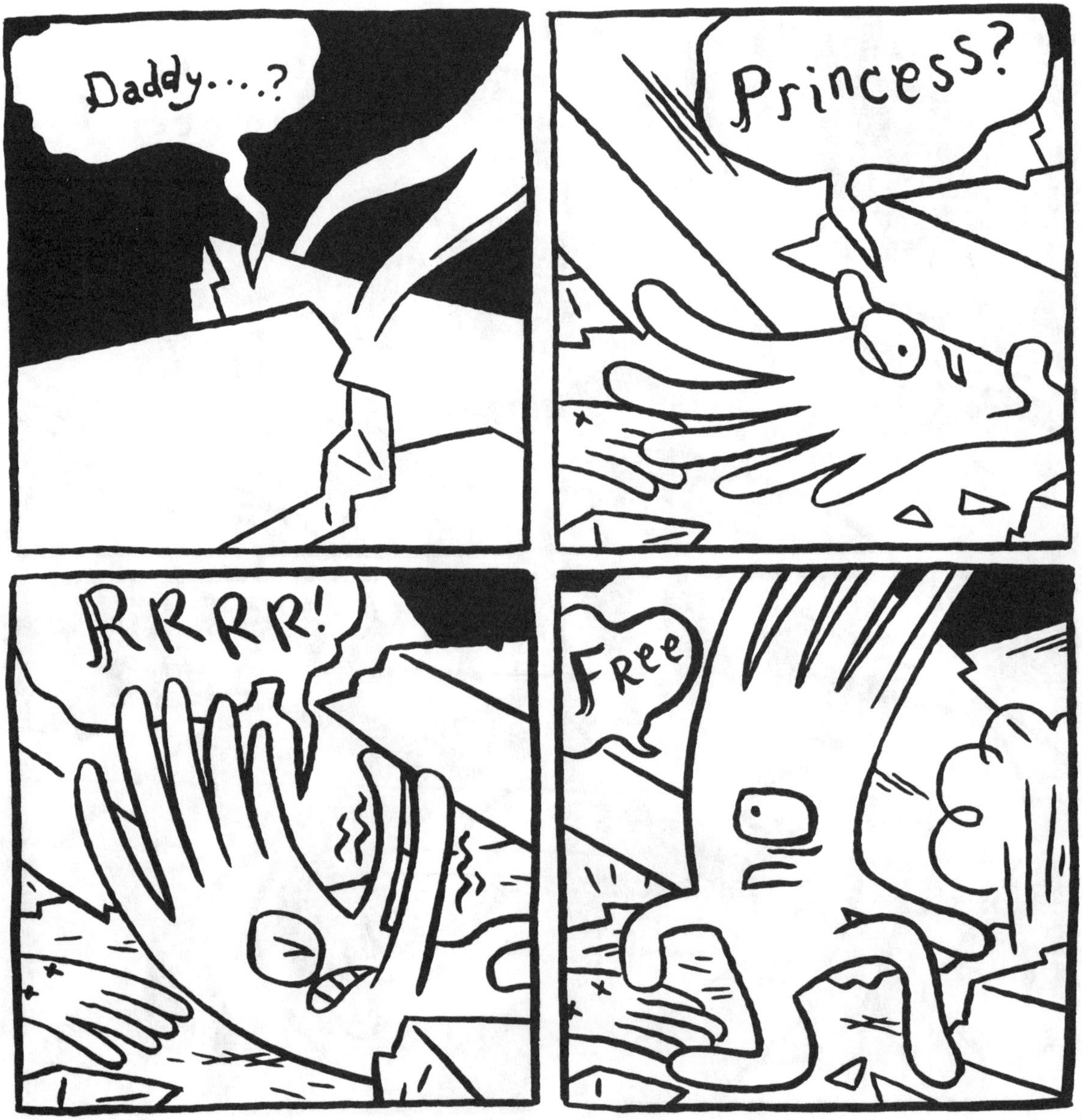
Daddy....?
Princess?
RRRR!
Free

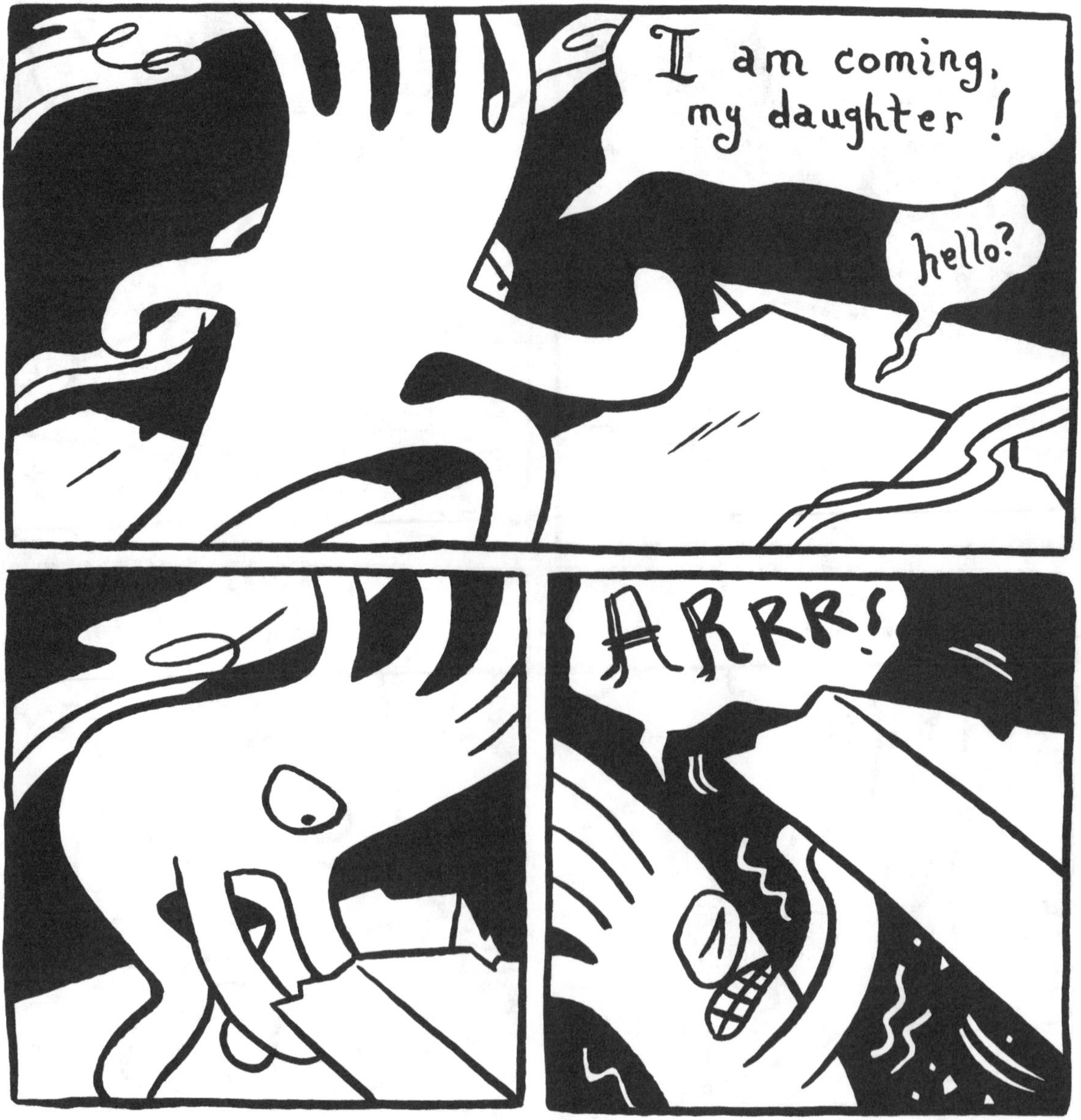
I am coming, my daughter !
hello?
ARRR!

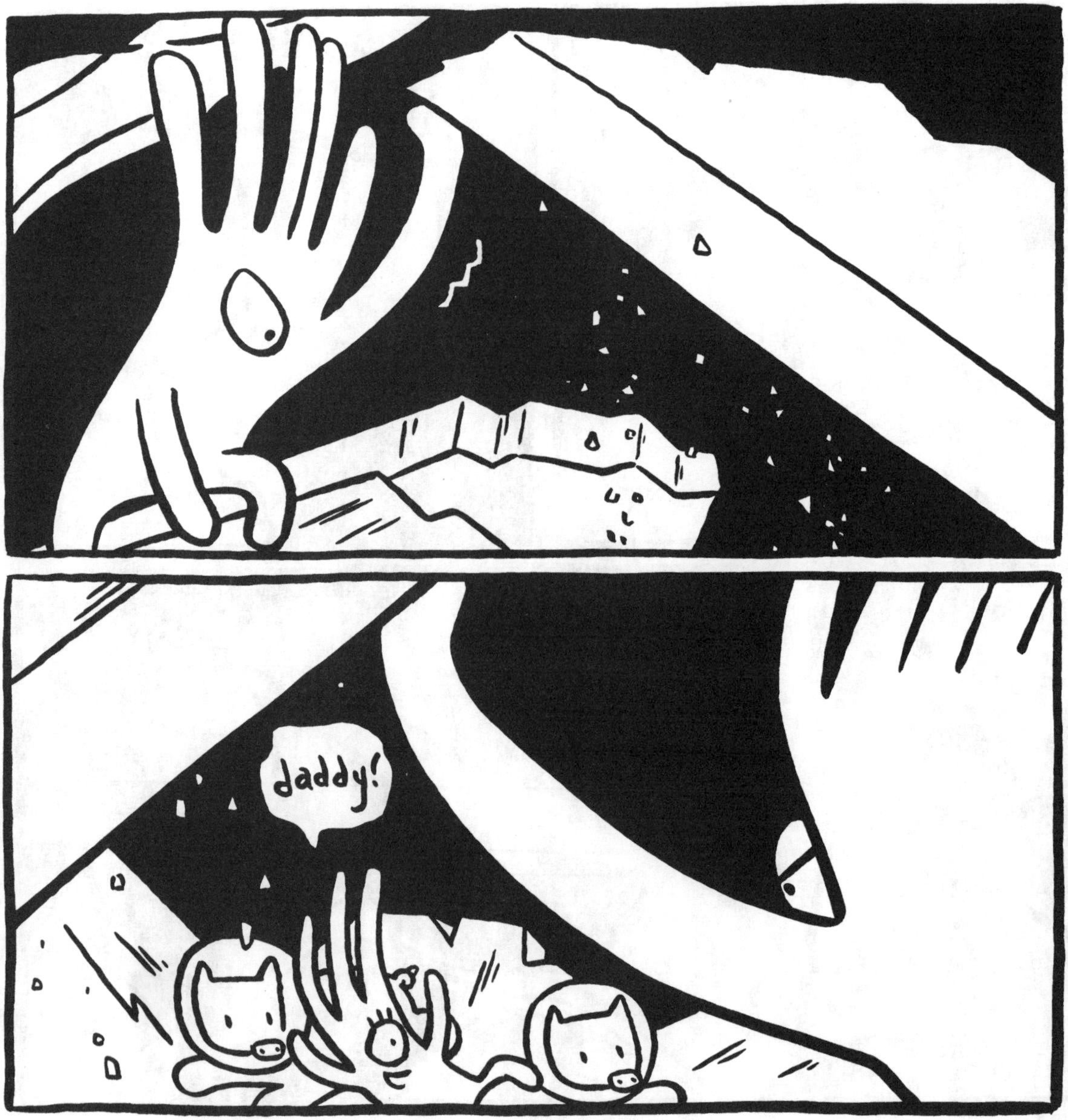
daddy!

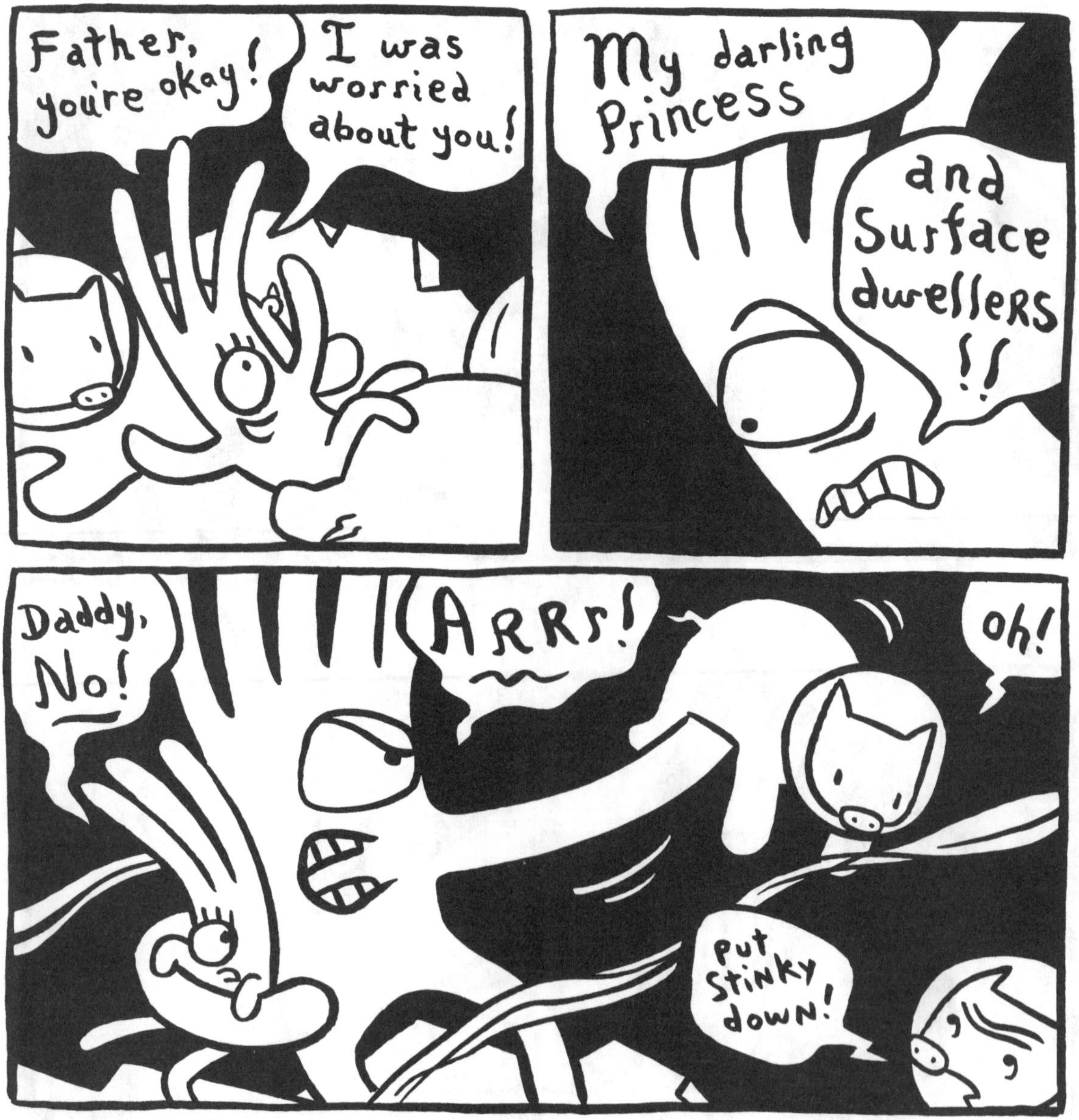
Father, you're okay!
I was worried about you!
My darling Princess
and Surface dwellers!!
Daddy, No!
ARRr!
oh!
put Stinky down!

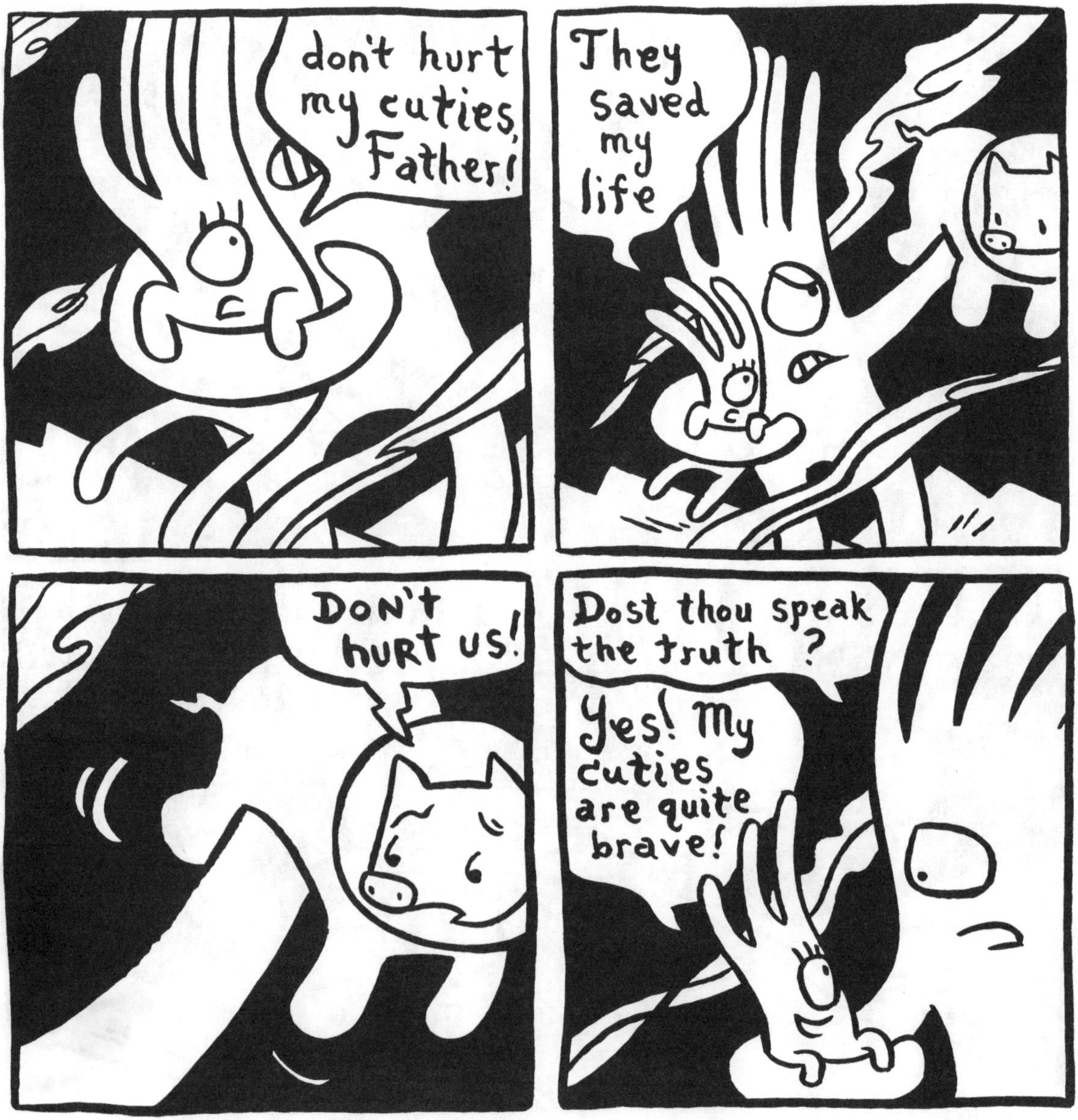
don't hurt my cuties, Father!
They saved my life
DON'T hURT US!
Dost thou speak the truth ?
Yes! My cuties are quite brave!

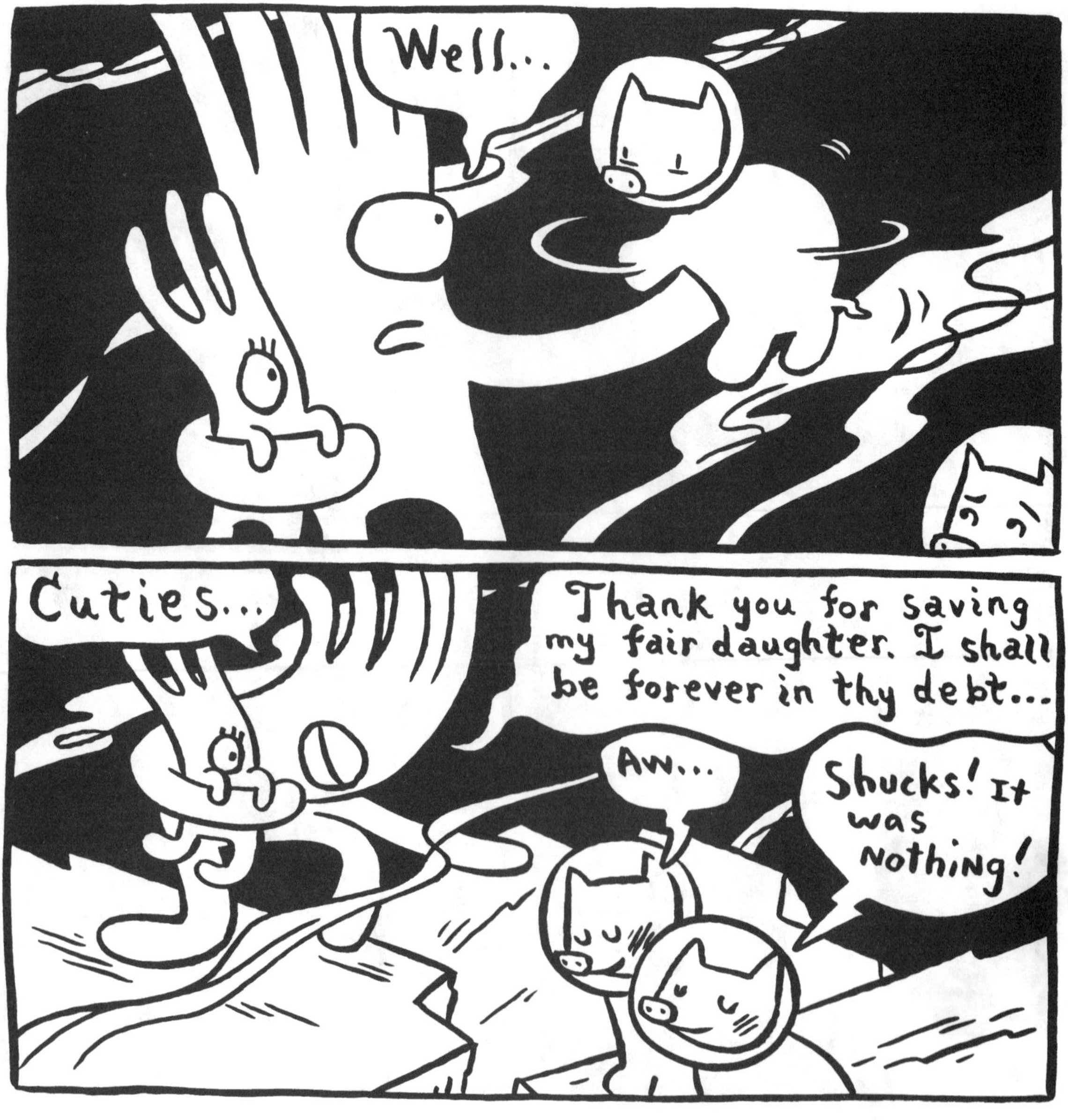
Well...
Cuties...
Thank you for saving my fair daughter. I shall be forever in thy debt...
Aw...
Shucks! It was nothing!

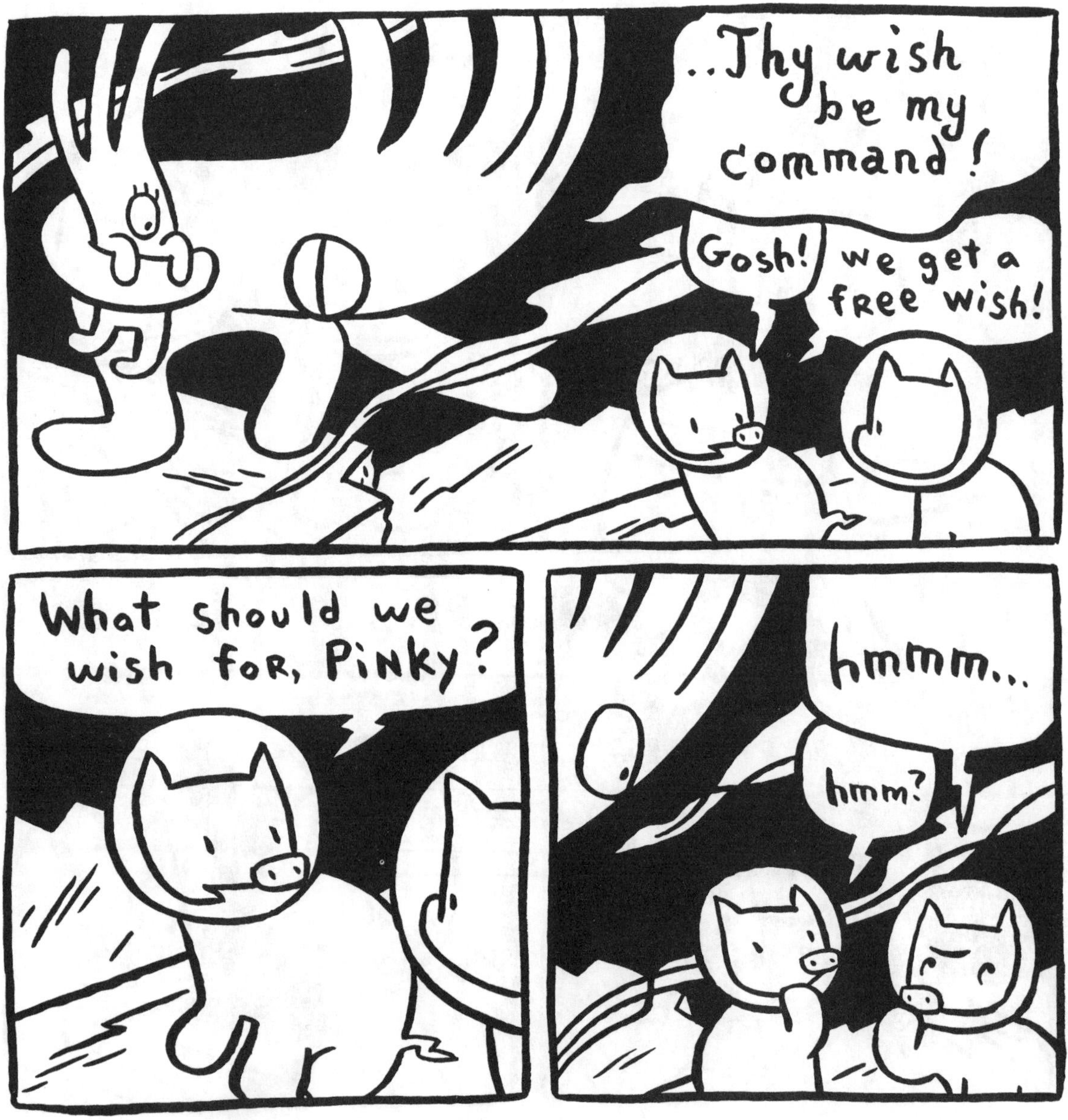
..Thy wish be my command!
Gosh!
we get a free wish!
What should we wish for, Pinky?
hmmm...
hmm?

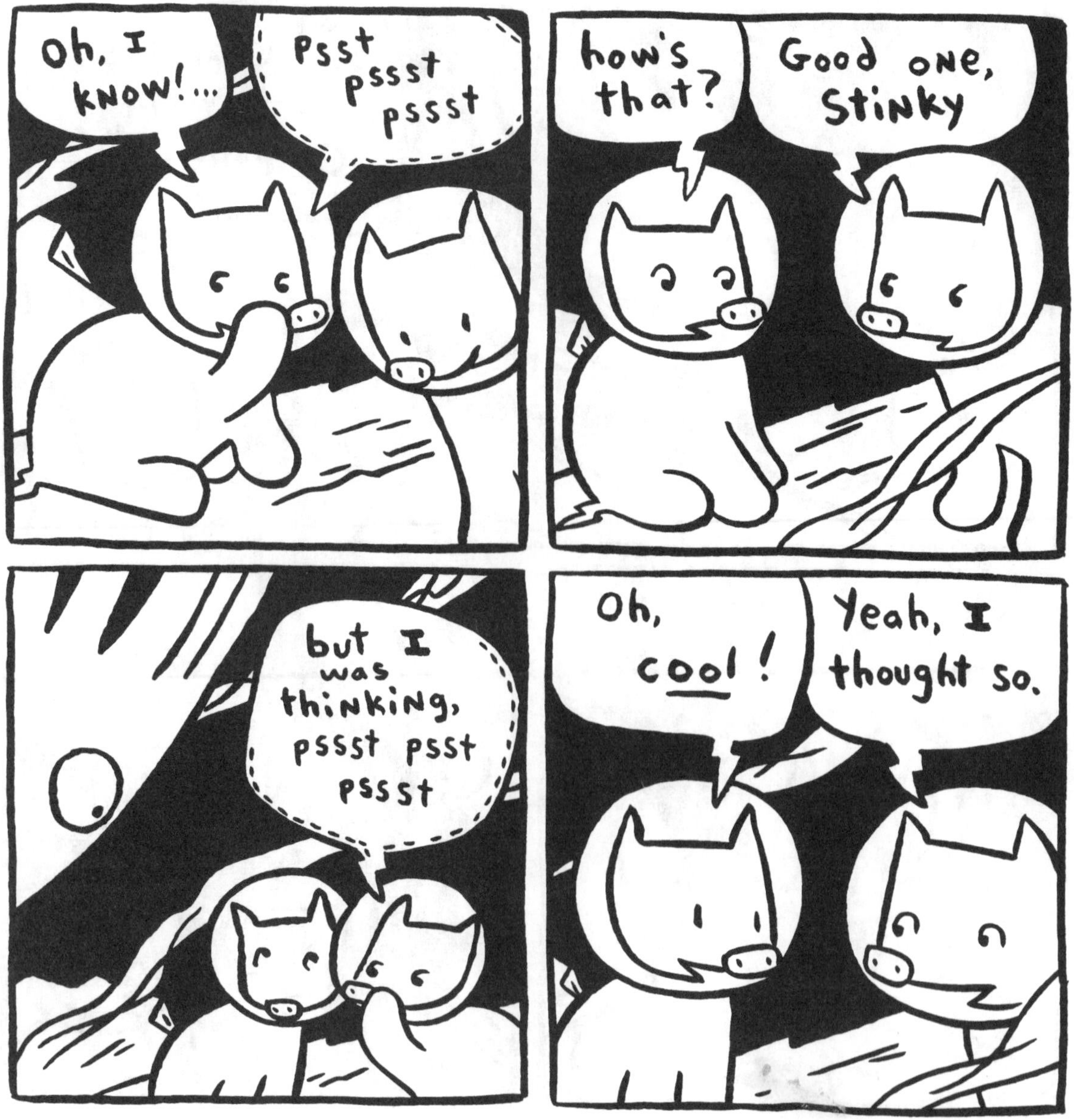
Oh, I know!...
Psst pssst pssst
how's that?
Good one, Stinky
but I was thinking, pssst psst pssst
Oh, cool!
Yeah, I thought so.

We're ready, Mr. Moon King
and what dost thou desire?
Kisses?
Well, actually, Pinky here would like to have our rocket ship repaired...
So we can continue exploring space..
... But Stinky was wondering if we could have a big party celebration and invite all our friends
tee hee

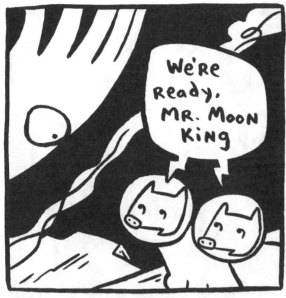

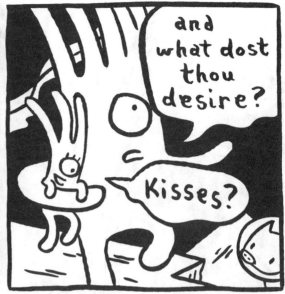

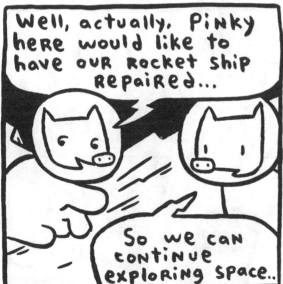

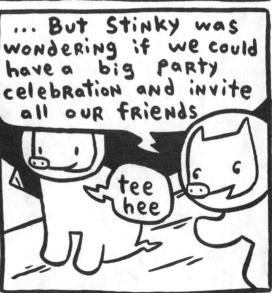

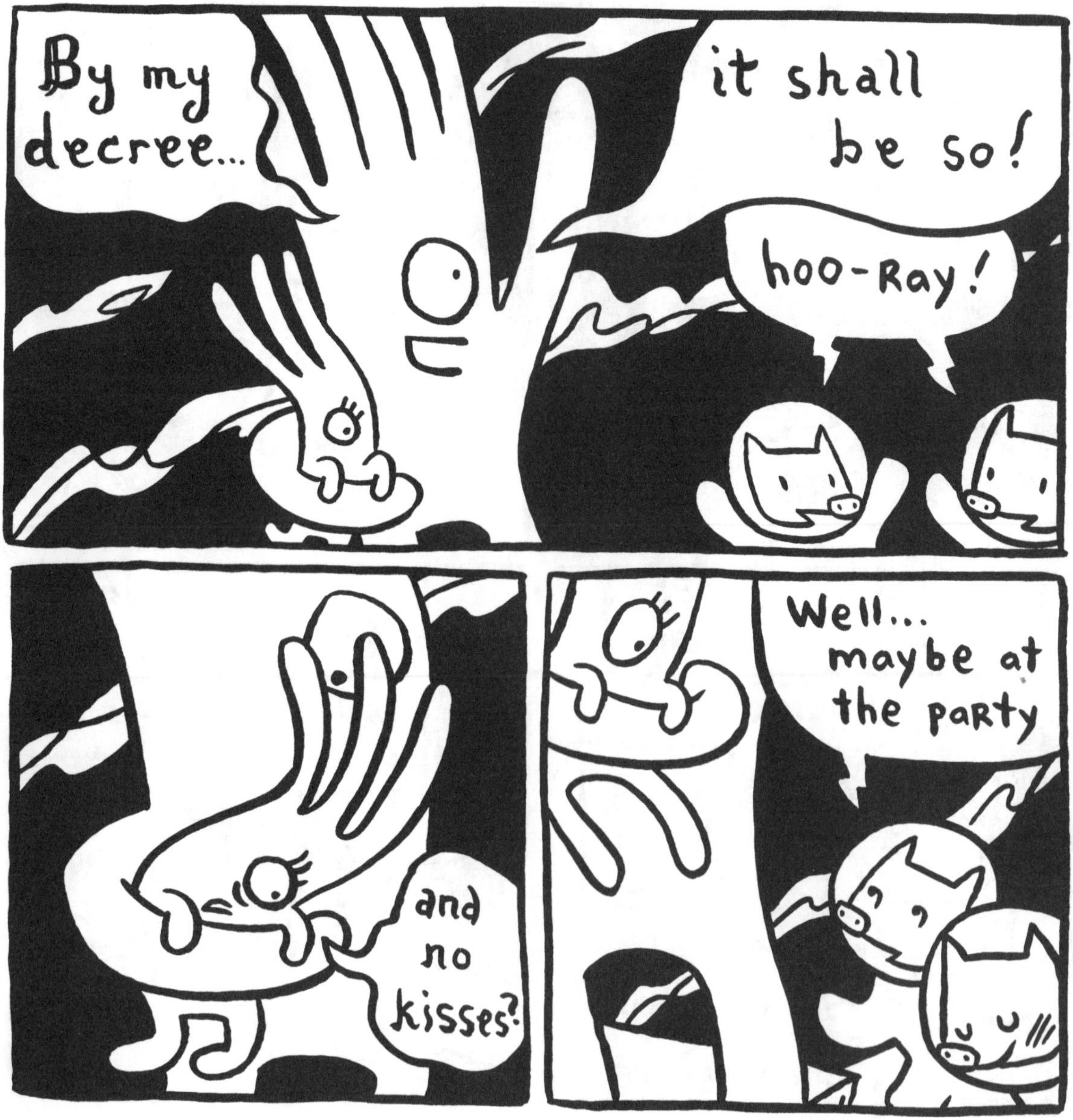
By my decree...
it shall be so!
hoo-Ray!
and no kisses?
Well... maybe at the party

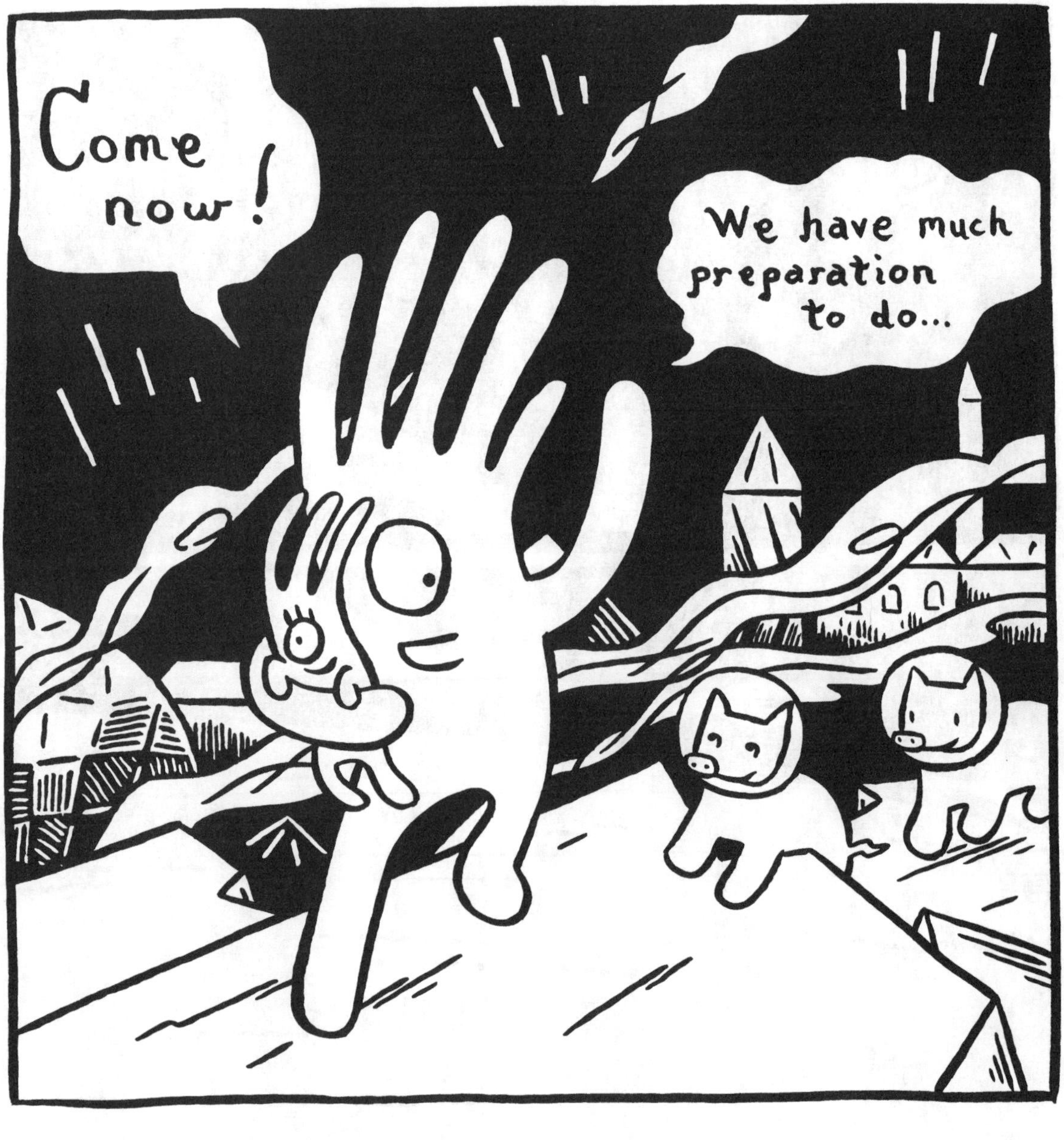
Come now!
We have much preparation to do...

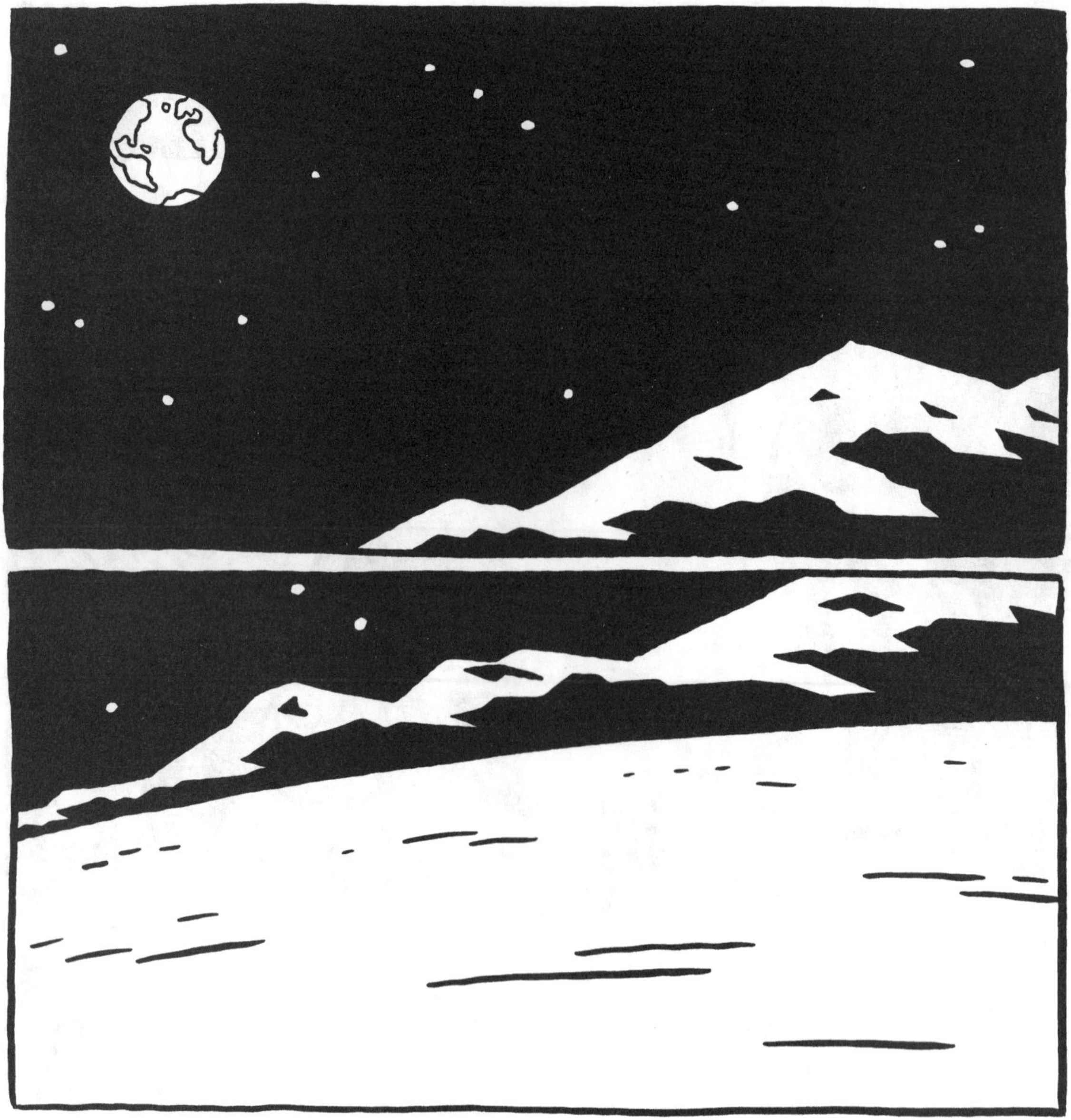

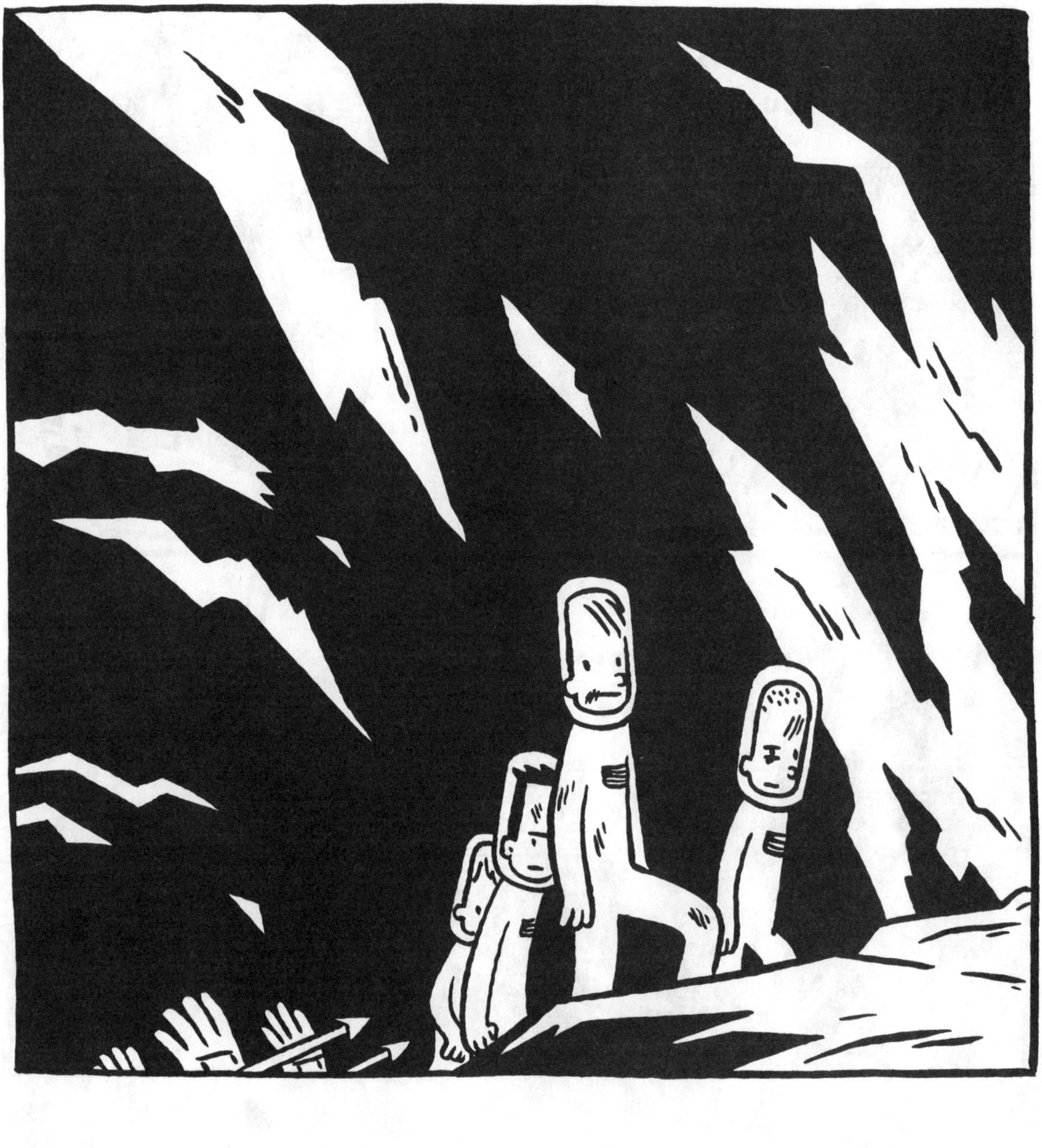

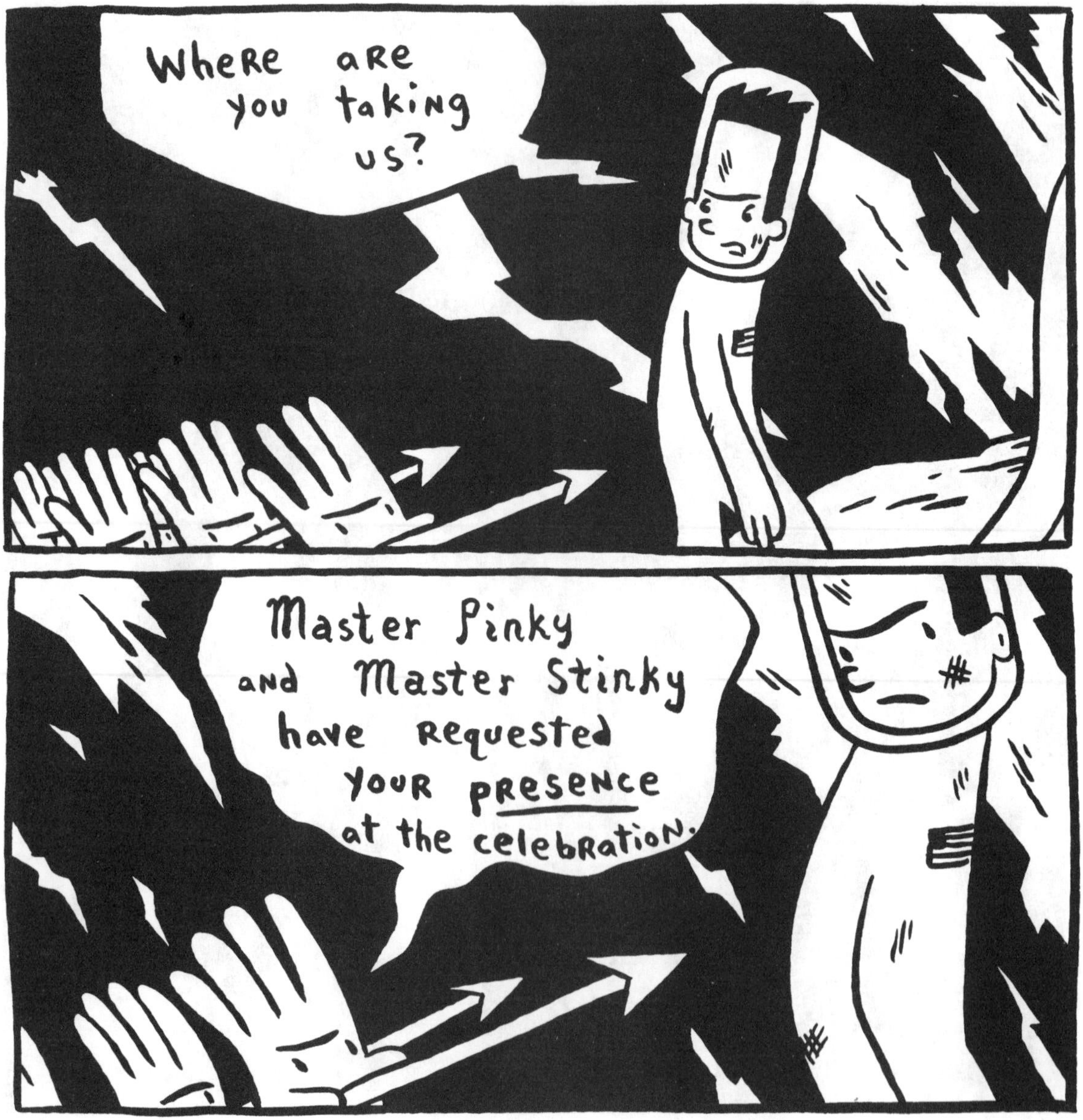
Where are you taking us?
Master Pinky and Master Stinky have requested your PRESENCE at the celebration.

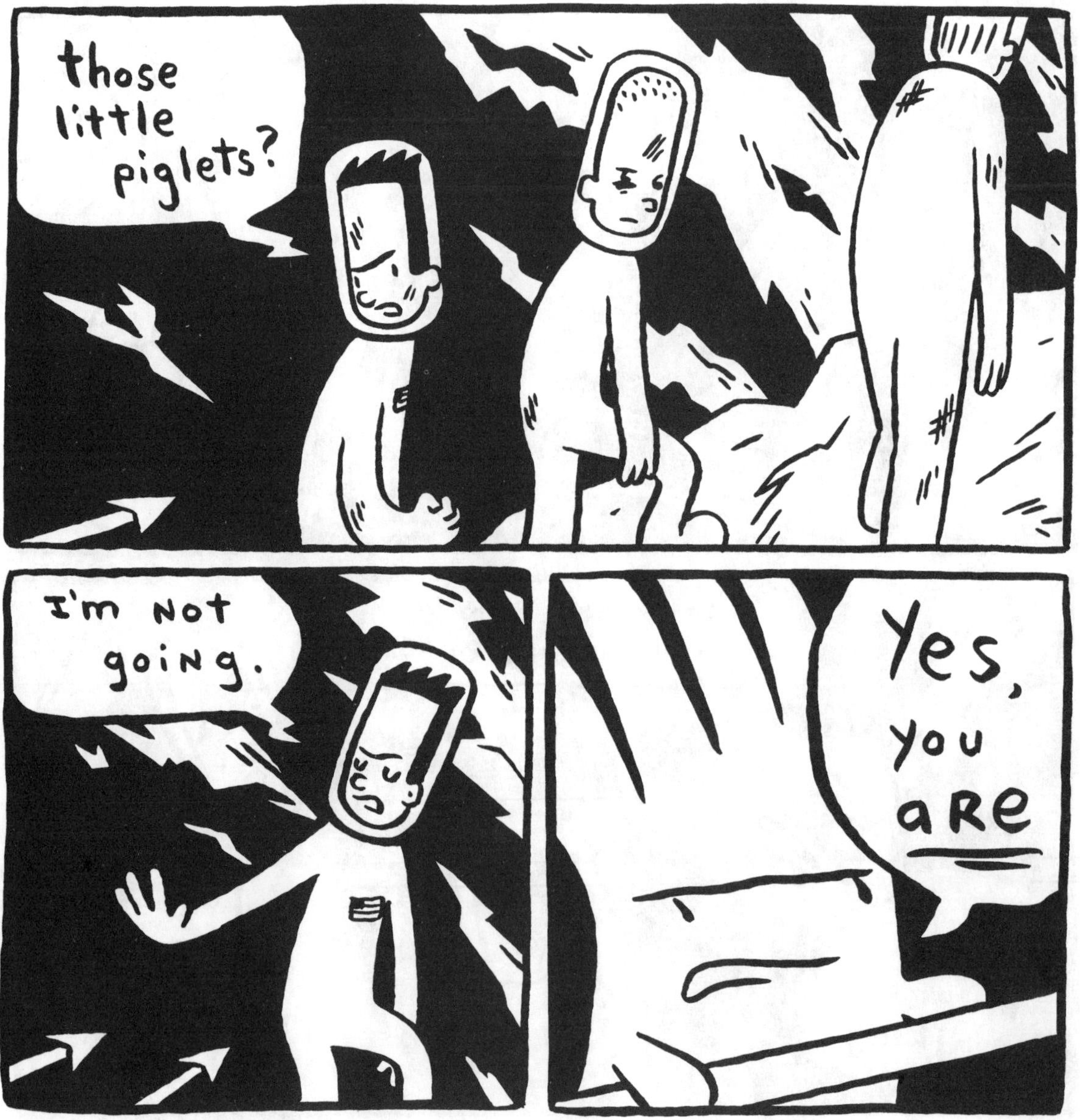
those little piglets?
I'm not going.
Yes, you are

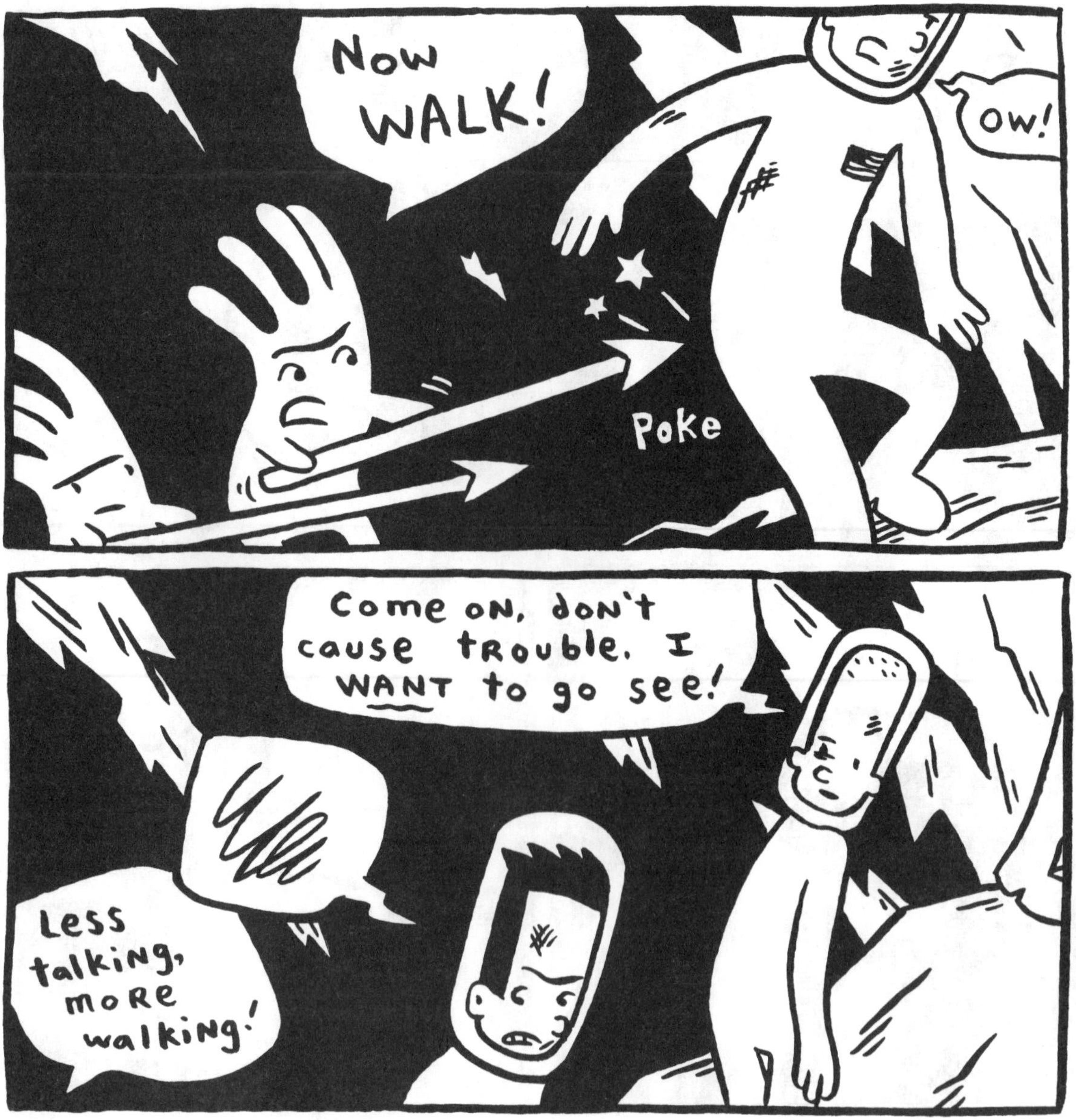
Now WALK!
OW!
Poke
Come on, don't cause trouble. I WANT to go see!
Less talking, more walking!

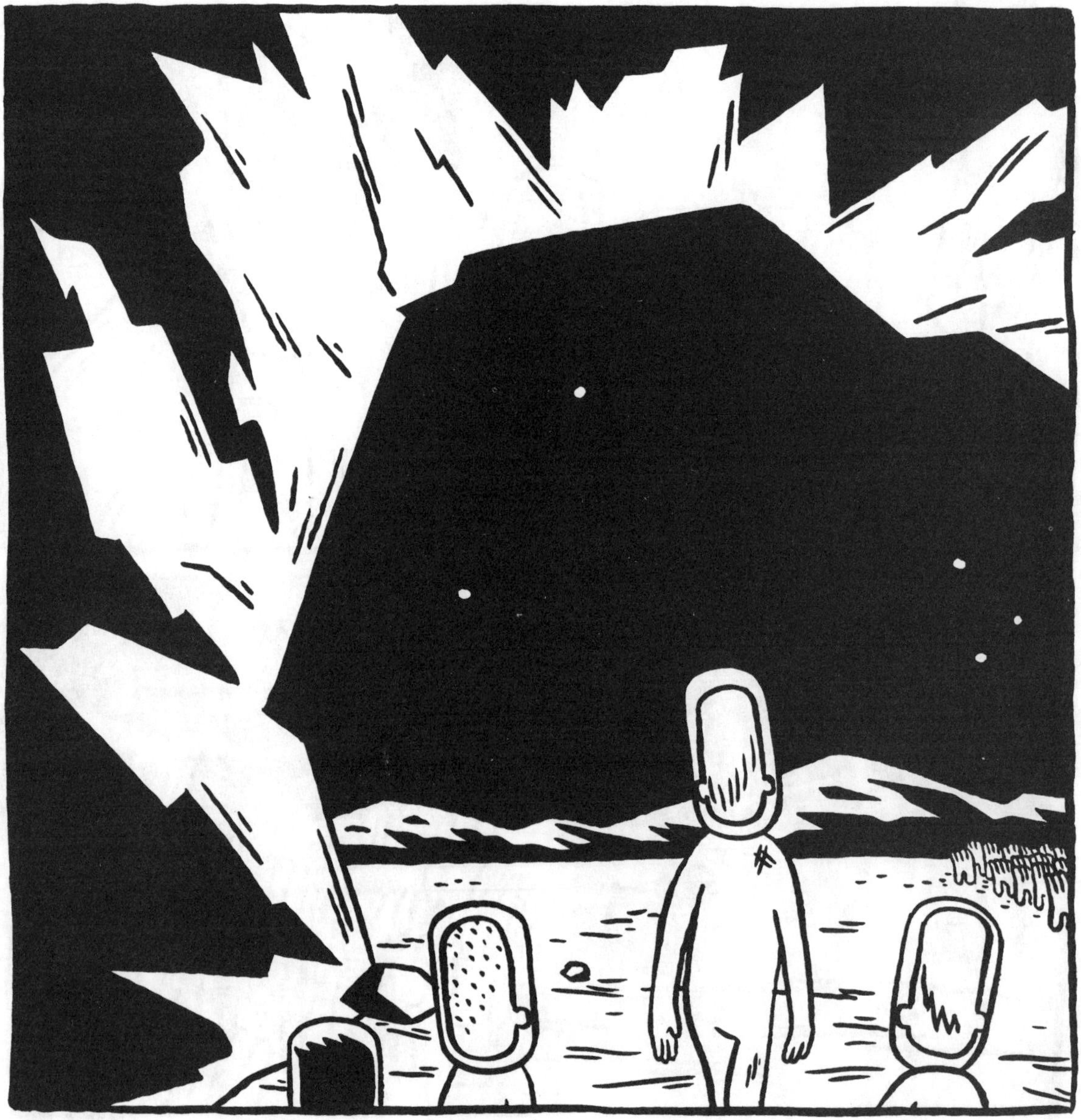

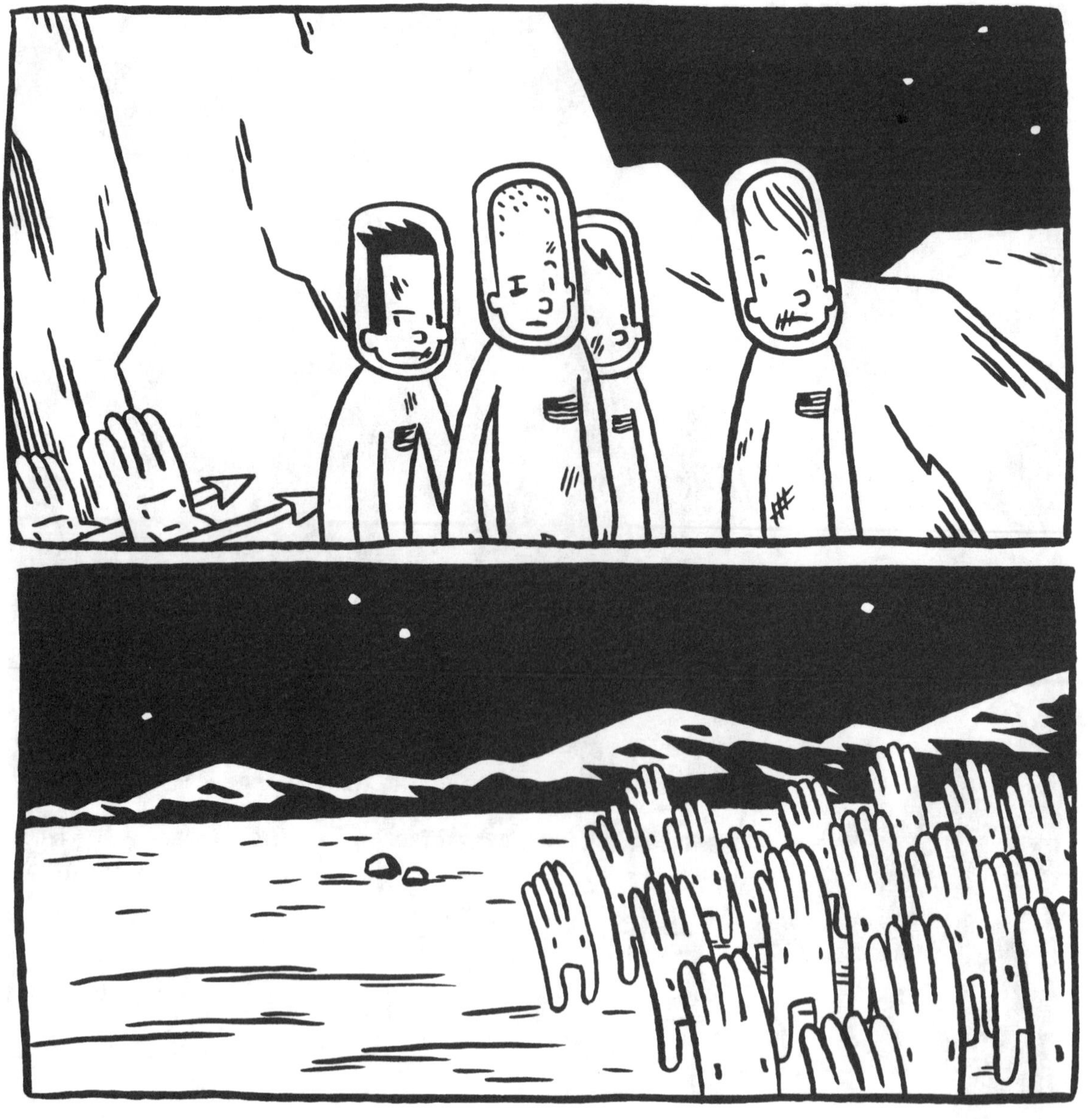

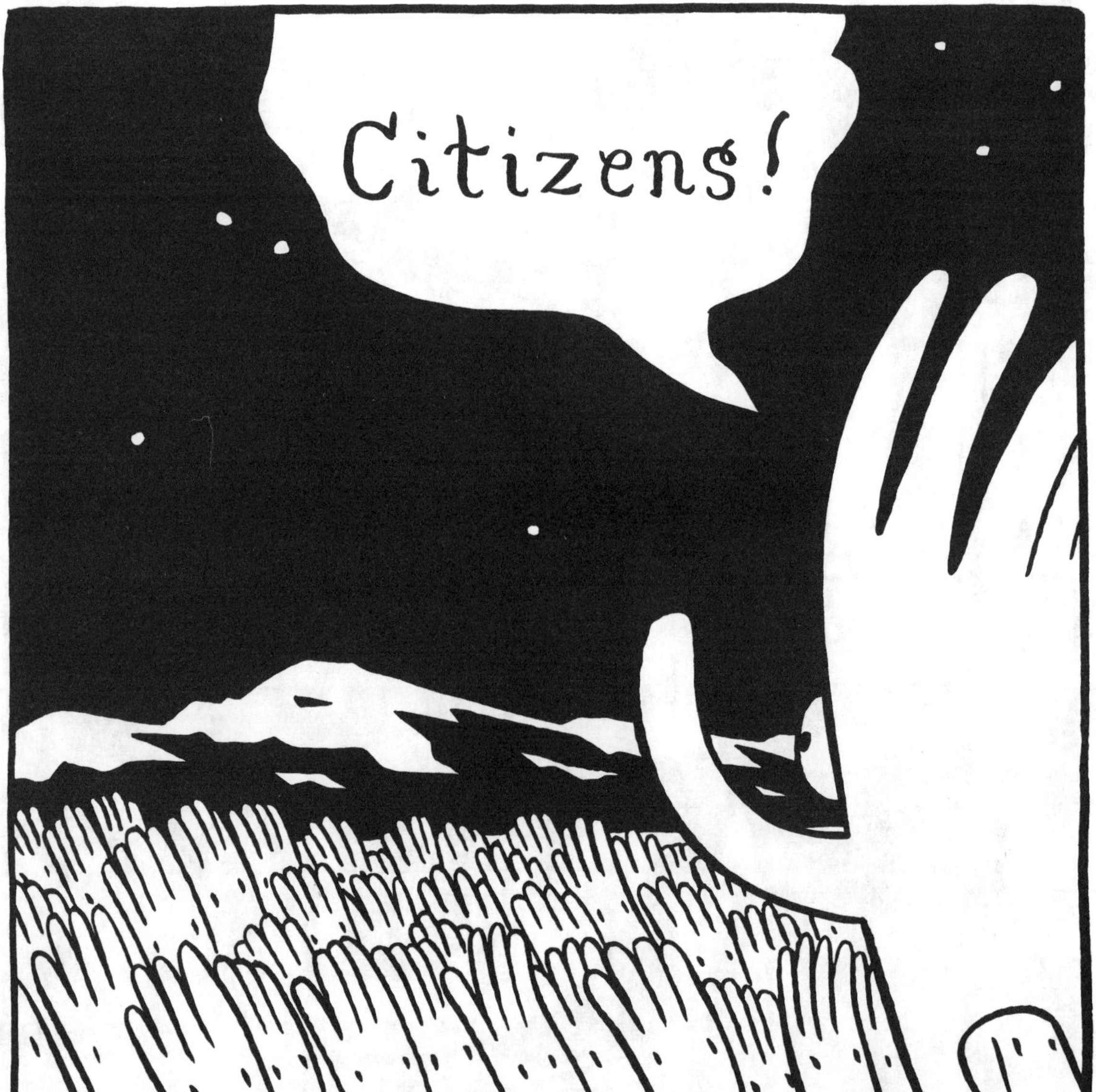
Citizens!

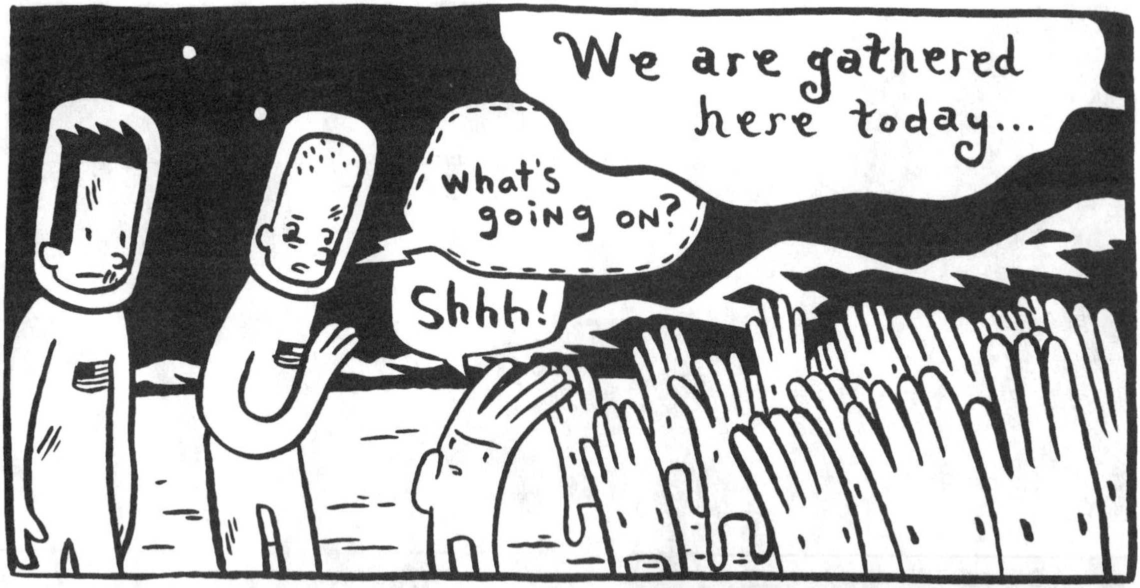
We are gathered here today...
what's going on?
Shhh!

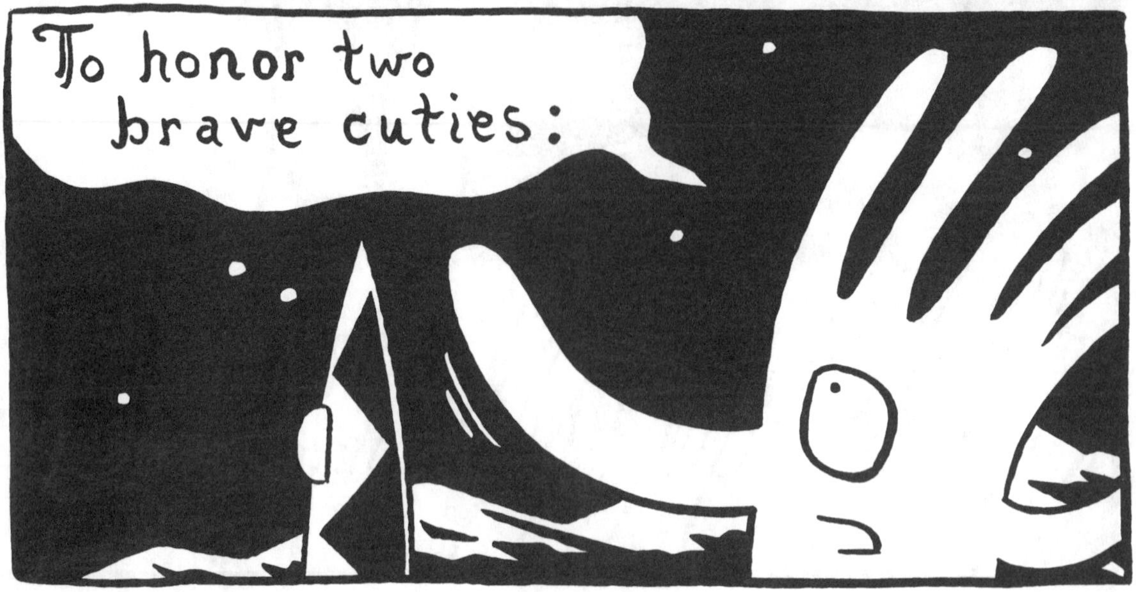
To honor two brave cuties:

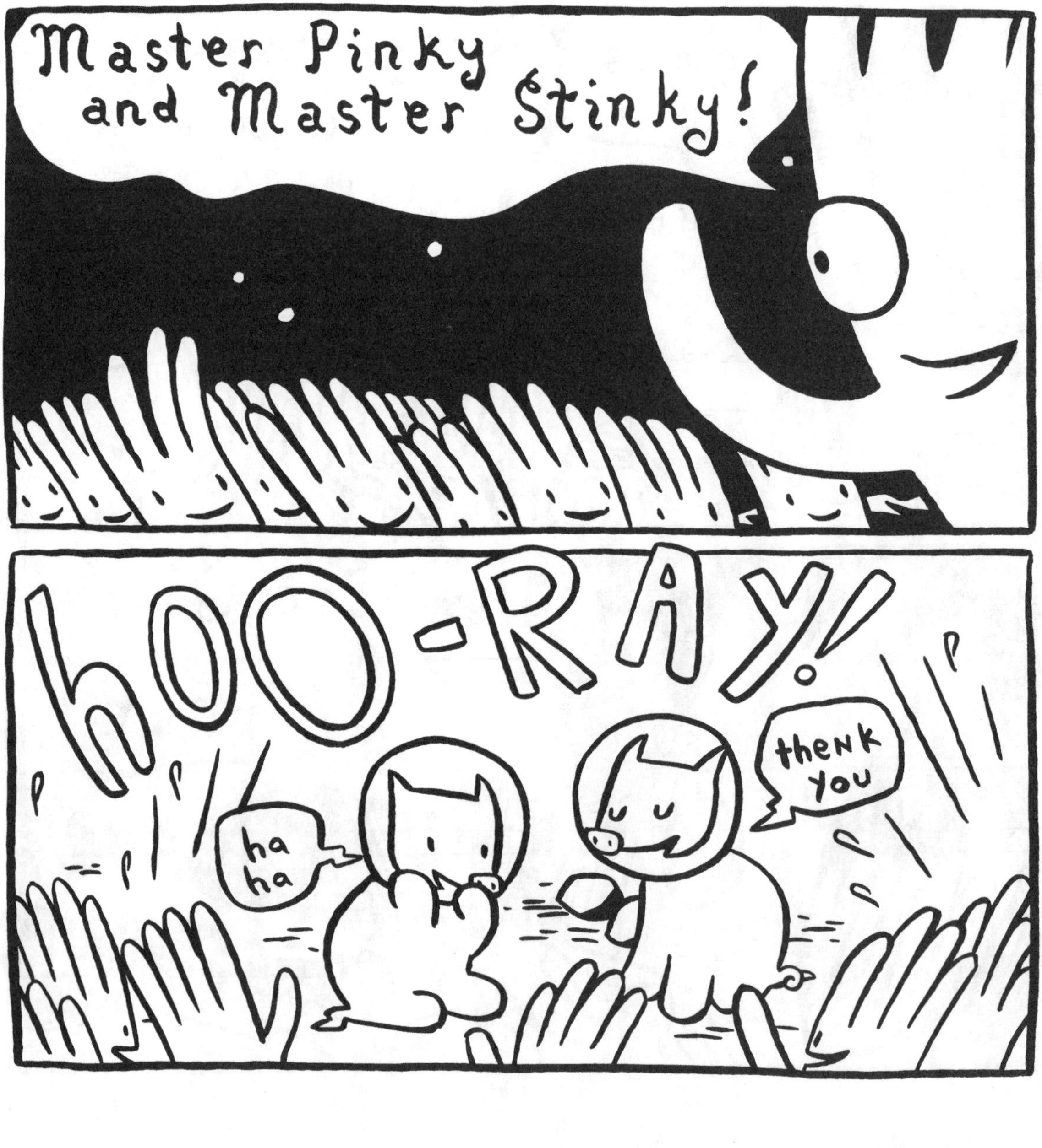
Master Pinky and Master Stinky!
HOO-RAY!
ha ha
thenk you

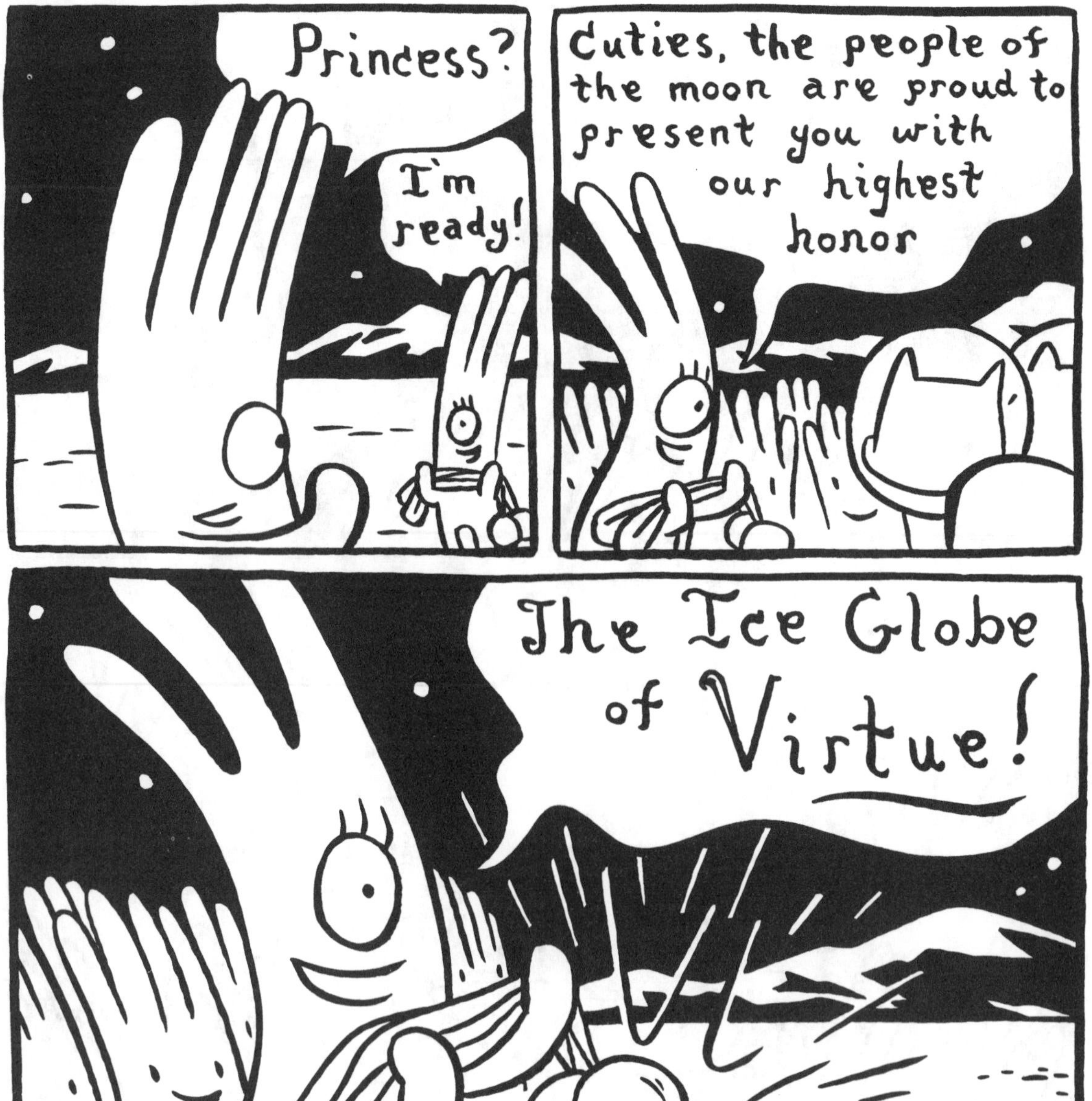
Princess?
I'm ready!
Cuties, the people of the moon are proud to present you with our highest honor
The Ice Globe of Virtue!

Master Stinky
...and Master Pinky
May the Great Spirit guide you on your journey to Pluto!

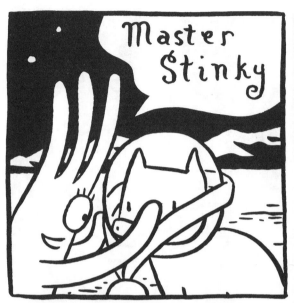

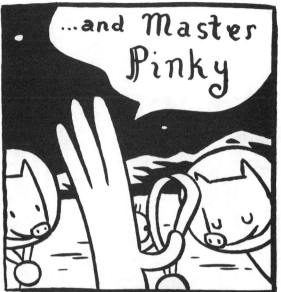

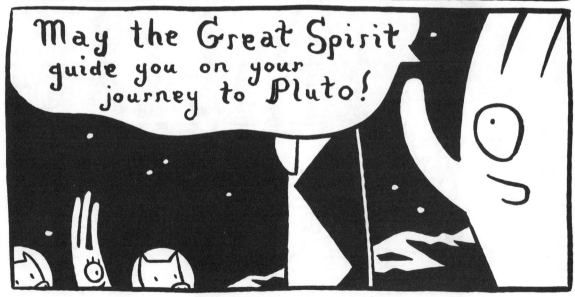

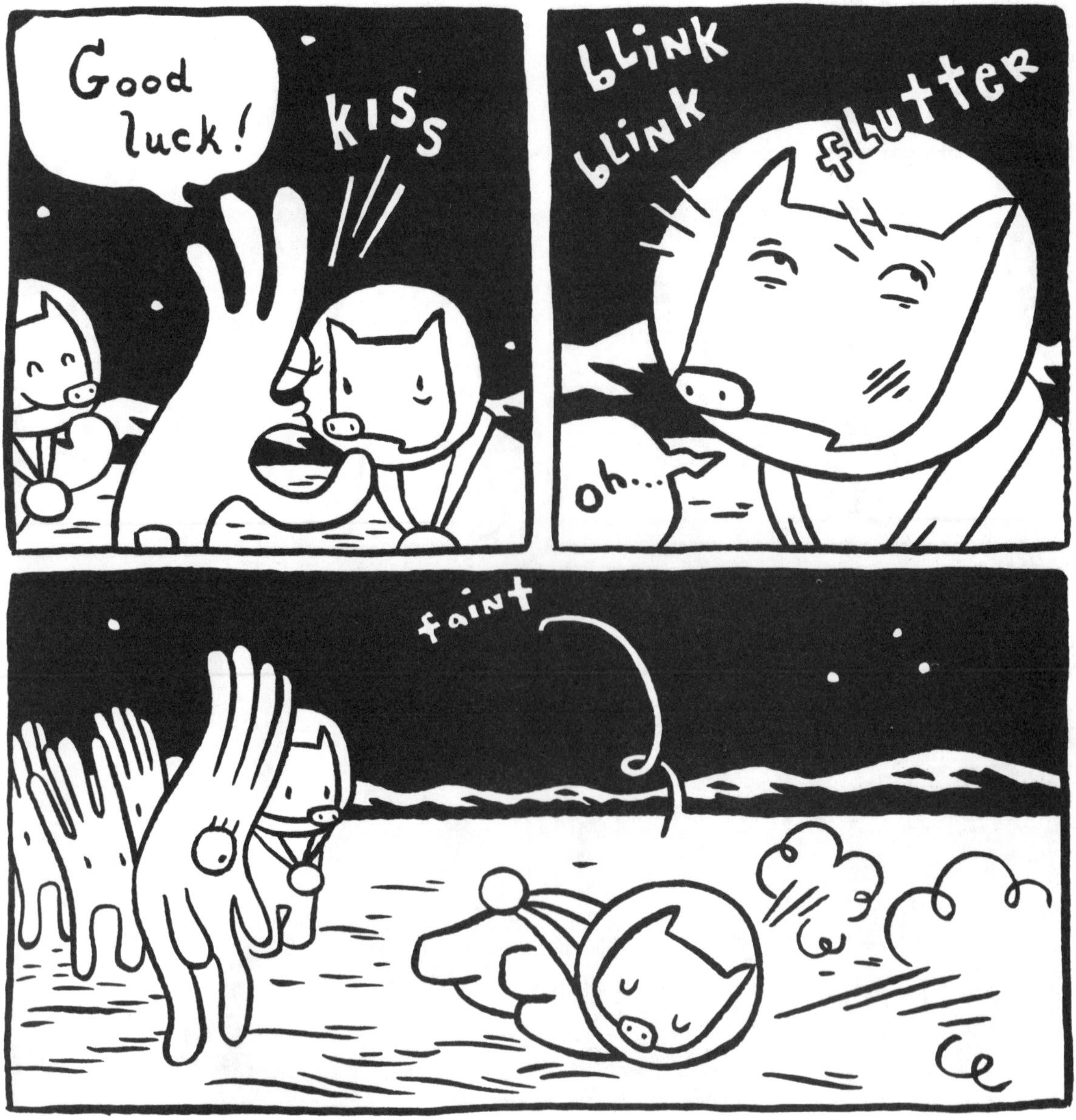

Good luck!
KISS
blink
blink
flutter
oh...
faint

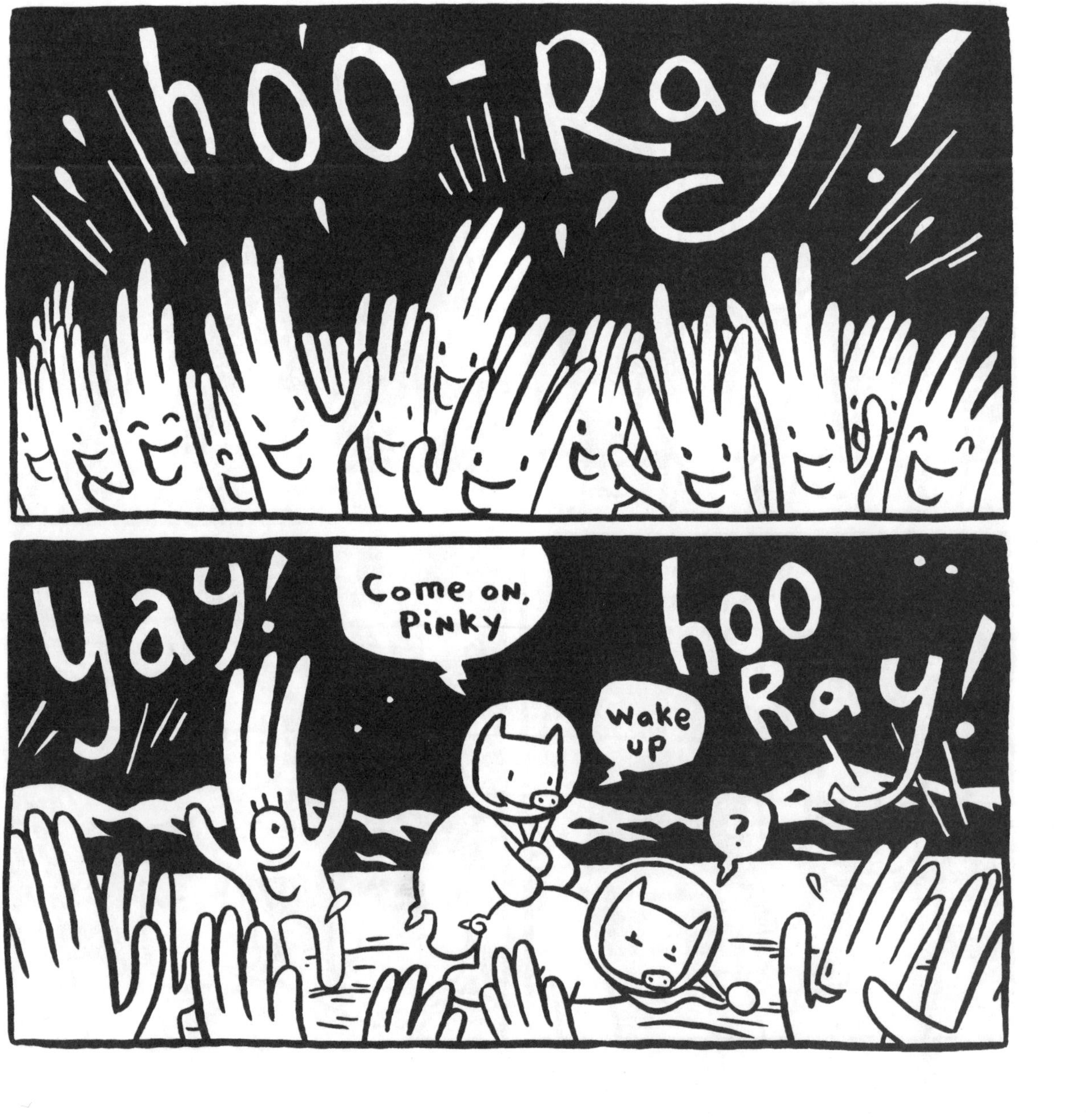
hoo-Ray!
yay!
Come on, Pinky
hoo Ray!
wake up
?

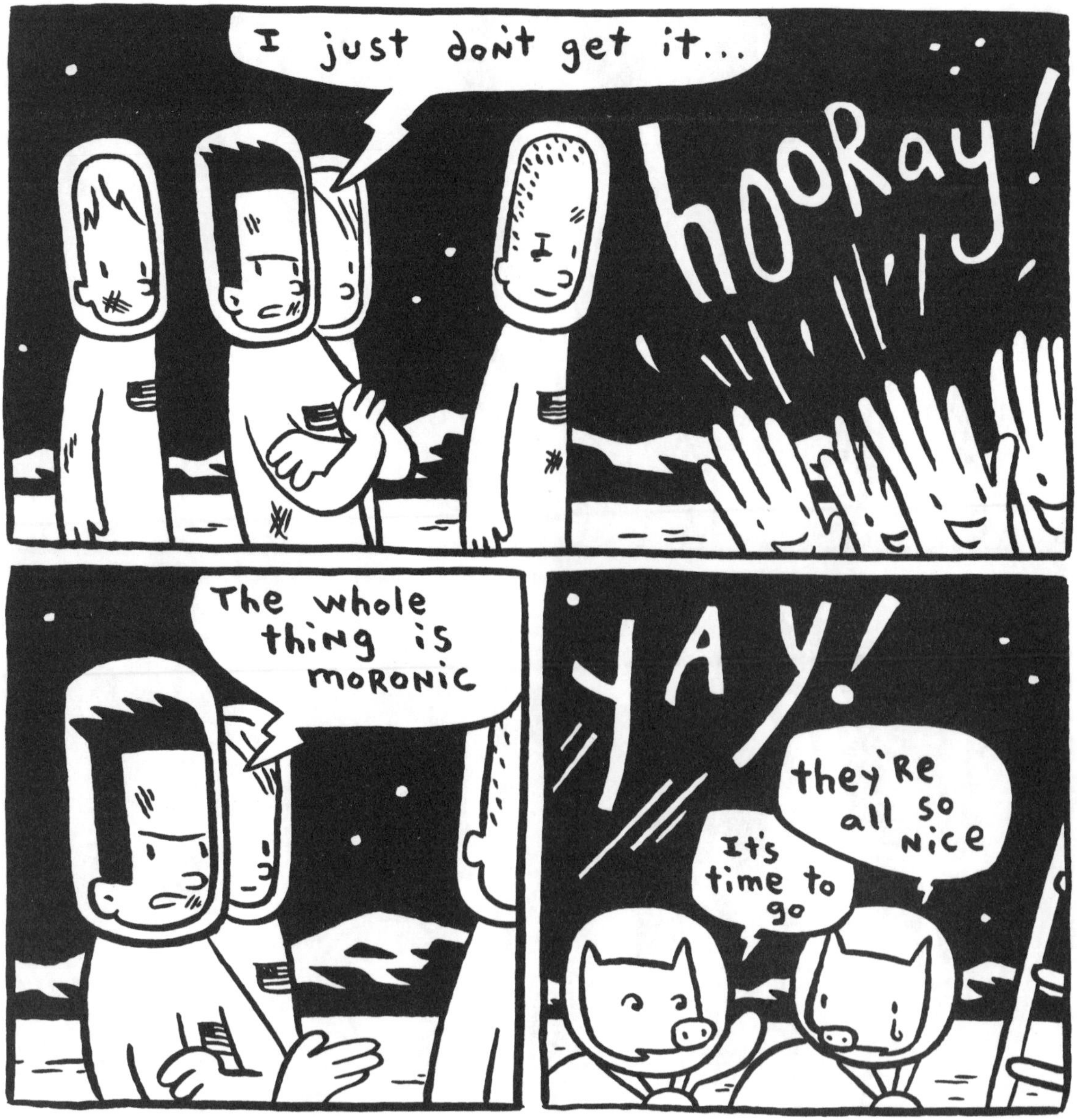
I just don't get it...
hooray!
The whole thing is moronic
YAY!
they're all so nice
It's time to go

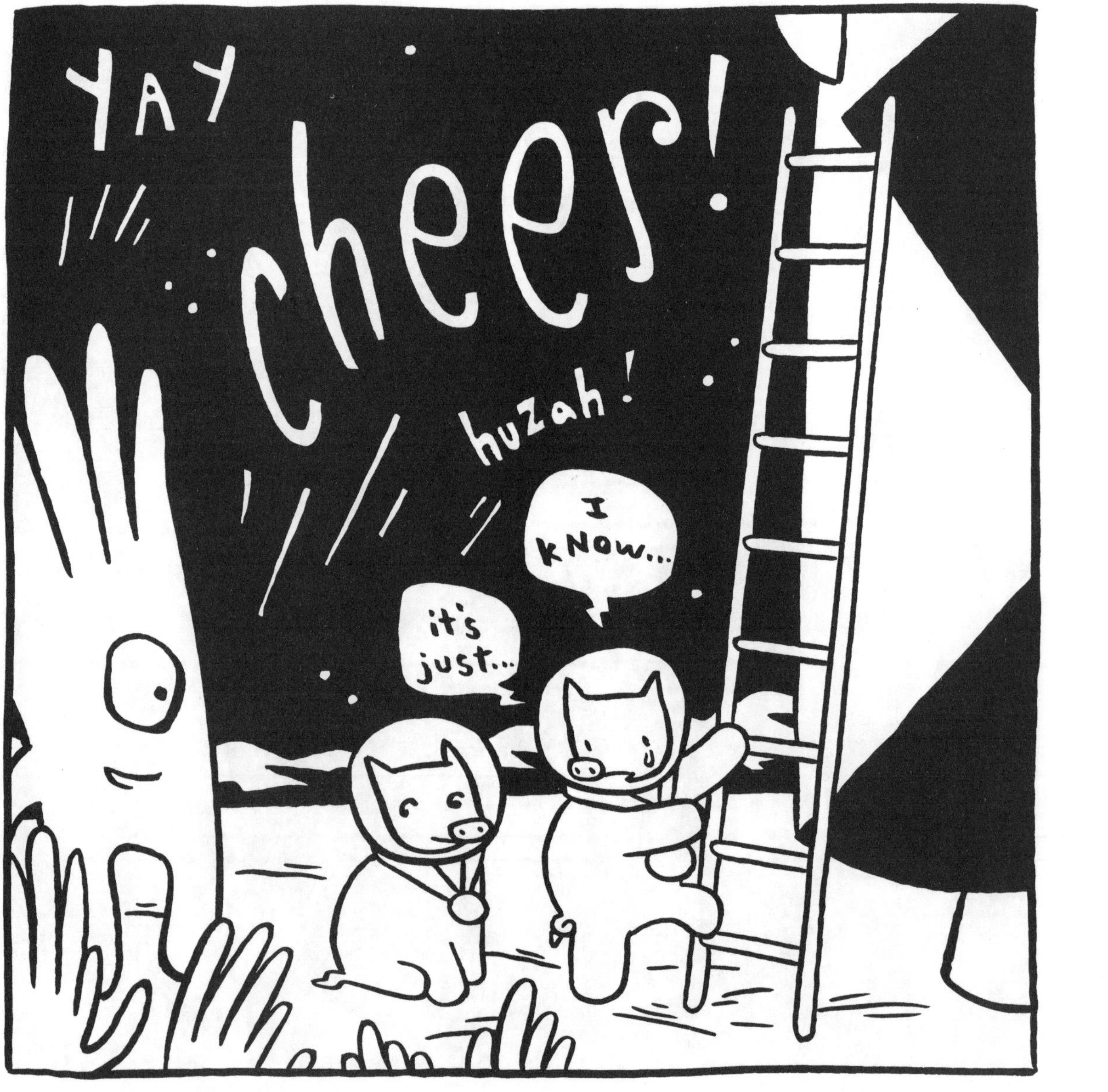
YAY
cheer!
huzah!
I KNOW...
it's just...

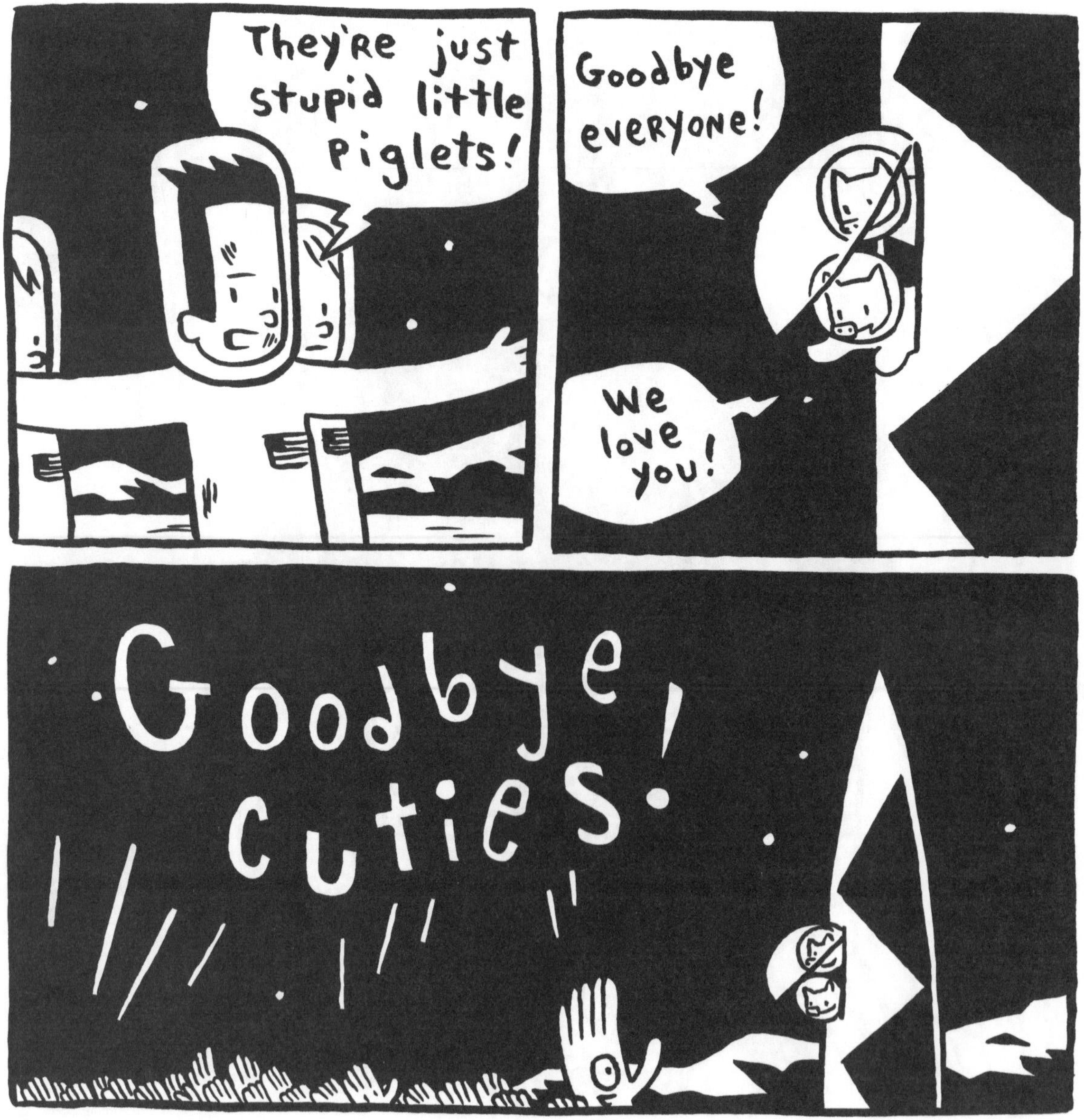
They're just stupid little piglets!
Goodbye everyone!
We love you!
Goodbye, cuties!

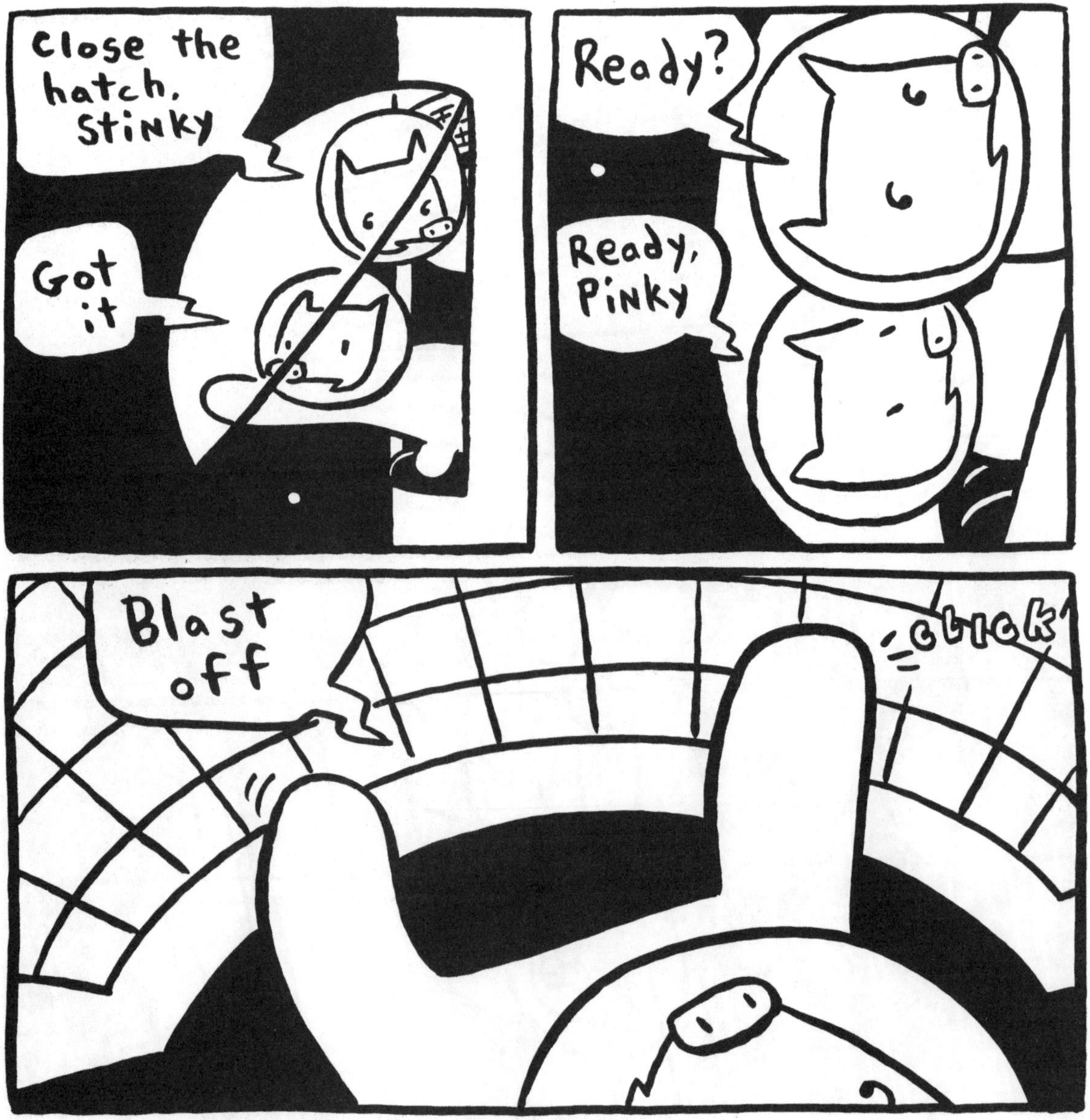
Close the hatch, Stinky
Got it
Ready?
Ready, Pinky
Blast off
click

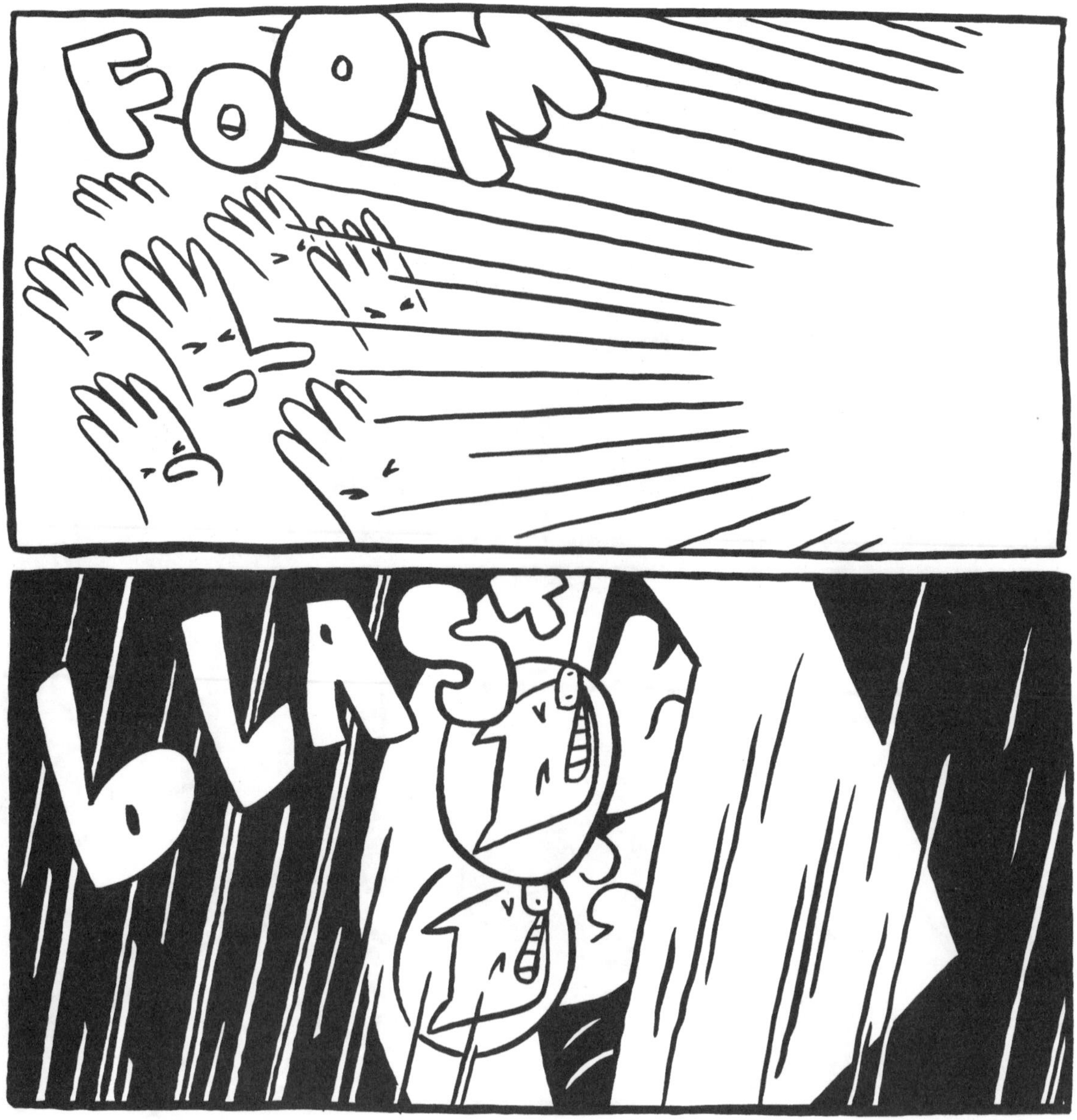
FOOM
BLAST

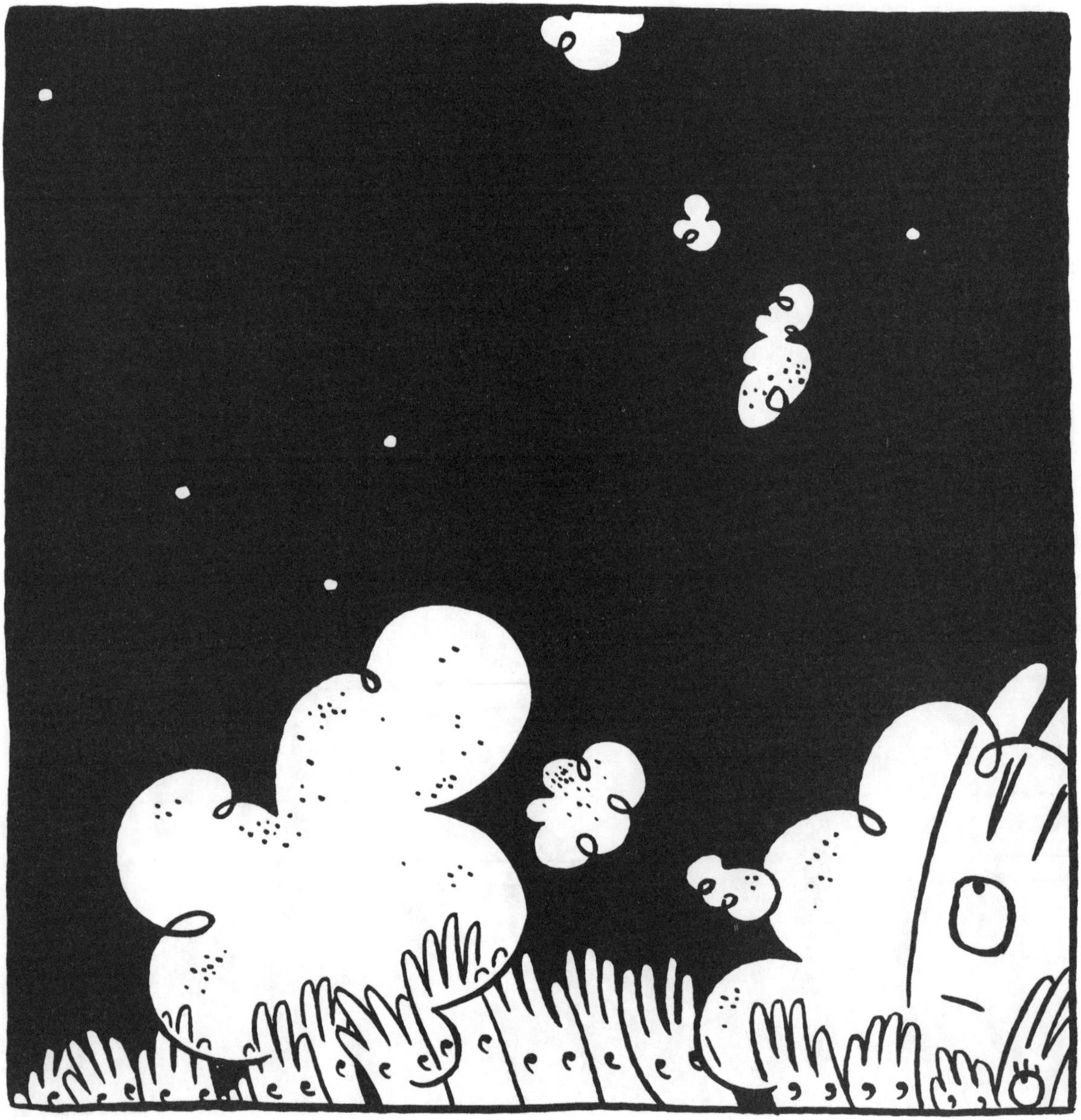

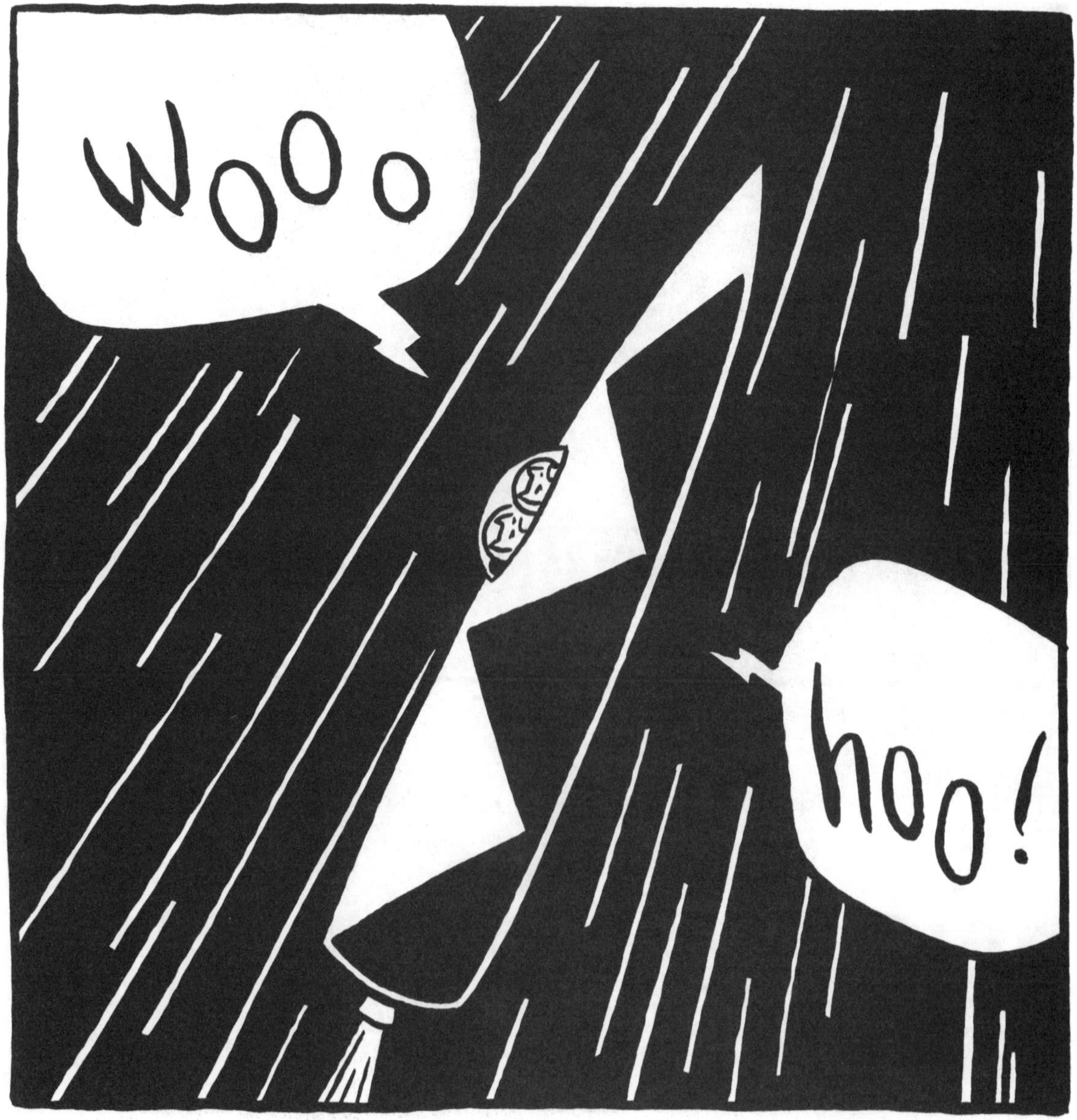
WoOo
hoo!

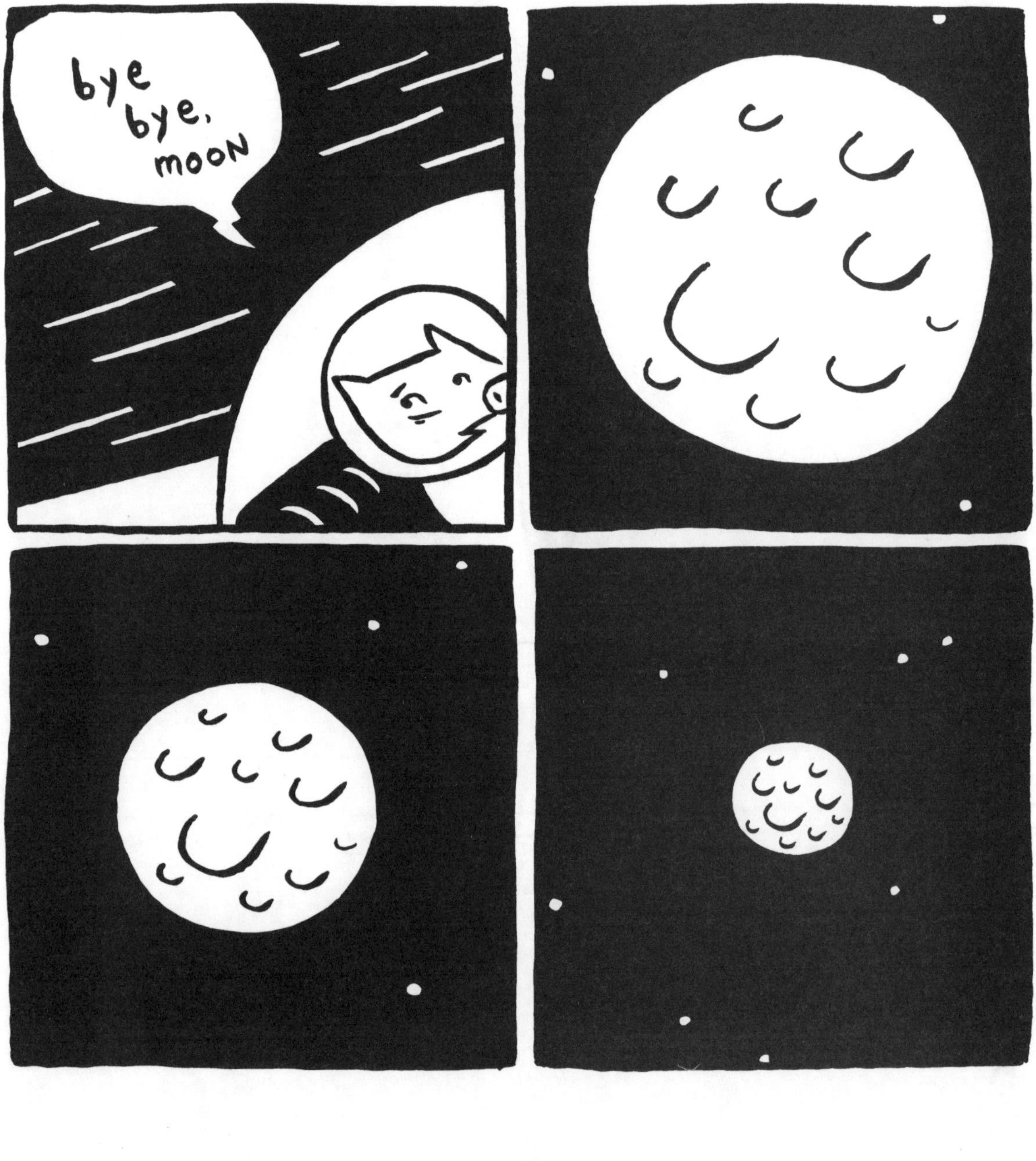
bye bye, moon

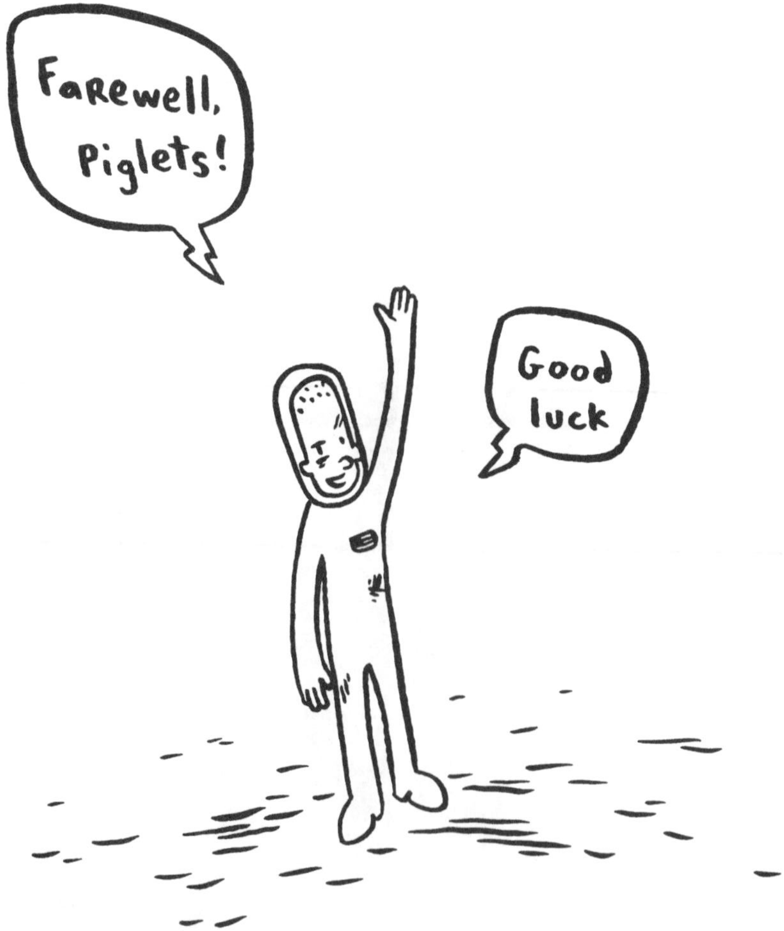
Farewell, Piglets!
Good luck

James Kochalka is more powerful than an evil genius, yet he stands on the side of goodness. With his wife Amy, and his cat Spandy, he lives in a small apartment in Burlington, Vermont. Patiently, he awaits the day he is needed to rise up and save the universe. This book took eleven months to complete. He is already hard at work on his next project.

JAMES   KOCHALKA
P.O. BOX 8321
BURLINGTON, VT
05402

james@ indyworld.com

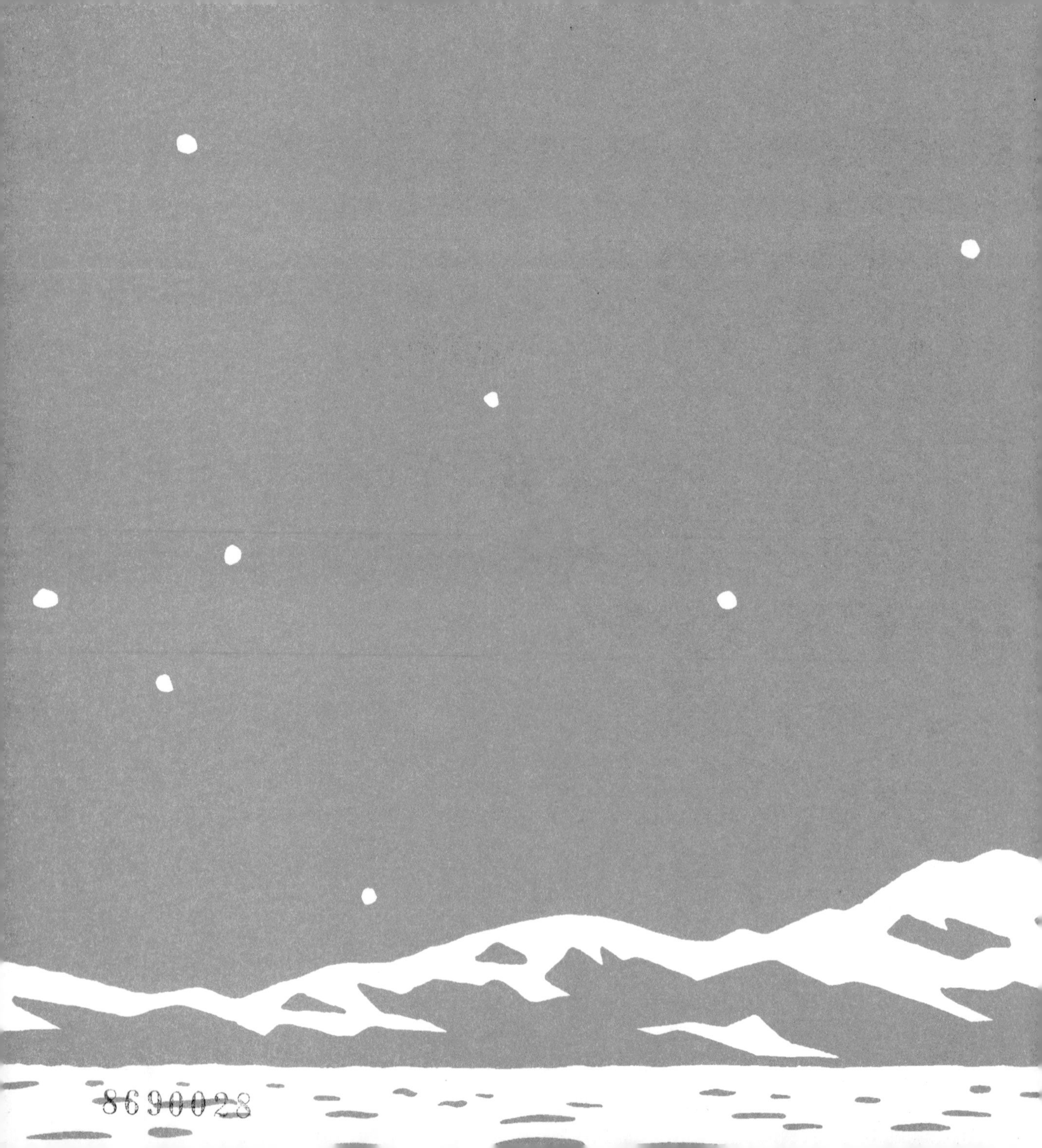